The Fire Theft

The
Fire
Theft

Mark Graham

VIKING

VIKING
Published by the Penguin Group
Penguin Books USA Inc., 375 Hudson Street,
New York, New York 10014, U.S.A.
Penguin Books Ltd, 27 Wrights Lane, London W8 5TZ, England
Penguin Books Australia Ltd, Ringwood, Victoria, Australia
Penguin Books Canada Ltd, 10 Alcorn Avenue,
Toronto, Ontario, Canada M4V 3B2
Penguin Books (N.Z.) Ltd, 182–190 Wairau Road,
Auckland 10, New Zealand

Penguin Books Ltd, Registered Offices:
Harmondsworth, Middlesex, England

First published in 1993 by Viking Penguin,
a division of Penguin Books USA Inc.

10 9 8 7 6 5 4 3 2 1

PUBLISHER'S NOTE
This is a work of fiction. Names, characters, places, and
incidents either are the product of the author's imagination or are used
fictitiously, and any resemblance to actual persons, living or dead, events,
or locales is entirely coincidental.

LIBRARY OF CONGRESS CATALOGING IN PUBLICATION DATA
Graham, Mark, 1950–
The fire theft : a novel / by Mark Graham.
p.   ; cm.
ISBN 0-670-84870-0
I. Title.
PS3557.R2158F57   1993
813'.54—dc20   93-6727

Printed in the United States of America
Set in Primer
Designed by Ann Gold

FOR MOM, DAD, GLORIA,
CHRIS, AND JOHN

Special thanks to John Graham, Hank Weirman,
Anne Peterson, Mark Moore, Susan Manchester,
Tom Cella, Stephen White, P. J. Scardino,
Suzanne Gluck, and Al Silverman for their
energy, their encouragement, their enthusiasm.

Thanks and love to Erin and Colin.

PART I

1 The ferry out of Calais was dangerously overloaded.

Among the endless procession of vessels that daily traversed the frigid waters between this French seaport and Dover's Admiralty Harbor twenty-two miles to the west, it was *unofficially* recognized that at best half were truly seaworthy. The *Spirit of Long Life* was one of those in the wrong half. Even at anchor the ferry groaned under the burden of its excessive load, two hundred and thirty-two people, sixty-two vehicles.

Hardly a majestic picture, the *Spirit of Long Life*'s hull was a bleached shade of orange. A cancerous rust spread indiscriminately across its face. The ferry's superstructure hinted of a white paint long since turned gray. Its funnels were a fatigued and weathered blue.

On the most idyllic day in spring, the *Spirit of Long Life* could manage the trip between Calais and Dover in just under three hours, a minor miracle. But this was the first week in March and the winter wind off the North Sea had a cutting edge to it. A legion of thunderheads marched defiantly across the sky. Not a day made for miracles.

Departure was seven minutes away. The harbor gate had already closed. The harbormaster, by then content with his pipe and tea, saw the beastly black Mercedes roll to a halt before the gate. It carried diplomatic plates. A tiny American flag flapped on the antenna. The harbormaster emerged from his house even as the driver leaned on his horn. Though the ferry's vehicle bay was already crammed from bulkhead to bulkhead, the harbormaster, a diplomat in his own right, ordered a half dozen bicycles hoisted into the luggage bin. He waved the Mercedes aboard.

Moments later, a woman on foot climbed over the gate. She was wearing khaki shorts and hiking boots. A bulky wool sweater hung well below her waist. Her hair was cut boyishly short, a convenience of style that was also a compliment to her lithe, sinewy figure. Without a word, Jaymin Bartel took the harbormaster by the hand and curled his bony fingers around a five-franc note, effectively silencing any protest he may have been contemplating. She bounded aboard the loading ramp at the rear of the ferry. Climbing an iron ladder normally reserved for crew members only, she paused long enough to light a cigarette. She peered back into the vehicle deck, at the Mercedes. Jaymin knew the driver and his companion would stay with the car the entire trip. She also knew that the colonel, as planned, had boarded the ferry ten minutes earlier.

Lingering a moment longer, Jaymin was struck by the sight of an apparent stowaway pulling himself effortlessly from among the bags of lamb's wool stored in the back of a farmer's flatbed. He was a dark-skinned man. Wild eyes stared out from a cadaverous face. He was dressed in a sackcloth pullover, a pair of filthy drawstring pants, and sandals worn through at the heels. He carried an oil-stained duffel bag over his shoulder. A long narrow tube protruded from the end of the bag. There was a familiarity about him that Jaymin couldn't place. Curious now, she watched the stowaway closely as he climbed the rear stairs to the passenger deck. When his gaze fell with inordinate attention upon the Mercedes, Jaymin felt compelled to follow him.

In a makeshift lounge passengers drank beer and wine from plastic cups. Jaymin saw the stowaway pause at the door. It was obvious by now that he was searching for someone. His reaction, however, suggested just as clearly that he wasn't finding the person, and he pressed on.

The restaurant was crowded. It smelled of beef and curry. The stowaway wove doggedly among the tables, his head pivoting. He paused only once, and then only for an instant. With growing impatience, he returned to the corridor.

A line stretched from the duty-free shop. The bartering was spirited. A man waved wooden dolls in the air. A woman shuttled between cotton rugs and imitation bronze statues. French wines were being sold in bottles or cases. While Jaymin viewed this as the logical place for a rendezvous, the stowaway moved on with little more than a glance.

They entered an open chamber that served as the ferry's main passenger compartment. People of all stations loitered among the benches and booths here, smoked, made idle conversation, and slept. Jaymin closed the distance between herself and the stowaway; she saw a change register on the man's haggard face, a glint of life lighting his dark eyes.

The focus of his attention proved to be neither a man nor a woman, but rather a young girl. She was standing next to the railing, thumbs hitched under the straps of her backpack, gazing into the channel's turquoise waters and watching a school of playful dolphins. A Polaroid camera dangled from a strap around her neck. Though alone, she seemed, Jaymin thought, quite content.

And though the stowaway approached her cautiously, it was clear to Jaymin that his appearance was unexpected. The girl took a quick step away, obviously repelled by his slovenly dress and chiseled face. The indigent man bowed diffidently, keeping his distance, yet there was no mistaking the girl's guarded posture. She looked down at his outstretched hand, but didn't take it.

They exchanged words. The stowaway bowed again. He offered his hand once more and this time the girl shook it, though her body language spoke clearly of her reluctance. She put her back to the railing, and Jaymin saw that she had fair skin and auburn hair pulled back into a ponytail. A strong nose and wide mouth affected a maturity beyond her years. My God, Jaymin thought. That face. I know that face. "Marion." She said the name aloud, her eyes and heart struggling with an image her head insisted wasn't true, and was thrown back into a past she had tried for so long to bury.

The orphanage walls had been like a prison for Jaymin until Marion's arrival. Their friendship had blossomed from the first moment, the one and only time in Jaymin's life she had experienced such instantaneous communion. Marion led Jaymin into a world of books and music. Jaymin led her into a world of boys and makeup and never-ending mischief. Marion discovered laughter. Jaymin discovered tears. They had been inseparable.

A year and two months after her arrival, Marion had been formally adopted. Jaymin died a little that day. They vowed to write. At first, Marion did write; but her new family moved her to Maine, then to Colorado. Soon after, the letters stopped. "Marion."

Jaymin searched this young girl's face, looking not for similarities but for differences. Her auburn hair was longer, the ponytail braided, but the tint was identical to Marion's; Jaymin had spent hours combing that hair, wishing hers was as thick, as glistening. There was a severity in this girl's gaze, a worldliness; Marion's eyes had laughed constantly. And even if their high cheekbones had been cut from the same mold, Marion's lips had not been so full as this girl's. Jaymin shuddered. This was wish fulfillment, nothing more. The girl resembled Marion, but she was not Marion.

Melancholy now, Jaymin slumped in a nearby chair. The girl and the stowaway had moved to a port-side bench. Jaymin saw the man laughing, the gaiety forced and unpracticed, and a jolt of sympathy played upon the girl's face. That was Marion, too; always there with a word of encouragement, a joke to ease the pain.

Jaymin forced her eyes beyond the ferry's streaked and cloudy windows. A veil of mist hung in the air. Fishing boats congregated around a vast island of kelp. On the horizon, navy vessels were like tiny motes in the eye.

When Jaymin looked back, the stowaway was lifting the metal tube from his duffel bag. He was whispering, a bent finger resting against his nose. He held the tube out to the young girl, but she shook her head, her arms folded across her chest.

If her refusal left the stowaway momentarily nonplussed, Jaymin could also see that it fed his determination. His gestures were increasingly adamant, even pleading, and Jaymin realized now that this was more than just a gift. From her vantage point she guessed that the tube was some sort of lightweight metal alloy, aluminum maybe, twenty-four inches long, and clearly sealed at the top.

In the end the young girl accepted the tube, though it wasn't clear to Jaymin whether he had forced it upon her or if she had been convinced by his sincerity. Nonetheless, she slipped off her backpack, loosened the top flap, and slid the tube inside. The stow-away watched feverishly as she tied the flap down again.

He rose. His last words must have carried a warning, or a threat even, Jaymin thought, for the girl seemed to shrink in her seat. Then the man turned on his heels, his retreat quick and unflinch-ing, his baggy pants fluttering with each stride.

2 Jaymin's immediate impulse was to introduce herself to the young girl. To ask her name. To touch her hair. To share the memories her angular face had evoked from Jaymin's childhood. Yet the impulse, Jaymin realized, was driven by sentiment and nostalgia, attributes she despised. Instead, she set out after the stowaway. His interest in the Mercedes had piqued her curiosity; now the exchange of the metal tube had turned curiosity into something more.

Jaymin followed the stowaway back along the corridor and into the lounge. He found an empty chair in the corner. Jaymin took a stool at the bar. She ordered Scotch. Under normal circumstances she would have had two or three by now. The drinking had become a disturbing habit; her superiors had warned her against it. But the acquiring of bad habits had always been easier for Jaymin than ridding herself of them.

Jaymin forced her thoughts back to the stowaway. He knew about the Mercedes, that much was clear, but what about its cargo? It was a foolish risk; they should never have agreed to bring a sample into England. And if the stowaway *did* know about it, then what? Jaymin shook her head. She ordered a second drink. She stared over the rim of the glass, her mind racing. Where had she seen this ragged man? When? The questions continued to nag at her, and nagging questions, Jaymin realized, often heralded the coming of trouble. She considered alerting the colonel, but immediately dismissed the idea.

She heard the stowaway order tea. He dug into his pocket for what, given his expression, was probably his last franc. When the tea came, he held the cup with the thumb and middle finger of both hands, exactly as Mother Superior had done twenty-two years ago at the orphanage.

Act like a lady, Sister Immaculata had repeated on a daily basis. *You're not a boy. Get out of the trees and put on a dress. Break another window and you'll spend a week locked in the closet.* Jaymin had spent many a week locked in the closet. And then she had learned. Being a girl had its advantages. A pretty white girl growing up in a New York City orphanage. Cigarettes, pot, fresh fruit. In exchange for what? A hand on her breast. A peek inside her shorts. It hadn't lasted; soon they had wanted more, and the advantages weren't so appealing. She had learned to fight, and to survive, or at least what she perceived *then* as surviving. It was a monstrous feeling, Jaymin thought now, another of life's hard-learned lessons down the drain.

Jaymin laid five francs on the bar. She followed the stowaway out into the corridor. He pushed through the crowd toward the stern end of the ship. Metal stairs rose to the nearly deserted main deck. The wind, redolent of sea and salt and diesel, bit into her skin. She stationed herself at the railing off the bow. The stowaway paced. Beyond, less than an hour away, rose the chalk-white cliffs of the English coast. Before her, the square-cut ferry and the unrelenting water waged their own private war, and the lofty spray of this encounter touched her face. A moment later, the acrid scent of cigar smoke filled her nostrils. Jaymin recognized the smell and tensed.

The colonel settled himself against the rail. He spoke to the side of Jaymin's face. "Will you come to my bed tonight?"

Jaymin answered in a tone as bland as pudding. "You keep asking. I keep saying no."

"You don't mix business with pleasure."

"Who said anything about pleasure?"

"You're not struck by the anticipation?"

"Your sense of self-worth is astoundingly misplaced, Colonel." Now she turned, pinning him with a gaze of absolute indifference. "In fact, I'm struck only by the anticipation of ending this ordeal and getting paid."

The colonel had never admitted to any affiliation with the military, but Jaymin had at least been given that much information. She had long been tempted to dismiss him as shallow and unimaginative, but the scope of their enterprise suggested otherwise.

She put her back to the railing again and felt the pressure of the tape recorder concealed beneath her shirt. The volumes of tape she had accumulated were enormous. The tapes were insurance, even evidence, though should they ever be discovered they would most certainly also be a death warrant.

"You talk of payment, and yet you speak with such irreverence to your paymaster," she heard the colonel say. He had become accustomed to her flippancy, and drew with seeming contentment upon his cigar. "Curious."

"When I was ten I'd let the boys have a peek at my underwear. Would that make you happy?"

Though he laughed, Jaymin worried that she had gone too far. A moment later, static cracked over the ferry's public address system, announcing their approach to Dover. Jaymin heard the ballast tanks opening off the bow and the influx of water as the tanks began to fill. A town materialized in the valley between the cliffs. Fortifications took shape atop them. The ferry merged with an entourage of freighters and Hovercraft. As Jaymin watched the stowaway descend the steps back to B deck, she again considered sharing her suspicions with the colonel; but it was obvious that he was still involved in his own fantasies over her.

He said, "Our ordeal, as you call it, is two weeks from completion. That should give you sufficient time to decide what makes me happy." He blew a fountain of smoke into the air. "You've checked our cargo?"

"Why? To make sure those two goons of yours haven't dozed

off? Sorry, that's not in my job description. I fly the plane and anything else that needs flying. I arrange transportation. Would I have hired those two? Probably not."

"Look into it anyway," the colonel said. When Jaymin saw the tiny white envelope he was holding in his palm, she flinched. Her reaction pleased him, and he said it again. "Look into it anyway. As a personal favor to me."

"I'm cold," Jaymin said. She snatched the envelope from his hand. "I'm going downstairs."

She started away. Knowing the anger she felt was directed more at herself than at him, Jaymin slipped the envelope into her pocket.

She tried anticipating the stowaway's actions. Unless she was mistaken, he had already spent the last of his money. The restaurant would therefore be no more practical than the lounge. Which left the passenger compartment or the vehicle deck. He was not among the many passengers loitering in the former, but Jaymin was quick to spot the young girl who so reminded her of Marion, her childhood companion. Oh, if only she could turn back the clock. The girl was seated now with an elderly woman.

Following the impulse she had ignored earlier, Jaymin stopped, smiled, and said, "Hello."

Eyes cast downward, the girl smiled shyly in return. "Hi."

The metal tube, Jaymin noticed, was still tied beneath the flap of her backpack. She said, "I know this is very bold of me, but you remind me so much of a friend I once had, I was wondering if it would be all right to ask you your name?"

"Angela."

"Angela!" Jaymin was curiously relieved. Also pleased. She said, "I'm Jaymin. Are we excited about visiting the great harbor of Dover?"

More confident, Angela glanced up. "I'm meeting my dad."

"Well then, he's very lucky." For Jaymin, the impulse to speak to this girl evolved; now it became a curious desire to know more about her. Where was she from? What did she do for fun? How old was she? Simple things. Yet Jaymin could not translate this desire into words. She said only, "I hope you enjoy yourself."

"You, too."

In the passageway, a sense of urgency overtook Jaymin and she half-jogged to the stairs leading down to the vehicle deck.

The woman who had befriended Angela Kaine was a fountain of chatter. A scarf held a tangle of gray hair in place, and she peered through round wire-rimmed glasses. She introduced herself as Ms. Sara Birchfield, from Coventry, sixty-eight years and three months old, and out on holiday as usual. Ms. Birchfield worked a crossword puzzle even as she talked. The talking inevitably led to meddling.

"Where's your mum and dad, for heaven's sake? A twelve-year-old girl traveling alone. I've never heard of such a thing."

"Thirteen," Angela corrected. There was a part of Angela that desperately wanted to say, "Not that it's any of your business," but she didn't. Instead, she said, "They're divorced."

"Oh, I'm sorry, child. It must be difficult."

"Lots of things in life are difficult."

"Don't be silly. Life is not supposed to get difficult until you get to be my age, young lady. So? Have they remarried?"

Angela sighed. "Mom almost did. Two years ago. Now we live in Paris and she says French men have a warped way of thinking, whatever that means."

"To be sure," Ms. Birchfield agreed. "And your dad?"

"Not Dad. I think he's still hurting from the divorce."

"It takes time sometimes. Take my word on that, child."

Angela had ceased listening. She was thinking instead about the woman who had stopped to say hello minutes before. The boots and the tomboy haircut didn't matter, Angela thought; they couldn't disguise how beautiful she was, her delicate features, almost like a doll's. But neither could the woman's beauty disguise her sadness. *Jaymin.* Angela had never heard the name before. She liked it.

"I have to go to the bathroom," Angela said to Ms. Birchfield suddenly. She jumped to her feet. She glanced about the room but Jaymin had gone. "You'll keep a watch on my backpack, won't you?"

"Can you find your way all right? Well, I imagine a twelve-year-old girl can find the loo quite capably, yes."

"Thirteen," Angela corrected.

"Oh, dear me, that's right. How forgetful." Ms. Birchfield waved her on. "Don't worry about your backpack, and, for goodness sake, don't dawdle. We'll be in port in a matter of minutes. Do you hear?"

Vehicles could be loaded into and unloaded from the *Spirit of Long Life*'s belly from either end of the vessel. The bow doors which opened onto the vehicle deck were hydraulically operated. The doors were closed upon departure by the ship's quartermaster. Nonetheless, the quartermaster's duties during a crossing also included navigation and signal communication, and often extended to outright piloting of the vessel. The closest thing to a permanent attendant on this deck was the machinist and his assistant in the engine room a floor below.

The vehicle deck ran the entire length of the ship. Unobstructed by the bulkheads and watertight partitions common among most seafaring vessels, cars and trucks on this deck could be tightly loaded and quickly unloaded. This was both a strength and weakness—a strength in terms of economics and convenience, a weakness in terms of safety, for as it was, it took as little as six inches of water on the deck's open floor to roll the vessel onto its side in even the slightest turn.

In still water, the bow doors on a vessel as antiquated as the *Spirit of Long Life* rested six feet above the waterline. When the vessel set sail, a bow wave collected under the prow. When the ballast tanks were full, as they were when the ferry approached port at high tide, this wave crashed spectacularly over the spade which extended out from the car deck. The bow doors, therefore, represented the last line of defense against flooding; an infallible defense when properly sealed.

The control panel that operated the doors was housed in a tiny booth the size of a closet. The control room door was by regulation routinely locked, but, as was often the case in ferries sailing out of French ports, the key had been left in the lock.

Jaymin stopped halfway down the steps. She looked out over the cars to the bicycle port and the Mercedes parked there. The driver was now perched on the front bumper. He was cleaning his fingernails with the point of a pocket knife. His companion was circling the car, nervously wrapping a rolled newspaper against his leg.

Jaymin scanned the deck, bow to stern. She caught sight of the stowaway emerging from behind the bumper of a rusted-out pickup. He carried the duffel bag in one hand, a heavy club in the other. Perplexed, she watched as he crept from car to car, making his way at last to the control booth. The alarm Jaymin felt when she saw him turn the key and step inside the booth left her momentarily paralyzed. My God, what was the son of a bitch doing? The answer was only moments in coming. Even above the roar of the ferry's engines, she heard the pressure release of the bow doors, like the hiss of a cornered alley cat. A crack appeared between the doors; a shaft of light filtered through, and then water. Jaymin realized at once that she could not reach the control booth in time. Her first thought centered on the Mercedes. Her second, inexplicably, was of the girl named Angela.

The crack in the doors widened. Jaymin saw the emaciated figure emerge from the control booth. From his duffel bag he produced a small compressed air tank. Yet even as he turned to face the bow doors it became clear that the water was rushing in at a rate far faster than he had anticipated. He backpedaled, then ran, struggling as he did so with the air tank. The first onslaught of water caught up with him. He was lifted into the air and thrown against the front bumper of a delivery truck. His limp body disappeared from sight.

Jaymin turned and bounded back up the stairs. She knew there was nothing she could do about the Mercedes, but there might be some hope for the girl.

Stephen Kaine watched the distant approach of the *Spirit of Long Life* from a jetty in the world's busiest port.

In years past, when the White Ensign ruled the high seas, the entire British fleet had dropped anchor in Dover. Today, there were no clippers or cruisers, nor carriers or battleships. Rather, there were fleets of fishermen and rusted freighters, embattled tankers and passenger ships teeming with people.

Throughout history, change had been Dover's most constant companion. The Romans fortified it, William the Conqueror captured it, and the Dauphin of France besieged it. It was a gateway and escape route for every king from Henry V to Charles II. The harbor had been gutted by man and silted over by the eastward drift of the sea so many times that history had lost track. At last count, seven million wayfarers passed through Dover every year. Ferries transported a million cars. Thirty ferries a day, and not one had ever sunk.

It was the perfect time of day. The early evening sky had ripened into a canopy of purples and pinks. Storm clouds marched irresolutely from the east. On either side of the city the cliffs rose from the sea, stark white barriers conspiring unsuccessfully to hold at bay the ubiquitous changes of man and sea. Even in the pale light of evening, the chalk that made up these walls radiated.

Stephen Kaine was two hours off the archeological site in Glastonbury. He had found time to shower and shave, but the sport coat he wore had been thrown over a pair of blue jeans and a work shirt. Kaine possessed the strong nose and long chin of his Scottish ancestors, but the dark, narrow eyes bespoke his Italian blood. When deep in thought he could often be found with one hand to his forehead, pushing back a shock of black hair. His Macbeth pose, Angela called it.

Four months had passed since her last visit. Too long for a father to go without seeing his only daughter. A thirteen-year-old changed in four months. One day a child running naked on the beach, the next a young woman locking the bathroom door behind her. An indifference to boys that is suddenly a confused interest. Dad, I don't care if the boys like me or not. How do you know if you're in love with someone? Did you and Mom fall out of love, or wasn't it real to begin with? Can you love more than one person at a time?

Kaine saw the ferry's running lights dancing above pools of

yellow light. For a time, it appeared motionless, not a ship atop the sea at all, but rather one emerging from it. Struck by this apparent apparition, Kaine stepped to the end of the jetty, his eyes narrowing. The ferry looped past the southern breakwater. By this time the infusion of ballast into the bow tanks had plunged the nose of the vessel well into the water. The bow wave had climbed above the prow and spade, and water was breaking through the open bow doors at the rate of fifty tons a minute.

And then the unspeakable happened. As the *Spirit of Long Life* inched into the main channel, Kaine watched in horror as the ship began an inexorable roll onto her port side.

3 On the bridge deck of the *Spirit of Long Life*, the ferry's captain swung the engine controls full astern; his intent was to reverse the pitch on the vessel's two main propellers and thus bring the ship to a stop. But it was too late; they were already listing at a thirty-degree angle to port. There was a momentary pause, a pause as fleeting as a last breath. Then a bellow of bending steel and yielding timbers filled the night.

The ferry slew over on her beam-ends and started to sink. The captain, his first mate, and the quartermaster were wrenched from their stations and flung down upon the port side of the bridge. Icy water rushed over them.

A level below, in the restaurant, dishes and silverware tumbled from tables bolted to the floor. Glass shattered. Jaymin raced in, tottered, and caught hold of a table. Then her feet gave way and she came down hard on the floor. Instinctively, she forced herself backward against the increasing pitch of the deck. Sliding, she hit hard against what was the port-side bulkhead. The impact destroyed for the moment her ability to breathe. But she recovered quickly. She grabbed the frame of a door and wrapped a leg around it.

Throughout the restaurant people clawed at tabletops and chair legs. A man, desperately balancing a briefcase in one arm and bracing himself between two chairs, lost his grip. Screaming, he plunged past Jaymin's outstretched hand and crashed through a port-side window. The sea, as black as coal, gobbled him up.

The tumult of rushing water filled Jaymin's ears. Lights flickered. She saw sparks and smoke, an acrid scent filled her nostrils, and then the room was encased in darkness. The bulkhead was barraged by flying luggage, food and bottles, and people, bodies cast down like stones. Blood splattered across Jaymin's face. Screams filled her ears. The stench of fear was so palpable she could feel it; so strong it almost took her, as well.

Then the rising water began to swirl around her. Its first touch stung, and Jaymin cursed the sea and ferries and everything remotely related to water. And why, for God's sake, was she pursuing a girl who was nothing more than an open window on memories she didn't need?

The flood seemed to rise in a moment from her waist to her chin. Thinking the water might serve as an ally, Jaymin relinquished her grip on the door and allowed the flood to bear her up into a passageway outside the restaurant. Not an ally at all, the water attacked, and the fierce pull of its current threw her against something hard and jagged. A sharp pain ran down her back. Finally, she broke the surface. Anguished voices filtered down from a half dozen directions.

Jaymin had been wearing two wool sweaters, and by now they were waterlogged and quickly draining her of strength. Treading water, she struggled out of each. Then she loosened the strap that held the tape recorder against her lower back and set it adrift. She reached down and unlaced her work boots. Still the water rose. More than by the pounding of her heart in her ears, Jaymin was amazed by her own equanimity. Her eyes focused on a faint glimmer overhead, a skylight perhaps, or more likely a starboard window in another passenger lounge.

Broken glass floated atop the water. A woman's scarf rode upon the surface. A pair of shoes bobbed in unison. An eruption of air bubbles broke around her, and a man's motionless form popped to the surface. He floated face down. His arms were extended at his sides, the sleeves of his coat like inflated tires. She yanked his head out of the water and he coughed. She dragged him toward the floor, now the wall, and crawled toward a table she had seen. The best she could do was to hook his arms over one of the legs, which seemed to bring him to life. They clambered up and out of the water.

Only now, in her bra and khaki shorts and shivering almost violently, did Jaymin realize the implications of the water temperature. The cold would eat people alive in an hour, probably half that.

Moments later, like a rampant disease, the water reached the table. It crept above Jaymin's ankles. When it reached her knees, it stopped.

The door to the lady's bathroom in the restaurant was locked, so Angela Kaine wandered out into the passageway.

As she neared the stern end of the vessel, the pungent smell of diesel assaulted her. Angela's first impulse was to take the stairs up to the main deck. She could watch their docking in the cool breeze. Her dad would be waiting. They would wave and blow kisses to one another. She would take a dozen pictures and he would complain about the results later. Why hadn't she brought her backpack?

At the end of the corridor there were stairways both up and down. The former led to the main deck, A deck. The latter to the car deck, C deck, and to storage lockers on C subdeck. A sign gave notice of rest rooms on the subdeck, and Angela pushed open the door. She was at once overcome by the drone of the engines, by the stark cool that radiated from the steel bulkheads, and by the urge to hurry.

The rest rooms were located in a passageway much narrower than those on the passenger deck. A second sign read EMPLOYEES ONLY. Angela knocked at the door indicating WOMEN, and let herself in. A pronounced suction inhibited her entrance; the same suction drew the door shut behind her. The room was tiny and claustrophobic, with a stainless steel stool, a sink with cold water only, a cracked mirror, a wall rack with paper towels, and a recessed trash bin. She hooked her camera over the door latch.

Angela was washing her hands when the water overwhelming the vehicle deck immediately below her caused the ferry to list suddenly onto its side. She was thrown against the door and came down face first on the floor. A scream caught in her throat. A sharp pain exploded across her rib cage and robbed her of breath. In the pause that followed, Angela listened and prayed and then gasped in the wake of a horrendous clamor. Had the ship collided with another vessel as they entered the harbor? It was all Angela could think of. An instant later, a languishing roll set the ferry on its side. Angela rolled with it, free-falling against the rest-room door, and then clawing like a wild animal to right herself.

When she was on her feet again, the din of bending steel and cracking timbers gave way to a sound far more daunting: that of water crashing through the corridors beneath her. Now, despite the pain in her ribs, she straddled the door, grasped the handle, and pulled. The door refused to budge. She changed positions, searching for better leverage, and tried again. It was useless. Either the latch had been damaged, or the weight of her fall had caused it to bind.

By now the echo of rushing water was all around her. She was besieged by an overwhelming sensation that walls were collapsing in upon her. Panicked, she fell to her knees and pulled and pushed and threw herself against the door. The bathroom light blinked, and blinked again. The connection sparked and sizzled and the bulb died.

In total darkness, Angela's panic and fear spiraled, gathering despair and disbelief, and she curled into a ball of total concentration. Her camera lay broken at her side and she drew it near. She listened without moving. What moments ago had seemed an unceasing bombardment of sound was now a growing force directly beneath her.

The *Spirit of Long Life* had gone down so quickly that there had been no time for a distress signal. Fortunately, Dover's Admiralty

Harbor was teeming with activity at six forty-five in the evening. The first alert had been sounded by the captain of the dredge *Xanthi*. A crewman had noticed an odd sagging in the ferry's running lights. The captain picked up the ferry's blip on his radar and saw, with great foreboding, that she had moved out of the channel into much shallower sea. When the *Spirit of Long Life*'s lights vanished altogether, the captain raised a harborwide alarm and turned his own vessel in the direction of the ferry.

Running, Stephen Kaine's first instinct had been toward a line of harbor tugs docked along the south jetty. He saw one with smoke rising from its exhaust funnel.

The tugboat had already weighed anchor when First Skipper Tanner Thorpe spotted Kaine, his arms frantically raised, his jacket flagging behind as he ran.

"The ferry . . . ," Kaine called out.

"We know. On our way," a crewman shouted in reply.

"My daughter's on that boat. I've got to get out there."

The crewman cast off just as Kaine made the leap from the dock to the tug's filthy lower deck. Even as the tug came about, he climbed the stairs to the pilothouse.

"Water temperature's forty degrees this time of year," the first skipper said without preamble. He was gnarled and gruff. A stocking cap pitched forward on his head and brow. His cheek bulged with chewing tobacco. "Blame it on the bloody North Sea, if you like, but a body submerged in anything that cold has about twenty-five minutes. Your daughter?"

"Angela. She's thirteen."

"God have mercy." The first skipper shook his head, jammed the throttle arm as far down as it would go, and then slapped at it just to be sure. "Angela. In Greek it means 'messenger.' To us Scots it means 'on the wings of an angel.' "

Kaine stared out the window. "In any language," he said.

Two Royal Navy cutters, a second tug, and four fishing boats had joined the pursuit. Overhead, two helicopters threw shafts of light across the water. When the ferry came into view it was apparent that it had somehow slewed out of the channel and come to rest on the seabed, its port side submerged in forty feet of water. What remained of the vessel's orange hull formed an eerie, rounded island. Its starboard propeller stood helplessly inert above the waterline. Lifeboats were still firmly affixed to their davits aside the hull. The sight stole every ounce of hope Kaine had left; and then he rallied back. Angela was strong and smart, he told himself. She wouldn't be easily defeated.

Eleven minutes after the *Spirit of Long Life* had gone down, the harbor tug, appropriately called *Broadside*, its floodlights ablaze, rammed the rubber fenders along its bow end into the ferry's stern. Fishing boats toured the waters surrounding the capsized beast and found the sea alive with people. The navy cutters had dropped men and lifeboats into the water.

While First Skipper Thorpe held the tug's nose tight against the ferry, Kaine and two crewmen leapt onto the hull. Over their shoulders they carried coils of rope, in their hands they held flashlights; it was all the tug had to offer.

Kaine followed a helicopter spotlight across the hull and stopped when he heard cries.

Peering into the gloom of a passenger lounge, Kaine came face to face with the wide-eyed stares of suddenly hopeful people. Dozens of them. Some treading water. Others clutching desperately to anything afloat. Tinny, weak voices filtered up to him, the lackluster chorus of souls slowly freezing to death.

Kaine secured one end of the rope to a davit and followed the other end down into the water thirty feet below. Now he realized that the beseeching looks he had seen were shock-induced; hands pawed at him from every direction. Another rope landed in the water next to him. He directed his first efforts toward the unconscious, while his mind ran wild with worry over Angela.

The eyes of a young boy, seemingly dead, his hair colored with blood, responded to the beam of the flash. Kaine tied the rope under his arms. He shouted, and the body was hoisted up.

It continued. An elderly man with glazed eyes; a woman with her baby dangling from her teeth; a teenage girl with two badly maimed wrists and a snow-white face. The burden of choosing who was to go and who was to wait settled upon Kaine even as the cold turned his limbs to ice. A diver from the Royal Navy joined him.

Together, they chose and tied and shouted. Minutes passed. The ropes absorbed water like a sponge and grew more slippery with each load. Some, too weak even to grab hold, plunged back into the water; one landed squarely on Kaine's shoulders and drove him under.

When he reemerged, the navy diver grabbed his collar. He slid one of the ropes beneath Kaine's arms and said, "It's a tomb now for those that are left. It will be yours in another two minutes."

Logic had been drilled into Jaymin's head since before she could recall. In the beginning it was an orphanage tenet: Life logically approached can be overcome. The streets of New York solidified the message. Since then it had become a personal credo at constant war with her essentially freethinking intuition.

Logically, Jaymin knew that the ferry should be submerged in a harbor channel a hundred feet deep. Nonetheless, taking the logic a step further, she realized the ferry had somehow settled itself on the sea floor outside the channel. She also understood that high tide was yet to come, with consequences she could only imagine. It didn't matter, she thought; they would be rescued by then.

Outside, a full moon surfaced above the horizon. A silver mist hung in the air. Stars glittered faintly through the window thirty feet above her.

Gradually, Jaymin's eyes adjusted to the dark. She saw an older woman supporting herself on the leg of a table, blood spurting from a wound on her temple, a sickly sheen coating her face. With her free hand she clung desperately to the arm of a young girl, just below her. A floor that was now a wall. A chair that was now a stepping-stone to survival. The girl was waist-deep in water and her teeth chattered uncontrollably.

"Give me your hand, sweetheart," Jaymin called from her perch.

The words served to arouse the girl; she turned her eyes in Jaymin's direction, but disorientation had turned to confusion and she said, "Mummy?"

"Give me your hand," Jaymin repeated, this time with more firmness. The girl reached out and Jaymin pulled her through the water, up onto the ledge. She tried speaking but the words and the chattering came out in a flood of tears. Jaymin held her. She massaged her legs, her feet, and her toes. The chattering receded. "If I'm going to hold you like this, you'd better at least tell me your name, don't you think?"

"Lucy."

"Scared?"

"Yes. What's happening? Are we going to die?"

Jaymin shook her head. "No, sweetheart, you're not going to die," she said flatly. "That's a promise."

First Skipper Tanner Thorpe's son, Connor, the youngest crewman on the harbor tug *Broadside*, was charged with the care of those survivors now crowding into the tug's main cabin. He stoked a roaring fire in the coal stove, brewed tea, and scoured the vessel from stern to bow in search of clothes and blankets.

Eighteen and hardly a man of the world, Connor was himself in a state of semi-shock. He watched a woman fall on her knees in front of the stove and burst into tears, an old man whose clenched fists refused to open, and a child with only the head of her doll clutched in her arms asking if anyone had seen her mother.

Connor was a savior; a cup of hot tea and he was a bloody savior. He watched as four bloated bodies were lined up on the ferry's hull. He watched as the near-dead were airlifted by helicopter to the Dover hospital. He watched the American—Kaine his father had called him—traversing the hull with his head hung down. Connor could see that the mere act of walking was a painful task for the man. Kaine's hands shook, and he worked them feverishly in an attempt to regain circulation. Water dripped from his clothes as he eased himself over the tug's bow and onto the lower deck.

"Mr. Kaine." Connor held out a cup topped with steaming tea. Kaine's hand shook as he raised the cup to his lips. The tea had no taste, but the heat of it sent sparks of revival coursing through his system.

The woman on her knees before the stove grasped Kaine's hand. "Dear God, bless you," she said. Kaine looked back at her with an expression void of recognition, void of emotion. "You saved my life. And my husband's. God bless you."

Kaine looked away. "I need clothes," he said to the first skipper's son.

"You can't go back out there."

Kaine climbed the steps to the pilothouse; he didn't want the woman's gratitude nor the boy's sympathy.

When Tanner Thorpe saw him, he growled, "We've done well, considering. The busiest harbor this side of hell and who turns up first, a bunch of fishermen. Angela?"

Kaine shook his head. "No."

"Fuck me. We're running out of time. Tides changing," Thorpe said bluntly. His son appeared at the head of the steps, a pair of blue jeans and a wool shirt in his hands. "What's this about?"

"He's going back," Connor said.

His father snarled. "I don't know what you're thinking exactly, Mr. Kaine, but your body won't be worth a shit the minute you hit that water again. Just so you know."

Kaine didn't answer. He peeled off his wet clothes, kicking them angrily aside. The jeans were too short, the wool shirt like a warm glove.

The first skipper persisted. "I just saw you save about twenty lives out there, mister, and if you think I'm about to let you go—"

"And I'd trade every one of them for a glimpse of my daughter, Thorpe." It was an empty statement, Kaine knew that. Empty men were full of such statements, he thought. He drained his tea. "I know what you're saying. I do. And I appreciate it. But Angela is in that boat. Not in this tug drinking tea and warming her hands next to a wood-burning stove."

He started down the steps.

"All right, then. Stubborn as a bloody Scot," the first skipper shouted. He unbuttoned his shirt and peeled off a sleeveless, rubberized vest that twenty years ago might have passed for a wet suit. He tossed it in Kaine's direction. "Take this at least. Who knows, maybe you'll drown in five minutes instead of two."

Kaine pulled it on. "Thanks."

"Use your head while you're down there, will you? A dead father's not much use to anyone."

Jaymin crouched on the rounded leg of a dining table. Her toes had gone numb. She had given up her place on the ledge to an elderly man who, by some miracle, had managed to keep a grip on his cane. Lucy sat on his lap now. For the last several minutes Jaymin had been holding the girl's baby brother. He was two, Lucy had said, and as Jaymin pressed him against her skin, willing body heat into him, she could feel the violent pounding of his heart. Somewhere down below their parents fretted and hung onto life by a thread. The water rose with the tide.

Overhead, a light stirred. Then other lights and the sound of footsteps. Then voices. They've come, Jaymin thought. Thank God. Thank God? The words startled her; she had never thanked God for anything. She had begged Him for death a few times, but never had she been thankful for life. Now, knowing what was about to come, she shielded the baby with her arms. On impulse, she kissed his forehead. A moment later, she heard a sharp pounding, and the pounding brought a rain of glass down upon them.

"It's okay. We're safe now," she whispered in the baby's ear.

This time the ropes that were lowered into the crowded lounge were equipped with harnesses. Four men, two in scuba gear, entered the chamber via a nylon rope ladder.

"There are children down here," Jaymin called out to them. "Please hurry."

One by one the children were hoisted to safety; oddly reluctant, Jaymin relinquished the baby, his tiny hand clinging to her outstretched finger until the very last.

By Kaine's estimate it took less than five minutes to get the children out, but he couldn't help but wonder how many others, languishing in the freezing water, would lose their lives in those minutes. Most could not even loop the harness over their arms without assistance. Two were unconscious. One dead. The woman perched on the leg of a table refused to go until the water was clear of the other passengers. Kaine could see she was half-frozen, her arms wrapped futilely across her chest.

"My daughter is in this boat somewhere," he said to her out of sheer desperation. "She's thirteen. Reddish blond hair. She wears it in a braid." What was he saying? How could this woman, this survivor of death, have any notion of what he was talking about? But it didn't stop him. "She would have been carrying a blue backpack and a camera, and wearing a jean jacket—"

"Angela," she said breathlessly. "Angela. And you're her father . . ."

"You've seen her!"

"Before the accident. Oh, God. Before the goddamn accident." She covered her face with her hands. The harness carried an unconscious man upward; water from his sodden clothes poured down on them. "She was in the restaurant. I said hello to her; she introduced herself. Oh, God, it all happened so fast. I'm so sorry. I . . ."

"We have to get you out of here." Kaine could see her strength flagging even as they spoke. Remarkably, she refused the harness a last time, then he coaxed her in. Kaine climbed the rope ladder, following her; here was a ray of hope, his only clue.

Kaine helped her aboard Tanner Thorpe's overburdened harbor tug. He wrapped a blanket around her shoulders.

"Which restaurant?" he asked. "She was in the restaurant, you said. The one we just came out of?"

"No. No, I don't think so. No. On the other side of the ship. The port side. But I'm not sure she was still there when the ferry went down. She may not have been." Jaymin hung her head. Then she rallied. Her green eyes flashed, beacons of hope. "She was strong, I could tell that. I got out, so can she."

The corridor beneath Angela's feet filled with water forty degrees cold. For the most part, the pressure seal on the rest-room door behind which she was trapped had, to this point, held.

But it was more than the water or the shifting of the ferry that fed her panic; it was the complete and utter darkness that overwhelmed her. Light had ceased to exist. A heaviness weighed upon the air. It was not only the water pressing in around her, but the metal surrounding her. If she could only catch her breath, Angela thought, she could surely think more clearly.

She stared at the illuminated numbers on her digital watch, as if something so small and so insignificant could serve as a lifeline, a security blanket. A bright yellow 7:53 stared back at her. They had been due in port at seven fifteen. They had been ten or twelve minutes away when the ferry sank. Good, she told herself: clear thinking. And then she even managed a laugh; her bladder was full again. The stool looked down at her from the ceiling. The sink lay sideways on the wall. Peeing on the door in the bathroom was something she might have done seven or eight years ago when she was mad at her mom. Now she was thirteen; even here in the dark the thought embarrassed her.

What Angela found most puzzling was the speed with which the ferry had sunk. A ship this size sinking in less than a minute? Surely someone had seen it happen. Surely her dad had watched their arrival. He always did. There, she thought: a reason to hope.

The ferry shuddered. Bulkheads groaned and water lapped against the walls. Angela adjusted her footing and felt a pool of water collecting at the base of the door. Her shoes were at once soaked.

A revelation struck her. *The tide.*

Panic struck again, then surprisingly abated. A voice said, "You're alive, you're still breathing, you still have a chance. Do something."

She unstrapped her watch, adjusted her footing again, and sat back against the cool metal of the sink. Her hand searched until she found an exposed water pipe. Then, using the face of her watch, she began tapping. Too weak, she knew. The idea was good, though. She took the tin shield off the toilet paper dispenser, bent it in half, and tried again. Better. Louder. She chose a pattern. *Tap, tap-tap, tap-tap.* Clear thinking; she congratulated herself. The pattern would distinguish the tapping from the sound of any loose pieces of metal rattling about the hull. *Tap, tap-tap, tap-tap.*

4 An hour and fifteen minutes later, the search was temporarily suspended. With the onslaught of high tide, in this part of the world a turbulent affair, especially at full moon, the ship was deemed dangerously unstable. Divers provided by the Royal Navy were ordered out of the water. Volunteers were sent back to shore. The bodies of the dead, Kaine heard the regional commander say, were not worth risking the lives of the living. As it was, the commander estimated that there had been between one hundred seventy-five and two hundred people aboard. Survivors up to the moment totaled a miraculous one hundred twenty-two. The dead numbered twenty-one, including the captain and his first mate.

Kaine's outrage at the suspension of the search was tempered only by the distinct possibility that Angela had been rescued without his knowledge.

Once ashore, Kaine discovered that both survivors and corpses had been transferred to facilities throughout Dover. The dead, he was told, had been taken to Saint Mary's Church, atop the eastern cliff. A church turned morgue; Kaine couldn't face it, not yet.

As for the living, the hospital had taken on the more critical cases, though several had also been airlifted to London. The Dorian

Boys School gymnasium had been transformed into an infirmary.

Kaine made the decision to begin his search there. He wasn't sure why. Calculate the odds and take your best shot up front, something like that.

He hailed a taxi.

"She's not here," Jaymin said when she saw Kaine enter the gymnasium. Jaymin had been given a large blue and red sweatshirt with the words CHURCHILL HAD HIS FAVORITES written across the front. The sleeves were rolled up above the elbow. Her leather hiking boots had been replaced by a pair of high-top tennis shoes. Her face glowed a vibrant shade of pink.

"You checked. Thanks." Kaine studied her; there was a feline quality to her gestures and her stride. The speed of her recovery impressed him. "How are you?"

"I'll live."

Blue wrestling mats covered the gym floor. Most of the survivors huddled around kerosene heaters. Blankets were wrapped around bent shoulders. Steam rose from broth-filled cups.

Kaine hurried through the facility despite Jaymin's assertion, and she stayed at his side. "I hate to even mention it," she said, "But I heard one of the doctors say they were using some church up on the eastern cliff as a . . . as a . . ."

"I know," Kaine said. "I haven't quite worked myself up to that."

A nurse gave Kaine the address to the Dover County Hospital. Also three phone numbers to the facilities at Chamberlain General Hospital in London. He used the phone in the school's office but all three lines were busy.

"The hospital is on the edge of town," Jaymin told him. "I can't bear another minute in this place. Mind if I come? I have a car. A rental. The agency dropped it by earlier."

Kaine found himself thanking her again, mildly curious about her motives, and chastising himself for not just accepting her concern as genuine. Her face captivated him, a face full of contradictions. In one way, it resembled a schoolgirl's, angelic and open; yet there was a hardness, as well, in the depth of her gaze, in the bird-of-prey slant of her eyes, in the brusque delivery of her words. It was this element of hardness that reminded him of Danielle, his ex-wife, a quality he had invariably been attracted to.

Dover, the city, lay nestled in the valley between Castle Hill and Shakespeare Cliff. For all its quaintness, Dover had the cosmopolitan air of a city that was used to seven million people a year tramping through its narrow streets. French restaurants were as plentiful as English pubs. Street signs were written in two languages. In contrast, Georgian houses looked down from the hills to the south and Regency cottages from the north. Whitewashed fences and gas lamps illuminated the night.

The hospital was located at the apex of the valley floor. Ambulances were parked at odd angles before the entrance.

Hypothermia proved to be the main affliction here. Blankets and oxygen and hot tea were the primary antidotes.

The attendant at the information desk allowed Kaine a moment to study the list of survivors airlifted to Chamberlain General in London. Angela's name was not among them.

Accident victims had been bedded in empty rooms in pediatrics and in surgical recovery rooms. Doctors labored over a cardiac case. The man's wife wept in the next bed. In a room normally reserved for intensive care patients, two babies rested beneath heat lamps. An emergency appendicitis case lay next to a woman breast-feeding an infant still blue from the water. A family of four celebrated their reunion. The elderly woman in the bed next to them had tubes feeding into her nostrils and a blue backpack cradled in her arms. A metal tube stuck out from beneath the flap.

"That's her," Jaymin said, taking Kaine's arm. "Angela's lunch companion."

"Her backpack," Kaine muttered. Restraining himself, he moved with quiet steps to the woman's bedside and saw the name tag at the foot of the bed: Sara Birchfield. He pushed a chair up next to the bed. He had hoped for a smile to ease the woman's apprehension, but couldn't manage it.

"I'm Stephen Kaine," he said softly. "Angela Kaine is my daughter."

"Oh, dear God." Almost desperately, Ms. Sara Birchfield labored into a more upright position. "Tell me she's safe. Please. Tell me she's asking for her backpack." Tears pooled in her eyes as she viewed the lack of expression on Kaine's face. The tears spilled and ran down her ashen cheeks. "No. Please, no. She can't be dead."

Jaymin said, "She hasn't been located yet. We're still hopeful."

Sara Birchfield shook her head, shock still clouding her wits. "She called me Sara. I so liked that. Oh, please God. Why couldn't you have taken me instead? She was so young . . ."

"My daughter was sitting with you." The words came out more brusquely than Kaine had anticipated. "Do you remember?"

The woman nodded. "We had lunch. She kept an old lady company. She called me Sara. I'll never forget that as long as I live . . ."

"Now you have her backpack. How did that happen? Please. Try to remember."

"But I do remember. I'll always remember. She needed a visit to the loo. A rest-room stop before we docked. What I think she needed more was a break from her luncheon companion." A rueful smile touched her face. "I tend to talk, you see, even when I don't have anything to say. Angela, well, she—"

"Which bathroom?" Kaine asked gently. "The one in the restaurant?"

Sara Birchfield stared down at her blanket, at the backpack held in her hands. "Yes. Yes, but they were locked, and there was a line. I saw her wander out into the hallway outside the restaurant. I promised to keep an eye on her pack. Through it all, it stayed on my arm. I can't tell you how."

"She walked out into the passageway? Which way? Did you see?"

"Right. She turned to her right," Ms. Birchfield answered without hesitating. "She should have gone the other way. There are loos outside the lounge. A woman my age takes note of such matters first thing. I thought of going after her, but what kind of sense, I told myself, would that have made? The poor thing was trying her best to get away from me. She was well-mannered, you know. And bright as a penny. My goodness, she talked like a college professor."

Past tense, Kaine thought: *Was* well-mannered. *Talked* like a college professor. *Is* and *does,* he told himself. Is and does.

Ms. Sara Birchfield held Angela's backpack out in two hands, her eyes averted. "I wish to God He would have taken me instead."

"I'm glad you made it," Kaine said in return.

All that remained was the inevitable visit to Saint Mary's Church, for this night at least, a morgue.

The irony of this was not lost on Kaine. Saint Mary's stood atop the eastern cliff in the shadow of the incomparable Dover Castle, a great castellated gun platform, built for war, from the Iron Age to the Romans, from the Saxons to the Second World War; yet, still unmistakably a castle, with stone walls twenty feet thick, with crenellated guard towers, with heavy timbered gates.

Saxon stonecutters built the church a thousand years ago from slabs of gray granite. The English introduced stained-glass windows and gilded sconces.

The road wound up the back side of the eastern hill. As they came upon the church a helicopter dropped yet another victim at the entrance. Jaymin waited in the car.

Rough-cut granite steps and massive wooden doors led Kaine inside. Soldiers occupied the vestibule. The bodies were positioned in rows along the center aisle of the nave. Kaine gave Angela's description to the county pathologist, a ragged man who carried anger and sympathy in the same tote.

"Six kids so far. Five girls, two around your daughter's age. Two hours ago as alive and vibrant as butterflies. In the name of God, what a waste." He drove a pencil down hard on his clipboard. The church had taken on an ambrosia of formaldehyde and incense, a most disturbing amalgam. "You'll have to look and it isn't pretty. These kids weren't walking around with papers on them."

Angela was not among the five. By now Kaine had buried his feelings so deep that relief lay dormant beneath a shroud of numbness. He looked beyond the bodies to the altar; Jesus, gazing down from his cross, seemed to share the feeling. On his way out of the

church, Kaine managed to ignore every waterlogged body save one:
that of a man, covered from the neck down by a white sheet; his
gaunt and leaden face was one Kaine would never forget.

"Ras. Ras Haydar." Kaine touched his forehead. His eyes
strayed to the tiny wire basket that hung from the side of the gurney
and contained the dead man's personal effects. An English sixpence
on a leather thong. A waterlogged coin purse. A ticket stub from
the French railway, Marseilles to Calais; it was dated March 4,
three days ago. And a pewter chess piece in the shape of a dragon.
For Kaine, the chess piece evoked a memory; he had seen a set of
such pieces once before, at the Karmin-Yar site on the Black Sea.
The set had belonged to the French archeological liaison on the
project, Maurice Dreyfuss. He and Kaine had been rivals, or more
accurately adversaries; Dreyfuss had replaced Kaine as Karmin-
Yar's chief archeologist when Kaine was dismissed six months ago.
But how would Ras Haydar have come into possession of the piece?
And why? Kaine leaned over the body, touching the forehead again,
and allowed his free hand to gather up the pewter dragon. He
slipped it into his pocket even as the pathologist approached.

"You know this man?" The pathologist managed to exude relief
and disbelief in the same breath. "He was found on the vehicle
deck of the ferry. Somewhat unusual, I'm told. Do you?"

Kaine hesitated, then glanced down at the face again. "He was
a co-worker. It makes no sense that he would have been on that
ferry. None."

"Perhaps not. Yet, here he is." The pathologist glanced beyond
Kaine to a man watching them from the shadows of the vestibule;
they exchanged the briefest of nods. "He carried no papers. Does
he have a name? Perhaps any next of kin I should know of?"

Kaine drew away from the body. In truth, he didn't know that
much about Ras Haydar. Only that Ras was a hard worker. Only
that the bleak hills of his Cappadocian homeland had provided him
with a life of destitution, growing knee-high wheat and raising
undernourished sheep. Only that Kaine's discovery of the ancient
city of Karmin-Yar had sparked new life in Ras's people and rekin-
dled a dormant pride. There was also a brother who had died, Kaine

remembered that, but the details of his death had remained a mystery.

"Well?" the pathologist said.

"His name is Ras Haydar." Kaine glanced down at the body again and then shook his head. "That's all I know."

Jaymin sped from the heights of the eastern cliff to the harbor like a person with a death wish. The instant she stopped, Kaine jumped out of the car and cornered the regional commander. "My daughter's still out there," he said, "She's in that ferry somewhere and I'm standing here on shore with your leash around my neck."

"I can sympathize," the regional commander replied.

"That's commendable," Jaymin said, "but it's not enough."

"To enter that ferry now is to put one's life—"

"It's my life," Kaine argued.

"I can't allow it. In this harbor, your life is my responsibility."

"I relieve you of your responsibility."

"Get within a thousand yards of that ferry, mister, and I'll have you behind bars for twenty-four hours."

The harbormaster intervened, drawing Kaine aside and laying a structural blueprint of the *Spirit of Long Life* on a table. Together with Jaymin and the ferry's purser they reviewed the ship deck by deck. With a single peculiarity, the *Spirit of Long Life* resembled the majority of ferries on the Dover-to-Calais line. D deck, the lower of four decks, constituted the engine room, machinist shop, and crew's quarters, all off limits to passengers. C deck had been specifically constructed for the cars and trucks which represented the life blood of the business. Regulations prohibited passengers from either staying with their vehicles during the course of a crossing or from returning to them at any time prior to docking—but these regulations were not easily enforced, the purser confessed. Subdeck C, the peculiarity of this ferry, was an addendum to its stern section and located directly above the vehicle deck. The blueprint, being ten years old, suggested a dead space with uses as yet unspecified.

"But that was then," the purser said. "Along about five years ago, the space was cleverly converted into storage sheds. Lockers, as it were. I keep a change of clothes down there, that sort of thing. Just easier than traipsing all the bloody way down to D. Course we had to twist the company's arm a turn or two about the loos."

"Bathrooms."

"Yes, well, of course they're not actually big enough for a bath, you see, but then you Americans have grandiose taste, I've come to realize."

"Where?"

The purser penciled in both the storage lockers and the loos. "Though I must tell you honestly that as things stand now the water level—"

"Is there a sign?" Kaine interrupted. "For passengers on the deck above? Or are they strictly for the ship's own people?"

"They're the most modern little things on the whole bloody vessel. Which isn't a monumental statement, I might add. Still, the company thought we'd better make them available to everyone. So sure, there's a sign, off the stern end."

B deck was the assemblage of restaurants, lounges, and rest areas assigned specifically for passengers.

"You were both down there," the purser said, looking hastily from Kaine to Jaymin. "If there's a bloody place to hide from the water, then I don't know about it. And what the water didn't bury, we've given a reasonably thorough going over."

"All right, then, what about A deck?" Jaymin said.

"If she'd gone topside," the purser answered with a grain of optimism, "then she'd sure enough have been thrown into the water."

But the harbormaster shook his head. "The sea is clean. That's the one thing we're sure of. She's in there," he said, nodding toward the structural blueprint and then out to the harbor. "If she was on the ferry, then she's still on the ferry, and it greatly distresses me to say it."

Kaine had ceased listening. His attention was focused on the blueprint section detailing subdeck C. Angela had left her backpack; had she gone to the main deck it would have been with the intent of watching their landing, and there would have been no reason to return below. A wrong turn had nonetheless led her to rest rooms a flight of stairs below, and Angela was adventurous enough to have sought them out. It was a hopeless bit of logic that was all Kaine had to pin his hopes on.

Angela had been tapping—a vigilant *tap, tap-tap, tap-tap* sequence—on and off for nearly three hours. She was doing it, she knew, more as a measure of self-control than with any genuine hope of rescue. The ship was surely alive, but the sounds were nature's own, not those of men searching. Sounds like that of rushing water, inconsistent streams which convinced Angela that other pockets of air existed throughout the ship, that perhaps a part of the ship remained above water. *Clear thinking.* Sounds like rusted hinges screeching in the night. Sounds like tree branches cracking under the weight of a heavy snow. Sounds like breakers slapping down on a sandy beach. Sounds that in time took on a familiarity, as do the groans of an old furnace in a drafty house, or the constant creaking of wooden floors.

The jolts of genuine fear came with the sudden and totally unpredictable shifts in the ferry itself. The result of the changing tides; Angela had reasoned this out, but the reasoning hadn't lessened her fear. The ferry would lunge forward, climbing the sand bar upon which it had come to rest, settle for an instant, and then slide. It would rise up in the water, slowly, effortlessly, and then, without warning, be cast down again, shudder, groan, and slide farther.

Then a wave of absolute quiet would ensue, a wave of utter motionlessness, a lull interrupted by a distant creak or a jet of water or a sigh as clear as if another human sat opposite her. And then the ferry would take flight again, thrust itself against an immovable force, and flop back down like a weary boxer. Angela would grasp at the water pipe or at the base of the sink, her heart crawling into her throat, holding on as if her very life was at stake.

She dozed off at ten thirty. An hour and ten minutes later she was thrust from this temporal escape by water now ankle-deep on the bathroom door. The water was icy cold. It caused the air temperature to plummet.

Because leaving her feet in the water would prove disastrous within minutes, Angela's only recourse was to straddle the wash basin protruding from the wall. One foot came to rest in the wash bowl, the other on the water pipe. There was essentially no head room; she twisted her upper torso, turning it sideways against what once was the ceiling. The cold of the metal permeated her cotton pants in the first instant, but it was not as cold as the water now stalking her.

Theirs not to make reply, theirs not to reason why, theirs but to do and die. Into the valley of death rode the six hundred. Angela wanted to laugh. The problem with an English school in the heart of Paris was that you might as well have been in an English school in the heart of London. What French writers? What French poets? Keats, Housman, Tennyson. *Theirs but to do and die. Into the valley of death* . . . Not so funny.

Angela took up the bent metal from the toilet paper dispenser. The water pipe was out of reach now. In the dark she searched and found the light fixture. Its metal casing was the same metal alloy as the basin and the stool. *Tap, tap-tap, tap-tap.* She peeked at her watch. It was one thirty-five. Have a plan, her dad who never had one always said. Okay then. No sleep; to sleep would be to invite disaster. Clear thinking. Yes. And no Tennyson.

5 First Skipper Tanner Thorpe poured ouzo in his coffee. He filled his mouth with chewing tobacco. He gestured with both the bottle and the can, but Kaine shook his head.

The harbor tug's pilothouse, a rounded room, was a tight fit for three people. At the head stood the ship's wheel. Before it lay the compass. The engine controls were positioned on either side of the wheel. Bell pulls hung beneath the windows. A long brass pipe, called the speaking tube, was attached to a side wall next to the window. Both the bells and the tube were, in this day and age, considered antiquated methods of communicating with the rest of the ship, but it was clear that Thorpe reveled in their use. Stretched across the ceiling, within easy reach, hung the whistle cords that allowed the skipper close-quarter communication with the various ships in his charge. The most modern devices aboard were the radio and telephone, and though Thorpe disdained both, he was generally on one or the other.

The hot plate that huddled in one corner of the navigational table was another device in constant use. A bunk was propped in one corner, and Jaymin had stretched out on it. Her eyes were closed, her hands behind her head. First Skipper Thorpe paced, and drank, and spat tobacco juice into a coffee can on the floor.

Kaine sat in one of two director's chairs. Angela's backpack rested upon a small circular table before him. Kaine toyed with the straps and a side-pocket zipper, and then fondled the top flap.

Their somber mood reflected a day and evening of sobering events. They waited because the regional commander deemed it necessary. The search would resume at four forty-five in the morning, an hour before dawn, and not a moment before.

The first skipper, a full-blooded Scot, swore. "Bloody, filthy English."

Idly, Kaine peeled the flap back. At the top of the pack lay the metal tube. What was it? Kaine's curiosity could not bring him to break the seal, not without Angela's permission. But it was obviously a Paris acquisition, he decided. A gift to herself, or from her mother.

Danielle had been in Paris two years now. Her promotion to IBM's international office there had been something of a coup. Since their divorce, a series of relationships had fallen apart on her, each as they became more serious, and now she was content, she had told Kaine, to be alone. Their divorce hadn't been what people call messy. The one and only point of contention had been custody of Angela, and Kaine had lost that battle. Ten weeks during summer break and two weeks over Christmas holiday, take it or leave it. Some settlement.

Kaine set the tube aside. Angela's key ring, with the Scottish medallion Kaine had found at the Cathedral of Mother Mary on the Isle of Lewis six years ago, was hooked to an inside zipper. A tattered square of pink and blue material from a blanket given to her when she was born fell into Kaine's hand. Only once had they talked about her giving the blanket up. Angela had argued that friends of absolute trust were rare enough and her blanket was as absolute as they came. To argue against such logic made no sense, Kaine realized, and so he hadn't. Under the blanket lay a journal, the contents of which Kaine had never been privileged enough to share. Now the words on the cover were illegibly smeared. There was a book called *A Wrinkle in Time*, and Kaine thumbed absently through its water-stained pages. A girl who read for the pure pleasure of the words, he thought. There was a change of clothes and a pair of ballet slippers. A silk case contained tiny pearl earrings. At the bottom of the pack he found a hairbrush and clips and a hair dryer she never left home without. There was also a Walkman and five tapes.

Tanner Thorpe bent over the table. He ran a cracked and bleached finger over the book and the earrings and the silk case. When he got to the clothing, he withdrew the finger. He turned aside and a stream of chewing tobacco juice exploded at the bottom of the coffee can. He slapped the wheel, paced, and swore again. "Fuck me. What's the time? Filthy English. What are we waiting for, the new moon?"

Jaymin's eyes snapped open. She rolled noiselessly onto the edge of the bunk, running her fingers pensively through her short-cropped hair. For a moment, she watched Kaine as he repacked Angela's things; he handled each item, she thought, as if it were a fragment of an ancient earthen chalice. The way only a father could.

She arose without a sound. She poured two fingers' worth of the first skipper's ouzo into a tin cup and drank it down in one swallow. The liquor was like fuel. "You know what I say, Mr. Thorpe? I say we forget the new moon. I say to hell with the Regional Commander and his petty threat of arrest. I say we get out to that ferry and find that girl. And I say we do it now. Right now. What do you say?"

Thorpe's stern gaze fell heavily upon Jaymin. Her expression in return was no less grave; she neither blinked nor wavered. Thorpe pulled his stocking cap an inch farther down his brow. "I say your companion here suffers from a corruptible sense of the law, Kaine. Don't get me wrong, but I find that rather attractive."

Kaine held his breath. "Is it possible?"

Thorpe threw up his hands, pacing, the exasperated elder. "We're a bloody harbor tug, aren't we? We can go where we want, pretty much any time we want; that's why this traffic jam of a harbor works. The exception at the moment is that ferry. You may consider the regional commander a fool, but he's got about a dozen armed boats out there making sure his foolishness is being steadfastly adhered to." Thorpe took a strong pull on his ouzo bottle. He wiped his mouth with the back of his hand. He winced, but not from the alcohol. "Then again, unless I'm very much mistaken, which happens now and again I must tell you, they'll not be patrolling the ferry seaside. Why should they? A waste of manpower. It's too shallow, given the sandbar that ferry's up against. His boats can't get any closer than this tug. Then again, we've a two-man raft down below that might just be worth the risk. And make no mistake about the risk."

"I accept the risk," Kaine said.

"Very noble. If the risk were only yours to accept."

"True."

"And that's only half the problem," Thorpe was quick to add. "The regional commander's right about the tides at the moment. Very unfriendly. That ferry's bouncing around out there like a rubber ball. And even if it wasn't, it's more than just a matter of a thirty-second plunge in a cold lake."

Kaine looked beyond the pilothouse window to the harbor. He nodded in agreement. He said, "In 1980, an archeological team I was a part of found the remnants of prehistoric cave dwellings at the base of the Rock of Gibraltar."

The first skipper's eyebrows raised. "The base of Gibraltar is a hundred feet underwater."

"I learned to dive," Kaine said, his train of thought unbroken. "Very well, in fact."

Thorpe looked grim. He launched a stream of tobacco toward the coffee can. Then he opened the pilothouse speaking tube and called down to the engine room. "Connor? You down there, boy? Fire the engines up. We're on the water in five minutes, hear? Then bring up that scuba diving equipment from the storage locker. And do it posthaste."

At two twenty-three a.m., the seal at the base of the rest-room door of subdeck C on the *Spirit of Long Life* gave out and water began leaking through in earnest. It rose up to a point just below the water pipe of the washbasin before jarring Angela from the throes of a fitful sleep. Without hesitating, she untied her shoes and peeled off her socks. Then she dropped onto her knees.

The rest room, on its side as it was, afforded no more than five feet of head room. By the time Angela located the leak, the room was half full.

Using two hands to work the wool sock into the crease along the door required submerging herself totally in water. Angela, much to her athletic mother's chagrin, was an inadequate swimmer at best; her most irreconcilable fear had always been of putting her face in the water.

Ours not to reason why, she heard herself mumble. *Ours but to do and die.* Oh God, if I get out of here alive I'll read Tennyson and the Bible every day. Promise. She drew a deep breath. *"Into the valley of death* . . . She plunged into the water. It stung, but she was better prepared for the cold this time. The sock held. She came up for air, half-starved for it, and without waiting plunged into the water again. As she was checking her handiwork, the ferry lurched forward. Angela's hands slipped and her head was thrust against the bulkhead. She came out of the water gasping for air, crying and swearing. Scared because this had been more severe than the shifting she had become accustomed to, the rising and the falling, the resettling. This had been more like a collision, or a tremor.

The impact had jarred loose the makeshift repair Angela had fashioned along the doorjamb, and the sock floated to the surface. It grazed Angela's arm and she gasped. Horrified, she wrenched the sock from the water, filled her lungs, and dropped to her knees again.

Angela knew she was in trouble. The force of the blow had somehow extended the break along the seal. The inflow was irreversible now. She forced one sock into the gap and clamped down on it with her right foot. The other sock she worked with increasingly stiff fingers along the seam. Her lungs burned. She turned her back to the wall, inched her left foot toward the seam, and stood up. Water oozed between her toes, now numb and aching. The water was chest-high. Angela covered her face with her hands. Her tears were warm.

The harbor tug *Broadside* settled in the swells a half mile beyond the southern breakwater of Dover's Admirality Harbor. First Skipper Tanner Thorpe had ordered all interior and exterior lights extinguished. It was a dangerous tactic. Thorpe was putting his career on the line and Kaine knew it. The tension showed on the first skipper's face and in every gesture.

The pilothouse door opened. Connor Thorpe walked in with a distressed look on his face. "Everything all right?"

"What could be better?" his father answered gruffly. "The raft?"

"The raft's in the water. We'll have to risk the outboard. It's too far to row. Wind's blowing out off the cliffs, though, so that's a bit of luck as far as the sound carrying." Connor shuffled his feet and got to the point. "It makes no sense to me that woman being the number two on the raft. I know these waters, she's . . ."

"The lady's going. I need you here. This tug's jumpier than I am, and anyone can push the tiller on an outboard. Subject closed." Thorpe threw a sidelong glance in Kaine's direction. "Give Mr. Kaine a hand with his gear."

"There's not much air," Connor said, carrying the oxygen tank out the door and down to the lower deck.

Kaine struggled into the wet suit; it was a size too small. He buckled the weight belt around his waist and a dive timer around his wrist. Connor held up the cylinder of compressed air and Kaine thrust his arms through the shoulder harness. He buckled the straps across his chest. Then he checked the pressure gauge.

"An hour and ten minutes' worth," the first skipper's son estimated. "Enough for what you have to do, one way or another."

Kaine acknowledged this life-and-death declaration with a remote nod. He adjusted the demand regulator on the mouthpiece. In a waterproof handgrip he stored a screwdriver, crowbar, ratchet set, and eight-ounce hammer. He strapped a long-bladed knife to his calf. In his hand he carried a watertight flashlight. Over his shoulder he coiled a length of rope.

Jaymin scrambled from the raft back onto the lower deck. "We're in for an interesting ride," she said. "I've been in bathtubs bigger than that thing." She walked around him, businesslike and maternal, checking his air tank and tightening straps. Finally she made eye contact. "Ready if you are."

They climbed into the raft. Jaymin pulled the starter cord. She adjusted the idle and tried again. The tiny outboard sputtered and started. Connor released the mooring. The night sky had an iron-ore cast to it. The wind bit into Jaymin's bare legs. A flask materialized from the pocket of her leather coat. Kaine watched her. "Compliments of the first skipper," she said. She uncapped it, drank, and held it out to him. Kaine shook his head.

In the distance, a helicopter circled, the beam from its searchlight scoring the water. It made a pass over the sunken *Spirit of Long Life*. Like a great sword, the beam cut a path over the rounded hull and then withdrew.

Jaymin took the swells head on. They made surprisingly good time.

All around them, the sea was littered with detritus from the ferry. Yellow lifejackets bobbed with acute irony among suitcases and handbags. A leaf-patterned sundress floated atop the water. An open umbrella created a centerpiece around which bar napkins circled. A baby carriage lay half-submerged on its side. Swells of oil-rich water lapped at the ferry's hull and ringed it in black. Twenty yards from the vessel, Jaymin cut the engine. The main deck was now a towering wall of steel jutting from the water.

She paddled to the stern end. Kaine secured the mooring. He tied one end of his rope to the topside railing and launched the other end into the water. He was hesitant, fearing not the dive, nor the ferry, nor the tide, but what he might find, or not find.

Jaymin clutched his arm. "Good luck."

Kaine moistened the inside of his diving mask and pulled it down over his eyes. "I'll find her," he heard himself say as he curled headfirst into the water.

Kaine entered the ship via a hatchway on the main deck. His flashlight threw a shaft of gold into the gray water; it lit the gray bulkheads a pasty white. He found a stairwell and a man bobbing face down in a three-piece suit, the arms of his coat billowing with trapped air. Kaine swam quickly past. Powerful kicks drove him down the flooded stairwell to the stern end of B deck.

Here, if Sara Birchfield was to be believed, was where Angela had gone when she discovered the bathrooms in the restaurant were locked. The beam of Kaine's flash came to rest on the sign indicating the facilities on subdeck C. The door wouldn't budge. Kaine wrenched at the handle. He threw as much weight as he could muster against it. He jammed the flash against a head-high window and it became clear that the stairwell roof had caved in, that the doors were fast up against it. Without hesitating, Kaine curled back into the B-deck passageway.

He peered into the lounge. Wine glasses, remarkably undamaged, swayed in the water like dancers with a last surge of energy. Beneath them, shards of broken glass—from whiskey and gin bottles, from a bar-length mirror, from a pair of bifocals—formed a mosaic against the wall.

Floodlights filled a portside restaurant farther on, and for an instant Kaine was sure he saw other divers; his heart skipped a beat. But the divers were only shadows cast by the blades of an overhead fan swaying restlessly in the water.

Near the bow end of B deck Kaine discovered the main stairway to the vehicle deck below. He followed the beam of his flash into the tangled mass of cars and trucks there, but paid no heed to the destruction. It took him two minutes to swim back to the stern end of the vessel. An EMPLOYEES ONLY sign hung in front of a metal staircase. Kaine used the handrail to pull himself along. The subdeck-C corridor was narrow and bathed in blackness. Water completely overwhelmed it. A second sign indicated the employee lockers and rest rooms. Kaine drew up. The rest rooms were starboard and therefore above him. The beam of his flash came to rest on the word WOMEN. He could feel his heart pounding in his throat; a hole ate away at his stomach.

When he had said "I'll find her" to Jaymin, he had meant, "I'll find her alive." Why had he said that? He had said it, he realized, not out of certainty, but to create a bridge for himself, a threshold over which he might cross from despair to some semblance of hope, no matter how tattered.

He turned the flash around; if Angela was behind that door and there was somehow a pocket of breathable air, it would disappear the moment the door opened. He rapped at the door with the blunt end of the flash, waited, and then did it a second time.

He heard a *tap-tap-tap* and a muffled cry.

Oh my God. He lunged for the handle, but the door wouldn't budge. He tucked the flashlight under his arm and used two hands. Nothing. The muffled cry continued. Hold on, baby. Kaine ripped open his handgrip and reached for the crowbar. He forced it into the seam along the doorframe. He anchored his feet against the opposite wall and threw his weight against it. The door gave. Air bubbles seeped out. Kaine wrenched the door free with his hands.

Angela's face was pressed against the bathroom ceiling. The water was up to her chin. The air space was fast disappearing. She gasped; her eyes were spheres of hysteria. Kaine filled his lungs. He took the mouthpiece out and held it up in front of Angela's face. His pantomime was simple. He showed her. Release your air, take a breath, hold it, pass the mouthpiece back. Angela nodded furiously. He tried to calm her, helping her with the mouthpiece and stroking her hair.

After Kaine's departure, Jaymin had maneuvered the raft beneath an overhang created by an inverted crane platform. The helicopter had returned twice. There was no pattern to its patrol; on its last pass, its roaming searchlight had flooded the water surrounding the platform, shadows bouncing off the bow of the raft.

Jaymin's nerves stood on end; she felt as if she had been staring into the harbor's oily water for hours. One thing was certain, he had been down there too long.

Waiting, she reminded herself, was a kind of nightmare you wake up from only to discover that the blankets of your bed are blankets of reality, parables of what actually is. A rape at gunpoint. A plane crash you've actually been in and somehow survived. A brother, with needle holes running along the veins of his arm, who hadn't survived. Dreams that always came back to haunt her. Dreams that weren't dreams at all, but the life she had so scornfully led.

Jaymin stared into the water and found she was a spectator

whose detachment had suddenly abandoned her. She was experiencing emotion, emotion beyond the anger and the petulance, beyond the insolence and her own death wish. This wasn't in her gut where she carried everything else. This came from another place, from a place she visited so infrequently that it felt like a foreign land; this came from her heart.

In her head, Jaymin counted off the men who had, over the years, foolishly proclaimed their love for her. In return, she had been able to offer them only her indifference, her scorn. It was a state of mind. To use and discard. As it turned out, the words of Sister Immaculata at the orphanage had made an impression, had in fact created a life philosphy for her: *Love nothing and nothing will rob you of you.*

But it was not indifference she felt now. This was something vastly different. Staring down at the black water and remembering Angela Kaine's smile, Jaymin realized that here was one person she would gladly have died to save.

The sea at her feet erupted in bubbles.

Jaymin saw the dull glow of a flash rising up to the surface. She fell to her knees. Pressing as close to the water as possible, she saw two shadows. Then the rope at her feet was drawn taut.

Angela's face broke the surface first. She was drawing hard on the mouthpiece of the air hose. Her eyes seemed frozen with shock and surprise. Her round face was bruised and flushed. She pulled frantically at the mouthpiece and gasped at the onrush of real air. Jaymin reached into the water and hoisted her out. Angela collapsed in her arms. She shook uncontrollably.

Kaine pulled himself from the water. He touched Angela's face, pushing wet strands of hair from her forehead. "You didn't leave me," she said.

"Never. You know that."

"I was quoting Tennyson and swearing on the Bible and . . . anything I could think of. Oh God, when the seal around that door broke and . . ." She ran out of breath. Now she recognized Jaymin. "You made it."

"We both made it," Jaymin said. She took a fresh handkerchief from her jacket pocket and carefully dabbed the water from Angela's face. "You're quite a girl. You were down there a long time. I don't know if I could have done it."

Jaymin wrapped Angela in a goosedown sleeping bag Connor Thorpe had thought to throw into the raft. Kaine started the outboard. Fifteen minutes later, they were safely aboard the tug. Connor provided a roaring fire in the coal stove, fresh clothes, and three blankets. A pot of boiling water rattled atop the stove and a cup of weak tea was brewed.

Tanner Thorpe introduced himself. He looked her up and down, a wry smile twisting his ruddy face. "From the looks of her, I'd say she was worth the trouble."

"Believe it," Kaine replied.

The first skipper eyed him. "Close?"

Kaine shuddered. "Close."

Angela spied her backpack; she couldn't believe it had been saved. "I left it with a woman in the restaurant. Her name was . . ." Angela's brow furrowed. "I can't remember."

"Sara Birchfield," Kaine replied. He smiled reassuringly. "She's all right. And some way or another she held on to your backpack."

"Good. Because there's a . . ." Angela hesitated. "There's a present in it for you."

Jaymin served her tea, a light smile touching her lips. "Not the pearl earrings, I hope."

"No." Angela tipped her head, embarrassed. Then she looked at her father. "From a friend of yours. His name—"

"Let's talk about it when we get ashore, Angie," Kaine said. He knew at once who she meant. Ras Haydar. His suspicions about Haydar's presence on the ferry now had a measure of substance to them: the metal tube in Angela's backpack. Kaine put his arm around her. "Give yourself a chance to rest."

"We'll be docking in a couple of minutes," Connor Thorpe said. He paused a moment before stepping out onto the lower deck. "I'm glad you're safe," he said to Angela.

"He didn't make it, did he?" Angela said to her father when Connor was gone. Jaymin poured more tea.

"Who, Angie?" Kaine said.

"Your friend." She closed her eyes and pressed against him. "He's dead, isn't he?"

For a moment, Kaine let his imagination dwell on this insight. He turned his eyes curiously down at his daughter. Finally, he said, "No, Angie, Ras didn't make it."

Kaine carried Angela ashore. With the rescue operation still in a state of suspension, there was a line of empty ambulances waiting on the quay. Jaymin ran ahead. She returned with an RAF doctor whose only questions were where and when, not how; Kaine respected him for that.

On the way to the hospital, the doctor ran tests for hypothermia, took Angela's blood pressure, and twice examined her eyes. "We'll keep her in the hospital overnight," he told Kaine. "Just for precautionary measures."

The doctor found Angela a bed in the pediatrics ward between a jaundiced baby and a man with tubes feeding into his nose. She fell into a deep sleep almost at once.

"To be expected," the doctor said. "She'll be out twelve hours, maybe more. You look like you could use some yourself. Waiting here makes no sense. Give me a chance to do my job, why don't you?"

"If she wakes up—"

"I know where to find you."

Jaymin left the hospital ahead of Kaine. Her parting words were, "I'll bet you could use a few minutes alone with that daughter of yours, and I *know* you've seen enough of this face for a while."

Kaine looked at her intently. "Yes and no," he said, not certain why he had put it that way.

Jaymin drove straight to London, to the Belgravia Hotel on Brompton Street. She made a brief stop at her room on the fourth floor. From the bottom drawer of the nightstand she retrieved a small cassette tape recorder, a replacement for the one she had left on the ferry. She strapped it to her lower back. Then she returned to the lobby. The public telephone was situated in a corner across from the registration desk.

Before dialing, Jaymin clipped the dime-size microphone to the receiver and punched the record button on the tape recorder. She had taped well over a hundred conversations in two years. An obsession had grown out of this; excessive notes often rambled on for pages. Some broached subjects irrelevant to the tapes. Some confessed to emotions and feelings so deep that Jaymin would never consider sharing them with anyone, least of all her superiors.

She dialed the number in Lambeth, and the colonel answered after a single ring.

"Where have you been?"

"I didn't know I was on a time clock," Jaymin replied. By now she had identified the stowaway as Ras Haydar, and she told the colonel about the metal tube he had passed on to Angela Kaine.

"You're sure it was Haydar?" the colonel asked.

"You knew he'd come back to haunt us."

"But you didn't think it was important enough to mention while we were on the ferry."

"I wasn't sure. It was a mistake," Jaymin admitted. "I only saw the man once before in my life, and that was for about five minutes."

"You were stoned."

"I warned you and your friends about involving the likes of Haydar and his brother in the first place. They don't think like we do."

"Well, they're both dead now," the colonel said. "So maybe the ferry accident was a blessing in disguise."

"Meaning you won't have to be looking over your shoulder every five minutes."

There was a measure of relief in the colonel's sigh. "Vindictive, wasn't he?"

"Vindictive as hell, but revenge wasn't his only motive for sinking that ferry," Jaymin reminded him.

"You're certain he knew about the Mercedes?"

"He knew."

"And the tube he passed on to Stephen Kaine's daughter? You think there's a connection?"

"Of course there's a connection," Jaymin answered impatiently.

"Find out what it is. And find out about Kaine. He's the last person we need in our lives right now."

"I agree," Jaymin said. "And what about the Mercedes?"

"Scotland Yard will take care of the car. You just be there when they do."

"Does this affect our timetable?" Jaymin asked carefully. "Do we move it up?"

"The timetable stays the same until I say otherwise."

6 Kaine booked a room at a bed-and-breakfast on King Street, dropped his bag, and then returned to the street. A church bell echoed high atop the cliffs. Three singular gongs. Despite the predawn hour, there were people up and about, but they talked in hushed tones; they seemed to walk on tiptoes. It was the accident, Kaine thought. Who could sleep with that at your doorstep?

He jumped a trolley bound for the harbor. The smell of baking bread served to energize him, though not to eat. His preoccupation centered on the metal tube Angela had stowed in her backpack. She had been so quick to mention it. "A present from a friend of yours," she had said. Ras Haydar.

The first skipper and his son were drinking coffee in the harbor tug's pilothouse. Thorpe was toying with his bell pulls. Connor lay upon the bunk, his cup balanced on his stomach. He swung his legs into a sitting position the moment Kaine entered.

"Well?"

Kaine smiled wanly, nodding. "She's sleeping. The doctor kicked me out. A motel room didn't sound too appealing."

"Connor, my boy, I do believe we've just been complimented," the first skipper said.

"You risked a lot going out there tonight," Kaine said.

"All we did tonight was prove that risk is a bloody relative term, Kaine, and there's no denying that."

Angela's backpack was lying in a corner at the end of the bunk. Kaine set it on the circular table in the center of the pilothouse. He slid the metal tube out from beheath the top flap. He felt its weight, judged it to be an industrial metal alloy of some sort. A high-tensile steel, perhaps. Angela was a collector of maps and her walls were covered with posters, but this was not the type of tube a bookstore or poster shop gave away. A plastic epoxy had been used to seal the cap.

"So maybe our select company wasn't the only reason for your return visit, after all," Thorpe said, chuckling and fishing a pocket knife from his pants. "You'll need this."

Kaine sliced through the epoxy and unscrewed the cap. Despite the nature of the tube, a tightly rolled sheet of paper fell open to reveal a poster of Janet Jackson. She wore a black tuxedo adorned with gold and silver sequins and white gloves.

"Who's this?" Thorpe asked.

"Michael Jackson's sister," Kaine answered.

"Oh, naturally." The first skipper grinned. "How foolish of me."

Kaine spread the poster full-length across the navigational table. "She's an American singer," he explained.

"One of Angela's favorites?"

"I really don't know. I haven't seen my daughter in four months," Kaine said. He shook his head, obviously distracted.

"You were expecting something else."

"Your daughter said something about a present from a friend," Connor Thorpe said. "Did she ever say what?"

"I assumed she meant the tube," Kaine said. He examined it once more inside and out. The first skipper was rolling the poster up again when he stopped suddenly. He flattened the poster out and turned it over.

"What is it?" Kaine asked, hunching over the table.

"There's more." What the first skipper had discovered was that a separate piece of white parchment had been taped, with extreme care, to the back of the poster.

The parchment measured perhaps fifteen inches by twenty, and Kaine, once he had removed it, was astounded by what its surface revealed. It was a complete blueprint, sketched in black and red ink and remarkably detailed, of the city of Karmin-Yar. The words had been scratched along the bottom border.

The first skipper and his son crowded nearer. "Who or what is Karmin-Yar?" Thorpe said impatiently. "Speak up, man."

"Karmin-Yar was the northernmost city in the Persian Empire," Kaine answered, numbed by the discovery. "It was built in 519 B.C. The Persians considered it their second capital. The city was located on the Black Sea, in the Cappodocian province of Asia Minor. It was lost for over two thousand years, wiped off the face of the earth by an earthquake that reshaped the coastline of the Black Sea. I discovered its location five and a half years ago. The Turkish government gave me permission to uncover the site, and that's what I was doing until six months ago."

"You finished?"

"Hardly. The project is less than a third complete. I was released. My passport was confiscated. I was deported."

"Why?" Thorpe asked.

"Cost overruns."

"Everything runs over its costs. What were you using, gold-plated shovels?"

"We were under budget a hundred and fifty thousand dollars."

"I thought you just said . . ." As he looked hard at Kaine's profile, the first skipper's brows formed a bridge of concentration over his eyes. He took a drink of ouzo straight from the bottle. Then he said, "Two thousand years is a long time to be buried. Or should I say, a long time to suffer rediscovery after. Why do you do it?"

"Because knowing where we've been provides us with a key as to what we've become," Kaine answered without hesitation. "And besides, I'm good at it."

"Fair enough," Thorpe said, though the endorsement carried with it a grumble of dissatisfaction. Then he pondered the blueprint, the lines on his ruddy face deepening. "So then, what's your problem?"

"There is no blueprint to the city of Karmin-Yar. At least there hasn't been up to now, and some rather good minds have been working on the problem for a long time." Kaine sighed. "Historically, the Persians kept all their official documents at Persepolis, their first capital."

"Which, unfortunately, Alexander the Great burnt to the ground twenty years after Karmin-Yar disappeared," Connor Thorpe interjected. Kaine's eyes came up in appreciation. "The city and everything in it."

Kaine nodded. "Alexander thought that by wiping out Persepolis, he could in effect wipe out the whole Persian empire. And in some respects he was right."

"But not in others." The first skipper was impatient. He threw a second glance in the direction of the blueprint. "Someone obviously knows something you don't."

"So it would seem."

"Or they're guessing," Thorpe said. "Or extrapolating from what you already know."

"I don't think so. They've labeled every chamber. And two of the chambers we've already uncovered are labeled differently. And I'd say correctly."

A meeting hall was now a court library according to the blueprint, and an anteroom to the palace of Darius was now a bathhouse. The archeological expedition under Kaine's direction had also uncovered the city's ceremonial palace, the town square, the *apadana* or audience hall, an amphitheater, the Great Treasure House, and the house of the city's satrap and high priest. At the time of Kaine's unexpected departure six months ago, excitement had been running high at the discovery of the north portico of the harem of King Xerxes.

Structures as yet undiscovered or unidentified by the expedition, yet confidently depicted on this most remarkable blueprint, were the temple of Cyrus, the temple of fire, the palace of Artaxerxes, the king's court, the royal tombs, a second amphitheater, a market center and business district, and residential complexes of the elite and the not so elite. Within the city, the treasure house, though drawn in black as were the majority of the buildings, had been circled. The king's court and the fire temple, on the other hand, had been drawn in red; more curious still were the dotted lines of an access tunnel which connected the two. Why? Kaine wondered.

"The fire temple was the most important building in any Persian city. Its most sacred," he said. "The first built and the first destroyed in case of siege."

"The home of their eternal flame," First Skipper Thorpe ventured.

"That's right. And the exclusive domain of the high priest and priestess. Under penalty of death."

"And the king's court?"

Kaine gestured disconcertedly at the blueprint. "The king's court was where the King of Kings conducted his business. When he was in the city. And since the Persians' empire stretched from India to Eygpt, that was maybe once a year."

"And this one. The one circled in black. The treasure house. You said you'd already uncovered it."

"Eight columns, three walls, and the entire west portico. We were fortunate."

"And discovered what? In a Persian treasure house, it must have been extraordinary."

Kaine's hand brushed across his chin. "The vaults of the treasure house were empty."

"Empty?" Connor Thorpe expressed his disbelief by slapping at the bell pulls.

"That's exactly how the Turkish government reacted, or were convinced to react."

"Explaining your sudden release six months ago. Yes?" the first skipper said.

"I thought the Persians were noted for their benevolence," his son added. "Not their generosity."

"They taxed their realm to the point of bankruptcy. And they were only interested in gold and silver," Kaine replied. "Besides benevolence, the Persians' other outstanding trait was a manic distrust for anything that walked and talked. History suggests that the Persians kept their treasure in Susa or Persepolis, very close to home, where the king could keep his eye on it."

"An explanation the Turkish government didn't buy."

"Not after they found a talent of gold darics in my tent."

Now both father and son were staring at Kaine. "Is a daric what I think it is?" the elder asked.

"Darics were the standard gold coin of the Persian empire," his son answered. "A talent weighed in at about sixty pounds, isn't that right, Mr. Kaine? A fair amount of money. Well?"

"Like all darics, the coins were stamped with an impression of Darius himself. Very authentic."

"Is that an explanation?"

Kaine smiled briefly at the young man—a resigned, distracted smile—but didn't answer. He gave his attention back to the blueprint instead.

At that moment, a voice rose up from outside on the dock. "First Skipper Tanner Thorpe. Detective Superintendent Christopher Preble here. Scotland Yard. May we come aboard, please? First Skipper Thorpe. Are you there, sir?"

"Well, aren't we honored, given the conversation," the first skipper said. He took the blueprint over to the navigational table, laid it face down on Angela's poster, and rolled the two into a tight cylinder. He slipped it back into the metal tube, which he dropped into the chart rack. Then he said to his son, "Well? We can't keep the good detective waiting all night, now can we? Ask him aboard."

Detective Superintendent Preble was a large, hunched man. Patches of red drew attention to an otherwise delicate, featureless face. He smiled remotely, as if out of practice. His handshake was like a huge glove. His walk was more of a scud, as if a hand at his back pushed him encouragingly along. His eyes dissected the pilothouse with mechanical quickness.

His partner introduced himself as Detective Hennagan. In the area of size and posture they were a matched set. Hennagan, however, did not smile, nor did he shake hands. He studied the people, not the place. He eased into a chair and allowed the detective superintendent to conduct matters.

"Sorry to barge in like this, gents. I know it's been a damn brutal evening." Five people in the pilothouse was intolerable, but

Preble managed to stroll nonetheless. He ran a hand along the brass speaking tube, took a moment to study the barometer, and drummed lightly at the wheel. At the chart rack next to the table he toyed momentarily with Angela's metal tube. Then he turned, perched on the edge of the table, and misused his smile a second time. "It's Mr. Kaine, isn't it? Stephen Kaine? The archeologist?"

In reply, Kaine stepped up to the coffeepot. He filled a clay mug half full. "It's no secret."

"We've been informed that your daughter has checked into the hospital. That her condition is guarded, but that she is out of danger. I can't imagine your relief."

"News travels."

"It was the timing that raised a few eyebrows." The detective poked a finger into his ear and screwed his face into a knot. "However, knowing she is safe makes it that much easier to ask you to come by the station for a few minutes. We have a situation."

"Situation?"

The first skipper scoffed. "In the precise words of the *Oxford English Dictionary,* a state of being with regard to circumstances." Thorpe spat in the direction of the coffee can on the floor and missed by a foot. "It seems to me the circumstances are pretty clear, unless you're double-parked somewhere. So maybe it's the state of being surrounding the circumstances you're wondering about. I'm curious myself."

Preble bowed his head. Then he fixed Kaine with a look of incomparable patience. "You're familiar with a man named Ras Haydar. He was a co-worker of yours. His body was taken from the vehicle section of that ferry lying on its side out there in the harbor. Now the reason the ferry is lying out there on its side is because the bow doors of the vehicle deck were opened prematurely. We have a witness who will testify to this Mr. Haydar's presence in the control room at the precise moment of the accident. This same witness has suggested that Mr. Haydar engaged your daughter— Angela is her name, I believe—in a conversation earlier in the crossing. This witness also suggests that there was an exchange of some kind between Mr. Haydar and Angela."

"Other than the rudiments of a normal, good old-fashioned conversation, I think is what he's saying," Tanner Thorpe said, a languishing glance taking in both policemen.

"A metal tube," Preble said, fingering the tube in the chart rack. "Very much like this one, I would imagine."

"Probably only two or three like that in the whole world," Thorpe said, now giving his entire attention to Preble.

Preble in return acknowledged only Kaine. "A certain Ms. Sara Birchfield tells us . . . does that name carry any meaning at all with you, sir?" Now Preble disengaged long enough to shift his gaze toward Angela's backpack. He raised an eyebrow, then an open palm. "Yes, I guess that it does, doesn't it? Regardless, I'll ask you to bring the young lady's belongings along. And, perhaps, with your permission, we might have a look."

"Witness?" Kaine said finally. He set his cup down but didn't move. "What witness?"

"A witness who prefers to remain anonymous for the time being. Nonetheless, a witness whose credentials we have followed up on. A witness who is trying to help us discover the hows and whys of the tragedy of this evening. We were hoping the same from you, frankly."

"It's a bloody lead," Detective Hennagan chimed in at last, expressing impatience with them all, including his own superior. "We intend following this lead until it drops from exhaustion or bears the kind of fruit we're looking for. The same way we'll follow every lead we come across."

"And I intend being at Dover County Hospital the moment my daughter is released," Kaine replied. He ignored Hennagan in favor of Preble. "Don't ask me to be anywhere else."

"We'll make certain you're nowhere but," Preble assured him. He slid off the table. Again he said, "If you'll bring along Angela's backpack. And any other possessions of hers that you may have been given."

Kaine hooked the backpack over his shoulder. He stopped at the pilothouse door and looked back. "Whenever you're ready."

"That's everything?" Preble said, observing the room a last time.

"Just the pack," Kaine replied.

The detective tipped his head, his reluctance an open acknowledgment of the lie. "Fine," he said.

Nonetheless, when they were outside on the dock Preble stopped. He lit a cigarette, sent a fountain of gray smoke skyward, and peered out at the harbor. The air filled with the drum and drone of marine diesels. A foghorn sent a blanket of sound across the water. A thin mist tinged the air a sprightly silver; English fairy dust, the fishermen called it. Preble poked a finger in his ear again and turned a knotted face inland. The vast chalk cliffs towered above the roofs of Georgian houses, but it was clear to Kaine that these were of no interest to the policeman.

Preble hunched his shoulders, purportedly in response to the cool night air. Then he said to Hennagan, "See Mr. Kaine to the station. I feel we were a bit rude not allowing the first skipper to offer us a cup of coffee. I'll be along shortly."

7 Kaine faced the police in a stuffy, dimly lit room in a highly modern building that seemed drastically out of place in a seaside town on the coast of England.

While they waited for Detective Superintendent Preble's return, Detective Hennagan concentrated on Angela's backpack. He fingered and photographed every article. His thick hands knew nothing of grace or privacy.

Kaine clenched his jaw. "I'll repack it if you don't mind," he said to Hennagan.

"Fine. Be my guest." The detective shrugged. Then he lit a cigarette, smoked, paced, and studied the floor as if it might prove more revealing than the contents of the backpack. Kaine was running his hand over the cover of Angela's journal when Hennagan posed an unexpected question. He said, "Your daughter normally flies into London on her visits with you. Isn't that right?"

Kaine didn't answer for a moment. The detective's eyes came up and Kaine held them. Eventually, he said, "How would you know that?"

"Your ex-wife. Danielle. We spoke with her twenty minutes ago. She's very concerned, naturally." Hennagan crushed his cigarette out on the floor. "I'm sure you had every intention of calling her yourself."

In fact, Kaine hadn't even thought of it, and the oversight struck him harder than he would have expected.

"She asked about your well-being, by the by," the detective said.

"Did she?" Kaine replied. He was on the verge of adding, "I'm glad," but didn't.

"At any rate, it was your suggestion that Angela, if I'm not being too bold calling her by name . . . It was your suggestion that she take the ferry from Calais."

"That's true."

"Perhaps you could be so good as to explain the suggestion." Now Hennagan placed himself within an arm's length of Kaine, hands locked across his rumpled shirt; his eyes were a cold, stark blue, as disconcerting as they were penetrating.

"The cliffs," Kaine answered. He felt beads of moisture beneath his shirt and his eyes wandered. It was three forty-five in the morning; outside street lamps cast a yellow haze down on Maison Dieu Road. Kaine's ears picked out the lonely cry of a tug whistle. "A person should experience the cliffs of Dover. At sunset? Off the bow of a ferry? It's a sight you don't forget. Angela was excited about the idea."

"You didn't tell her about a certain stowaway she would be meeting, I assume," Hennagan challenged. "Ras Haydar. And now you'll tell me his presence on the ferry was a surprise to you, as well."

"I feel like I'm being interrogated, Detective Hennagan. Why is that?"

"Questioned, Professor Kaine. You're being questioned. There's a difference."

Hennagan didn't have time to explain the difference. A moment later, Detective Superintendent Preble entered the room. He did so without knocking. Under his arm he carried the metal tube from Angela's pack.

"Mr. Kaine was just about to explain his co-worker's presence on the *Spirit of Long Life*," Hennagan told him. "The stowaway? Ras Haydar?"

"Don't let me interrupt," Preble said. He laid the tube on the table in front of Kaine.

"There's nothing to interrupt," Kaine said. "Ras was a laborer on an archeological project I was in charge of some time ago. The city of Karmin-Yar, near the Black Sea. His family probably farmed tobacco or cotton. They probably raised sheep, too. Karmin-Yar was twenty miles from his home; I think that was as far away as he'd ever been."

Preble unfolded a piece of paper from his inside pocket. It was yellow and had the look of a fax reply.

"In fact, Ras Haydar, as you call him, was born in Istanbul in 1955, was reared in Ankara, and educated at London University. As of six months ago, he was a member of the Cappadocian secret police, working, as you said, undercover as a laborer at Karmin-Yar. What his official police duties were, we don't as yet know."

Preble watched Kaine's shoulders sag. The detective's expression never changed. He went on: "However, Haydar's problems began about the same time yours did. And were much the same. He was accused of tampering with historical artifacts found on official government property, which translates into simple theft in my book. Though, the way I understand it, not on the same grand scale as you."

"Lies."

"Surely. You were never charged. Neither was he, apparently. The Turkish government tried to find a connection between you and Haydar, but without success. Now he shows up on a Dover ferry bearing gifts for your daughter." Preble picked up the tube again. He turned it in his hands, slid his palm over the surface. "First Skipper Tanner Thorpe says he knows nothing about it, that the tube came out of his chart rack and therefore probably contains some obscure depth chart he's never had the pleasure of using. He has given us his permission to open the tube, and now, since it was ostensibly a part of your daughter's luggage, I will ask you for your consent. Do we have it?"

Kaine held out a hand. "May I look?"

"Please." Preble seemed eager for him to examine it.

While Kaine hoped for some evidence to the contrary, it was, to be sure, the tube in which the poster and blueprint had come; along the rim of the cap a crust of epoxy remained. Still, he returned it with a guileless shrug, saying, "You don't need my consent, Detective Preble. I know nothing about it."

"Very well." Preble uncapped the tube and a ream of oceanographic charts spilled out. He thumbed from one to the next, revealing an orderly replication of the reef line from Romney Marsh south of Dover, north to Kingsdown, and as far along the coast as Deal, near the mouth of the Thames. Neither the poster nor the blueprint was there. Kaine breathed an inaudible sigh of relief.

Outside, a harbor bell tolled. High tide had reached its peak and was now receding. Preble appeared neither shaken by the meaningless charts nor moved by the tolling bell. In fact, he yawned.

Finally he said, "It would appear we've kept you long enough, Professor Kaine. I'm pleased to know your daughter's been found. Of course, I'll expect to have a word with her when she's up to it. Detective Hennagan will see you back to the dock." Preble returned the charts to the tube, capped it, and tapped it thoughtfully against his palm. "Perhaps you'll see these charts back to the first skipper for me. With my thanks, of course."

Hennagan dropped Kaine at the Athol Terrace without a word. Remnants of the tortured rescue operation now nine hours old had evolved into the tortured preparations of a salvage operation just thirty minutes from commencement. Ambulances hovered at the ferry terminal. The Royal Navy stationed a dozen boats in the water. The *Spirit of Long Life* lay hunched upon a sandbar illuminated by the moving lights of helicopters and cutters. Thirty minutes. Kaine shook his head. In thirty minutes Angela would have been dead for two hours. What was it the regional commander had said? "The bodies of the dead were not worth risking the lives of the living." Well spoken, Kaine thought.

Night evolved. The crisp, cutting blackness gave way to a ghostly silver.

The Athol Terrace gave access to the eastern docks, which adjoined the south jetty. Along the jetty, arc lights spilled pools of glitter over the moorings of three harbor tugs, among them the one called *Broadside*.

As Kaine turned the corner he saw a man stepping off the tug's lower deck. He was short and squat, and even in this light, Kaine could see that his dress was more appropriate to the city than to the sea. He wore a three-piece suit and shoes with the high gloss of spit polish. The jetty lights reflected off his gold cuff links, and his sandy hair was swept back in a high wave.

The first skipper, with a stocking hat pulled low over his brow and his cheek bulging with chewing tobacco, followed the man outside. Thorpe paused on the lower deck, wrapping an arm around a four-foot-high steel bitt. Their voices, though guarded, carried over the water nonetheless.

"You'll be hearing from me," Kaine heard the first skipper say.

"Oh yes. And you'll be very much on my mind," the man replied. He started down the quay and two compatriots fell in at his side. Bodyguards. This was clear by their size, but also by their close attention to the surroundings.

Kaine stepped into a dockside phone booth and raised the receiver from the cradle. The bodyguards caught sight of him. One sauntered over to the booth, much the way a prospective caller might, and stood beside it. In response, Kaine feigned a heated conversation with an imaginary lover. He found himself nearly shouting, "Don't talk to me like I'm a goddamn child." He slapped the side of the booth and the glass shook. "Mother someone else if that's what you need. I've already got a mother."

Shaking his head, the bodyguard moved on, trotting to catch up with his partner and their well-dressed employer. Kaine slammed down the phone and stepped back out onto the quay. The man and his two friends moved swiftly along the eastern dock and turned left onto Athol Terrace. Kaine followed, not knowing why, but certain this scene had something to do with the ferry accident and Angela and the treatment he had just received at the police station—with one or all of them, he didn't know and didn't care. One and all, he decided, were surely related.

A century and a half ago, the terrace had been built on stilts, then on chunks of limestone, and finally on concrete pillars. The castle jetty was shaped from broken slabs of chalk and shone like blocks of ice as it stretched out into the water. Footsteps echoed. The cliff rose into the air, threatening and hypnotic; under its gaze the world's busiest harbor looked small and insignificant.

A jog in the road took the trio onto Townhall Street. A puff of smoke arose from their midst and Kaine caught the acrid scent of a cigar. Their pace slowed. The street meandered on cobblestones amid government buildings and the gardens of a city park. Their car was parked, half on, half off the curb, next to a bed-and-breakfast called Truly's.

It was a blue Toyota. The license plate was typically British. A simple black and white rectangle with four letters and four numbers: MSBD1403. Kaine memorized it. Then he saw the sticker on the right-hand side of the bumper. It read, MAXIM RENTAL, LONDON, OXFORD, BIRMINGHAM.

When Kaine returned to the tug, Tanner Thorpe was excited but didn't say anything about his visitor.

Kaine didn't pursue it. Instead, he laid the metal tube on the table. "You switched the poster and blueprint for the navigational charts."

"I figured I'd better move with a certain speed. That Scotland Yard gent would be back, quite naturally. He's English, after all. And you can always count on the English. Such redundantly correct folk. He knew about the tube, sure enough, just like he knows that his wife'll be wearing curlers to bed every Monday, Wednesday, and Saturday. So he asked you the question in a most courteous way, and you answered in a most American fashion. You lied. It wouldn't have been right to challenge you straight out, so he left and came back. Enough time for an old Scot to embellish the lie." Thorpe replaced the charts with the tube's original contents. He slipped the tube into Angela's backpack and handed it to Kaine.

"He knows better, of course, this Detective Preble of yours. Which brings up another thing about the bloody English: Their patience is disgustingly unlimited and they never give up. Do you hear? He'll be around."

"I'll remember that," Kaine said.

8 They released a wan but happy Angela from Dover County Hospital the morning of the following day. Kaine wrapped an arm around her shoulder.

Jaymin met them as they emerged from the front door. She raised a hand in greeting. Her stride was nimble and catlike, her lithe frame draped in an oversize leather coat. She wore makeup; a mere touch brought out the brilliance of her green eyes, the fullness of her lips, and carved out the slopes and valleys around her cheekbones.

"Well, young lady, I thought I'd better see if the color had returned to those cheeks of yours, but I guess I didn't need to worry. You look great."

Angela gave her a tired smile. "Thanks. You, too."

Jaymin touched her cheek, then turned an exploratory glance in Kaine's direction. "Truthfully, I just wanted to be here. Not to intrude. I hope it's all right."

"I'm glad you came."

"Me too," Angela said.

Jaymin took hold of Angela's hand. "Do you have a place?"

"On King Street. Near the harbor," Kaine answered.

"I saw your car," Jaymin said, laughing, and nodding in the

direction of the Honda. "I'd offer my services as a chauffeur, but I don't know if you trust me after our last ride together?"

"Good point," Kaine grinned. He handed her the keys anyway.

The bed-and-breakfast was a converted Georgian three-story. The day manager provided them with a key to Kaine's second-floor room, and also handed over the metal tube he had consigned to the hotel safe the previous afternoon.

Angela fell asleep almost immediately. Jaymin covered her with a down quilt and kissed her forehead. Kaine watched the interaction.

"When I first saw her," Jaymin said, "she reminded me so much of a friend I once had that I literally had to talk myself out of running up to her and throwing my arms around her." Jaymin turned away from the bed, crossing her arms. "But Angela is very much her own person, isn't she? More like Mom or Dad?" Jaymin instantly pushed the question away with an open palm. "Sorry. Don't answer that. Stupid question."

Kaine laid the metal tube in the bottom drawer of a freestanding dresser, then threw himself into the room's one overstuffed chair. Every nerve in his body tingled. The last thirty-six hours had provided him with almost no sleep. That his daughter was alive left him lightheaded, the relief was so overwhelming.

Danielle had called twice, once from Paris and again when she had reached Calais. She was due in on the next Hovercraft. Kaine couldn't trust his feelings. He admitted an undeniable interest in seeing her—but then she would almost certainly insist upon taking Angela back to France, and Kaine had no intention of allowing that.

His eyes were heavy with fatigue. He looked across the room at Jaymin. She had thrown her leather jacket on the floor in the corner. She was leaning against a narrow mahogany credenza, her arms folded across a heavy flannel shirt. There was an electricity to her presence, nervous yet controlled. A sensuality she seemed capable of turning on and off at will.

"What was her name?" Kaine asked.

"Who?"

"Your friend?"

Jaymin was momentarily embarrassed, then pleased. "Marion."

"Pretty."

"Yes, but I spend too much time in the past as it is," Jaymin replied. She tipped her head in Angela's direction. "She'll be famished when she wakes up. How about you? When was the last time you ate?"

"To be honest, a drink sounds better than food," Kaine said.

A wry smile hung on the corners of Jaymin's lips. "You read my mind." She pushed away from the credenza. "Don't move. There's got to be a bottle in this place somewhere."

She returned five minutes later. Kaine was stretched out on the bed next to his daughter. His arm was draped over Angela's shoulders and his eyes were closed.

The kitchen downstairs had provided Jaymin with a bottle of cheap Scotch and a plastic bag filled with ice. She took both into the bathroom. On the theory that even cheap Scotch was not meant to be tampered with in any way, she emptied the ice into the sink. She poured three fingers' worth into a plastic cup, and drank deeply while staring back at her reflection in a wood-framed mirror. But she couldn't bear it; she turned on the cold tap and splashed water onto her face, ran her fingers briskly through her hair. She reached into her bag of dogmatic quotes. *Whatever doesn't kill you, makes you stronger.* Nietzsche. Jaymin laughed. What trash, she thought.

Before the cynicism wore off, Jaymin carried her glass and the bottle back into the room. She stopped at the window. Beyond lay the harbor. The remnants of a ragged fishing fleet were creeping slowly out to sea; as if it were cursed, they were giving wide berth to the sunken *Spirit of Long Life.* From a distance, the ferry suggested a mammoth gray whale, entrapped and bloodied. A skirt of black oil draped about its lower body. With the tide, the skirt broke into islands and drifted toward shore.

Jaymin poured a second drink. Behind her, father and daughter had not moved. She observed their steady breathing a moment, drank, then moved with long strides to the dresser. The metal tube lay in the bottom drawer among bed sheets and bath towels. Kaine had obviously not shared its contents with the police, and this pleased Jaymin. She carried the tube across to the credenza. She drank again, stared, and suffered an unmistakable case of misgivings. This was particularly odd because Jaymin was rarely given to either misgivings or second guesses. She remembered Sister Immaculata accusing her of gross self-indulgence. She would say, "Don't you ever stop to think, child? Actions spur consequences, you know, and oftimes the consequences aren't so very pleasant."

As she often did, Jaymin raised her glass to the dearly departed Mother Superior. Her toast was always the same. "May you rot in hell, Im."

She emptied the glass. Then she opened the tube. She laid the poster on the credenza.

Unlike First Skipper Thorpe, Jaymin knew who Janet Jackson was: she was Michael's sister, though just not quite as pretty as her brother. For a moment, Jaymin's attention shifted back to the bed and the man lying there. Pretty was not a word she would have used to describe Stephen Kaine. He was too shopworn, too hard, too bruised by the sun and the heat and the sand. He was like the survivor of a long siege, who, in the end, steps away from it stronger. It was an image that attracted Jaymin.

The colonel had ordered her to find out more about Kaine, and about his daughter and the stowaway. And Jaymin would, but in her own way and for her own purposes.

She examined the poster a second time, then turned it over. The blueprint peeled away in her hand. When she saw the words Karmin-Yar at the bottom, an exasperated sigh passed heavily from her lips.

That the blueprint of the entire city could somehow have fallen into the hands of Ras Haydar was an extraordinary complication; it could very likely place their entire operation, and two years of work, in jeopardy. The implications were equally inauspicious for Kaine. Merely knowing of the blueprint's existence placed his life in danger. Angela's, too.

At that moment, Jaymin heard the bed squeak. Angela had turned restlessly, and with a low groan.

Quickly, Jaymin pressed the blueprint against the back of the poster, ran a finger over the tape that held it there, carefully recrafted the poster into a tight cylinder, and fit it neatly into the tube again. She replaced the cap and carried the tube back to the dresser, restoring it to its original place. Then she took her glass and sat with crossed legs in the overstuffed chair.

Less than a minute later, Kaine was perched on the edge of the bed, fully awake, contemplating her.

"I started without you," Jaymin said, hoisting the glass and tipping it apologetically. She hastened from the chair to the credenza, where she splashed Scotch into a second cup. Kaine saw her composing herself, drawing a deep breath, arching her back, and then releasing the air in a slow stream.

Finally she turned.

"Cheap Scotch at nine in the morning. Can you imagine?" She crossed the room and held out the glass. "Well, it's afternoon somewhere in the world. Sleep?"

"Some."

"Some!" Her lips curled with amusement. "The only time I sleep that sound is after a bottle of this stuff."

Kaine returned her smile, but there was an unnerving quality to it, a strain of irony. He tested the Scotch. It left a subtle aftertaste in his mouth and a pleasant fire in his stomach. He helped himself to more. "At nine in the morning, this could become a habit."

"We were lucky. There's a very accommodating chef downstairs," Jaymin explained. "He said there aren't a dozen Scotch drinkers in all of Dover. Hard to imagine."

Kaine rose. He toured the room, pausing at the edge of the bed and touching Angela's cheek. He paused again at the credenza and studied the label on the Scotch bottle.

Then he threw a quick glance over his shoulder, as if struck by some incidental revelation, and said, "How was it that you were on that ferry, Jaymin? You're a pilot, you mentioned yesterday. Why would a pilot with her own plane choose a three-hour ferry trip over a twenty-minute plane ride?"

"Why do you ask?"

"Curiosity. I like you. I'm curious about people I like."

"I'm more curious about people I don't like," Jaymin countered.

"It gives me a broader playing field for my curiosity. It's the cynic in me, I suppose."

"You're American."

"Is that supposed to explain my cynical side? You're American, and you seem pretty normal."

"I was born in Denver. Very normal."

"Very," Jaymin said. She measured the quality of his tone. It was clear he was probing, and now that she thought about it, maybe he had a right to. Fine, she would tell him a thing or two. "I was born and raised in New York. In the Bronx. Yeah, I know, I don't sound like it," she said. "It was okay. You learn fast. Well, at least I had to. My truly wonderful parents swept me under the rug when I was three. I went through three foster homes in five years and ended up at Saint Jude's Orphanage in Manhattan. Not a pretty place. I came out of it, though. Not unscathed, mind you; just enough to recognize the enemy when I see him."

Kaine considered this. Did the enemy have one face or many? Was a friend as easily recognized? Had the statement been a warning? In response, he said, "Do you know that the police think I was involved in the ferry accident?"

Jaymin shrugged. "I know they're watching you."

The glass stopped halfway to Kaine's lips. He held Jaymin's eyes again, then drank.

"The minute we left the tug," she said. "Two men. In civilian dress. Not very subtle. They were still with us when we arrived here this morning."

"You're sure it was the police?"

"They're the same in every city in every country in the world. Take my word for it."

Kaine smiled thinly. "I guess I'll have to."

"You can walk away from it, you know. That's what they're hoping for anyway. They may prove it was sabotage, but it's a different matter proving responsibility. Take Angela back to the States for a couple of months." Jaymin tossed out each phrase matter-of-factly. She moved her glass like an instrument of the obvious. Then she paused. "Were you?"

"Was I what? Involved in an accident that nearly resulted in my own daughter's death?"

Kaine stepped up to the window. The water beyond the cliffs was a deep aquamarine. Iridescent flecks danced upon its surface. In the sky, pockets of heavy white clouds hovered in a field of brilliant blue. At last, Kaine gave in to the relentless draw of the *Spirit of Long Life,* but the sight of its lifeless hull was too painful.

He took shelter in his original question. "Why *were* you on that ferry two nights ago?"

"Because I'm a liar and a thief and a cheat, and if I were you I wouldn't trust a thing I say or do." Their eyes locked, but only for a moment; there was a grimness to the confession that Jaymin seemed eager to step away from. She sighed and shook her head. "I own a Cessna 421. Well, that's the first lie. I don't own it at all; there's this very unreasonable bank in Manhattan and they own everything I have. Not my soul, as such, but since they own my plane the rest is academic anyway. It's an eight-seater, but I don't charter passengers. Only cargo, and I'm not particularly choosy as long as the money's right. And if the money's right it's just as well not to ask."

"That's one philosophy."

"My plane's in Calais with instrument problems. I had business in Dover. I thought the ferry might calm my nerves."

"What kind of business?"

"Is this still the curious friend asking?"

"I'm still curious anyway."

"Just business." Jaymin pushed the question away with her free hand. "There are times when it's best not to ask for more information than you need."

"Suggesting you were overpaid."

"The word *overpaid* should be stricken from the language, don't you think?" Jaymin's smile had a flirtatious quality to it, masking, Kaine realized, her unease. Then she said, "Well, anyway in most cases. Maybe with the possible exception of such idealistic fields as archeology, where I imagine the sheer joy of commitment and discovery makes the pay almost irrelevant."

"Sure. If you could only glean some type of edible substance out of commitment and discovery."

Jaymin laughed. "Yesterday you mentioned something about a dig outside Glastonbury. What's that about?"

"King Arthur's burial ground, some say."

"The Isle of Avalon? That's pretty ambitious."

Kaine nodded. "Back then, Glastonbury was surrounded by marshland. As the story goes, after Arthur's last battle, at Camlann, he was taken there. As a parting gesture, he commanded one of his knights, the loyal Sir Bedivere, to throw Excalibur into a nearby lake. And when he did, a hand mysteriously reached out of the water and swept the sword from existence."

"Good story."

"Another school of thought claims that the Holy Grail is hidden in the Chalice Well at the foot of the Glastonbury Tor. That after Jesus used the cup at the Last Supper, after his death, Joseph of Arimathea brought the grail here to England. Another good story."

Kaine emptied his Scotch. He pushed away from the window and crossed to the dresser. From the bottom drawer he removed the tube. He held it up.

"Did you find what you were looking for?" Kaine paused long enough to assure eye contact, but didn't wait for an answer. "You see, I don't ever sleep very deeply. On the one hand, I'd like to believe you were drawn to my daughter's poster. On the other, you don't look much like a Janet Jackson devotee."

"I'm not," Jaymin said quietly.

"Then tell me, what are you a devotee of? A minute ago, you called yourself a cheat and a thief. It occurs to me that you might add charlatan and sham to the list, as well. First you ingratiate yourself to my daughter and then you invade her privacy."

A look as cold and colorless as stone captured Jaymin's face. She said nothing.

"The police kept talking about a witness," Kaine said. "A witness who saw Ras Haydar and Angela exchanging discreet conversation and a metal tube. A witness who claims to have seen Ras Haydar at the controls of the ferry's bow doors moments before it went down. You! You're their witness. Aren't you?"

Jaymin looked across at the bed and the sleeping figure there, and her face softened. She said, "I didn't intentionally . . . force myself on Angela, Stephen. Believe me. My attraction to her was genuine. So was my concern. You have to believe that."

"Really? Didn't you also just call yourself a liar? Didn't you just say, 'If I were you I wouldn't trust a thing I tell you'? Now you say, 'Believe me.' " Kaine was suddenly overwhelmed with fatigue. Visions of Angela up to her chin in icy water swept over him. The woman in whose company he had found solace an hour ago was now an adversary. "All right," he said. "As naïve as it may sound, I'd like to believe you, Jaymin. Tell me how."

"What does the blueprint of Karmin-Yar signify?"

"You don't know?"

"How would I?"

"Then someone else will be asking you the same question and expecting an answer. Isn't that right? Who?" Kaine asked. "The police?"

Jaymin returned to the credenza. She capped the bottle and left an unfinished drink. "What are you saying? That I'm a snitch for Scotland Yard? Is that it?"

"Yesterday you said you had to meet some people. In London, you said. They sent you back, didn't they? So, tell me. What people?" Kaine recalled the man he had seen leaving the harbor tug the night of the accident, and his parting words to the first skipper: *You'll be very much on my mind.* Kaine used this, saying, "Does one of them wear expensive suits and gold cuff links? Does he travel with bodyguards?"

Jaymin drew a sharp breath. She stared at the floor. When she looked up at last, a shadow had fallen across her face, sadness tugged at the corners of her eyes. "I came back this morning out of concern for your daughter."

"That, and something else."

Again Jaymin said nothing. She gathered up her leather jacket and draped it over her shoulders. She crossed the room and stopped at the door. Now the sadness consumed her entire face.

"Something tells me we're destined to meet again, Stephen Kaine. Funny thing is, I'd like to make it sooner than later."

And then she was gone.

When Angela opened her eyes twenty minutes later, Kaine was seated in front of the nightstand poring over the blueprint.

"Daddy? Did you find it?"

Kaine moved from the chair to the edge of the bed. He held up the poster. "I imagine you know who this is."

"Wasn't there something else?"

Kaine showed her the blueprint. "I assumed this was for me."

Angela pushed herself up onto one elbow. She looked warily at the blueprint. "Your friend said something strange. He said, 'Tell your father that the deed will happen the third week in March. Tell him that's all I know.' "

"The third week in March?"

"What happens then?"

Kaine shook his head. Deed? What deed? He ran the message through his head again, but there was no time to ponder.

A knock at the door signaled Danielle Kaine's arrival.

She was a tall, striking woman, the antithesis of Jaymin. She threw her arms around Kaine's neck with almost the same vigor as she had embraced Angela.

This was not unusual. The one aspect of their marriage that had not suffered over the years was the physical part. In fact, they had carried on for a year after their divorce. It hadn't worked for Kaine, however: he was selfish enough to want both the marriage and the sex. But marriage and archeology were not favorable bedfellows. Life on an excavation site did not fit Danielle's image of home. Home, for most of their marriage, had been a three-bedroom farmhouse in the mountains outside of Denver. But it wasn't much of one, Danielle used to say, with a husband who lived out of a tent six months a year in countries she couldn't even find on a map.

So Kaine had moved his family to the West Coast and taken a full-time professorship at the university in Berkeley. That hadn't worked either; site work was still the most compelling part of the job for him, and he couldn't resist it. He had returned from his first six-month stint at Karmin-Yar five years ago to find an empty house and a three-page letter telling him it was over.

"I miss you," she said. They shared the overstuffed chair, she on the arm, and watched Angela deliberately sipping tea.

"How much?"

"Not enough to live out of a suitcase, if that's what you had in mind."

He wanted to touch her. "How's Paris?"

"The Frenchmen are tactless, and the women are snobs. I've become a workaholic as a matter of compensation. How's the English countryside?"

"Too good for the English people."

"Meaning you're still obsessed with Karmin-Yar." She held him momentarily with her eyes; they were dark like mahogany and as clear as springwater. Then she smiled and touched his shoulder. "I'm sorry. It's been hard, hasn't it? You worked a long time for that."

"Five years was long enough."

Now she looked at him with interest. "Translated?"

"Leaving wasn't the problem. It was how I left." He showed her the blueprint. He told her about the stowaway and the metal tube. "If the people at Scotland Yard are to be believed, Ras Haydar was working undercover for the Turkish secret police."

"Terrific. Yet he passes this information on to Angela, intending it for your eyes only, and then jeopardizes the plan by sinking the ferry. My God, Stephen, his messenger came within five minutes of drowning. It makes a grand total of no sense."

"The ferry went down incredibly fast; it's possible he didn't expect that."

"Okay, then there was something on the ferry he didn't want to reach shore."

Kaine thought a moment. "Or someone."

It was a chilling prospect that brought the conversation to a sudden halt. Impulsively, Kaine reached up and kissed her cheek.

"What was that for?" she asked.

Now he stood up. He took her hand. "We're too close to the

water and too close to that ferry. Let's see some of the Kentish countryside. We'll have a picnic."

Kaine consigned the metal tube and its contents to the bed-and-breakfast safe. A woman in the kitchen downstairs packed them a lunch. They set out in the beat-up Honda Kaine had borrowed from the Glastonbury excavation. They drove to Bishopsbourne, a tiny village trapped at the bottom of a wide valley. On their left sheep ambled in fields of wild grass. Well-tended hedges coursed along the roadway. Stone walls formed unobtrusive barriers between whitewashed farmhouses. A stream emerged from the grounds of a Kentish mansion, and they parked beside it. Danielle carried their basket to the edge of a cherry grove.

"My God, just like a family," she said, spreading an old quilt on the ground.

"This is different," Angela said. "I don't ever remember you two kissing."

"That's all we ever did," her mother corrected. "What we never did was talk."

The soup was cream of mushroom and Angela ate it all. The kitchen had also provided corned beef sandwiches; Angela ate hers and half of her mother's.

A man on a bicycle dismounted next to the stream. He held up a hand and called, "Good afternoon." A beat-up Mercury from the mid-1970s made two passes. The second time, the driver asked directions.

They drank tea out of a thermos and shared two banana-pecan muffins. Danielle asked about the blueprint. "I know the fire temple was the first building constructed in any Persian city. Was the king's court the second?"

Kaine shook his head. "The king's court was part of the current king's palace. In the case of Karmin-Yar . . ."

"Darius," Angela said.

Kaine smiled. "The First. Very good."

"How far did the rules of church and state go?" Danielle asked. "Was the king allowed into the fire temple?"

"Only the high priest and priestess. It was the Persians' most inviolate law."

"Then why the tunnel from the king's court to the temple?"

"I've been asking myself the same question."

"Obviously Darius considered himself more inviolate than . . ." Danielle paused; a glazed look had overtaken Angela's face. "Angie? Are you all right, baby?"

"I lost my camera."

Danielle's eyes narrowed. "A camera's replaceable, you're not."

"You mean dead is dead. I know, you're right," Angela said. "I was thinking about when Daddy was bringing me out of that ferry. We swam past this man. And he was dead. Real dead. But you know, his eyes were still open. And you know, they stared right back at me."

"Oh, baby, I'm so sorry."

"And there was this boy. He had to be about my age, I think. He was wearing a crucifix around his neck. And you know, after all that time, he was still holding the cross in his hand. Like he couldn't let go." Crumbs from her muffin spilled onto Angela's lap. She chewed very slowly. And then stopped. "I should feel lucky, I guess, shouldn't I?" She looked at them. "How come I don't?"

9 The Kentish barns looked like ancient Viking halls.
Manicured hedges traced the outlines of fields haunted by a history of war. The soldiers of Rome trampled them; William the Conqueror laid waste to them; warring armies from as far away as the Tigris and Euphrates rivers and the northern forests of Europe left their mark in blood upon them.

Since morning, a detour had been set up diverting traffic from the A2 highway leading into Dover onto Castle Hill Road. Kaine followed this road as it rose gradually onto a high plateau of wild grass. The plateau served as a throne for the great and ominous Dover Castle. The white cliffs plunged three hundred feet into the ocean; seemingly a stone's throw away lay the coast of Europe.

The road down from the castle meandered along a steep and narrow asphalt path. Walls of white fortified the inland side. Seaside, the road tumbled into forests of pine trees and slabs of broken chalk. The traffic Kaine anticipated hadn't materialized, and he wondered why.

A car fell in behind them. Kaine recognized it. A chipped and pale blue, it was the old Mercury they had seen outside of Bishopsbourne. It straddled the center lane and came upon them at a furious rate. Glancing into his rearview mirror, Kaine felt his stomach turn over. His initial thought was that the poor bastard had lost his brakes and had better turn the car into the mountain and take his chances before it was too late.

Then Kaine glimpsed the driver's face. He saw neither panic nor terror nor gritted teeth. What he saw instead was a cold, blank mask.

"Stephen, what is it?" Danielle, he realized, was reacting to his rigid posture and the sudden strain on his own face.

"Hold on," Kaine shouted. He swerved onto the shoulder of the road and the Mercury caught him on the left rear taillight. The Honda lunged forward, fishtailed, and sent a cloud of dust into the air; the tires rediscovered the asphalt and the car stabilized again. Angela screamed.

Danielle glanced out the back window. "Jesus Christ, Stephen."

"Grab hold of something," he said, surprised at the lack of emotion in his voice. "We're in trouble."

Sweat coursed down his forehead and face; his shirt was soaked through. In the mirror he saw the Mercury pressing down on them again. He jammed the accelerator to the floor and the car jumped ahead. Impact this time was hardly more than a nudge. They plunged into a series of quick turns. They swept past a tractor on the right shoulder and two bicyclers coming up the mountain on the left.

The driver of the Mercury obviously knew the road; he backed off a hundred yards before the hairpin. Kaine saw it too late, and the Honda spun a hundred and eighty degrees before he was able at last to bring it to a halt, hanging precariously on the shoulder. A retaining wall was built of split-rail pine; beyond it the mountain fell into a sea of tall trees. The Mercury surged around the bend. Accelerating, the driver set it on a collision course with the Honda.

Seconds before impact Kaine found reverse. He cut a half circle back onto the road. The Mercury braked, slid, and bounced to a halt in the oncoming lane. Its engine stalled.

The truck motoring up the mountain was filled with prison workers, a cheap-labor cleanup crew. The driver, Kaine would discover later, was probably drunk; the crew most certainly was. As it turned out, the driver of the truck slammed head-on into the Mercury without ever touching his brakes. Though they were traveling at a diligent twenty-five miles per hour, the impact was enough to send the Mercury lurching back with a severe jolt.

Kaine threw on the emergency brake and jumped out in an act of adrenaline and fury, not concern. He sprinted across the road to the Mercury. He wrenched open the door on the driver's side. He leaned in and saw blood spurting from the man's nose and mouth. The steering wheel and windshield were dappled in red. The man's head slumped against his chest, but Kaine saw the rising and falling of unconscious breath. He pulled the head back by the hair, looked into a barroom brawler's face, and then dropped it wrathfully back down.

The labor-crew chief spilled out of the passenger side of the truck's cab. He and half his crew jogged over. The driver of the truck hadn't moved; his hands still gripped the steering wheel and his mouth hung agape.

"Sweet Jesus," the crew chief murmured, peering through the front window. "Sweet Jesus, is he . . . ?"

"Dead? No." Kaine rifled the man's coat pockets and discovered a wallet and passport. He tossed his head toward the truck. "Do you have a radio?"

"Not one that works. Sorry." The crew chief ran a hand roughly across his chin, and Kaine used the moment to slip the wallet and passport into his pants. "Should we be thinking about moving him to a hospital, you suppose? Take him down to the clinic at the harbor? We could lay him out in the back of the truck."

"Don't move him," Kaine said. "Get a rag and some water, if you have it. See if you can slow the bleeding. But don't move him. I'll find a phone and have an ambulance sent up."

Danielle had walked halfway to the wrecked car. She stood with her arms crossed and a hand at her mouth. She took hold of Kaine's arm, gripping it, and whispering, "He was trying to force us off the road, for God's sake."

"He was trying to do more than that."

"We're taking Angie the hell away from here, Stephen."

Her grip intensified. Their eyes locked. "It's not as easy as that, Danielle. We can't leave."

"Don't tell me that," she argued. "Why? Does this have something to do with Scotland Yard? With Ras Haydar and that goddamn ferry?"

"We've been under surveillance since yesterday morning. The man on the bicycle in Bishopsbourne was one of them."

"The guy who waved and said, 'Good morning'?" Disbelief distorted Danielle's features. She clenched her fists and paced. "Then where is Scotland Yard now? If what you say is true, if you've been told not to leave Dover, and if we're under surveillance, then why aren't they here, right now?"

Kaine was struck by Danielle's insight but had no answer for it.

"Stephen, Angela's been through enough."

"I know." He turned toward the car.

Angela had opened the door on her side and was standing behind it. Danielle wrapped her arms around her. Kaine rested his hands on her shoulders. Angela's first question was the same as the crew chief's.

"He has a broken nose and a mouth full of broken teeth," Kaine replied. "He was lucky. So were we. He lost control of his car and now—"

"You said we were in trouble." Angela sat down on the edge of the car seat and peered back at him. "What did you mean by that?"

Kaine crouched down. "We need to find a phone. We have to call an ambulance."

"He was trying to drive our car off the road, wasn't he?" Angela said. "He was, wasn't he?"

Her face went slack. The freckles of her childhood were giving way to the ripeness of adolescence. Had he missed that? She was thirteen and the first signs of womanhood were touching her body. He had taken a vow of honesty the day she was born and now was on the verge of breaking it.

"Maybe," he said. Her eyes were much like her mother's, stern and unyielding. "I think so. And I think it has to do with your poster, with the blueprint of Karmin-Yar."

The manager of the bed-and-breakfast met them at the front door. Detective Superintendent Preble had stationed himself in the hotel pantry, his back pressed against the safe. In his hand he held a seizure order.

"The minute that metal tube passes the plane of this safe door, this order takes effect," he announced. "You can make it as hard on us as you want, but I'm going to have a look inside that tube."

"I think you should," Kaine said. He tipped his head in the direction of the hotel manager. "Sorry if we've caused you any inconvenience."

"The superintendent found our kitchen to his liking. I'm afraid dinner will be a bit thin tonight," the manager said dryly. He unlocked the safe and presented the tube to Kaine, who laid it in Preble's hand.

"You'll want to accompany me to the station, I would imagine," the detective said.

"I don't see why," Kaine replied. "The tube won't tell you who sank the *Spirit of Long Life* and I can't tell you why."

The manager passed Kaine his room key, and Kaine, Danielle, and Angela climbed the stairs to the second floor. The door was open. The room had been ransacked. The remains from Angela's backpack—her books, her blanket and clothes, her jewelry and key ring—were strewn across the bed. Kaine's suitcase, his clothes and sundries, had been similarly treated. The dresser drawer had been left ajar, the nightstand had been rummaged through, and the closet stood open.

They heard heavy footfalls on the stairway, the sound gaining volume on the hardwood in the hall. Kaine turned quickly about and came face to face with First Skipper Tanner Thorpe.

"Thorpe!" Kaine said.

"Forgive the intrusion. I thought I'd better check on the young lady's condition before . . ." Thorpe stopped in midsentence. "God have mercy. The police, I gather, are being more bold than usual."

"You gather correctly," Danielle answered without waiting for an introduction. When Kaine had seen to the formalities, Thorpe took hold of her hand.

"She's looking better, isn't she?" he said, peeking over at Angela and winking.

"Considering," Danielle answered. "She'll look even better when she's a couple of hundred miles away from this crazy country of yours. Please. No offense."

Thorpe glanced quickly at Kaine. "Something else happened."

Kaine told him about the incident on Castle Hill Road.

"God have mercy." The first skipper scratched diligently beneath his stocking cap. "You're in the bloody thick of something and you don't even know what it is, do you?"

"Our dilemma is more immediate than that," Kaine said. "Angela is too vulnerable here in Dover . . ."

"But the police have ordered you both to stay put until the matter of the ferry accident is made right. How bloody predictable. They're watching you but not doing a very good job of protecting you."

"Exactly."

"I hope you're not overly surprised," Thorpe said. Now he tugged at his stocking cap, drawing it minutely closer to his brow. "All right then, though it may not be my place . . ."

"Please, Mr. Thorpe," Danielle said. "Make it your place."

"All right then. If we did it quietly, it occurs to me that my tug might be a good place for Angela to stay until this matter is resolved."

"You can't be serious?"

"I am indeed. We spend twelve, sometimes fifteen hours a day on the water. What could be safer? The rest of the time we're docked at a restricted quay in the harbor. The harbor is under federal jurisdiction and Royal Navy authority. If Scotland Yard can be convinced that a grandiose case need not be made of it . . ." Thorpe shrugged. "Sometimes they do more harm than good, frankly."

"Stephen . . ."

"It's only a suggestion, young lady. Only a suggestion." Now Thorpe eased himself into the nearest chair, directing his attention to Kaine. "However, there is something you should know before you decide."

Kaine stiffened; a foreboding edge had crept into Thorpe's voice. "What's that?"

"I've been bribed. Early Tuesday morning when you were off with the police, a boldly dressed American offered me two thousand dollars for the blueprint of that lost city you're so interested in. Or, as he put it, for services of equal value."

"And?"

Thorpe took a round can of chewing tobacco from his shirt pocket. He tapped the top but didn't open it. "I lied about the blueprint, naturally. But I also took the money. I thought I might as well. Connor needs an education, and he won't get it on my salary."

Kaine decided against mentioning the man he had seen, or his two bodyguards. Instead, he said, "You didn't tell me."

"A Scot has to be leery of himself. He never knows whether he's going to betray someone until it actually happens."

"Wise philosophy."

"Ideally, there's supposed to be less guilt that way."

"If only life were ideal."

"My thought exactly."

"And what have you decided?"

"About the problem of betrayal? Only that the next time my American friend lays two thousand dollars on my table, it won't be free."

Kaine considered the vehicle he had seen the man and his bodyguards drive away in. The plates and the rent-a-car sticker.

"Obviously he knows my name."

"Yours and Angela's both."

"Stephen, this has gotten way out of hand," Danielle said. "We've . . ."

"You said he was American?" Kaine interrupted. "Are you reasonably certain of that?"

"Most Americans are reckless. Most of you give away too much. It's the way you walk, with your whole bodies. And you have a tendency to smile at the wrong times. You see, you haven't been around long enough. What? A couple of hundred years? And up to now it's all come so easily."

Kaine was interested. He moved from the credenza to the bed. "He was a businessman then, by his dress?"

"Could be. A hustler anyway. And one with a few hidden strings to pull, if you get my meaning."

"You mean you're playing games with someone you shouldn't be," Danielle suggested.

Thorpe popped the lid on the chewing tobacco and filled his mouth. "Probably right."

The admission brought a sudden halt to the conversation. Kaine broke the spell, reaching for Danielle's hand. "You have to return to Paris, you said. For how long?"

Danielle hung her head. "Two days at most. It can't be helped. I had every intention of taking Angela with me."

"I know," Kaine assured her. He pushed a shock of black hair off his forehead. Then he said, "I think we'll take you up on your offer, Mr. Thorpe. But we'll also keep the room at the bed-and-breakfast, for appearance's sake if nothing else. And I'll have a talk with Detective Preble."

"I think it's best," Thorpe replied.

"And if you hear from your American friend, you can give him a message from me. Tell him there is nothing at Karmin-Yar worth dying for. Tell him that as soon as Scotland Yard is satisfied, we'll be returning to the United States."

Unfortunately, Kaine didn't believe that Tanner Thorpe's "friend" would be that easily satisfied.

Kaine's archeological aspirations had begun when he was a boy, digging tunnels in his backyard.

One summer it had been a full-time devotion for him and three friends, Scott Laurie, Tom Seferis, and Wes Townsend, his best friend. They were inspired by a movie called *The Great Escape.* Fortunately for them there had already been a substantial hole created beyond the back fence of the Kaine household after Stephen's father uprooted a pair of wild elm trees. Scott was in charge of tools; he also collected wood for the supports and stole food from the local grocery. Tom found inventive means of concealing the dirt; he filled the neighbors' milk boxes and dropped bucketsful down the sewer drains. Kaine and Wes dug.

The first day they went down four feet, tunneled back beneath the fence, and broke off in two directions. The tunnel destined to reach Mr. Kaine's toolshed they dubbed Elvis. They called tunnel number two Fabian. It was directed toward the window well that looked into the basement of their next-door neighbors, the Shelbys. Mrs. Shelby, at thirty-one an "older woman," often exercised down there, in her bra and panties.

Every morning the boys would meet. Dig, conceal, eat, and fantasize. In the afternoon, they played Little League baseball and swam. Most nights they would camp out in their sleeping bags and spend hours in their underground catacombs with flashlights and popcorn and the *Playboy* magazines Scott purloined from the drugstore.

Over the course of the summer, Elvis grew fatter and deeper instead of longer. It became a grotto big enough for four boys, a cooler, a transistor radio, a lock box for their magazines and cigarettes, and Scott's Coleman lantern. Fabian never made it to Mrs. Shelby's window. Instead, they drove a shovel into a clay sewer pipe and Stephen's father called a halt to the project.

The one thing Kaine never told his friends about was the pocket watch he found buried next to that sewer pipe. It was gold-plated and beautifully etched. An inscription on the inside of the face cover read, SEYMOUR JACOBY, 1896. Kaine had, from that day forward, proclaimed himself an archeologist.

When he was sixteen, he had spent ninety-two dollars, two years' savings, to have the works inside the watch restored. To this day, he still carried it, the only piece of jewelry he had ever owned. The watchmaker responsible for its rebirth was a World War I veteran, and he had set the watch that first day to Greenwich mean time. Kaine had never changed it.

Now, after he had put Danielle on a Hovercraft back to Calais and settled Angela in with Tanner Thorpe and his son, Kaine, alone in his bed-and-breakfast room, reached into his pocket and withdrew the watch. A nacreous patina of age had captured its golden surface. The watch served as a prop, a buoy, a conduit of nervous energy. He opened it. Inside, on a snow-white face, gold hands revolved around elegantly Romanesque numerals. The watch read 2:55. Dover time was an hour later; in Karmin-Yar it was 5:55 and by now the site, Kaine thought, would have closed down for the day.

On the bed, Kaine laid out the passport and wallet he had taken off the man in the beat-up Mercury. There was no blood on the face staring out from the passport photo, but the pugilistic scowl was unmistakable. Empty black eyes peered from within a well of dark circles. Cheeks and jowls, thick and fleshy, hung beneath a weight of indifference. This one looked wounded, caged. A thin stubble of gray and black nested upon a broad, balding skull. The face, reason suggested, belonged to a forty-five- or fifty-year-old man. The date of birth on the passport reported a man born thirty-five years ago and residing in Washington, D.C. The driver's license in the wallet corroborated these facts. The man's name was Joseph Jankowski.

Kaine thumbed through the passport legend. In the last six months Jankowski had journeyed from either New York or Washington, D.C., to Istanbul, and on to Marseilles on seven occasions. The order never varied. His stays in Turkey were typically four to five days, whereas he rarely stayed in France more than twenty-four hours. Over the course of the same six-month period, Jankowski had visited England on three occasions. He had arrived in London less than thirty-six hours ago, had obviously been briefed about the ferry accident, and—because in Kaine's opinion this was not the face of a decision-maker—had received instructions concerning himself and Angela. Fly into London for an afternoon and drive three people off the side of a mountain, will you? Have lunch and fly back home. Sure, why not.

Finally, Kaine focused on the wallet itself. Inside, flap vents held a Virginia driver's license, a Citibank Visa card, a Citibank money-machine card, an expired membership card to the John Birch Society, a twice-folded piece of paper with two phone numbers on it, and a red poker chip. Plastic photo flaps were yellowed with age and contained but a single picture, that of a young, round-faced girl of perhaps eight or nine years. An inscription on the back read, *Ivana, 9/17/78.* The second flap contained a wallet-size medical card informing authorities that the cardholder was a registered hemophiliac. The announcement sparked a vivid image of Jankowski hunched over and unconscious at the wheel of the old Mercury, blood spurting from his nose and mouth. Kaine read the card again and felt little.

The wallet contained forty-five dollars, a hundred and eighty pounds, and two francs. In one corner there was a cash receipt for ten kilograms of acetic anhydride from a Marseilles establishment called Dumas Industries. Curious. A thug from Washington, D.C., buys twenty-two pounds of a common industrial acid during a twenty-four-hour stopover in France's most corrupt city. Why?

In another corner Kaine found a square of white typing paper. It was folded in thirds. Opened, it measured approximately two inches by three. There were segments of incomplete words on either side of the paper which indicated it had obviously been snipped from a fully typed page. The remainder read,

> *then from what we have detect*
> *ow in the possession of a Sov*
> *r. Jurgen Spire. His whereab*
> *nd there is evidence suggesti*
> *ledge heretofore undiscovered*

Jurgen Spire. Kaine stared at the name in amazement. There were only two legitimate authorities on the lost Persian city of Karmin-Yar. In the West, there was Kaine, the man who had discovered the city's whereabouts, had begun the process of recovering it from the mud and sand that had washed it from the face of the earth, and had been abruptly banished from the site six months ago. In the East, there was the man whose name was typed on the tiny square of white paper Kaine now held in his hand: Jurgen Spire.

Kaine had met Spire twice. They were, he recalled, like two moths drawn by the same bright light. He had expected competition and contention, and found, to his satisfaction, only mutual illumination. Kaine had offered the Karmin-Yar directorship to Spire, but the Soviet archeologist had cited his advanced years—though he was only fifty-eight at the time—as a polite way of declining. Now here was Jurgen Spire's name carefully blocked out in the wallet of a man who had, three hours before, made every effort to run Kaine, his ex-wife, and his daughter off the side of a mountain.

Kaine studied the paper again. "Then from what we have detected . . ." Detected what? Something to do with Karmin-Yar. "Is now in the possession of a Soviet archeologist, Mr. Jurgen Spire. His whereabouts is . . ." Is no secret, Kaine realized. Spire taught advanced archeology at the university in Leningrad. Yes, but what of his country house in the Crimea? Spire had once mentioned it to Kaine as the perfect retreat for a private session between the two of them. Kaine had, in return, suggested a log cabin in the southern mountains of Colorado, and both had laughed. Now it didn't seem so laughable.

Lastly, the cryptic note mentioned "evidence suggesting some knowledge heretofore undiscovered by . . ." By whom? By Spire? Or by the creators of the note? And furthermore, evidence of what matter? At Karmin-Yar, there were hundreds of matters yet undiscovered. Though five years had passed since the site's discovery, the project was embryonic in its development. Only a third of the city's ruins had been resurrected. Now there was a blueprint to confirm what remained. Was it possible that Jurgen Spire was responsible for the blueprint's discovery? Was there any other explanation that made sense? And if so, how had Ras Haydar come upon a copy?

Kaine was struck by the urge to hurry. He replaced all the contents of the wallet, less the cryptically typed note and the twice-folded piece of paper with two phone numbers listed on it. These he slipped into his shirt pocket.

10 How secure were the telephones in Dover, a town of twenty-five thousand? Kaine had no way of knowing.

He was now guilty of leaving the scene of an accident, though he had informed the police and hailed an ambulance. He was also guilty of larceny if not robbery. He doubted Scotland Yard would appreciate his intent. And he now faced the problem of following up on his leads without incriminating himself.

Kaine took the stairs up to the third floor. He found a linen closet stuffed with sheets and towels and boxes of tissue. On the floor lay a carton filled with complimentary samples of Scottish Mist shampoo. Kaine poured the box out, set the wallet and passport inside, and refilled it.

For a brief moment he studied the yellow slip of paper from Joseph Jankowski's wallet and the two phone numbers that were written there. One looked reassuringly American, with a three-number area code, a three-number prefix, and four-number suffix. The other he recognized as a long-distance configuration from the Cappadocian province of Asia Minor, another indirect reference to Karmin-Yar. With the paper safely concealed in his pocket, Kaine retraced his steps to the lobby.

He walked out into the street. It was crowded, a twenty-four-hour condition in Dover, but not so crowded that Kaine missed the towering figure of the detective named Hennagan standing in the doorway of an art gallery. Hennagan made no pretense as to his purpose there; he followed Kaine with his eyes and then walked at a discreet distance behind him. In Market Square, Kaine found a pub called the Prince Regent. Even in Dover they played darts and served roast beef sandwiches. The noise level struck Kaine as an advantage. At the bar, he ordered a Worthington E, a thick, dark lager. He watched the door for two minutes, but evidently the detective's orders did not include an accounting of the beer Kaine drank.

He left the mug untouched on the counter. At the rear of the pub he discovered two phone booths. One was empty. Kaine closed himself inside. The operator in Dover connected him with one in London. Kaine gave her his credit-card number for billing purposes, and the two phone numbers. He recited them in the order in which he wanted them placed, the first apparently a United States number—(703) 678-9803—and the second, ostensibly Turkish—2-29746-7-3.

"It will take a minute or two. Please hold."

Even as the tumult of the pub filtered into the booth, Kaine's thoughts turned to Angela. Her only visible reaction to the incident on Castle Hill Road had been fatigue. The fear or the terror Kaine expected had yet to exhibit itself. She seemed to view her tenure on the harbor tug *Broadside* as an adventure, not as a measure of security. Maybe this was good.

Kaine had often thought of his daughter as a survivor of the war between himself and Danielle. But the wounds were as unavoidable as they were undeniable, and they manifested themselves in different ways. Angela had trouble making friends, not out of insecurity or unfriendliness, but out of distance. Her teachers called her inattentive. She could absorb a science class completely and yet walk away from an exam half-finished. She could recite Whitman and Shakespeare from memory and yet fail to turn in the simplest assignments in literature. Her mother often would find

them, nearly perfect, in her backpack days later. Angela's passion
was the piano, yet her recitals often tended to be acts as remote as
the glimmer of a distant star.

"Sir," the operator broke in. "Are you there?"

"Yes, go ahead."

"Your first call is to Arlington, Virginia, U.S.A. I have that
number on the line, if you'd like."

"Please."

The number rang fourteen times; Kaine counted them off in
his head. He was a ring away from hanging up when a winded
voice answered. "Colonel. I'm sorry, I was in the can. Everything
on the up and up?"

"It's Jankowski," Kaine replied.

A shattering pause followed. "He's not here," was the eventual
reply. "You know he's not here. Why in the hell are you calling?
This number is for emergencies. Did something go the hell wrong?"

"Nothing went wrong," Kaine answered. "They don't want me
talking to London. You don't want me talking to you. You guys
want confirmation or don't you?"

"Hold on. Just hold the hell on for a second. Since when does
the colonel—"

Kaine slammed the phone down. "Colonel," he had said.
"Everything on the up and up?" "You know he's not here." Colonel,
Kaine thought. The man in the suit outside Tanner Thorpe's tug
had not been a colonel.

In time, the operator's voice intruded upon the silence. "Sir?
Are you there? I've confirmation on the second number, if you'd
like. Are you there?"

"I'm here."

"You were correct about the second number's Turkish origin.
Are you aware, however, that the last digit refers to an extension?"

"I can't say that I was."

"Extension three, in this case. I have an operator standing by
in Sinope. Shall I connect?"

"Thank you."

A second operator, her English heavily accented, took control of the call. She said, "Your call to Cide is being placed. One moment please."

Cide, Kaine thought; but was he really surprised? The town of Cide was located less than half an hour from the Karmin-Yar dig. The American and French contingents used it as a place of refuge. Two bars catered directly to their Western needs, and a restaurant had taken the enterprising step of introducing pizza to its menu. It was not uncommon for members of the site staff to keep motel rooms or trailers there on a permanent basis.

The level of static jumped as the call swept away from Sinope. A man answered, in a dialect that Kaine had taken two years to grasp. In English his greeting translated most correctly as, "The Black Sea Inn. May I help you?"

The inn was a dockside motel featuring fifteen or sixteen free-standing units. Kaine knew it well. The doors faced a gravel parking lot. The windows of dully painted bedrooms looked out on the water and the dozen or so boats that were normally docked there.

"Room three, please."

"Mr. Dreyfuss is not here presently. He asked that you leave your name with me. And any message."

"Dreyfuss!"

"Yes, sir. Who may I say is calling?"

"I was looking for Mr. Jones," Kaine replied.

"There is no Jones here."

Kaine set the receiver down. Maurice Dreyfuss, the archeologist who had been installed as the Karmin-Yar project director upon Kaine's release, and whose phone number shows up in the wallet of an American thug. Kaine leaned against the wall of the phone booth and closed his eyes. A knock on the door brought him rudely back to life. He opened it.

"This your own private box, mate, or can the rest of the world have a chance?" The man smiled as they exchanged places; Kaine studied his face as if every man had suddenly become his enemy.

Detective Hennagan took Kaine by the elbow when he emerged from the pub's front door.

"We'll take a walk, I think," he said.

"Where?" Kaine asked.

"You haven't seen enough of our lovely police station to my way of thinking. Nor to my superior's way of thinking, unless I'm very much mistaken."

"Has that ever happened?" Kaine wasn't in the mood to deal with Scotland Yard. "You being mistaken, that is?"

Hennagan didn't like the question. Neither of them laughed.

The metal tube, Angela's poster, and the blueprint of Karmin-Yar lay in an orderly fashion upon the desk of Detective Superintendent Christopher Preble. Preble was sporting the same oatmeal-brown suit and the same dour expression. For all that, he was still more affable than his partner. When Hennagan stepped out of the office to take a phone call, Kaine used the opportunity to test the depth of the two detectives' working relationship.

"Does the detective take everything so personal, or is it just me?" Kaine said.

"He'd love nothing more than to see us nail you to a post," Preble replied. "In case you were worried."

It was clear to Kaine that, though Preble had said this with a certain venom, it lacked conviction, as if he and his partner had parted ways on the matter. Kaine pressed the point.

"It doesn't sound like his confidence level is very high," he said.

"I might take that as an insult," the superintendent challenged.

"Or the truth," Kaine said.

Preble's eyes cut like a well-stropped blade. He reached into his pocket for a handful of red candies. He popped them one at a time into his mouth, still staring Kaine down. Cinnamon perfumed the air. When Hennagan entered the room again, Preble kicked out a chair from his desk and sat down.

He said, "A member of the Turkish secret police, a certain Ras Haydar, is installed at an archeological excavation in which you are the director and chief archeologist. His cover is that of a common laborer. What his purpose was, the TSP has chosen not to share with us. Later, you and Mr. Haydar are both accused of theft, oddly within days of one another, and yet the TSP finds no connection.

Neither of you is charged nor convicted, very rare treatment for the Turkish police. You say you hardly knew Ras Haydar. Yet there is a connection here, and you and I both know it."

"Baffling, isn't it?" Kaine replied.

"Assume with me," Preble continued, gesturing with candy-stained fingers at the desk. "Assume that Ras Haydar intended this blueprint for you. Assume he in turn opened the bow doors, which sank the ferry. Assume he intended the blueprint to survive but perhaps not himself. That makes this piece of paper"—Preble flicked his middle finger at the parchment upon which the blueprint was drawn—"at least minutely important. At least to Mr. Haydar. You, in turn, say it's inaccurate and meaningless."

"You entered my hotel room without permission. You left the place in a shambles. Then you wave a piece of judicial nonsense in my face and claim it gives you rights to my daughter's possessions. I guess I'm not in a very forgiving mood."

"I see. Well, try this one on. You left the scene of a fatal car accident." Preble dropped a candy into his mouth. "Yes, indeed, the driver, a Mr. Jankowski. He bled to death from injuries sustained in that accident. You stole the victim's wallet and passport. The first we classify as a misdemeanor, the latter something more serious. It could very well be that my mood too is becoming less than forgiving, Professor Kaine."

"And maybe it's time I bring the American embassy in on our problem."

"The American embassy. That's a meritorious idea." Preble rummaged through his desk and came away with a brown folder impressed with the official U.S. crest and addressed to Scotland Yard in London. "Would you care to know what your embassy is saying about you, Professor?"

Kaine shook his head; he had fallen neatly into Preble's trap. Six months ago Kaine had petitioned the American embassy in Istanbul over his expulsion. The results had not been favorable. The embassy had responded by instigating their own investigation of his activities at Karmin-Yar and subsequently throwing their full support behind the Turkish government. Upon his arrival in England, he had been summarily warned that his welcome would be contingent upon the results of that investigation, as yet incomplete.

"Something about an ongoing investigation and the possibility of charges pending, and so on, and so on," Kaine said.

"A good percentage of the population thinks you're guilty of some indiscretion, Kaine. The theft of art antiquities is one thing, but a half million dollars in gold is another. Add that to your questionable behavior here in Dover—"

"I assume you're talking about the twenty-five or thirty people I pulled from that capsized ferry lying out there in your beautiful harbor." Kaine punctuated the statement with a harsh breath. He drew a hand roughly through his hair. "Questionable behavior."

Now Preble cast an avuncular tip of the head in Kaine's direction, exasperated yet sympathetic. Then, without looking away, he spoke to Detective Hennagan. "Ever have one of those days, Paul, when tea just doesn't appeal?"

"If I have, I don't recall," Hennagan said.

Now Preble spoke to Kaine. "It's almost a sin to admit to a craving for a cup of coffee around this place, but it happens every once in a while. Join me?"

Kaine looked back at the crooked smile being candidly parlayed by the detective superintendent and knew it would be in his best interest to accept. "Thanks."

"Do us the honor, will you, Paul?" Preble said to the detective sergeant.

Hennagan wasn't pleased; it was an errand meant to remove him from the room for a moment, and they all knew it. "I'll probably have to brew the bloody stuff."

"Bring our guest some cream while you're at it." When the door was closed, Preble anchored his meaty arms on the table. "We're not getting anywhere, are we?"

"Not far," Kaine answered.

"To be candid, Mr. Kaine, I've never been very good at believing Americans," Preble admitted.

"No?"

"It's not so much a lack of sincerity as it is this feeling that you've stacked the deck in some way or another." Preble filled his hand with candy again. "But I have a hunch about you."

"In the field of archeology, a hunch is the next best thing to a solid fact," Kaine said.

"The man who died in that car accident up on Castle Hill Road was a former New York City policeman," Preble said. "There's bound to be an investigation. I've already heard from the FBI. I didn't bring up your name, but it's pretty inevitable unless I have some concrete reason not to."

"Your former New York City policeman tried to drive me, my daughter, and her mother into a forest of pine trees. Did you bring that up with the FBI?"

"No one, other than you and your family, have stepped forward with any information on that possibility. It doesn't give me much to go on. Especially given your eagerness to leave the scene. I want the man's wallet and passport, Kaine. And anything else you may have lifted from his person."

"They're back at my hotel."

"Fine." Now Preble fell back in his chair. He massaged the layers of his fleshy cheeks. "Okay, I can fend off the FBI for a time, but I need some upfrontness from you in return."

"The FBI doesn't upset me, Detective Preble. Someone taking potshots at my daughter does."

"Understandable. And this blueprint. Why all this mystery over the blueprint?"

"I've been involved with the city of Karmin-Yar for most of my career," Kaine said. He held up the blueprint. "I've never seen anything like this before."

"It's a fake then."

Kaine rose. He took Angela's poster and rolled it into a tight cylinder. He stared at the blueprint, but made no move to retrieve it. Finally he said, "Ras Haydar evidently didn't think so."

"I'm more concerned with the opinion of the esteemed archeologist, Stephen Kaine."

Now Kaine held the blueprint up. "A part of me wants to believe it," he said. "Another part of me doesn't want to admit that someone else was capable of finding what I couldn't."

He stared at the blueprint a moment longer, then returned it to Preble's desk and asked, "Your witness. The one who claims to have seen Ras Haydar enter the control booth to the *Spirit of Long Life*'s bow doors. There was no one else then? Only the two of them?"

Preble poked a finger in his ear and screwed his face into a tight knot. He said, "Just curious, I imagine?"

"Not at all. Ras Haydar isn't here to defend himself. Who's to say he wasn't the real witness? A witness turned victim. Has anyone else come forward? Were there any other bodies retrieved from the vehicle deck? Or was his the only one?"

It was clear by Preble's porous expression that the queries had struck a nerve—personal or professional, Kaine couldn't tell, but he tried to turn it to his advantage, to give Preble the opportunity to lie. He said, "I realize it's probably something you've already considered."

"Two others, in fact," Preble replied drily. "A couple of kooks who apparently couldn't bear to leave their Mercedes unattended long enough to get a beer and a sandwich." Preble shook his head. "No, Kaine. Your friend was the culprit. But the blueprint of some ruined city on the coast of the Black Sea seems a paltry excuse for the death of twenty-four people."

"We finally agree on something," Kaine said.

Preble escorted Kaine back to the bed-and-breakfast on King Street.

They climbed the stairs to the third floor and the maid's closet where Kaine had hidden Joseph Jankowski's wallet and passport. The detective superintendent watched as Kaine emptied the box of Scottish Mist shampoo onto the floor.

The wallet and passport were both gone.

"I thought we were playing this straight," Preble said.

"They were here two hours ago."

They talked to the manager.

"I've had a dozen people in and out of here in the last couple of hours, and no one who didn't belong. Could I have missed someone?" He shrugged. "I admit it, half the time my head's turned."

When they were alone again, Preble said. "You took the wallet and passport, so I know you went through them. And thoroughly, if I'm any judge of your character. And whoever stole them was after something. What?"

"He traveled," Kaine admitted. "A lot. And always to the same places."

Kaine explained about Jankowski's New York to Istanbul to Marseilles connection. He also told Preble about the basic contents of Jankowski's wallet, including the receipt for the acetic acid he had purchased in Marseilles.

Kaine's lies were lies of omission, for what he didn't mention was the slip of paper with the reference to the Soviet archeologist Jurgen Spire, nor the one with the two phone numbers he had called earlier. Why, he wasn't sure.

11 The rescue operation surrounding the *Spirit of Long Life* had taken a new direction. Now that it had been cleared, at last, of the living and the dead, the operation's attention turned to ridding the channel of the downed ferry itself, no small task.

Gigantic floating cranes were being positioned on one side of the ferry, but as such there appeared no definite plan for their use. First Skipper Tanner Thorpe reiterated the dilemma when he told Kaine, "It'll take a month to have that thing righted and out of the way if they don't get someone with half a brain out there. The Royal Navy thinks it's their problem, and Scotland Yard thinks it's theirs. I don't think the word *cooperation* has made its way into either of their vocabularies."

"Then the Mercedes will still be down there," Kaine said, donning scuba gear for the second time in three days.

"Move the thing before the renowned American archeologist has his look? Fuck me, never," Thorpe said sarcastically. "And you expect to find what exactly?"

The early-morning sun cut valiantly through a layer of mist, but there was no warmth in it. The first skipper steered the tug in the direction of a French cargo ship. A funnel aft of the wheelhouse threw a jet of black smoke into the air. Thorpe relayed instructions to the vessel's captain. When he replaced the radio mike, he looked Kaine over.

"This bogged-down mess of a harbor is off limits to anyone without official permission," he sneered. "Which I have, and you don't. And never will. Not by the order of the Royal Navy, the harbormaster, the ghost of John Paul Jones, or anyone else. You are a marked man, Kaine, and everyone and his brother is just waiting for you to make a mistake. I could lose my license just knowing your name, and it's getting to be a hard name to forget."

"I've asked too much of you already. I realize that," Kaine said. Angela had been onboard for less than a day and Thorpe was already calling her stay an apprenticeship. "I'm grateful."

"Fuck me. You mean that after this I'll have seen the last of you?" The first skipper launched a wad of chewing tobacco toward the coffee can that served as his spittoon, and hit it dead center. "I doubt it."

He used the old-fashioned bell pulls to signal his engineer to cut power to one-fourth. Then he gave Kaine a stiff glance. "The minute we get to this floating bucket of rust up ahead here, you're off. Use the port side and don't make a show of it. Oh, and do watch the propeller. Or maybe I didn't tell you. The propeller on a harbor tug the likes of *Broadside* is eight feet long. It's driven by an electric motor which is, in turn, fueled by a rather large generator, which is, in turn, powered by a sixteen-cylinder diesel engine capable of about sixteen hundred horsepower. I figure any man who gets caught in its way has a better chance of surviving a one-way trip through a sausage grinder."

"Thanks for the advice," Kaine said.

"Here's some more," the first skipper said. "We'll be back in the channel again in roughly an hour and twenty minutes. Your air won't last much longer than that so don't miss us. I don't need a thirteen-year-old orphan on my hands."

Kaine scrambled down the wheelhouse steps to the lower deck. Angela and Connor Thorpe met him there. She wore a life preserver over a red and black fleece jacket. Her hair was pulled back in a ponytail.

"Why do you have to go down there?" she said, sounding much like her mother. "How important can it be?"

"I'll be all right," Kaine assured her. He touched her cheek. "Promise."

Connor helped him strap the cylinder of compressed air onto his back and Kaine checked the pressure gauge. It wasn't encouraging.

"Ninety minutes, tops," the young seaman said. He checked the demand regulator on Kaine's mouthpiece. Kaine buckled the weight belt around his waist and Angela handed him the dive timer for his wrist.

"Good luck," was all she said.

The French freighter was small as such vessels go, but it nonetheless dwarfed the tug. The tug was trimmed with rubber fenders; still, the gentle tapping of its hull against that of the cargo ship produced a torturous squeal.

Kaine strapped a long-bladed knife to his calf. He pulled the diving mask down over his eyes. In a watertight satchel he carried the same tools that had aided him in Angela's rescue. In his hand he carried a high-powered flash. The tug had very little freeboard; the deck rested so close to the water that Kaine simply belly-rolled into the sea and was gone.

A film of harbor scum played upon the surface. Even this far from the wreckage, a veneer of oil was apparent.

Kaine dipped his head and kicked for the bottom. A unified school of tiny yellow fish flashed past. Five meters below the surface the sun's rays were cut in half and color diminished. Reds and yellows were now blues and greens. Thirty feet farther down, shades of gray and black took hold. Kaine switched on the flashlight. A family of albacore turned and fled. Seagrass danced. The sand churned beneath the huge beating wings of a stingray.

The vast bottom of the *Spirit of Long Life* loomed in the distance, a wall of black. The sharp crease of the keel reached out to him like an abstract work of art. The bodice of the hull became more rounded. The black mutated to a swatch of brown and finally to a rust-infested orange.

By now, the fallout from the wreckage had drifted far from its point of origin. A lampshade was a crown in search of a queen. The water held a lady's scarf in suspended animation. An opened umbrella suggested a UFO with a hooked antenna. And closer: a golf bag, a boiler pan, a suitcase strapped with duct tape and decorated with an ominous LONDON OR BUST sticker.

Kaine spotted two other divers touring the bottom. They were loaded down with photographic equipment; one with a camera on his shoulder, the other with floodlights held aloft. Kaine drew up behind a thatch of swaying seagrass and watched a third diver enter the vessel through a broken window.

When he was within a hundred yards of the ferry, Kaine circled to the bow. Across its face, the bow doors were clearly open, an empty, humorless grin. Kaine felt the relentless pull of the tide. He saw the ferry lurch forward; a cloud of sand kicked up at its side and settled again. A baby thresher shark snaked along the bottom.

Beyond the bow doors the ocean had scrambled the sixty-seven cars and trucks into an impossible jumble at the rear of the vehicle deck, C deck as it was called on the purser's blueprint. Kaine's flashlight illuminated a Volkswagen bug, an old Citroën, and the flatbed truck in which Ras Haydar had stowed away the day of the accident. Blotted sacks of wool bobbed and swayed. Drowned chickens were prisoners of a wire cage. Mosaics of broken glass crept across the deck floor and tossed the light of the flash back in Kaine's face.

Kaine felt like an eel. The cars and trucks forged a precarious maze of dead ends and false leads. Kaine stopped at a silver Audi and a black Peugeot. He snaked beneath an inverted panel truck. He burrowed through the broken windows of a Jeep. He wrenched open the side door of a beat-up Renault and stared into the open jaws of an eel that was no figment of the imagination.

The creature lunged. Its teeth clamped down on the car's doorframe, grazing Kaine's arm. Frustrated, the eel tore furiously at the frame. Kaine dove, even as he gasped for air. He plunged into the Jeep again, pulled himself into the rear compartment, and burrowed down behind the seat. He slipped the knife from the sheath beside his leg, then held his breath. The eel entered the Jeep, ugly head scanning. A body as sleek and long as a boa constrictor's followed.

Sixteen feet. When it was outside the Jeep, the eel's head coursed along the windows, fangs exposed. Its tail slapped hard against the sidewall and the vehicle shook. A school of mackerel caught its attention and it disappeared.

After a moment, Kaine got hold of himself. He exited the Jeep opposite the Renault. There was a narrow opening between an overturned pickup and a convertible with a demolished roof; Kaine inched through it.

He found the Mercedes squashed between the stern doors and a minibus. A bicycle was caught beneath the front wheel well. Doors both front and back were open wide. With the incoming tide, a loose bumper drummed against the side of the bus. Miraculously, a tiny American flag was still raised above the front fender.

In Kaine's mind, the intuition that had driven him this far was clearly defined as facts. A connection did exist between this car and the sinking of the ferry; a connection did exist between this car and Joseph Jankowski; a connection did exist between this car and the blueprint of Karmin-Yar.

Kaine began with the interior. Using the flash, he peered beneath the seats, under the dash, and in the glove compartment, which, most curiously, was completely empty. Using the long-bladed knife, he split the seat cushions and stripped them down to the springs. He sliced away the floor mats. Using the screwdrivers and hammer, he exposed the interior of the dashboard. He dismantled the roof and broke through the door panels. He razed the window ledge behind the backseat.

Outside, he pried open the trunk. He discovered a jack, a spare tire, and a tool box. Kaine rummaged through the box, tore out the trunk mat, and sliced into the spare. He took a hammer to the taillights. He swam around to the front of the car and accosted the headlights in the same fashion. He released the front hood. He searched the engine with the steadfastness of a man used to searching. He went so far as to unscrew the air filter and run his flashlight over the carburetor. He probed the side walls and dismantled the panel behind the dash.

Nothing. A nagging sense of futility ate into his confidence. He checked his dive timer. He had wasted fifty minutes.

He snaked between the undercarriage of the car and the side of the minibus against which it was wedged. He used the flashlight to probe the wheel wells and spooked a fish ablaze with the colors of a macaw. He moved along the chassis, taking in the frame, the suspension, and the transmission. When the light of the flash fell upon the flat metal box neatly tucked beneath the car's muffler, Kaine, hardly an automotive buff, realized he had stumbled upon the discovery he had been hoping for.

He used the crowbar to force the muffler and exhaust pipe aside. The box was new. Steel brackets and a series of four bolts, also new, secured it to the underside of the chassis. As yet, the ebb and flow of saltwater had left it unscathed. In a month, Kaine thought, it would be eaten with corrosion. As things were, the bolts turned easily under the pressure of the ratchet.

Once the box was freed, the weight of it most impressed Kaine; in his surprise, he nearly dropped it. He played the flash over its surface. Case-hardened steel, it was dark green, smooth, and, much like a safety deposit box, had been fitted with a two-key lock system.

Kaine doused the light. He replaced his tools and looped the satchel over his shoulder. With the box cradled in two hands, he started back toward the bow. While the reappearance of the eel played most prominently in his mind, a great ball of yellow light suddenly materialized at the bow doors. The light entered the open doors and brought the impression of day to the dark of the vehicle deck. The silhouette of two divers came and went and came again. Now Kaine saw the camera poised on the shoulder of the one. The other moved the floodlights in an orderly fashion from one side of the deck to the other.

Kaine slipped behind the bed of an overturned truck and momentarily held his breath.

In slow sweeping strokes, the light moved from bulkhead to bulkhead, from ceiling to floor, and finally set its sights on the destruction. The camera followed. Methodical though they were, the divers nonetheless slowly closed the gap between themselves and Kaine.

It was in the afterglow of the floodlights that Kaine saw the stairs leading up to subdeck C, the same route that had led him to

Angela what seemed an eternity ago. The battered and mangled cars were his ally now. He hid behind bumpers and beside upended wheel wells; as the light approached, he ducked into their shadows. He breathed intermittently, timing the release of his air with the turning of the camera crew's heads. The subdeck stairs were now effectively blocked by a wide-bodied car of some kind and a barricade of twisted bicycles, but Kaine managed to squirm through the car's smashed windows into the passage.

The ferry shifted. Overhead, Kaine heard the dull thud of footsteps. He had less than five minutes' worth of air left. At the head of the subdeck stairwell, he forced the door open a crack and nosed through.

B deck proved to be a repository of vivid memories. The cries of the weak and the dying, the weight of life-and-death decisions, a woman's body crashing down upon him, the cold sucking life from his own body like a ravenous sponge.

He swam. Though the living and the dead were gone, the ferry held an afterlife, surreal though it was. Drinking glasses had somehow ridden a tide of water into the corridor. A restaurant table had broken away from its base and, with three chairs and a man's raincoat, swayed in a doorway.

How had a brown and white puppy ended up outside a restroom door, his head twisted and tongue lolling from his mouth? Kaine's skin crawled at the sight. So the dead were not all gone, he thought. Had the dog's owner survived? If so, would he ever own another dog after this?

Work crews busied themselves in every room: two or three men in scuba gear clearing debris or using torches to secure welds. To see sparks underwater was an eerie sight. Kaine moved through the water as if he belonged; no one challenged his presence. The box had the effect of a miniature treasure chest.

An observation deck off the bow end of B deck was submerged in twenty feet of water, and Kaine surveyed the surroundings from here. Then he dove. He used the heavy steel box as a sinker and found the bottom seconds later. He swam fifty yards before pausing. Then he curled behind a stand of swaying seagrass and peered back. He couldn't shake the feeling that he was being watched. There, upon the observation deck. But he wasn't sure, and for the moment his concerns were more immediate.

He sucked a last breath from his air tank and surfaced. His lungs ached.

Swells rose and fell around him. The dead ferry lay fifty yards to the east; men and machines fed upon its body. Divers grouped around its hull. Helicopters hovered above it. Cranes encircled it. To the west, in the middle of the channel and steaming in his direction, Kaine spotted the harbor tug *Broadside*. Connor Thorpe stood on the bow peering through binoculars. Kaine saw a hand thrust in his direction and a plume of black rising from the funnel as the tug picked up speed.

He swam in bursts underwater. By now, the steel box was a dead weight dragging him down; his arms burned. As the tug approached, Kaine dove a last time. He resurfaced on the starboard side, out of view of the ferry.

The first skipper paused so briefly that the tug never actually came to a standstill; Connor hoisted Kaine aboard. The tug circled back into the main channel and set out for the harbor's latest arrival, a passenger ship flying the green, white, and red flag of Italy.

Angela helped Kaine off with his air tank. She hugged him tightly. "What took you so long? I was about to send out a rescue party."

Kaine kissed her forehead. Then he struggled out of his flippers. He allowed Connor to carry the box up to the wheelhouse, where he dropped it on the chart table.

Tanner Thorpe stared first at the box and then at Kaine. He said, "I don't suppose it makes much sense to underestimate you, does it?"

"It was bolted to the underside of the chassis," Kaine explained. "Very neat."

The first skipper studied the two-key lock. He shook his head in dismay. "Not without a blow torch or a stick of dynamite. How important is the box?"

"Not the box," Kaine replied. "It's what's inside."

Thorpe tossed his head in the general vicinity of his son. "Take the box down to the engine room. And don't make a mess of it. Do you hear?"

Angela followed Connor down the stairs and then the first skipper radioed the harbor. Pleading engine trouble, he requested another tug take charge of the passenger liner. The harbor agreed.

Connor and Angela reappeared moments later, faces flushed with excitement.

"Well?" his father asked.

Connor laid the box on the table again. The face of it was scorched and blackened. "I thought Mr. Kaine would probably want the honor."

Kaine hesitated.

Tanner Thorpe understood, saying, "I guess you've got a decision to make, don't you?"

"What does that mean?" his son asked.

"Nothing," Kaine answered quickly. When he raised the lid, the seal gave way, hissing. Inside, a silk cloth lined the box. Beyond the folds of the silk lay a sculpture of solid gold so brilliant and so finely appointed that Angela gasped.

Now Kaine took it in his hands. Designed in four hinged sections, it opened into a circular headpiece bejeweled with rubies and emeralds. Four finely etched crests were slotted into the headpiece and rose in gentle arches above it.

"A crown," Connor Thorpe whispered.

"Yes. The crown of the Persian high priestess, Sharana Ni." Kaine recognized it at once. "Its design is Persian but the craftsmanship is typical of the Cappadocians. Sharana Ni was the first mistress of the fire temple at Karmin-Yar."

"From that city of yours," the first skipper said.

"The Persians weren't typically nomadic, but the Cappadocians were. They designed everything with ease of travel in mind. And since the high priestess would never travel without her crown, the collapsible design was ideal."

Kaine found himself in a state of semi-shock. That he could be on the waters of the Strait of Dover holding one of the most sacred artifacts of ancient Persian life was, on the one hand, dumbfounding, on the other, frightening. But did it also open another door on the sinking of the ferry? Were Ras Haydar's religious convictions of such depth that he would revert to measures so extreme to reclaim such an inviolate treasure? Kaine was an archeologist, and the crown was an archeological wonder. But to risk one's own life and the lives of hundreds of others for a crown and a previously unknown blueprint?

Kaine withdrew the silk cloth from the bottom of the box. Beneath it lay six rows of gold coins. Angela looked on in awe, Connor with intense curiosity.

"My God, now what?" his father exclaimed.

Each coin was stamped with a kneeling archer, the image of Darius the First, ruler of the Persian Empire from 521 to 486 B.C., and master builder of the lost city of Karmin-Yar.

"Darics. The standard gold coins of the empire," Kaine told them. "Ninety-eight-percent pure gold."

"A system of trade based on gold?" Thorpe mused. "Is that what you're saying?"

"Their system of trade was based on the barter system," Kaine said remotely. "Meats, grains, textiles, services. That kind of thing . . ."

Kaine's words trailed off. He was still grappling with the breadth of this discovery. Despite his assertions about the crown's design and its convenience for travel, the fact was that the high priestess of the fire temple dared travel on only the rarest occasions. The coronation of a new king, a marriage in the royal family, the death of a parent, perhaps. And only then if the event didn't conflict with a holy day, of which in the days of Sharana Ni there were an overabundance. Was it possible then that, by some stroke of good fortune, Sharana Ni had been away from Karmin-Yar at the time of the great earthquake? Had the crown then been lost or stolen?

"Well?" the first skipper interrupted, his voice strained with impatience.

"It was their taxation system that was based on gold," Kaine replied. "Gold or silver. Objects or coins, it didn't matter to the Persians. They melted it all down anyway. The silver was stored in ingots, or bars . . ."

"The gold they made into coins in Darius's image," Connor
Thorpe said. He pinned Kaine with dubious eyes. "The same gold
you were accused of purloining six months ago, and which cost
you your job."

"Accused of purloining but not convicted of," the first skipper
pointedly reminded his son. But the tone of his voice was less
convincing when he posed his own query to Kaine. "Didn't you say
you'd uncovered the treasure house at Karmin-Yar before you were
so ungraciously relieved of your job?"

"That's right."

"And it was empty."

Kaine nodded. "Completely."

"Could the Persians have had time to prepare for the earthquake, say by transferring what was in the treasure house to some
safer site?"

"Earthquakes of that magnitude don't normally issue advance
warnings, Mr. Thorpe. And besides, we've found enough skeletal
remains to convince us that it happened fast. Very fast."

A chill that was neither the water nor the wind ran down the
length of Kaine's spine. He wrapped his arms around Angela's
shoulders and stared out through the pilothouse window. The glass,
he saw, reflected back an image of a man caught in the penumbra
of what he thought he knew and facing the harsh reality of endless
unknowns.

That the Persian Empire encompassed both the Cappadocians
and the Scythians was not an unknown. Nor was the fact that both
tribes had settled upon the Great Silk Route from China; Karmin-
Yar had purposely been built upon the route. Gold and silver were
natural vehicles of commerce. The Cappadocian gold hoards were
legendary among archeologists. Their artisans turned gold into jewelry and bookends and statues honoring everything from horses to
governors. The Scythians, though nomadic and continuously at
war, forged gold-embellished chest plates and helmets so finely
polished that enemy soldiers, legend held, turned in horror from
the very reflections they cast.

The Persians, however, maintained a benevolent approach to

the traditions and cultures of the tribes in their empire. Their only insistence was upon the tributes paid to their King of Kings. First to Cyrus the Great, then to Darius, then to Xerxes. The tax, as with the Medes and the Babylonians and the Assyrians and a host of others, was extracted in the form of precious metals. The Persians, though benevolent, were also maniacally untrusting. Darius once wrote, in the cuneiform language which he himself developed, that the Cappadocians were essentially "snakes beneath the skin." The Scythians in their pointed hats "carried daggers beneath their smiles and blood on their lips." Not the kind of description bestowed upon neighbors held in high esteem.

The only written record ever discovered in reference to Karmin-Yar was found in the foundation records in the city archives of Persepolis. Again the words were attributed to Darius. He said, "A Treasure House amongst the heathens by the Sea shalt be as decorative as a honey jar in a high tree in winter."

Over the years, Kaine had interpreted this to mean that the tributes made by "the heathens by the sea" were quickly removed from their areas of influence, logically as far away as Persepolis. When he had found the Karmin-Yar treasure house empty, he had been disappointed, but he had also found in this emptiness a confirmation of his interpretation of Darius's words.

Now a new logic intervened. Here was the crown of the high priestess of Karmin-Yar in company with the gold of taxation. The crown, by law, might be removed from the sacred fire temple, the domicile of the eternal flame, but only in the company of the priestess. Under threat of death, once the flame was lit, only the high priest and priestess were allowed to enter the temple. The Cappadocians and the Scythians honored this tradition with the same fervor as their conquerors. Now a blueprint of the city had fallen into his hands, and it showed, among other things, a tunnel linking the palace court of the King of Kings with the inviolate fire temple. Why? Had the King of Kings violated his own sacred tenets by using the fire temple for purposes other than the keeping of the eternal flame?

Kaine looked beyond the reflection in the window now. The

white cliffs were blindingly beautiful. The harbor churned with activity. Beneath his feet, the tug's massive engine droned and the pulse of it could be felt in every nerve in his body.

As the tug scudded along toward the south jetty, Kaine's attention was drawn to a small dockside gathering obviously awaiting their arrival. He pressed closer to the window; the hair on the back of his neck stood on end.

The group was four in number, all recognizable. Jaymin wore blue jeans and a leather jacket. Erect and unmoving, she stood well away from the others, her legs spread, her hands buried deep in her pockets. What was she doing there? Her dark expression was no more readable than a closed book. Detective Superintendent Preble stood quietly, his hands busily feeding red candies into his mouth. Detective Hennagan paced robotically at his side, a matched pair, those two. The harbormaster looked gray and tired; he held a clipboard across his chest, and disgust tugged at the lines of his weatherbeaten face.

First Skipper Thorpe shook his head and spat.

"Ugly," he said, now tossing his head toward the four. "Damn bloody ugly."

"What do they want?" Angela asked.

"You stay up here after we dock," Kaine answered. He replaced the gold coins, six rows, thirty pieces. He laid the silk cloth in the box and carefully repacked the crown of the High Priestess, Sharana Ni. He closed the case. Outside, he saw Connor Thorpe bound ashore with a bow line in his hand. The rubber fenders of the tug caressed the dock, and the first skipper cut the engine.

"They won't be handing out any awards for bravery, you might have guessed that by now," he said to Kaine.

"Well informed, aren't they?" Kaine replied. "How much trouble are you in?"

Thorpe snorted. "The harbormaster there is a gent by the name of Hennessy Jones. We go back forty years. Shipmates we were. He'll slap my wrist to make the detective superintendent happy and then apologize in private later."

Together they ambled down the pilothouse steps to the lower deck. Kaine carried the steel box under his arm. He looked from Jaymin to Preble and back again.

"Well, fuck me," Thorpe bellowed. "A bloody welcoming party. Unnecessary, but damn lovely. And of course you brought champagne."

"First Skipper Tanner Thorpe," the harbormaster announced in a stern voice. "Your vessel is now my vessel. Come with me, if you will."

Thorpe raised an eyebrow in Kaine's direction. He whispered, "The champagne is actually rum and he keeps it under lock and key in his office. Good luck."

"You're effective as hell in trying a man's patience, Professor Kaine," Preble said, once Thorpe and the harbormaster had made their way up the dock.

"I scuba dive for pleasure," Kaine said to Preble, though his eyes never left Jaymin. Eventually, he stepped ashore. "I thought the ferry presented an ideal opportunity."

"And it proved fruitful, I see. Excellent." Preble threw an inquisitive glance at the box. "You saved us the trouble of sending down our own man and in the process placed another black mark next to your name. You seem determined to force my hand and I don't know why."

"You keep threatening me with arrest."

"And you see my threats as token bluffs?"

"I see you recognizing that arresting me solves nothing," Kaine replied.

"American bravado?"

"Not bravado, confusion. Earlier you mentioned that two men had foolishly stayed with their automobile during the crossing of the *Spirit of Long Life*. You mentioned a Mercedes-Benz. What you didn't mention was the car's diplomatic status."

"That only serves to explain their desire to remain with their vehicle, as far as I can see."

"Good," Kaine replied. He started up the dock. "Then we can both get on with our business."

"If it were only that simple." It was Preble who issued this statement, but Detective Hennagan who stepped into Kaine's path. "There are other forces involved in something as complicated as this ferry accident. You don't seem to realize that. Or perhaps you do and have chosen nonetheless to butt heads with those of us in a position to be of service."

"Other forces?" For a moment, Kaine peered back down the ramp at Jaymin. She was staring across the harbor at an outgoing ferry, her angelic features both stern and passive. Yet she was acutely aware of him. Kaine saw that in the tilt of her head and in the set of her jaw. Then, like a man whose curiosity had given way to disappointment, he said it again. "Other forces."

"The box," Preble said. "I'll have to ask you for it, please. The rightful owner will be grateful, I'm quite certain. And I'll recommend that he not press charges."

"You're aware of the box's contents then?"

"That, I'm afraid, is not a factor here." Preble favored Kaine with an avuncular smile.

"Since the rightful owner of what's in this box died two thousand years ago, I'd say it's very much a factor. Either that or Scotland Yard is playing politics. I didn't know that was Scotland Yard's purpose."

"Can we move this thing along, Detective Preble?" Jaymin snapped. She faced them now. Her hands came to rest on her hips.

With that, Kaine held the box out by the handle; he held it out to Jaymin specifically. "You're right. We're wasting time, aren't we? You have people to answer to and we don't want to keep them waiting, do we?"

It was Hennagan who relieved Kaine of the box and Preble who thanked him. Like bookends, they retreated, leaving Kaine and Jaymin momentarily alone.

Jaymin's hands returned to her pockets and her steps were quick and sure as she set out along the dock. But when she was an arm's length from Kaine, she paused. Their eyes met and lingered. And though they both seemed on the verge of speaking, they likewise seemed to realize that there was no explanation that would suffice, nor words capable of bridging the gap that separated them.

Still, Kaine noticed that Jaymin's stride, as she made her way toward shore, was less confident than before. Furthermore, he reflected that, try as he might, he could not tear his eyes away from her.

12

An hour ago, watching the two Scotland Yard detectives walk down the jetty with the crown of Sharana Ni in their possession, Kaine had been reminded of the American he'd seen aboard the harbor tug *Broadside* the morning of the ferry accident. The man and his two bodyguards had driven away from the scene that morning in a blue Toyota Camry with a bumper sticker on the back advertising Maxim Rental of London, Oxford, and Birmingham. One of those bodyguards, Kaine realized now, was unmistakably the late Joseph Jankowski.

On the chance that Maxim had expanded from the three locations noted on its bumper sticker, Kaine checked the phone directory. They hadn't; the company's nearest outlets were still in London, seventy miles to the west.

Kaine drove the rusted-out Honda out of Dover and into the Kent countryside.

Rain hung in the air. It was as if an artist lacking in colors had mixed a steely gray with forest green and washed it over the day. In the valleys between low, lush knolls sheep grazed. A man worked on the steep roof of a stone church. A spiral bell tower loomed above him; it rang ten times. Along a row of thatch-roofed houses, boys in short pants played soccer and their voices rose in odd harmony to a train whistle. A field of hops rose upon the back of a treeless slope. Beyond the field a swath of orange flowers bloomed.

As he drove, Kaine considered Jaymin's defection—a description he couldn't help using—to the "other side," and realized the logic of it. Still, he harbored some fleeting hope that she was being manipulated in some way, and without recourse—by the man in the expensive suit perhaps, or by the colonel with direct connections to an unlisted number in Arlington, Virginia. What he could not forgive was the theft of artifacts of history for profit. The crown of the high priestess Sharana Ni belonged to the world now, a tiny fragment in the legacy of mankind's evolution.

A pall hung over the sprawling city of London. A blanket of clouds threatened to engulf it. A corridor of thick mist followed the meandering course of the Thames River. Two thousand years ago the Romans threw a wooden bridge across the river and a city was born. The old city, the city of the Romans, the Saxons, and the Normans, still represented the commercial center of the city nineteen centuries later.

Kaine crossed the Tower Bridge.

The car rental company he sought was located a block off Fleet Street. Distinguished by a narrow blue awning, it was sandwiched between a bakery and a branch of a Japanese bank. Kaine parked in a loading zone in front of the bank.

The rental office suffered from a lack of ventilation. A fan hung from the ceiling and cranked nervously. Travel brochures lined an unoccupied counter. A stout, buxom woman with a page-boy haircut and a tight leather skirt sat at a desk, a computer slave tied to her master.

She was exceedingly polite. "May I be of assistance?"

"I'm afraid a car with one of your stickers on the rear bumper sideswiped my car and left a healthy dent in the front fender," Kaine answered. "The driver didn't think it was necessary to stop."

"I'm dreadfully sorry."

"I thought I'd come here before I went to the police."

An awkward moment followed this statement; the woman obviously didn't know whether to be grateful or not. She offered Kaine a seat next to the desk. "You're certain the car was one of ours?"

Kaine described the blue Toyota, and the driver, as if he had seen them in broad daylight. He gave her the license number.

"May I ask when this happened?"

"Tuesday morning in Dover. It was probably six or six thirty. I was on my way to breakfast."

The woman was busy typing the information into her computer. "Dreadful."

"Unless I'm mistaken, your renter was drunk."

Kaine moved to the edge of the seat and turned in the direction of the computer. A directory of Maxim-owned vehicles rolled across the screen. Eventually, the woman brought the directory to a stop and used a long, brightly painted fingernail as a pointer.

"Yes, it is indeed one of our cars. A Toyota Camry, just as you said. Let's see where it is these days, just to be sure we're on the right track." She typed in a series of numbers and a rental contract materialized. The woman expelled an exasperated sigh. "It went out the day before. Tuesday. Not from this office, from the one off Knightsbridge. Unfortunately it hasn't been returned yet, so it's going to be a bit difficult to confirm until it is. You understand."

Kaine wasn't listening. His attention had come to rest upon the name on the renter's contract: Paul Hennagan. Hennagan! Kaine almost said the name out loud. The Scotland Yard detective. The computer had taken information off his driver's license. The address was an apartment in Folkestone, a small coastal town that was Dover's nearest neighbor. An obscure signature, hardly more than a scribble, had been scratched across the line at the bottom.

Now the woman was shaking her head, and Kaine heard her complain. "I never like it when they pay in cash. I'm always suspicious." She turned her gaze up at Kaine, in hopes, he imagined, of a sympathetic nod. When he was unable to produce it, she said halfheartedly, "It will be necessary to give an accounting to the police. I know it's an inconvenience . . ."

Kaine rose, and the absence in the gesture was reflected in the absence of his reply. "Thanks for your help."

He turned for the door. "Wouldn't you like to leave your name?" the woman called out.

"I'll talk to the police," Kaine said as he walked out.

But Kaine didn't go to the police; he paid a visit to the American embassy instead.

An attaché sat in a cubicle at the rear of the embassy's grandiose lobby. He had a wedge-shaped face, feminine in its narrowness and delicacy. A receding hairline had left patches of ivory skin flanking a tuft of reddish brown hair. Nervous and dispirited, the attaché glared at Kaine with bloodshot eyes, a deep crease piercing his forehead.

The Mercedes-Benz at the bottom of Dover's Admiralty Harbor was fitted with diplomatic plates and carried an American flag on the fender, but during the course of Kaine's search it had rendered no registration papers or official documentation of any kind. Its very presence on the ferry would present a starting point for any investigation into the wreckage; Kaine had spent enough time on foreign soil to know this. His experience had also led him to an understanding of embassy employees. They were slaves to common courtesy; in return, they reacted most positively to acts of rudeness.

"You're missing a car," Kaine said bluntly to the attaché. Kaine allowed his identification to be scrutinized, but not without an exaggerated sigh. He leaned heavily on the desk and tapped at the surface with his fingers.

"A car?" The attaché said the word as if trying to grasp an alien concept. His lips were a ruby red and he turned them into a severe pout. "Forgive me, but I haven't the slightest idea what you're talking about."

"A Mercedes," Kaine replied. "Black. Shiny. Leather interior. Very nice."

The attaché's forehead took on an extra furrow. "There's an overabundance of Mercedes in London, sir."

"I didn't say the car was in London. Nor on English soil, for that matter."

"Yet you say it belongs to us."

"You know the miniature red, white, and blue flags you people put on the front fenders of your cars? It had one of those. You know the black and white plates every diplomatic vehicle in the world uses? It had a set of those, too."

"Where, if I may be so bold, did you see this mysterious car, if not in England?"

Kaine scooped up a paper clip from the attaché's desk and casually straightened one end. "When I know for sure it's yours, I'll tell you. I don't want to saddle you with someone else's problem."

"You're very thoughtful." The attaché viewed the paper clip as one would a "sold" sign on a highly coveted jewel. His eyes shifted. "You obviously have a special interest in this car," he said to Kaine.

"If it doesn't belong to you, then it belongs to me." Kaine ran the end of the paper clip beneath a fingernail. "As a loyal American, it's the least I can do."

"Very patriotic," the attaché said drily.

The embassy fleet was logged into the computer and every car was accounted for. The attaché passed this information on to Kaine as if nothing less than a formal apology would make up for the time he had wasted.

"Good," Kaine said, giving every indication that the matter was settled.

"After all that you didn't get the license plate number?" the attaché called out, his voice tinged suddenly with disbelief.

"Naturally."

The attaché scowled. "It might help. This is assuming you're really trying to help."

"FRMA101."

"The embassy house in Marseilles, France," he answered at once. He struck out at the keyboard with newly discovered vigor; his interest level, Kaine saw, rose even as his bony fingers typed.

Kaine, in return, became an ally. He leaned on the desk again. Exasperation dissolved into a pool of mutual conspiracy. "That makes sense," he said. "The car was on a ferry from Calais."

"Crossing into England?"

"Dover."

"Which actually makes no sense at all."

Kaine saw a renewal of nervous tension, and he took this as a positive sign. "Why not?" he asked.

The attaché's tongue traveled nervously over his lips. He said,

"Because a 101 license plate number is only found on vehicles at the disposal of the embassy's administrative director."

Mentally, Kaine reviewed the embassy hierarchy as he remembered it, and said, "Who would answer only to the ambassador himself, in Paris."

"That's true, but hardly the point. The point being that the administrative director in Marseilles, Carl Davis, died of a heart attack four months ago. His successor has yet to be named."

"And the car?"

"It was reported stolen three days ago."

"From where?"

"From the embassy motor pool in Marseilles. From a card-operated garage three floors below ground."

"An embassy employee then."

"That is a question for the police. Our question is, where is the car now, and obviously you have the answer." The attaché resumed his adversarial role. "I'm really not in a big hurry to ring for our security people, but I suppose you know I will."

Kaine straightened. His gaze wandered aimlessly, as did his thoughts. Only now did it occur to him that he had been cold ever since his rescue efforts in the *Spirit of Long Life;* a chill had seemingly burrowed beneath his skin and taken root in his bones. For now, it was the embassy's marble floor tiles. They seemed to radiate a coolness all their own, and Kaine had the sensation of standing in a mountain stream.

He shuffled his feet unconsciously. His eyes settled momentarily on a huge photograph on the wall behind the desk. It was a garden portrait of Prime Minister Margaret Thatcher and President George Bush. Between them stood a second, shorter man. His fingers were intertwined over a rounded paunch, and diamond rings sparkled on either hand. He wore a silk suit that, opposite the Iron Lady's boxy jacket and pleated skirt and the president's typically lifeless ensemble, looked nothing short of pretentious.

Now Kaine saw the attaché reach for the telephone, which caused him to smile. He said, "Your car is on the vehicle deck of a ferry called the *Spirit of Long Life*. Unfortunately the *Spirit of*

Long Life is submerged in fifty feet of water in Admiralty Harbor in Dover."

Plane and oak trees marched at Kaine's side as he walked through Hyde Park. At the park entrance, he stopped next to the Marble Arch. The sun burned through a layer of gray mist and he absorbed a full minute of its rays.

The sun evoked a memory, which produced a dull ache in his stomach. His mother had been a consummate sun worshiper. They had spent holidays together—Kaine was an only child—at a beach house in Southern California. The house stood on a cliff. Every day they built sand castles and christened them with exotic names like the Eagles' Aerie or the Fortress of a Thousand Dragons. Kaine's father had paid for the house in cash, a fact he took immeasurable pride in. The trouble was, he never spent a single day there with his son and wife. He used it instead, Kaine discovered later, for his occasional trysts.

Kaine's mother had died in a plane crash when he was fifteen, her first solo flight ending up in a ball of flames on the side of a mountain fifteen minutes from Denver. Though his father had been in Africa at the time, Kaine had blamed him for her death, had vented the pain of her loss on him, and had vowed eternal hatred.

Kaine jogged across the street and entered the campus of the University of London. As he climbed the stone steps to the Institute of Scientific Studies, his memory opened another wound. No, he no longer hated his father; he had simply been stripped of any respect he may have ever had for the man. The result was indifference, and by now, the side effects on Kaine were well documented. He had never been a team player; he had never been in one spot long enough to develop those skills. His pursuits had always been of the solo variety: swimming, fencing, sculpting. And though these were not without their rewards, the problem was overcoming the emptiness that often accompanied them. The emptiness, in turn, had dreadful consequences on the ego. Kaine's only recourse had been more solo pursuits, and archeology was perfect.

Now he was seeing that part of himself in Angela and felt helpless to derail it.

The institute was built like a church. The ceilings rose to glorious heights, the arches were carved of stone, and the windows were framed in heavy slabs of wood and accented with quarrels of colored glass.

The chemistry department was hidden away in the basement. The door to the environmental lab Kaine was seeking stood ajar. He knocked, then stepped quietly into a large, singular chamber overwhelmingly scented with ammonia. Stout wooden tables lined four walls and were heavy with equipment. Long workbenches ran through the heart of the room, and gas and water lines formed asymmetrical grids above them.

There were no students. An antiseptic silence was broken only by the lone professor who stood before a blackboard drawing a model built of abstract formulas and words like *transferases,* and *isomerases,* and *enzymes.* He was a barrel-chested man with a graying beard and a sharp, narrow nose. A hospital green smock cast him more in the mold of a medical man, though the Nobel prize he had received eleven years before was in honor of his theory on cell reproduction. The Nobel had stolen Dr. Julian Persoff from the classroom, his first love, and made him a prisoner of research.

Kaine had walked into Persoff's office for the first time nearly fifteen years ago. In his hand that day he had carried a temperature-controlled storage box containing three clay jars from the ruins of a Scottish dolmen. The first jar harbored holy water, the second blackberry wine, and the third human blood. The latter was atypical of the Scots in every way and had perplexed Kaine ever since.

The sudden activation of a device called a spectrometer shook the doctor away from his preoccupied state and informed him also that he had a visitor.

"Stephen Kaine, good Lord." The spectrometer spat a ream of paper into Persoff's hand. Then he shook Kaine's hand, and did so with zest and vigor. "It's been two years, and I didn't even get a card last Christmas. You're obviously not dead, so I can't bring myself to forgive you."

"You've earned a gray hair or two since then," Kaine remarked.

"And you haven't." Persoff scowled. "How dare you retain your youth?" He reached beneath an enclosed fume hood and reduced the heat under a narrow glass funnel. "You'll drink tea, I assume."

"I don't want to disturb you."

"Of course you do," Persoff replied. "And I am immensely grateful."

On a shelf in the center of the room a row of glass beakers were held at odd angles by stainless steel support clamps; beneath each beaker a blue flame burned. Among the beakers were jars containing methanol and buffer solution, polishing alumina and distilled water, baking soda—and one jar with the words ORANGE PEKOE TEA written across the front. Persoff uncapped the lid, filled two tea balls, and dropped them into stoneware mugs. He poured hot water over them. Then he apologized for the smell in the room.

"Never pour ammonium hydroxide down the sink." He waved a hand in front of his face. "Good Lord, it smells like forty cat boxes in a closet."

Kaine laughed. He was staring at the periodic table of the elements over the blackboard. He tested his memory. "Hydrogen, helium, lithium, beryllium, boron, carbon . . . ?" He drew a blank and looked up. "Nitrogen? Are you sure?"

Persoff followed his eyes to the table. "The truth of it is, the only people I know with that thing memorized are scared freshmen. That's why we keep it on the wall." He served Kaine his tea. "But don't tell me the periodic table of the elements brought you all the way to London."

"No. Acetic acid did," Kaine replied. From his inside coat pocket Kaine withdrew the piece of paper upon which he had written the name of the chemical company from which Joseph Jankowski had purchased ten gallons of acetic anhydride. "I was struck by the quantity."

"On the one hand, acetic acid is the most popular acid in the world," Persoff said, studying the paper. "On the other hand, you're right. You don't see that many folks bringing it home in ten-gallon jugs. Which brings us to Mr. Jankowski. Who or what is he?"

"A former New York City policeman who tried to run me, my daughter, and former wife off a mountainside in Dover." Kaine told the chemist the story. "I found a copy of the purchase order in his wallet."

Persoff screwed his face into a knot, then pursed his lips. "I don't recall ever hearing of Dumas Industries."

"Is it important?"

"Only in so far as I rarely forget a name. Or a face, or anything else, I'm afraid. It's a disgusting curse."

"What do people do with the world's most popular acid?"

"They make vinegar, didn't you know?" Persoff scoffed, then chortled. "Which is true, but what they do mostly, my archeological friend, is use it in the acetic anhydride form for producing cellulose acetate, which in its most practical application is used in the making of plastics. Cellulose acetate plastics can take almost any form you want." Persoff dramatized the point by removing his eyeglasses from the pocket of his smock. "The frames? Cellulose acetate plastic."

"Somehow I don't picture Mr. Jankowski in the eyeglass business," Kaine remarked. "What else besides vinegar and plastics?"

"Aspirin."

"Not this guy."

"Heroin."

"Heroin and Marseilles." For a moment, they drank tea in silence. Then Kaine tipped his head. "It was my impression that the French government had taken care of that combination years ago."

Persoff shrugged. "The past is your department. Mine is an endless series of forays into the land of make-believe."

He set his tea aside and spent a moment in another room removing slide samples from a drying oven. When he returned, he had a gallon bottle in his hands. The liquid inside was clear; outside, two words were typed beside a chemical formula: ACETIC ACID. He took the cap off. "Don't get too close."

Kaine did, leaning directly over the mouth. He pulled back quickly and winced. "Strong."

Persoff threw an open palm in the air. "I'm glad I didn't say anything about not drinking it."

"How's heroin made, Julian?"

"To be truthful, heroin isn't much more than the chemically

bonded synthesis of acetic anhydride and morphine." Persoff waved
Kaine over to a workbench and a pair of stools. He pushed aside a
stack of papers. "Naturally, morphine is the key ingredient. The
acidic bond simply fortifies the morphine and makes it ten times
more powerful than your ordinary medical variety."

Persoff yawned, but the yawn gave him renewed energy. "All
right then. You start with ordinary opium poppies; in this case,
ordinary is a relative term, of course. After the poppy flowers, it
produces a seed pod about the size of an egg. After the petals fall
off, the pod produces a milky white sap. The sap is opium. How do
you extract pure morphine from opium? You add the opium to hot
water. When it dissolves, you add everyday lime fertilizer. After a
bit of filtering the solution is heated again, this time with concentrated ammonia. In the end, the morphine weighs about a tenth of
what the opium did."

The chemist stared out into space, stroking his beard. Kaine
waited.

"Then it gets tricky," Persoff said. "I can't detail the exact process for you, but essentially a ten-kilogram production of heroin
requires ten kilograms of morphine and a like amount of the acetic
anhydride. The two have to be heated together very precisely."
Persoff looked around him. "Now that I think about it, you could
do a good job of it in a lab like this. A very good job. After six or
eight hours, you've created an impure form of what's called
diacetylmorphine."

"Heroin."

"An unsatisfactory variety, yes," Persoff answered. "The diacetylmorphine is made less impure by treating it with water and
chloroform, then with sodium carbonate, then with alcohol and
activated charcoal. Now you're getting somewhere. A little ether,
a little hydrochloric acid, and you're talking about something that's
perhaps eighty or ninety, sometimes ninety-five percent pure. And
it all begins with a rather lovely, innocuous-looking flower with
orange and white blossoms."

"Poppies."

13 Jaymin had made the mistake of mentioning the Belgravia Hotel to Kaine during those bleak hours after the ferry accident when they were searching for Angela. She had reserved a room for the week, she had said, though she wasn't sure whether or not the sheets would ever be turned down. Kaine had taken this to mean that the room might never be used. But he had studied Jaymin over the last four days. Like every estranged warrior who takes an impossible stand against the world, she would need a sanctuary. A place to hide, a place to toss aside the armor of her belligerent struggle, a place to rekindle the fire. During their last encounter, on the docks off the south jetty early this morning, when Kaine was forced to relinquish the crown of Sharana Ni, he had seen the ebbing of that fire. That her most basic instinct would eventually force her to seek sanctuary, he reasoned, was only logical.

The Belgravia Hotel was located on Brompton Road across from Knightsbridge. Decades of daily polishing had left a green stain on the stone around the brass markings at the entrance. A hand-stitched awning formed a gray canopy from the curb to the doors. The doors were heavy mahogany highlighted by panels of frosted glass.

Her room, the front desk informed him, was on the fourth floor. Kaine opted for the stairs, climbing them two at a time. In the hall outside her room, he stood for a moment lost in the numbers on the door: 411. The juxtaposition of his motives rendered him momentarily immobile. He wanted answers. He wanted her, too. He would not, he realized, get both.

Without knocking, he reached for the handle, turned it, and the door opened.

Jaymin sat on the edge of the bed huddled over the nightstand. She held a hypodermic needle in her left hand. Her right hand formed a tight fist. She had twisted a red bandanna around her right bicep. Veins bulged from her forearm. The serum inside the syringe was golden brown in color. On the nightstand, a white envelope formed a crucible for white powder. A candle burned. Beside it lay a bent spoon tinged with the black carbon from its flame. An eyedropper was plunged in a small tumbler of water. A swatch of cotton had been torn from a larger roll and lay next to the tumbler.

Kaine stared without confusion; his visit with Dr. Julian Persoff had prepared him.

Jaymin stared back. She blinked away a moment of bewilderment. "Only a fool leaves her door unlocked in the heart of downtown London. Only a degenerate walks through a closed door without knocking."

"Finish it," Kaine said, his eyes locked on the heroin. "Then we'll talk."

Jaymin's hand shook as she laid the syringe next to the envelope. Her skin was chalky. Her full lips were parched. A bead of sweat hung from the bridge of her nose and she brushed it quickly away. Her shirt was open at the front, merely tied in a knot below her ribcage. She loosened the bandanna and rolled the shirtsleeve down over it. She drew a deep breath. Finally, she pushed strands of damp hair off her forehead, seeking an element of composure.

"We'll talk first," she told him. "I'm not the sociable type."

The room was dark behind drawn curtains. It reeked of sulfur. A secondary smell, like that of sweet mustard, caused Kaine a moment of dizziness. He overcame it with his own display of cynicism, saying, "That's curious. What type are you exactly?"

The candle flickered, throwing incongruous shadows across her face. "The type who says none of your fucking business about twice a day."

Kaine closed the door. Without moving, he took in the rest of the room. The Belgravia had been granted four stars for its understated opulence; a woman in blue jeans shooting heroin into her arm was part of a bad dream. The curtains were lace and satin. The soap and shampoo were perfumed and complimentary. An Old World chandelier hung from the ceiling. The headboard above the bed was hand-tooled, and from the post nearest the nightstand hung a shoulder harness and holster, empty. The gun lay in the middle of a queen-size bed. It was an American-made nine-millimeter Smith & Wesson; its polished finish suggested the pride of its owner. Beside the gun lay a tiny cassette recorder fitted with an elastic waistband and a disc microphone the size of a dime.

"You know why I'm here," he said.

"You're playing amateur detective." Jaymin seemed more concerned with the recorder than the gun and swept it from Kaine's view.

"I've searched most of my career for the crown of Sharana Ni, Jaymin."

"That qualifies you to play cops and robbers?"

"I'm not *playing* at anything."

"Maybe you chose the wrong profession."

"It's a profession that leaves you a little cynical about the human race, if that's what you mean."

"There's more involved here than a fucking crown worn by some nomadic princess and a couple of gold coins the world has gotten along just fine without for two thousand years, Stephen. Sorry to disappoint you."

"Drugs," Kaine said simply. There were too many telltale signs. Ras Haydar's message to Angela. "Tell your father that the deed will happen the third week in March. That's all I know." The third week in March, the opium harvest. Ten gallons of acetic anhydride,

the prime bonding agent used in the production of heroin, purchased by a New York City thug in Marseilles. Now this scene with
Jaymin. Kaine said it again. "Drugs. Heroin."

"It's the toast of the marketplace again. Didn't you know that?
Or have you been locked away in your world of trinkets and fossils
for too long? Well, maybe not the toast just yet, but let's say it's
riding the growth curve again. Oh, not like this." Jaymin hitched
up her shirtsleeve again. She tightened the knot on the bandanna.
"You know what's in now, Stephen? You know what's got people
excited now? Now that coke has peaked. Now that pot is almost
passé. It's called smokable heroin.

"The crackheads are cooking the stuff up with their rock. They
call it 'chasing the dragon.' Makes it almost tolerable. Up quick,
down easy. The trendies in New York and LA, you know the ones,
with no values and even less direction, they mix it with grass or
sprinkle it on a cigarette. They call it . . . what? In vogue, I suppose.
But China White is not like coke. It comes with a built-in convenience factor. It doesn't have to be cooked or nuked or anything.
No treatment at all. Just light the shit up.

"See, this is one of those watershed times in the history of drugs
that no one will see until it's too late. New product, old sources.
Ten years ago the news was good. The Turks set fire to their opium
fields, the Mexicans cut back, the Soviets invaded Afghanistan, and
the government cracked down on the Mafia. Just like that, prices
skyrocketed, which happens to be the best eradication program of
them all. Now the Soviets have given up on Afghanistan, and the
Turks got lazy. Or wise, maybe. After all, their people were starving.
Poppies produce sixty times the income of wheat. And goat's milk?
Be serious."

Jaymin marched into the bathroom. She cleaned out the syringe
in the sink. She carried it back to the nightstand and passed the
needle through the flame of the candle.

Her voice summoned energy from the process. "But in Turkey
it's more than just a complacent local government. Now there's a
new marketing vehicle. A new intermediary, someone with the
goods to make the vehicle run the way it's supposed to."

"Who?"

"What do you think happened when the producers in South America saw their coke business leveling off and the walls closing in over in their own countries? I'll tell you. They started looking for new ground to break, that's what."

"Ras Haydar didn't open the bow doors on the *Spirit of Long Life* in the name of some South American drug dealers."

"Don't be foolish."

"Don't tell me they're not related."

Jaymin ignored him. "Things began to happen in earnest about two and a half years ago when a gentleman by the name of Meo Monastero took over the Turkish government."

Kaine's eyes narrowed; he raised a hand. "Which coincides nicely with the infiltration of the Karmin-Yar site by the Turkish secret police," he said.

"I'm not surprised," Jaymin replied. "Monastero promised his people prosperity. Within two years there were ten thousand acres of mountain farmland cranking out raw opium, about seven hundred metric tons of it, and two hundred labs turning it into low-grade morphine." Jaymin tossed her head in the direction of the envelope on the nightstand and the white powder inside. She used the eyedropper to fill the base of the blackened spoon with water. She used the tip of a nail file to lift a wedge of the powder from the envelope. She held it out for Kaine's inspection, her expression aloof, yet weak. "Which down the road translates into about seventy tons of this shit."

The muscles in Kaine's neck constricted. He said, "Down the road; places like Marseilles."

Jaymin tipped her head, as if mildly impressed. "Buy two kilos of morphine from one of those hilltop labs and it might cost you eight hundred dollars. Pick a route. By the time you reach Ankara it's worth two thousand. In Istanbul, the same two kilos gets you five thousand. After the morphine has been transformed in a lab in a place like Marseilles, you stash what is now only a kilo—a kilo of this shit—in the back of an overstuffed chair and ship it off to Amsterdam or London or New York. Portside in Europe, the kilo is now worth fifty thousand dollars wholesale; in New York, a hundred and fifty thousand and the package hasn't even been opened. Dilute it down about ten times and now it's an eight-hundred-thousand-dollar product.

"Am I getting through to you yet, Stephen? A dollar's worth of this stuff at the source in the Daglari Mountains yields a thousand dollars on the streets of Manhattan. Not exactly goat's milk or wheat."

Now Jaymin consigned the powder to the water and stirred momentarily. Kaine saw the heavy sagging of her shoulders. Her head moved from side to side. A sigh so irrevocable and powerful passed her lips that Kaine was compelled a step farther into the room. She held the spoon above the flame. A repugnant odor permeated the air. Tears pooled in Jaymin's eyes and tinseled the sides of her cheeks. Her lips parted.

"Don't," Kaine said, venturing closer. "I can help. Let me help you. Please."

He said the words even as another part of his brain spat out the inevitable question, How? How would you help her? Empty words of philosphy and consolation? A good, old-fashioned scolding? How, exactly?

Jaymin rolled the swatch of cotton between her fingers. A tiny pellet took shape and she dropped it into the spoon. Kaine watched the pellet expand, slowly absorbing the liquid. Now tears fell in silent cataracts onto Jaymin's shirt and lap. Gathering the syringe into her right hand, she stabbed the needle into the cotton. As she drew the plunger back, a golden brown serum filled the cylinder.

Restraining himself, Kaine stepped back, but turning away was impossible.

Jaymin's hand shook. The spoon tumbled onto the nightstand, upsetting the water, and carrying the glass with it to the floor. The shattering glass had the effect of either shaking Jaymin out of her remorse, or reminding her of the overpowering need she was experiencing. She paused long enough to look Kaine's way.

"I wish you could help," she said, suddenly calm. She closed her fist. "I'll be fine in a minute."

Kaine turned to leave. But at the door he stopped, his hand unable or unwilling to work the handle. He heard Jaymin sigh again, this time in an outpouring of relief.

"Don't leave," she whispered. "There's Scotch in the bathroom. Pour two. Please."

As if he were incapable of doing otherwise, Kaine did so. When he returned from the bathroom, Jaymin's tears had been replaced by a glaze of sweat. She was on her feet, pacing like a cat behind bars. Her eyes were pinned and glassy.

"Addicts shoot for the nod, for the float. I do it for the energy." The energy, as she called it, permeated her voice. "Sorry about the emotional display. I don't know where that came from."

"Maybe it was less of a display than you think," Kaine replied, his voice, in return, businesslike and unaffected. But the room was small; he could feel the heat of her presence. "When you said you wished I could help, it sounded like you meant it."

"I wouldn't take everything I say so seriously. As a matter of fact, I wouldn't take anything I say seriously." They drank Scotch. She couldn't rid herself of his eyes, his absolute attention; then she gave into it, seeking it even. Eventually she said, "Is Angela safe?"

Kaine hesitated. "I think so."

"Why don't you take her home, Stephen? Wherever that might be."

"You suggested that before."

"Yeah, and I'm suggesting it again."

"After what happened on the docks this morning, I can see why."

"Did it ever occur to you that there are a few things in this life you just can't control? That maybe you're doing more harm than good? Forget about Karmin-Yar and that fucking crown. They're ghosts from your past. Give it a rest. And all this bullshit about drugs. It has nothing to do with you. Let us . . . me worry about that, why don't you?"

She stopped dead center in the room, so close that when she turned they were nearly touching. Her skin was as pale as ivory; it glistened. Her lips were damp now, slightly parted. Her breath was sweet, and it brushed the side of his face. His hand moved unconsciously to the small of her back. His mouth grazed her cheek, moving slowly down to her lips. His eyes fell upon a pool of moisture gathering in the hollow of her neck. A single bead broke free and fell to her chest. Like a tiny jewel, the bead traveled between her breasts, and Kaine followed it until the knot of her shirt absorbed it. Unable to stop himself, he traced its path with his fingertip.

Was this why he had come, after all? Disgusted with himself because he didn't really know the answer, Kaine dropped his hand and stepped slowly away, hiding behind a question he knew she would never answer. "Us, you said. Who is us? The man in the expensive suit and gold cuff links? The colonel?"

Jaymin's eyes closed. Her shoulders sagged. "Let it go. Haven't you and your family had enough close calls?" Now her hand twitched and the Scotch trembled. "I don't want you or Angela to get hurt."

Now the trembling touched her voice. She retreated, stepping into the bathroom and reemerging with the bottle. "Don't ask me to choose. I've already chosen. Don't ask me to explain. I can't."

Kaine toured the room like a man tracking butterflies; every nerve in his body tingled. He followed an impulse to the nightstand. Jaymin had called the powder in the envelope China White, yet diluted and heated it turned a golden brown. Now the impulse was curiosity. Kaine touched a finger to his tongue, dabbed the fingertip into the powder, and brought it back to his tongue again. The taste was harsh and biting, as was the smell.

"Don't ask," he heard Jaymin say. She was beside him now, closing the envelope and storing it in the nightstand drawer. She extinguished the candle between two fingers.

"Don't ask?"

"How or why," she said, gesturing toward the nightstand.

"It's not my affair."

"The problem is, you like me. Maybe more than you should."

"Maybe."

"So does Angela. Which is hard to fathom."

"Her first impressions are generally accurate," Kaine said. "And she trusts them."

"I'll quit when it becomes a problem."

"I'm sure."

"It helps me focus," she said.

"On?"

"On me."

"That's an answer?"

"If I don't, no one else will."

"Which obviously explains your interest in Karmin-Yar," Kaine said.

Jaymin sighed. In a gesture as natural as shaking hands, she snatched the shoulder harness from the bedpost, slipped it through one arm and over her head, and swept up the pistol from the bed. She checked the safety and then worked the gun snugly into the holster. Finally she carried the cassette tape recorder into the bathroom. She closed the door. When she emerged again her shirt was buttoned down the front and she was tucking the tails into her pants. She threw on a worn leather jacket.

Then she said, "You're not in a position to understand my interest in Karmin-Yar, Stephen. Moreover, you'd probably be surprised by what does interest me."

Kaine decided that he was being too easy on her; there was a spark but no flame. He purposely showed her his back and said, "What interests you is obvious, Jaymin. Easy money, illusive answers, and quick fixes. Obvious."

"Try the art of the Baroque," she snapped. Her voice had a predatory element to it, electric. "Try modern architecture. Try quantum physics."

Kaine was pleased. He displayed an element of guarded interest. "I see. Rembrandt then, or Rubens. Frank Lloyd Wright or Le Corbusier. Max Planck or Albert Einstein."

Kaine came about. The room was so small and her presence was so dominating. She had taken her stand, so close that Kaine could see the flaring of her nostrils, even the tiny cracks in her parched lips. Her tongue ran quickly over these and they flushed with the infusion of moisture. Her breathing was labored and harsh. She moved not a single muscle, and Kaine dared not disturb the moment, though he wanted more than anything to reach out for her.

Now her voice was calm. "I prefer Vermeer to Rembrandt, actually, and Caravaggio makes my heart sing. Mies van der Rohe stirs me more than Frank Lloyd Wright ever could, and though Paolo Soleri wasn't very practical, I'd live in one of his mud huts in a minute. And yeah, I admit to having Einstein's photograph on my wall back home, but I carry Stephen Hawkings's book in my suitcase."

"Good taste." Kaine tipped his head, but a compliment was taking it too far; he knew it the moment it left his mouth.

Jaymin broke away. "Yeah, I've got great taste, all right."

There was an empty shoe box on the floor next to the night-stand, and she laid it open on the bed. The bent spoon, the candle and its holder, the syringe and the bandanna, the eyedropper, the matches, and the cotton all fit neatly inside. Ignoring the broken glass on the floor, she opened the nightstand drawer. She removed two thick phone books. The shoe box slid into the back of the drawer, and the books, once replaced, camouflaged the box nicely. Then she took the folded envelope and tucked it gently in the breast pocket of her leather jacket.

When she was satisfied, Jaymin glanced briefly in Kaine's direction, her face taut and remote. "What about you, Stephen?" she asked. "What is it that interests you? Beyond the artifacts of the dead and forgotten?"

"Answers. Like why it was necessary for someone to sink a ferry carrying two hundred people in the middle of Admiralty Harbor? For the sake of a gold crown or the blueprint of a lost city? Is that possible? Like why my daughter's life has twice been put in jeopardy? Like why the police don't seem to have any answers? Things like that interest me, Jaymin."

"I should have known. The singleminded man. Good luck." Jaymin lit a cigarette. She blew smoke aggressively toward the ceiling. "You know what I was hoping you'd say, Stephen? Naïve and foolish me. I was hoping you'd say, 'At this moment, I'm interested in you, Jaymin. You and only you. In making love to you until we collapse from exhaustion. In tasting you. In being inside of you. In coming with you over and over again.' Not in some . . ." She threw her hands in the air. "Not in some ferry accident that's over and done with."

From the dresser top, she gathered up her keys. She strode to the door, embarrassed, but stopped before opening it. Now she turned and offered him the most open and honest look he had ever seen. "I've never said anything like that to a man before. God forbid. But you know why? Because I've never wanted a man before, not really. So I've said it, and I'm glad. Lock the door on your way out, will you?"

Kaine stood in an empty room and the emptiness gnawed at his insides. He had stood by and watched her shoot heroin into her arm and felt outraged and helpless and desirous all at the same time. The singleminded man, she had called him. Danielle would surely have agreed. Not a very attractive label, Kaine thought.

He left the hotel without enthusiasm. It was cold when he stepped outside. The mist had taken on a solid quality, like fragments of glass. His breath crystallized as it left his mouth.

There was, he thought, a missing ingredient; it went beyond the crown of Sharana Ni, and beyond the hints of drug smuggling. Kaine wondered if he would find that missing ingredient in the Crimea, with the one man in the world who knew as much about Karmin-Yar as Kaine himself did.

14 The galley of the harbor tug *Broadside* was situated off the main deck between the cabin fore and the bunk room aft and directly beneath the pilothouse. It was tiny, consisting of a stove with two electric burners, a butcher-block table the size of an oil drum, three backless stools, and cabinets laden with canned food.

Angela had effectively taken over the butcher-block table. Atop it lay a water-stained copy of Madeleine L'Engle's *A Wrinkle in Time,* a tape player Connor Thorpe had lent her, two cassettes, and Angela's new Polaroid, her mother's parting gift. An open can of beef stew sat upon one of the burners. Steam rose from slowly erupting bubbles. Tanner Thorpe stirred the contents with a wooden spoon. He allowed Angela the privilege of licking it clean. A space heater churned at their feet. They drank hot tea from tin cups. The first skipper spiced his with a generous splash of ouzo.

"Why you and not me?" Angela said, her eyes on the ouzo bottle. " 'Cause you're old and I'm not?"

"Old? Who said anything about old?" Thorpe grasped the ouzo in one hand and showed Angela the mouth of the bottle. "Put a finger right in there."

Angela did so, and Thorpe tipped the bottle until the liquor spilled over her finger. "See what you think."

Angela plunged the finger into her mouth and gagged. "Poison."

"Close enough," the first skipper agreed.

The tug was off duty. If the first skipper had a home on dry land, Angela wasn't aware of it. Tonight, they were alone. Connor Thorpe had gone off with a cousin and a friend. The friend owned a car. They'd be back later, was all Connor had said.

"You say you don't know where my dad is," Angela said, "And now you say you don't know where your own son is. Don't you know anything?"

"This is what I know," Thorpe replied. "I know you can't control everything that happens around you, no matter how much you may want to. Worse yet is *trying* to control everyone around you. People tend to resent a controlling hand almost as much as they do the prying eye. I also know you talk more than a girl of thirteen should, and I know when I'm too hungry to argue."

Angela stared with dismay at the can on the stove. "And this is dinner?"

Tanner Thorpe ladled stew into tin bowls. The spoons were silver. He said, "This or nothing."

"You're taking me out for ice cream later though, isn't that what you promised?"

"I said that?"

"A meal like this deserves dessert," Angela responded. "As hard as we worked today, we deserve dessert."

"Fuck me . . ." The first skipper caught himself, but too late. He scowled, but it was the scowl of a doting patriarch. "All right, then, all right. Dessert after."

Angela graced him with a satisfied smile. She had grown rather fond of the first skipper, rather quickly. A commitment very unlike her. From the table, she silently raised her camera and caught Thorpe with the serving spoon in his mouth. The photo rolled out of the mouth of the camera and began instantaneously to develop.

"Damn modern invention." The first skipper snatched the photo from Angela's hand, but, despite his annoyance, became transfixed at the evolution of his own face on the paper. He grimaced at the result. "You could be held liable for something as frightening as this," he said, handing it back. "Do us both a favor and destroy it immediately."

"Not on your—"

A voice called to them from the quay outside, interrupting her. "First Skipper Tanner Thorpe, are you there? Tanner Thorpe. May I come aboard, please?"

Angela watched the first skipper's face tense, his hand course zealously over his chin, and his eyes recede behind narrowed lids. "Who is it?" she whispered.

"Go into the bunkroom and stay there," Thorpe replied. "Be silent and be patient."

"Why?"

"At once, Angela Kaine. Do you hear?" He threw his thumb in no uncertain terms in the direction of the curtain that separated the galley from the bunks. Then he extinguished the galley lamp and pulled the louvered doors shut behind him. He stepped into the cabin.

Angela emerged from behind the curtain again and followed him. She stopped at the louvered doors and peered through a slot created by two missing slats. The cabin beyond consisted of two cushioned benches, an overstuffed chair, and a wall-mounted side table. A hinged door led out to the main deck and the first skipper held it open. A man clambered aboard.

"I hope I'm not intruding," he said. His voice had a brusque, grating quality that Angela didn't think fit his diminutive stature. "I thought a visit was in order."

"I've been expecting you, Mr. Davidson," Thorpe replied. He didn't move. "What shall we talk about?"

"May we perhaps talk inside? These Dover nights catch me by surprise."

"People expect the English Channel to provide them with a Mediterranean breeze for some odd reason," Thorpe said. Angela followed the man's passage into the cabin. "They end up freezing their asses off and wonder what went wrong. Unfortunately, the prevailing wind here is from the north, off the North Sea. Very deceptive."

"I'll remember that."

Angela was struck by the man's double-breasted suit and maroon vest only because they were so out of place on the tug; cuff links glistened from the end of his sleeves; diamonds flashed from the ring fingers on each hand. And she was struck even more by his face, a wide and fleshy pulp from which cold, pale eyes peered. A wave of sandy hair was combed high on his head.

Thorpe motioned him into the overstuffed chair. He switched on an electric floor heater. From the side table, the first skipper poured ouzo into a pair of tin cups. He chose the bench opposite the chair.

"You've come to talk about Mr. Kaine, I might well imagine," he said, consuming his ouzo in a swift, practiced swallow. "And my response is that you've gained for yourself a rather formidable adversary. Unfortunately, or perhaps fortunately, one who doesn't have much to go on, as I see it."

"Where is he?"

"He's in London attempting to find out what happened to that crown and those gold coins. Why, I can't imagine."

Angela held her Polaroid close to the opening in the door. She stared at Davidson through the viewfinder. Her finger toyed involuntarily with the shutter release.

Davidson tipped his head back and swallowed the ouzo without a grimace. He said, "Tell me more."

"He's trying to track down the car from that wreckage. The Mercedes. He knows it's a diplomatic vehicle, and he has a license plate number."

"And?"

"He's scared. His daughter's almost been killed twice. He doesn't trust the police."

"He said that?" Davidson asked, as if it were of some importance. "The police in general, or the police on this case?"

"He's an American. I think that means he lacks faith in the police as a whole."

"What has he said about the map?"

"A blueprint of his city? What do you think? He's up in arms. He's baffled. He's fascinated."

"Does he know where it came from?"

"The stowaway—"

"Does he know where it came from, First Skipper Thorpe," Davidson repeated laconically.

"It's my impression that he doesn't." Thorpe raised his shoulders. "He knows the woman's involved."

"Very obvious. I'm looking for the unobvious. That's what two thousand dollars buys."

"Your two thousand dollars bought you an ally." Thorpe gestured with a gnarled, bent finger. "Where's the money now?"

Davidson nodded, a distracted, paternal nod that suggested that the response had not surprised him. A moment later, he withdrew a small snubnosed gun from inside his suit coat, a .38 Special with a stubby cylinder attached to the end. The sight of it sent a shudder through Angela's body. Her hands shook and the camera shook with them.

"Tell me more," she heard Davidson say again.

"He knows the woman's got help. The police tipped him off to that. They kept talking about the rightful owner of the crown, and Kaine intends on finding out who they were talking about."

"Kaine's in London, you said. London's a big city. Where in London?"

Angela could see Tanner Thorpe studying the end of the gun as it bore in on his chest. Sweat flooded from his forehead into his eyes, stinging. On his face, she could see the internal debate. His words suggested that the debate had not been resolved. "He was going to the embassy for one, about the car. To find the woman, Jaymin, for another. And he mentioned a stop at the university, but said it had to do with a project he's been working on in southern England."

"Did you believe him?"

"I saw no reason not to."

Davidson hesitated. It seemed to Angela that he asked the next question with more care than the others. "How much has Kaine said about the stowaway? The one called Ras Haydar?"

"He's confused," Thorpe admitted. "He says the Turks are guided more by emotion than logic. Sinking the ferry was serious business. Were the blueprint and the crown reason enough? I think that's what Kaine is asking himself."

A distant look captured Davidson's face, and his nod added a fatalistic air to it.

"Where's the girl?" he demanded eventually. "Kaine's daughter. Angela. We know she's staying with you."

"How in the bloody hell would you know that?"

"Let's just say that Scotland Yard is being cooperative. Where is she?"

"She's gone into town with my son. But I've questioned the girl with every device I know and her father has told her nothing."

"Of course he hasn't. That's not the point."

"She trusts me," Thorpe muttered.

Angela tried making sense of what she was hearing. She played the viewfinder over the first skipper. She studied his face and found it unreadable. Finally, she leveled the camera once more on the man in the suit.

She heard him say, "You made a similar claim concerning her father, if I recall."

"He entrusted me with the care of his daughter," Thorpe argued. "Is further proof really needed?"

Davidson poured ouzo into the first skipper's cup. "Drink it," he ordered. Thorpe did so and Davidson topped off the cup a second time. "Does Kaine know that you took money from me?"

"To deceive, one must entice with a show of good faith," the first skipper replied quickly. "I told him you offered me money. I also convinced him that I didn't take it."

At Davidson's urging, Thorpe drank a third and fourth shot of ouzo. "What else did Kaine tell you about the map?"

"That it's a fake." Thorpe chuckled. "He's too close to the situation to believe it could be real."

"Good. That's very good." Davidson tipped the barrel of the gun in the direction of the ouzo and Thorpe drank. "And the crown of Sharana Ni fits into this in what way?"

"You want me to say it?" The words slurred slightly. "He thinks his precious discovery has become a device for profiteers. Artifacts for money. Is he right?"

Davidson filled the cup again, but this time Angela saw that the directive to drink was steadfastly dismissed by Thorpe. She almost cheered. Then Davidson's voice intervened. He said, "I think your allegiance has wavered, First Skipper Thorpe. Most unfortunate."

"Allegiance is not a virtue easily bestowed upon the vermin of the earth, Mr. Davidson," Thorpe replied. "And rest assured there is nothing unfortunate about it."

Through the narrow scope of the camera's viewfinder, Angela saw the impact these words had on Davidson's face; it was like a slow leak stealing shape from a balloon. Then she watched in horror as he pulled the trigger. A dull thud was eclipsed by a low groan, the first skipper's only reaction to the attack. The shot was accompanied by an orange flash that caused Angela a moment of blindness, of paralysis. Yet somewhere between the second and third shots she managed to snap off two pictures from the Polaroid, sending flashes of blue light back at Davidson.

Momentarily confused, he watched Tanner Thorpe's heavy frame pitch to one side. Then his eyes came to rest on the louvered doors. The paralysis Angela had experienced moments ago still gripped her. Her camera dangled from the fingers of one hand; in the other she clutched the swiftly developing photos.

Davidson screamed and dove for the door. He fell heavily against it. Like a distorted claw, his hand thrust through the opening left by the missing slats.

Simple instinct caused Angela to lunge backward. She stumbled even as she turned, crashed into the butcher-block table, and lost her grip on the camera. She jammed the photos into her jacket pocket, freeing her hands. Then she scrambled through the curtain into the bunkroom. Behind her, she heard the first skipper's killer throwing his weight against the doors and the sound of wood splintering. The bunkroom was lit only by the dim rays of the moon as they filtered in through a single porthole. Still, attached to the far bulkhead, Angela saw the rungs of a steel ladder.

Frantic, she scrambled up it. Twice her foot slipped, the second time nearly sending her sprawling to the floor. A cut opened on her forehead. She glanced back. The louvered doors fell open with a heavy crash, and she heard the man named Davidson growl.

The steel ladder led to the pilothouse above; Angela knew the layout by heart now. For some reason she would find hard to explain later, she threw her full weight against the tug whistle. Its shrill call amplified across the harbor.

"You silly little bitch." Davidson was on the ladder now, and the words rang with a terrible venom.

15

As evening cast its eerie shadows over the Kentish countryside, it was as if all nature were suddenly in a hurry.
Outside Faversham, a deer dashed in front of Kaine's headlights.
A mile past Canterbury, a formation of geese descended upon a
sun-streaked lake. Endless acres of fruit trees shook in a brisk and
chilly breeze. The blooms of adventurous flowers took shelter now
by folding their petals in upon themselves.

Consciously or not, Kaine set his pace accordingly. Narrow
roads scurried over grassy knolls, and his headlights illuminated
the blanket of moisture deposited by a late-afternoon shower; for a
brief instant, the wild grass glistened. He drove recklessly; unusual
for Kaine since his thoughts often wandered when he was behind
the wheel. But maybe that was the point, he thought. Focus. Keep
his mind off the smell of acetic acid in Dr. Julian Persoff's laboratory
and the sight of a hypodermic needle pricking Jaymin's slender
forearm.

Outside of Bishopsbourne his attention was diverted by the
ruins of a Norman castle. The moon's silver light caromed off stone
walls. On either side of the road, clusters of blooming hops hung
from poles and strings. From the high ground above Dover, an

enclave of lights sprang forth between chalk ridges. The harbor beyond threw back a reflective field of iridescent crystals.

Kaine took the Maison Dieu Road through the heart of town directly to the harbor. He parked below the east cliff along the Marine Parade. Behind him, a helicopter prepared for departure; Kaine fled from its powerful downdraft and the cacaphony of its rotors and came away with the shriek of *Broadside*'s whistle in his ear.

There was something so unnerving about the sound, its proximity to the docks and its seemingly endless duration, that Kaine was at once on guard. As he approached the castle jetty, his stride lengthened into an uneasy jog. When the tug came into view, he drew up suddenly. At the same moment, he saw Angela virtually leaping down the pilothouse steps to the lower deck. Her fear catapulted across the water; Kaine felt it as surely as if it had been his own, and then he was running. He saw Angela trip while crossing the deck. She used one of the main bitts to right herself.

Behind her, charging out of the pilothouse door, he saw a man in pursuit. Kaine recognized him even from afar as the American who had offered Tanner Thorpe two thousand dollars. In the gray gloom of early evening the object in the man's hand glistened.

"Angela." His arms pumping, Kaine raced behind the car ferry terminal. Above him, by Kaine's reckoning not more than a hundred feet, the fierce wind of the helicopter bore down on him. Still, he concentrated on the tugboat. He saw Angela scrambling over the rubber fenders along the tug's outer hull. She leapt onto the quay, found her legs, and ran. Kaine called her name again and again, but the distance between them was still too great and the tumult of the helicopter was deafening.

Angela reached the dock moments before her father did. She hesitated, her head pivoting in either direction. Kaine saw her; she was hunched beneath an arc light, her silhouette clearly defined in a circle of tawny yellow.

She heard his footsteps and recoiled; then she heard her name. "Angie."

"Dad." Angela threw herself into his arms. The heat of her

efforts manifested itself in a sheen of sweat across her brow, yet she was trembling.

"It's okay now. It's okay," her father soothed. Then more urgently. "What happened? Where's Thorpe?"

"He's been shot." Angela's breath came in short, burning gasps, brittle and hot. "A man named Davidson. He shot Mr. Thorpe in the chest. He saw me. He's coming."

Kaine glanced back at the tug. Davidson was scrambling over the side onto the quay. The helicopter had dropped down along the quay adjacent to the tug and was now hovering. Davidson climbed aboard. Kaine saw him motioning to the pilot, then gesturing with the gun. The helicopter rose above the quay, but only a matter of feet. Davidson perched astride the open door and leveled the gun in two hands.

Now Kaine grabbed Angela beneath the arms. "Come on, Angie. Come on."

He dragged her in the direction of a clapboard dock house, the nearest structure of any consequence. Out of the corner of his eye he saw an orange flash. Wood splintered over their heads. They made it to the corner of the house and crouched down; Kaine shielded Angela with his body. The helicopter pursued them. A second bullet tore into the concrete at their feet. Pressing against the wall, Kaine led Angela along the side of the building to an old-fashioned porch. A light burned within the house, and Kaine beat on the door. He tried the door handle. They couldn't wait; the helicopter was upon them. They fled to the far corner of the building. A row of metal-hulled lifeboats were hung along the wall. They huddled there as Davidson emptied his gun, his last bullet caroming off the nearest lifeboat and ripping into the water.

Suddenly, the wind abated and the roar diminished; the helicopter had broken off its attack. Kaine scrambled out from behind the boats and watched it bank in the direction of the city, gain altitude, and accelerate. He stood there a moment, realizing that in the dim of evening he had never gotten a clear view of their assailant.

When he returned to Angela's side, she had retrieved the photos from her jacket pocket. Her hand shook as she stared down at them.

"I don't know what made me do it," she said, meekly passing them to her father. "My finger just pressed down on the shutter release. It just happened."

Kaine's initial enthusiasm quickly dissipated. The flash from the gun had effectively obscured the face in both photos. A shock of wavy hair stuck out above it. Identification was impossible.

"I'm sorry," Angela said, seeing his expression.

"Don't be," Kaine said quickly.

"His name is Davidson. Or at least that's what the first skipper called him." She shook. Tears streaked her face. Kaine wrapped his arms around her. "He was cruel and vicious, Dad. Evil. Just evil."

The door to the dock house opened timidly. A gray-haired, white-bearded man peeked out. He ventured out onto the porch. When he saw Kaine and Angela, he blurted, "What the blazes is happening? What was that I heard? Did I hear . . . Good God, man, it's late. What—"

"Call the police and an ambulance."

"Is the girl—"

"Tanner Thorpe has been shot," Kaine interrupted again.

"What in the name . . . Good God."

The brick red that was the man's normal color retreated with such swiftness that Kaine expected him to falter, but instead he turned in one drunken pirouette, stomped into the house, and grabbed the radio mike.

Now Kaine took Angela's hand and they hurried back down the dock to the south jetty. "He's dead, Dad," Angela repeated again. "I know he's dead."

"Wait here," Kaine said when they reached the tug.

He jumped aboard. When he opened the cabin door, he saw that First Skipper Tanner Thorpe had crumpled onto the floor. Blood pooled beneath his left arm. Three bullet holes scored the front of his plaid shirt, now thoroughly soaked in red. A look of peace, however incongruous, had captured his face. Kaine pressed two fingers against the carotid artery in his neck. There was no pulse. Color seemed to retreat from Thorpe's ruddy face even as Kaine looked down upon him.

The wail of sirens spoke of the efficiency of the old man in the dock house.

Scotland Yard arrived sixty seconds before the ambulance. The doctor had been on call since the ferry accident. His face had a saprogenic pallor to it. He swore even as the old man from the dock house wept. Angela touched Tanner Thorpe's face as the hospital attendants carried him to the ambulance, but her tears had given way to a look as empty as the night.

Detective Superintendent Christopher Preble demanded the photo Angela had taken of the man called Davidson. Photo. Singular. Kaine had slipped the second of the two photos into his jacket pocket; Scotland Yard had ceased to impress him, and since the two photos were indistinguishable, he didn't feel as if he were obstructing anything, much less justice.

Studying the photo, Preble shook his head. A crooked smile could have signified relief or dismay or the pure acceptance of fate's long reach. Kaine couldn't tell which.

"When she's up to it, we'll have your daughter sit down with a sketch artist," Preble said after Angela gave her stony account of the incident.

"You won't find him," she said coldly. "You keep blaming all the wrong people and they always end up dead. So far we've been lucky, that's all."

"She should see a doctor," Preble said, looking from the girl to her father.

"She's seen enough doctors. And what's more, she seems to be making perfect sense," Kaine replied. Then he threw an open hand in the direction of the photo Preble was still clutching. "Whoever *he* is was on board the first skipper's tug early Tuesday morning, as well. He offered Thorpe two thousand American dollars. As a retainer of sorts."

"Offered? And did the first skipper take the money."

"His son needs an education."

"His son needs a father more." Preble was disgusted, as if he had lost control of something he should have had under his control. "Offered him two thousand American dollars. As a retainer, you say? For what exactly?"

"For the privilege of knowing what I was thinking," Kaine answered. "I underestimated its worth."

"Or this moron"—Preble struck a fleshy finger at the photo—"overestimated it."

"Either way."

"Either way." The retort rang heavy with irony. "Either way suggesting Thorpe had served his purpose or had second thoughts about his commitment."

"I found the crown of Sharana Ni attached to the undercarriage of a Mercedes-Benz with diplomatic plates—"

"From the American embassy in Marseilles. We know that. And we know you made a nuisance of yourself at the embassy here in London. You've caused enough trouble, Kaine. Now your daughter is the sole witness to a murder. We'll put her in police custody, find a place for her to stay. She'll be safe—"

"Safe? I imagine Tanner Thorpe's son would beg to differ with you."

"As I told you before, Angela's not to leave the county, under any circumstances," Preble said. "Nor are you. I'm sorry, but it has to be that way. You can make it as easy or as hard on yourselves as you wish, but you're here to stay until this matter is satisfactorily concluded."

"Fine. But I'll make my own arrangements for her safety."

"That's your choice, of course, but you'll let me know what those arrangements are, won't you?"

Kaine's hesitation was brief. "I'll let you know."

That night, Angela rebuffed her father's attempts at conversation for the first time in memory. She refused food and slept only fitfully.

When Angela saw her mother step off the Hovercraft from Calais the following morning, she left her father standing at the ferry terminal and ran against the grain of the disembarking throng with as much speed as she could muster. She collapsed in Danielle's arms, tears streaming down her face.

Kaine watched this scene with a strange blend of relief and detachment. Had he lost her? Was it possible that Angela had come to perceive the horrendous events into which she had been thrust over the last five days as his failing, his responsibility? Moreover, could she be blamed if she did? She was, after all, in his care. Her life had been twice threatened. Now she had witnessed an event that would stay with her forever. Angela had often complained about life in Paris, that it was hard simply because it was so foreign. But at least she had been safe there, Kaine thought. At least she had been safe.

She and her mother walked toward him arm in arm. Danielle raised a hand in greeting. She wore a severely conservative business suit, tan skirt and matching jacket over a high-collared silk blouse, and looked magnificent. As she neared, he saw that signs of weariness and stress lined her sharply cut features. She allowed Kaine to embrace her, and then held on a moment longer.

"I should have never left," were her first words. "Fucking business. I don't know where my priorities are."

"It's not your fault," Kaine said. They stood for a moment with Angela between them, her arms wrapped possessively around her mother's waist. "Talk about priorities. I was in London, playing amateur detective."

"You should have been here," Angela muttered.

"You're right, Angie, I should have been here."

"We both should have been here," Danielle interjected, and then skillfully changed the subject. "I am sorry about that man, the first skipper. I liked him despite his manners. And his poor son. I can't imagine."

They walked, with Angela between them, back to the terminal. Lines of cars rolled off one ferry while similar lines filed onto another. Pedestrian traffic funneled into fenced walkways and onto the Athol Terrace. Upturned heads gawked at the sight of white cliffs towering hundreds of feet above them. The rank scent of diesel was no match for the sight, nor was the mechanical roar of a harbor shuffling twenty ships an hour to and from its doorstep. But the cliffs could just as easily have been an empty desert to Danielle; she graced them with not so much as a glance. Instead, she ran her fingers through Angela's hair as Kaine led them along a narrow dock ramp to the castle jetty. Their car was parked behind a pump station on Townwall Street.

Kaine opened the door to the backseat. He hoisted Danielle's one bag, ducked in, and laid it gently on the seat. He glanced through the back window and caught a glimpse of Detective Sergeant Paul Hennagan slipping into the doorway of a curio shop. Kaine's first thought, weighted heavily with cynicism, was that obviously Scotland Yard only extended its trust so far. His second was that perhaps Hennagan was wearing his other hat now. That of the heavy for a man named Davidson, a killer in a double-breasted suit and gold cuff links. In either case, finding a safe haven for Angela was not going to be a task easily realized.

They returned to the bed-and-breakfast, but Kaine asked for a different room. "I'm packed," the manager told him. "I've got five people waiting for the room you've already got."

"I don't want you to rent the room we've already got. I'll pay you a week in advance on it, but I need something else, as well."

"More mystery and intrigue?" A resigned sigh accompanied the crooked pursing of the manager's lips. He stared across the lobby and saw Angela curled up on a couch with her mother. "I've got a room with a pair of broken-down beds in the basement. My daughter's two kids use it when they're in from Norwich. I'll have one of the lady-help throw on some sheets."

"Is there an exit, other than the front door?"

The manager looked fatigued. "By law we've got fire escapes snaking down the front of the building, but I don't suppose that's what you had in mind."

"We're being watched," Kaine said directly. "My daughter has seen enough of Dover, but her freedom of movement is under a certain amount of scrutiny."

"Ah. To the point at last." He unhinged his eyeglasses and

stroked the bridge of his nose. "We run our own laundry service. Also in the basement, two doors down from the room you'll be using. We had to install our own vents. The one above the washers comes off easily enough. You'll try not to make a mess of things, won't you?"

16 Unlike the bed-and-breakfast rooms on the floors above, the basement room contained no television and no bathroom. It had been fitted out with a half kitchen, however, and a small refrigerator was stocked with frozen pot pies, eggs, and butter. Cabinets contained utensils and dinnerware. An old ceramic stove had two functioning gas burners. In the far corner, next to the beds, stood a pinball machine.

While Danielle set about lighting the stove, Angela stole away to the pinball machine and discovered that it had been rigged to operate without tokens. Kaine, meanwhile, explored.

A stool and shower, he discovered, had been installed in a closet next to the stairwell. Four bicycles hung from the ceiling joists in the hall. The maintenance man had set up shop in a room lit by a single bulb and littered with tools.

In the laundry room, two industrial dryers revolved; they sent torrents of hot air through rectangular shafts and out a vent along the side of the wall. A woman filled a huge washer with sheets and towels. A second washer clicked into its spin cycle. The vent the manager had mentioned was different from those attached to the dryers. It was a simple wall-mounted unit used, apparently, for ventilation purposes only.

Kaine returned to the maintenance shop and helped himself to a set of screwdrivers, a flashlight, and a step ladder. He waited until the woman in the laundry room had finished her task, then used the ladder to ascend to the top of the washer.

As it turned out, a four-foot square hole had been inexpertly cut into the building's brick wall. A wooden frame had been hastily laid into the hole, and the vent had been attached to the frame by eight screws. The screws came out easily. Kaine balanced the vent atop the washer.

He switched on his flashlight. It was a sizable opening, set at ground level. Beyond stood a building so close that he could almost reach out and touch it. He straddled the frame and peered out into the gloom. A cobbled walk ran between the buildings, hardly big enough for a man on foot. He climbed out, extinguished the light, and jogged to the end of the path.

He emerged at Market Square. The square teemed with activity. Kaine crossed a footbridge spanning the River Dour. He scanned King Street for loiterers of a suspicious nature. Across from the bed-and-breakfast entrance, Hennagan sat behind the wheel of a green sedan. Another man walked the block corner to corner and back again; he and Hennagan made eye contact. At the bus station a block farther on, two uniformed policemen conversed with a woman at the ticket counter.

Back in the basement, Kaine returned to the hall and the bicycles hanging from the ceiling there. He eased two of them down and walked them into the laundry room. Somehow he managed to maneuver the bikes through the opening above the washer, then stand them on the path between the buildings.

Over chicken pot pies, Kaine told Danielle and Angela about Detective Sergeant Hennagan and the rental car he had traced to the agency in London.

"This Scotland Yard detective is in league with the bastard who shot First Skipper Thorpe?" Danielle was incredulous. "And he's watching our daughter? Haven't you told anyone?"

"Mom, the man who shot Mr. Thorpe came right out and said that Scotland Yard was cooperating with them," Angela said.

"How?"

"Policemen are bought and paid for in Dover just like they are in every other city in the world, that's how," Kaine replied.

"This is incredible, Stephen, and I'll never forgive you."

"Do you remember our trip to Cornwall fifteen years ago? The fishing village on the coast?"

"Of course. Dodman Point. Our belated honeymoon. The wind blew like hell for two weeks. It was the best vacation we ever had. All we did was screw all day. How could I forget it? I've never felt more energized in my whole life."

Angela laughed, embarrassed. "Haven't you ever heard of being subtle?"

"Subtle never gets you anywhere, my child. Believe me."

"How come you two got divorced?" she asked suddenly. "You still like each other. It's so obvious."

Danielle didn't answer; her eyes fell upon Kaine, and he wondered if there was an explanation worthy of the question. He dropped back in his chair and said, "The motel we stayed in was called the White Rain."

"That was before we knew what it was like to have money, when we still knew how to have fun." This was not Danielle's way of expressing sarcasm, only irony, and Kaine understood. She said, "The White Rain motel. I remember. And you want me to take Angela there, don't you?"

"If I thought we could get her out of the country—"

"Can we get her out of Dover, Stephen?"

"If the police aren't actually watching the airport or the train and bus stations, they'll at least have notified the security people there." He told them about the laundry room and the bicycles. "Take the bikes past Market Square. It's crowded at this time of night, so you'll blend in well. There's a cab stand on Biggins Street, about a mile south of the square. Take a taxi into Folkestone; it's fifteen or twenty miles down the coast. Have him take you straight to the airport. Charter a private plane."

"What about the assholes watching our hotel?"

"I'll take care of Hennagan and his friends," Kaine said. "Register at the motel in Dodman Point in your mother's maiden name."

"You remember my mother's maiden name? I'm impressed."

"I always liked your mom." Kaine threw out a smile like a lifeline. "She had your sense of humor."

"After all this time I think I'm beginning to recognize a compliment when it comes my way," she replied. "What about you? What are you going to do?"

Kaine withdrew the photo Angela had taken of Tanner Thorpe's killer. He laid it on the table. A vague image lurked behind the orange flash of his gun. The deeds kept mounting, like fallen soldiers, and Kaine wandered among the carnage seeing the outstretched hands of the wounded and the dying. His own daughter had come to see him as . . . as what? An ineffective pawn? A bumbling interloper? An unsuspecting fool? No, Kaine thought, chastising himself. If Angela was angry or disappointed or afraid, she had every right to be. And their relationship was built of better stuff than that, and he knew it.

"There's a face in here," he said eventually, taking possession of the photo again. "If I can find the face, maybe we can . . . get to the bottom of all this."

"Why?" Danielle demanded. "It's that damn city, isn't it?"

"No," Kaine said simply. "It's me."

"And you can walk away from it when you're done?"

"I finally know why I had to find Karmin-Yar," he answered. "Now I know why I have to walk away from it."

When they were in the laundry room, Kaine kissed Angela's cheek. He gave Danielle a brief hug. "Give me five minutes. And don't use the flashlight unless you have to."

"What's that, your inexpert way of saying be careful?" Danielle said nervously.

"More like my inexpert way of saying I'll be thinking about you every minute."

Danielle was a moment replying, and though her smile was sad, it was also genuine. "I think we can accept that."

Kaine took the freight elevator to the first floor. He exchanged a brief nod with the night manager, who gestured in the direction of a bespectacled man seated in the lobby. The manager mouthed the word "Police." Kaine allowed himself to be seen and then walked out the front door. He crossed the street. The man on the corner was instantly alert. He walked halfway down the block and stationed himself at the bed-and-breakfast entrance.

Hennagan, Kaine noticed, had vacated the green sedan. He was now seated at a window table in a café called the Crepe Garden. He was talking into a cellular phone, while watching Kaine from behind an open menu. When Kaine walked into the café, the policeman displayed his complete surprise by sliding a hand beneath his overcoat.

"You won't be needing your gun," Kaine said, taking the seat opposite him. "I'm not planning anything dramatic. Sorry."

"Just dropped by for an informal chat, is that it?"

"I couldn't decide whether to talk to somebody at the American embassy or your superiors at Scotland Yard. Then I thought I'd give you a chance to explain first."

"Is that a fact?" A scowl consumed Hennagan's huge face. He laid the phone on the table and drummed at the Formica top with the fleshy side of his fist. "Explain what exactly? Why I have to spend my precious time baby-sitting a second-rate archeologist and his ex-wife while my first and only wife sits at home alone and nurses a plate of cold fish and chips? Well now, professor, you can find your explanation in hell as far as I'm concerned."

Kaine leaned across the table, tempering his voice. "Explain what you and Joseph Jankowski were doing two nights ago on the south jetty with a man in a suit that costs more than you make in a week. A man who tried to bribe First Skipper Thorpe with two thousand dollars, and who drove away from the scene in a car rented by you from the Maxim rental car agency in London. A man who returned to the harbor this evening and paid the first skipper back with three bullets in the chest."

Hennagan responded with a look as cold and menacing as a coiled snake. His drumming fist paused in midmotion. The fingers opened and closed. Twice. And then a third time. In time, the drumming resumed.

"I don't like you, Kaine. You're the kind of man who thinks the world was made just to keep you bloody amused. But you're also not a man who trifles, and I wonder why you're trifling with me now."

"The Maxim office I visited was in central London, off Fleet Street. The woman pulled the records up on her computer. You didn't use the Fleet Street office, though, you used the one off Knightsbridge. She had a copy of your driver's license on file. You live in Folkestone on Wilton Road."

Kaine searched for a reaction and found none; Hennagan was a study in concentration. Kaine heard Jaymin's voice: *You're playing amateur detective.* He moved uncomfortably in his seat.

"You're not lying," Hennagan said mutely. "But why the bloody hell are you bothering to tell me? Haven't you had enough trouble?"

Suddenly, the loose skin around Hennagan's eyes and cheeks came together in narrow slits. He reached for his phone, hurriedly speaking to someone on the other end while drilling Kaine with a new intensity. "Check their room for the girl and the woman. Quick."

The reply was sixty seconds away. "Gone, goddamn it."

"The manager," Hennagan ordered. "He's been too chummy. Find out what he knows. Break the place up if you have to."

Kaine held his breath, at the same time commanding himself to hold Hennagan's gaze. "In the basement," came a harried voice over the phone. "The filthy rogue."

"I'm on it," came another.

"Check the bloody laundry room. Do it fast."

The reply came some moments later. "Gone. Out the window. Can't see a thing. I'm on the hunt."

"Meet me at the car," Hennagan said to the one in the lobby. He stood up, but without the haste Kaine would have anticipated. "I like you better than I did five minutes ago, Mr. Kaine. But you play a dangerous game."

17

The Defense Department building in Chatham was now called the Chatham Institute of Technology. Set upon the banks of the River Medway, it occupied a parcel of ground once reserved by the egocentric Henry VII for the docks and shipyards of his prodigious Royal Navy.

These days, the institute's research had nothing whatever to do with the high seas. Instead, it dealt primarily with the development of killing devices from space.

It was Saturday. The parking lot was nearly empty.

As Kaine drew up before the security gate at the front of the facility, he noticed the swastikas that had been burned into the esplanade along the fence.

"Skinheads," the guard in the control booth told him; he scrutinized Kaine's identification. He checked his log and placed a phone call. "An appointment with Dr. Daniel Stone. I got it right here. Happy Dan, we call him. Never in my seventeen years here have I seen the man smile."

Though the Medway was a formidable body of water, the institute towered above it, the building's steel and glass exterior serving as a modern-day reflector of blue-green water and ships of commerce.

Kaine passed through a metal detector at the building's entrance. His attention was drawn at once to the video cameras that monitored the outside entrance he had first come through. He watched for a moment, finding the procedure remarkably effective. Cameras had been mounted on the control booth from three vantage points. He saw a car pull up at the entrance. When the guard asked for the driver's identification, she looked directly into one of the cameras. The image of her face was frozen and instantaneously enlarged. A copy of the enlargement was transferred to the control booth via a laser printer.

"Does everyone get the same treatment?" Kaine asked the guard monitoring the video display.

"Everyone," he said. "Queen Elizabeth, Maggie Thatcher, the ghost of Elvis Presley. Everyone."

When Kaine was finally led into Daniel Stone's third-floor office, they shook hands. Stone's grip was weak and clammy. He didn't return Kaine's smile.

The two men knew each other by reputation only. As a sideline to his aerospace assignments, Stone had often done computer analysis for archeological sites all across the British Isles. When he had got to be the best at it, he had started charging for his time and now was rarely called upon. He hadn't yet come to realize that archeology was generally a nonprofit venture, and that skill wasn't as crucial nor as scarce as money.

"Can't quite understand your call, frankly," he said. "I've been blackballed by your crowd as of late, and I must admit I kind of miss those historical sojourns."

"Lower your rates," Kaine suggested. "You'll find you've been missed a bit yourself, I imagine."

"You're kidding? Money?" Daniel Stone was three years Kaine's junior but looked ten years older. More than his premature baldness, it was the sallow hue of his skin. He scoffed. "Money, huh? Always money."

"Crazy, isn't it?"

The room was a cold one in every sense of the word. Cool air poured from vents in the ceiling. Lifeless mainframe computers lined two walls. White benches held row after row of white and beige desktop computers. White tiles. Stone wore a white, loose-fitting jacket. His shirt and tie were an uncomplimentary powder blue. Fortunately, someone had placed a pair of Norfolk Island pines in one corner, a splash of grand color which was the room's saving grace.

From his jacket pocket, Kaine withdrew the Polaroid Angela had taken of Tanner Thorpe's killer. He passed it over to Stone.

"This doesn't look particularly archeological to me," the scientist said. "Gunpowder, yes. Invented by the Chinese a couple of thousand years or so ago, wasn't it?"

"Actually, I think the Chinese were more interested in the entertainment value of the firework," Kaine said, easing into the purpose of his visit. "It really began with the Asians. They were the first people to dabble with various combinations of saltpeter and sulfur . . ."

Stone's eyes sparkled in amusement. "Saltpeter and sulfur? Huh."

"The basic formula for early gunpowder. They got close when someone added charcoal. Unfortunately it seems that history doesn't like to credit the Asians with much of anything, so in 1292, when some guy by the name of Roger Bacon added young hazelwood to the recipe, people started calling *him* the father of gunpowder."

"Fair enough," Stone said. "But that's history, not archeology. And the Polaroid, that was some crazy American named Land, wasn't it? A color film that develops pictures even as you watch. How could he lose? Speed and wonder in a single product, the American dream."

"Right," Kaine said. "But there's no negative."

Stone studied the photo, frowning deeply. "And no face. Which is exactly what you're after, isn't it?"

"Is there a way?"

"Scotland Yard is experimenting with an idea or two on this very problem," Stone replied, tugging on the loose flesh below his jaw. He looked intently at Kaine. "You've approached them, of course."

"They consider me part of the problem, not the solution."

"Are you? Part of the problem?"

"In the sense that a physician gives a measure of sight to the contented blind man."

"Ah, yes, you're making perfect sense."

"Is there a face behind that gun blast?"

Stone chortled. "You're actually suggesting I infuse some enjoyment into my day. Humph, you are a cruel sort, aren't you? Well, come along, Mr. Kaine. We'll see what we can see."

The staccato of their footsteps took them past the mainframes to the gallery of desktops. Stone slapped at each like a paternal grandfather and finished his tour in a small cubicle enclosed by privacy partitions and furnished with a computer of seemingly grander design than the others.

"This is the one we're after," Stone said, drumming at the screen. "It's a twenty-inch job, uncommonly high resolution, plus a wonderful little addition called a graphic coprocessor."

He rolled what looked like a simple copying machine up next to the computer and made two cable connections. He opened the machine to reveal a glass surface beneath which an array of lenses and tubes were arranged. Stone laid the photo face down on the glass and then closed the machine again. He flipped a switch and a mechanized purr filled the room.

"For your information, a scanner. Purpose? So the damn computer knows what it's spending its time analyzing. Simple."

"I like simple," Kaine announced magnanimously.

"Then maybe you should leave now," Stone scowled. He sat down at the keyboard. He talked and typed at the same time. "This is not the computer you find on a stockbroker's desk or in an accountant's office, rest assured. It's equipped with a parallel processing capacity. Very unique. Furthermore it's cleverly linked with sixteen RISC elements."

"You don't have to explain," Kaine said. But Stone did.

"RISC is an acronym for reduced instruction set computer. Feel better?"

"Like a new man."

"Then try this on. This computer is linked into those mainframes over there. Those mainframes have an object library in their memories that covers everything from single-cell amoebas and the quartz constituents of an amethyst to the fifty ways you can make a cheeseburger and the exact size and shape of Kim Basinger's breasts. It knows the composition of every flower or tree ever grown. It knows every artificial ingredient ever added to food or fertilizer or sleeping pills. It knows the bone structure of humans dating back two million years. Fill in the blanks between all that nonsense and you'll realize how much data we've fed into that library. Why? So the computer has the ability to learn. Learn how? Through extrapolation. Impressed?"

"Highly."

Stone typed. Upon the screen above the computer flashed an enlarged facsimile of Angela's photo. It had been broken down into a series of muted rectangles, hundreds of them.

"Two things to remember," Stone said. "All that wonderful information I just told you about? The computer stores it how? In a series of polynomials, or for your benefit, just think of them as mathematic equations, millions of them."

"Kim Basinger's breast as a mathematical equation," Kaine mused. "Got it."

Stone pushed on. "The computer has read your photo in the same way. Every curve, every line, every shadow, every change in color. Every aspect of it. A polynomial. I've told the computer to eliminate as much of the diffused light obscuring the face as possible. It's like looking beyond the clouds that obscure Neptune or Pluto from the eyes of the Jupiter probe. Then we get into a process of pattern recognition; in scientific terms we call it a simultaneous fifth order solution. More simply, the computer takes what it sees on the photo, then it returns to its object library. It saves what it sees as familiar, and discards what it doesn't. The process involves exercises known as edge detection, and detail enhancement, and pattern matching."

"In other words, the computer starts guessing," Kaine said.

"And with incredible speed. When the guessing starts to make sense, it starts to extrapolate, which leads to gradual enhancement of the photo." Even now the images on the screen fluctuated. "The rectangles that you see now will start to take on curves, which will take on dimension."

"Like adding flesh to bone."

Stone shrugged. "Simply, if not scientifically, speaking."

"How long?"

"Eight to twelve hours. Call before you come," Stone advised. "Oh, and it's not cheap, this computer time, I hope you realize."

"We'll have lunch sometime. On me," Kaine said. He peered back at the computer screen. "And when it's done, I'll have a face worthy of a name."

"Not at all," Stone corrected. "You'll have a face. The name is your problem."

18 The telephone booth outside of Canterbury stood at a crossroads, alone and exposed. Kaine closed himself inside and glanced hurriedly about. A signpost displayed wooden arrows pointing in three directions. Over hills golden with flowering hops meandered the coastal route to Ramsgate and Margate. Through verdant meadows and fields occupied by oblivious cattle led a two-lane road back to Dover. The village of Canterbury lay to the east. Kaine could see half-timbered cottages bordering cobbled streets. Overlooking the village stood the most breathtaking church Kaine had ever laid eyes on, the Cathedral of Canterbury.

He dialed the overseas operator in London. He gave her the Arlington, Virginia, number he had taken from Joseph Jankowski's wallet. The phone number was his only link to the "colonel." More important, by far, was the colonel's involvement, if as yet unsubstantiated, in the events of the last six days.

A man answered, and Kaine recognized it as the same voice from his previous call. This time, however, his greeting was abruptly delivered. "Password."

Kaine's deliberation was only a matter of determining in his own mind a suitable response. Contrition would get him nowhere.

Hesitation would be a dead giveaway. He settled instead on the blunt and forceful approach.

"Fuck you and your password. You tell the colonel I have his associate's neck in a noose, and if I don't get a personal audience within the next four hours, I'll be sending gift-wrapped packages of that neck to Scotland Yard, the FBI, and every newspaper from London to San Francisco. Am I making any sense?"

The pause that followed the reply told Kaine he had made an impact.

"I don't have shit to say to someone throwing around threats like a Mafia hitman," was the eventual answer. "Now you got no password, I got nothing to say."

"How does Polaroid sound?" Kaine replied evenly.

"Unacceptable."

"How does a Polaroid print that will see the colonel's associate convicted of murder in the first degree sound? Are we getting any closer to your password?"

"You've got two minutes," was the response.

"And you have thirty minutes. By then I'll have found another place from which to call. By then you will have for me a telephone number of London origin at which I can contact the colonel personally."

Kaine hung up. He followed the first arrow through the farms of the Isle of Thanet to the coastal town of Ramsgate. Ramsgate stood at the foot of its own chalk cliffs, and the harbor was a sanctuary of ketches and yawls. Pigeons were as plentiful as seagulls. The phone booth here stood in the shadows of an unlikely obelisk honoring King George IV.

The man in Arlington answered after the first ring. "Talk."

"I'll talk to the colonel, or I'll talk to Scotland Yard. The choice is yours." Kaine considered the abruptness of his retorts and tried anticipating their effect. He said, "This is a matter that goes beyond murder and we both know it."

"I need a name."

"No names."

"If it's money you're interested in, you'll have to be more convincing."

The very mention of money suggested to Kaine that he had made an impression. He said, "We have a great deal to talk about before the subject of money arises."

"I haven't been able to locate the colonel. Without his consent, I have no authority—"

"That you have no authority is obvious. That I am running out of patience is equally obvious. You have ten seconds."

The impending silence seemed longer. In his head, Kaine counted to ten and then started over. When he got to four, the man said. "At three o'clock London time, you will call the following number." Kaine copied it down. He recognized it as, in fact, a London number. The man ended with a veiled threat. "I hope you know what you're doing."

"I don't," Kaine said in return. "Which makes me dangerous, doesn't it?"

Kaine ordered breakfast at a harbor café. The bread was homemade and steaming hot. An omlette lost its appeal the moment it was served. Despite the impressive offering of beers listed on the menu, he washed it down with a Coke.

When he drank, Kaine drank Cognac or Scotch, but never at ten in the morning, a blatant half-truth that made him think of Jaymin. A woman who drank Scotch like water and who quoted Stephen Hawkings from memory. A woman who admired Caravaggio and cooked heroin over a candle. A woman whose physical presence stirred him as few women ever had but whose self-disdain left him cold and unsympathetic. She was a formidable adversary who was also a danger to herself, which made her a danger to him and to Angela.

The feelings were too conflicting; Kaine pushed them aside. He had to move. He drained his Coke and stood up.

His call wasn't due for another four hours, and he could place it from any booth within a hundred miles of London. The image enhancement of Angela's Polaroid wouldn't be completed until this evening, and Kaine couldn't bear the thought of staring at the variable changing of tiny dots on a computer screen.

Hennagan.

The detective sergeant's name filled Kaine's head as he drove the coast back to Dover. An undercurrent of respect had entered Kaine's thinking about the man. A man very much in control of his own reactions, Hennagan had registered hardly a trace of emotion in response to Kaine's accusations about the rental car and his affiliation with Tanner Thorpe's killer—but had this exercise in self-restraint been due to the extent of Kaine's knowledge or to the nature of the knowledge itself?

Kaine remembered now that Hennagan had given away one thing during the various interludes they had been together. He had mentioned the night shift: on at midnight, off at ten the following morning. "By then I need a shot and a beer," Hennagan had said. "And the closer to the station, the faster the relief. I practically pay old Brickstone's rent every month."

The police station was located on Saint James Street in Market Square. A ten-minute walk put you in touch with a dozen pubs. Brickstone's was one of these. It fronted an alley next to a bookstore. A wrought-iron guardrail led down three stairs to a narrow landing. Beneath an elaborate coat of arms a single word had been carved into the wood: BRICKSTONE. A sign out front read, IF IT SWIMS, WE SELL IT.

Through the door, Kaine smelled beer and frying fish. He saw Hennagan at the bar, a beer held between fleshy hands, deep in conversation with a skittish man who looked as much in need of a transfusion as of a drink.

Kaine positioned himself at the back of the pub. Along one wall there was a shellfish display which featured pink prawns, coal-black winkles, peanut-shaped cockles, clams as big as silver dollars, lobsters as plump as a man's forearm, and live eels. Kaine could hardly bear the sight.

A waiter had no sooner set a pint of ale in front of him than Hennagan got up to leave. The detective had finished neither his beer nor his shot. Kaine followed him at a distance.

Hennagan's car was actually a van in need of a paint job. He took the Folkestone Road south along the coast. The road rose steeply, settling upon the flatlands high above the sea. The wind blew fiercely. In time, the road descended the cliff, weaving among vast fields of broken chalk, like white boulders. The road emerged eventually in the town of Folkestone, a shabby reflection of Dover, less quaint, less cosmopolitan.

Kaine anticipated that Hennagan's eventual destination would be his Wilton Road home, but the detective stopped instead at the emergency exit to the local hospital on Radnor Park Road. He emerged ten minutes later in the company of three hospital attendants. The four men hoisted sealed cardboard boxes that were quickly stowed in the rear of the van.

On the road once more, Hennagan showed no sign of returning home. Instead he drove straight for the A20 expressway. He stopped at a petrol station and made a phone call from a public box. His next stop was in Canterbury, at the back of the great cathedral. This time it took two men to carry a single crate from the rectory to the van. His assistant in this endeavor proved to be a slight figure in clergyman's robes; when they parted, Hennagan wrapped his arm around the man and they shared a laugh.

In central London, Hennagan picked up two laundry-size bags from a packing house near the Liverpool Street Station.

In a working-class neighborhood in the East End, in the Tower Hamlets, he stopped again. He used a parking meter and bought two hours' worth of time. In a housing project next to a textile mill, he carried in the two bags from the packing house. A light illuminated a third-floor room. The drapes were drawn.

Twenty minutes passed. Kaine climbed out of his car. The van was parked a half block up the street. Kaine strolled up to the vehicle and tugged at the doors. Both front and rear were locked.

The diner across the road was called Lester's Chop House, home of "London's Noted Cup of Tea." Kaine stepped inside. Working-class men sported T-shirts under tattered vests. Factory girls wore nylon stockings under fish-stained smocks. There were men in suits and ties and fedoras. There were women in heels.

A table emptied at the window, and Kaine took it. The menu was written on a chalkboard. Entrées like; eggs, bacon, and beans; pork sausage, chips, and beans; tomato and toast; or new potatoes. Kaine was neither hungry nor thirsty, but there was a crowd, and now there were people waiting for tables. He ordered tea and marmalade toast.

He saw movement beyond the curtain on the third floor of the tenement across the way, but no indication of its nature or intent. Four sealed cardboard boxes, a crate worthy of two strong men, and two well-filled laundry bags. A Scotland Yard detective with an obvious array of outside activities. What was he doing here? Kaine wondered. And then, with increasing cynicism: What am I doing here?

His tea and toast arrived. Kaine dabbled with the cream and made a mess of the honey. The toast was burnt exactly the way Lester's patrons liked it.

The woman at the table opposite him glanced up from her own cup of tea and smiled at him, a blatantly flirtatious smile. Kaine was used to the more "dignified" approaches of women who thought it was the man's place to make the first move. The change was refreshing; he tipped his head pleasantly.

The woman dropped her eyes, blushing even as her smile broadened. She had a mass of blond hair, permed and teased, and pulled haphazardly off her head. Makeup highlighted huge blue eyes, but her lips were full and moist and deep red without the aid of lipstick. Young, Kaine thought. Too young.

He adjusted his chair for a better view of Hennagan's van. He saw a city street crew positioning barricades beneath an overhead power line in front of the tenement. A maintenance crane blocked half the street, and a man was perched in a motorized basket at the end of the boom.

When Kaine reached back for his tea, he realized the woman was studying him. When their eyes met, the set of her jaw was quickly replaced by a more relaxed expression. She settled her chin on a bridge formed by her hands. Not *quickly*, Kaine thought. *Expertly*. Did she do this kind of thing that often, or was it something else?

She wore a loose-fitting cotton tank top. Her skirt was leather and tight around crossed legs. The wear on her boots had been meticulously camouflaged by a coat of black polish. She touched the rim of her cup to her lips and said, "You're not going to say anything, are you?"

"You're sure?" he answered. It was a clumsy response.

"Well, I suppose I could be preparing myself for the inevitable disappointment." Her voice had a throaty, earthbound quality to it and was more educated than Kaine would have expected for this part of London. "But let's face it, you don't belong here. You don't look the part."

"Really. Should I be offended?"

"You're tan. You look healthy. No one in the East End gets tan, not even in the dead days of summer."

"What do the people in the East End do during the dead days of summer if not enjoy the sun?"

"The same thing they do every bloody day of the year, silly. Try to escape. You see, this is one of those places where you wake up one morning and this chill runs down your back because you just know you're in trouble. You're stuck. Really stuck. The more you fight, the more stuck you get, and the more you bleed." She reached out her hand. "Anyway, I'm Shelley Christian."

"You don't look stuck, Shelley Christian," Kaine told her.

"I'm sitting in a burned-out diner after a morning in a floral shop selling flowers to obnoxious old women and fighting off the petty, disgusting advances of a boss with bad breath, talking to a man whose name I don't even know and dreading the thought of going back to an empty apartment in four hours that by then will have seemed more like ten. That's pretty stuck."

"I've felt stuck before," Kaine said evasively. This wasn't right. It was too easy. "A friend once told me that being stuck was really only a matter of thinking too much about *what* you were instead of *who* you were."

"Good theory," Shelley Christian replied. Her chin came to rest on her hands again. "This was a good friend, I take it."

My once and former wife, Kaine wanted to say. But he didn't. He shook his head, then concentrated on his tea. He looked beyond the window to the street and Hennagan's van.

"You're waiting for someone," Shelley said.

"No," Kaine answered. "Nothing like that."

"It's okay if you are. A friend?"

For a moment, Kaine glanced Shelley Christian's way. "No," he said again.

Looking back, Kaine saw that the city crew had extended its barricade. Warning signs alerted pedestrians and drivers to the hazards of the task they were performing. Kaine stared momentarily at the man in the motorized basket at the end of the boom; he was maneuvering a power line in two hands.

The light in the room on the third floor of the tenement house went out. Moments later, Hennagan appeared at the tenement doors. The woman who bade him farewell was dressed in nurse's attire. Her smile had a grateful look about it.

"I'm sorry, I have to go," Kaine said, pushing away from the table. Then he stopped a moment. "You said you worked in a floral shop nearby. Can I ask which one?"

Shelley Christian stared, her teacup suspended in her two hands. "Why? In need of a dozen roses, are you?"

Kaine shook his head. "Just curious."

He saw Detective Sergeant Hennagan reach for the door of the van at the exact moment that the high power line fell from the hands of the man in the motorized basket above. The line struck the top of the van and sent seventeen thousand volts of electricity searing through the vehicle's metal frame. Seeking an exit into the ground, and finding none in the van's rubber tires, the current entered Detective Hennagan's body via the door handle and sent his heart into a severe spasm, and his body into spasmodic convulsions. The van vibrated and sparked. The sparks caromed in a thousand different directions. Hennagan's hair sizzled. His skin charred and peeled. A rank odor filled the air even as Kaine bolted into the street. Heat radiated in waves. Paralysis struck every soul within a half block. After what seemed an eternity, the man in the motorized basket raised the cable back into the air; only then would Hennagan's hand release itself from the door handle. Only then did he crumple to the ground.

19 Kaine was the first person to reach Hennagan's side. He pumped the detective's heart and then pounded viciously upon his chest. While the nurse from the tenement looked on in horror, Kaine pressed two fingers against the carotid artery on the side of Hennagan's neck. There was no sign of a pulse.

Kaine gave the police a false name and a hotel in downtown London for his current address. They asked a dozen questions. No, he hadn't seen anything suspicious. No, he couldn't describe any of the work crew. He watched while the police opened the boxes and crates in the back of the van. The cardboard boxes contained secondhand shirts, sweaters, and blue jeans. The crate contained sixty pairs of shoes.

"He was bringing them to the shelter in the Hamlets," the nurse cried. "There are so many kids down there without a thing to wear, don't you know? He was just trying to see they had something to keep their bodies warm. Sweet Lord, have mercy." Kaine listened in awe. "He was such a decent man. Just a good, caring man. He and his wife didn't have any family of their own. These kids were their family."

The constable tried consoling her. "What shelter, miss? Please, try to remember."

The nurse brushed tears from her face; she used a flood of anger to calm the quavering in her voice. She thrust her jaw out. "Mother Mary's Shelter for the Homeless. In the East Hamlets. You must know the one. Off Lindley Road. Every month he made the rounds, to churches, to different groups he'd contacted. He'd pack it up and deliver it personally. He brought us blankets for the clinic today. Just now. Not five minutes ago. Two bags, fifteen or twenty blankets. He never got anything in return, never expected it. Now look at him."

Shelley Christian was standing at Kaine's side. "You knew him," she said.

"As a matter of fact, I didn't know him at all," he replied.

"When I asked you if you were waiting for someone, you said, 'No, nothing like that.' Is this what you meant?"

Even as this wall of contradictions closed in on him, Kaine listened to the sound of her voice. She wasn't scared, nor frazzled. Nor was she suspicious. Her accent had flattened out. He had been right. Now she was watching him.

He said, "What I meant was, it's remarkable the way life shapes you, the way it lifts you like a wave out at sea and carries you, with or without your consent, and dictates this course or another, or this direction rather than another, all of which may or may not have anything to do with your own vision."

"I know what you mean," she said. "I heard someone say he was a policeman. Are you in trouble?"

"Where were you born?" Kaine asked. "Here in the East End? In the Hamlets?"

She crossed her arms. "Do you always answer a question with a question?"

"The nurse mentioned a shelter on Lindley Road. I think I'd like to pay a visit. How would I get there, do you know?"

She covered her hesitation handsomely, saying, "Take a cab. I've wasted enough time."

"I'm sorry. That's right, you have to get back to work. The shop. Can I drop you?"

Shelley Christian had already turned to go. She glanced over her shoulder. "No, thank you. I'll walk."

But she didn't walk. A block from the café she slid behind the wheel of a well-preserved Volkswagen bug. She didn't return to a job at a floral shop either. Instead she led Kaine straight to the American embassy on Grosvenor Square, where she parked in the employees' lot.

Kaine didn't stop. He'd learned enough. He circumvented Hyde Park, drove through Belgravia, passed Buckingham Palace, and used the Westminster Bridge to cross the river into Lambeth. Houses stood like stone statues here, cramped and narrow. Pubs and grocery stores had a way of popping up next to one another. A confectioner sold rock candy and taffy. A bookseller specialized in out-of-print classics and first editions. In a shop devoted entirely to the making and selling of umbrellas, canes, and whips, Kaine asked for the use of the telephone.

He placed his call to the local number he had obtained earlier from the man in Arlington, Virginia.

The voice on the receiving end spat words like a hammer hitting nails, gruffly and pointedly. The voice was also American, Kaine was certain of that.

"You've been looking for me. I'd like to know why."

"Because you have a serious problem, Colonel," Kaine answered.

The pause that followed was filled with unspoken calculations. "Do I?"

"You're careless," Kaine answered. "Your whole organization is careless. You hire men like Joseph Jankowski, men without half a brain, and then wonder why things go awry."

"You spoke of a problem."

"You and your organization had Detective Sergeant Hennagan of Scotland Yard killed. That I can't prove. You also had First Skipper Tanner Thorpe of the harbor tug *Broadside* killed. That I can prove."

"Then perhaps you'll be so kind as to tell me how?"

"One of your friends pulled the trigger, Colonel," Kaine replied. "But this wasn't one of your Joseph Jankowski types. This is the type that doesn't like to go down alone. The type that thinks the going will be easier if he has company on the way down."

"I'm interested. All right. Is that what you want me to say?" the colonel answered calmly.

"He was photographed in the act. The police have a witness. And I have a face. Maybe the witness doesn't concern you, but the photo should."

"Why are you telling me this? Just hand the photo over to the police and be done with it."

"I have a feeling you have more influence than the local police. Also more to offer," Kaine said carefully.

"I see. And what do you propose?"

"An exchange."

"The photo and the negative in return for . . .?"

Kaine hadn't thought of a price. "Half a million."

"That's a lot of money."

"But then there's a lot at stake, isn't there?"

"Yes, as a matter of fact, there is. So let's be done with this. I'll meet you—"

"You'll meet me at the Chatham Institute of Technology in two hours," Kaine said.

"Why there?"

"Because one place is as good as another, and I have the photograph," Kaine answered.

A pronounced pause told Kaine that the pros and cons of the location were being considered. "Fine. The Chatham Institute in two hours."

This morning at the institute, Kaine had taken note of the projector room listed in the lobby directory, and he mentioned it to Turnbull now. "On the second floor, number 245," he said. "And leave your hired help at home, Colonel."

Kaine returned to the Chatham Institute of Technology via the New Kent Road.

He found the routine of security exactly as it had been eight hours before. The guard at the gate, the video process at the entrance, the escort to the third floor.

"Your timing is that of a man in a hurry," Dr. Daniel Stone said, his brows dancing with curiosity. "Or perhaps that of a man skirting some matters of legality. Is that possible?"

"I've involved you more than I should have, let's put it that way," Kaine admitted.

"You're talking to a man who detests involvement at any level. Maybe you should tell me about it."

"Do we have a face yet?"

Like a patient father figure, Stone accepted this parry. He marched Kaine past the bank of mainframes and the blank faces of desktop computers to the cubicle in which Angela Kaine's Polaroid was being processed.

Indeed, a face stared out from the twenty-inch screen. In color. The clouds created from the blast of the gun had been effectively erased. Formations of broad and undefined rectangles had now taken on curves, and with the curves had come the slow evolution of depth. The process of edge detection—of a jawbone, of an eyebrow, of the bridge of a nose—had given way to the guesswork Stone had earlier referred to as line enhancement. The thousands upon thousands of dots of color that created the image were now noticeably smaller, creating shadows, and flaws, and even character.

It was a broad face, fleshy, overfed. Thick brows arched above eyes that reflected a profound lifelessness. A wave of perfectly tended hair rose above a high forehead. There was a hint of familiarity about the face, Kaine was convinced of this, but the seeds of recognition were not yet ready to germinate. The computer continued to process, to digest, to extrapolate, and every adjustment registered on the screen. Yet the sequencing had slowed dramatically, as if fact had taken over from pure guesswork. Like a slide projector, the screen now flashed a new image every two seconds.

Kaine studied the circular clock on the far side of the wall. It read four fifteen. The colonel's scheduled appearance was an hour and fifteen minutes away. Kaine used his hand like a stiff comb. "How long?" he asked.

Stone recognized his impatience. "Believe me, the computer is far more impatient than either you or I, and you may rest assured I speak from a broad history of impatience. Its focus has narrowed now, as the reduced speed of the changing images suggests."

"Then it's close. How long?"

"Long enough for a cup of hot coffee and an explanation from you," Stone said. "Trust me, the computer will make no bones about informing us of its success."

Stone proved true to his word; the coffee was not only hot but the color of an inkwell. They sat on stools staring at the computer screen. Expressionless, Stone absorbed Kaine's story about the killing on the harbor tug and understood that much had been left out—whether by design or necessity, Stone didn't ask, and Kaine respected him for that.

Instead, Stone asked about the colonel. "A military man? You're certain?"

"He was called that by his accomplice in Virginia, and his voice bears it out. He seemed confident in his ability to get inside the institute."

"For a man who deals in facts, you have few at your disposal," Stone snorted. "You're leading him to the projector room on the second floor, aren't you? Why? To show him the results of our experiment with the Polaroid? To show him that you do in fact have the information you've suggested you have? How foolish."

"My goal is to identify the man. When he arrives at the front gate he'll be forced to give his name. His face will be on film downstairs."

"And you intend on being downstairs in the video room when he arrives. Of course." If there was approval in Stone's brief smile, it was also weighted with concern. He said, "Then this colonel of yours will need to think that our experiment with the Polaroid has failed."

A series of low beeps told them the computer had completed its task. The screen was motionless. A face etched in primary colors glared back at them; the color, Kaine found, proved a hindrance to recognition. Stone switched on the laser printer sitting on a shelf adjacent to the cubicle. He typed a command into the computer. Computer and printer reacted simultaneously, producing a black and white replication of the face on the screen. The man who had calmly put three bullets into Tanner Thorpe's chest peered back at them. Where the colored image on the screen had effected artificiality, the black and white print infused life. Yes, Kaine thought, he had seen the face. But where?

He looked up and found himself the object of Stone's rather acute attention. "Know him?" Stone asked.

"No. Do you?"

Stone shook his finger at Kaine. "I promised you a face, not a name, remember? And so a face you have."

Kaine watched Stone adjust the contrast on the photo and run off two more copies. These he placed in Kaine's hands. "For you," he said. "May they serve you well."

"May they serve First Skipper Thorpe well."

"Indeed. And with that in mind, we will ask the computer to do something it doesn't much like doing. We will ask it to regress."

Stone placed himself in front of the keyboard. He introduced a series of commands into the machine, and the reaction was instantaneous. What Kaine saw was the gradual distortion of the killer's face, the rapid deterioration of the work the computer had done over the last nine hours.

"We'll take it back a couple of hours," Stone said.

The result was a face similar in structure, even in contour, to the prints Kaine held in his hand, but one without resolution, and certainly one without the properties necessary for positive identification. Stone printed it out.

"To the projector room," he said.

In shape and size, room 245 put Kaine in mind of a private movie theater. Stone placed the distorted print in an overhead projector. He turned off the lights. The print came alive on the screen.

"Not much to look at, is it?" Stone said. His eyes expressed delight. He rubbed his hands together. "Your friend, the colonel, will be pleased."

Stone fell into the seat next to the projector. "I'll wait for him here," he said. "I'll explain the difficulties involved in getting a clearer picture, also your great disappointment in finding it so. You, on the other hand, had better get yourself to the video room downstairs. I'll let the guards know you're coming. They'll be thrilled with a bit of intrigue. It'll liven up their day."

"Thank you," Kaine said.

"I should thank you, actually," Stone said. "I feel useful for the first time in . . . in a while."

Two guards sat in the control booth peering nonchalantly into nine television screens; three of the nine played upon the institute's entrance. The guards offered Kaine a portion of horsemeat pie, a half basket of onion rings, black tea, and cigarettes. As a matter of courtesy, Kaine forced down two onion rings. He sipped tea and listened to one of the guards expound upon their system.

"Every six months or so, we get a new toy. The fun lasts about a week. Our biggest problem really is putting boredom in its proper place, if you know what I'm saying."

"Like most jobs," Kaine said.

A car rolled into view.

"Honda Prelude. Right off the lot it looks like. A rental," the guard said automatically. He copied down the license plate. The Prelude came to an abrupt halt at the gate. "Occupants, two. Man and woman."

Kaine felt sick. "He has a passenger?"

"Yeah, that a problem?" the guard asked. Kaine shook his head in reply. "Huh. You look like it's a problem."

The guard at the gate signaled the driver to roll down his window. He did so. He gazed out. The camera mounted on the gate caught his profile through the reflections of the front window. The booth camera looked directly into his face, a face hard, chiseled, and stern. His hair was cut close to the scalp, ears wide and eyes minute slits. The shot was frozen on one of the televisions.

"Can I get your name, please?" Kaine heard the guard ask.

"Turnbull."

"Identification, please, Mr. Turnbull."

"Colonel Turnbull," was the blunt reply. He produced a simple leather folder.

"Excuse me, sir. And your passenger, Colonel Turnbull?"

"My assistant, Ms. Jaymin Bartell." The camera caught only a glimpse of Jaymin's profile, but Kaine recognized the curves and valleys of her face as if he had known her for years.

There was a second exchange of identification, and Kaine heard the outside guard say, "Fine. And the purpose of your visit, sir?"

"Admiral Avery is expecting us."

The guard nodded. "I hope you enjoy your stay, Colonel Turnbull. There will be someone to meet you at the front entrance."

"Unnecessary," Turnbull snapped. "We'll walk through the front door like everyone else."

"Whatever you say, sir."

"Who is he?" Kaine asked as another camera followed the car down the drive and into the visitors' parking lot.

"You don't know?" the guard said. The television fed a copy of the still photo into the guard's hand and he passed it automatically into Kaine's. Then he referred to a leatherbound log book. "Turnbull, William F. Full bird colonel, U.S. Army. Currently assigned to the U.S. National Security Council. Also a member of the President's Foreign Intelligence Advisory Board. Age forty-seven. Born—"

"Thank you," Kaine said. He was in the process of putting the copy of Turnbull's photo into his pocket next to the ones of the man called Davidson when the guard interceded.

"Sorry. I know it's only a copy, but it can't leave the premises." He held out his hand. "Property of the institute and all that."

Colonel William Turnbull wore tan slacks and an olive green polo shirt, open at the neck. He walked with military correctness, however, and acknowledged his required escorts, by rank a corporal and a sergeant, with military stiffness.

Jaymin walked a half step behind, a concession to her role as the loyal assistant. She didn't look the part. Her hands were buried in the pockets of her leather jacket. No briefcase, no clipboard, no deferential look on her face. She wore khaki shorts. The corporal stared at her legs.

The sergeant offered a brief, very correct salute. Then he said,

"Sir, I'm sorry to inform you that Admiral Avery is not due back at the institute until five forty-five. It was the understanding of his office that you were not expected until six. I've also been told to inform you that champagne and canapes have been ordered, and lastly that the admiral hopes you'll join him for dinner."

"You're very kind, and reasonably correct," Turnbull replied.

Jaymin knew that Turnbull had a genuine affection for the English, almost certainly because the English seemingly had in return a muted affection for no one at all. Not a dislike so much as a patented lack of interest, he had told her on the way in. They were curious, but not so much that their curiosity needed to be satisfied. They were taciturn and to the point, much like himself. Jaymin had been tempted to laugh; while her affection for the British had more to do with heritage and dignity, she had never thought of Turnbull as a soul mate to the likes of Churchhill or Queen Elizabeth.

"There is one thing the admiral may have failed to inform you of," Jaymin said, directing her attention to the ranking sergeant. "That while Colonel Turnbull waits, Admiral Avery's office has something planned for him in the projection room on the second floor."

"I assume you know where that is," Turnbull added.

"Yes, sir." The sergeant held the elevator doors open, and Jaymin and Turnbull positioned themselves at the center of the car. "May I assume someone is meeting you there, sir?"

"We're to make ourselves at home."

"Yes, sir," was the reply. "I'll see to it that tea and coffee are made available to you and your companion."

"More importantly," Turnbull said, "see to it that we're not disturbed."

The second floor was dedicated to plush conference rooms, utilitarian auditoriums, and two corridors of unnumbered offices. The floor tiles were speckled gold. The projection room was located directly across from a lounge where Jaymin glimpsed a table of weary defense officers drinking Canadian whiskey. Her eyes twitched at the sight. There had been no time to prepare for this unexpected visit to the institute; Jaymin had listened to the tape of Turnbull's telephone conversation with Kaine and recognized his voice at once. Her presence at the institute had not been a request. Six hours had passed since her last fix, and her control was waning; the thought of a large Scotch was almost more than she could bear. Damn you, Stephen.

Double doors swung open onto a minitheater encased in total darkness except for the muted reflection of an overhead projector. "I'll get the lights, sir," the corporal hastened to say.

"Not necessary," a voice from the heart of the theater announced. A moment later, a small desk lamp illuminated a slide projector, a sound board, and a man in a white smock. "It's Dr. Stone, gentlemen. I'll see to our guests' needs from here on out. Thank you."

"Yes, sir."

The doors closed. Colonel Turnbull reached out for the wall switch, and, with the flick of his wrist, filled the room with light. His hand didn't move. In a silence dampened only by the hum of the projector, a mutual appraisal followed.

"You were expecting someone else," Stone said. Jaymin saw an ironic twitch spread across the doctor's sallow face, then an expression of disbelief; he obviously recognized Turnbull. Jaymin had seen the look before, and it meant trouble every time.

"I don't know you," Turnbull said bluntly. He dropped the light switch and again the room fell under the spell of the desk lamp and the overhead spot. He strode guardedly down the aisle and entered the row where Stone manned the projector. Jaymin eased into a seat in the row behind them. "Well?"

"But you do, Colonel Turnbull. You do. We met two years ago at the International Aerospace Symposium sponsored by our wonderfully insipid United Nations. We actually joined forces momentarily on the pro side of the stratospheric defense argument. Your newspapers took to calling it Star Wars."

"Stone. Dr. Daniel Stone." The admission, Jaymin saw, rang with the same fatalistic irony Stone himself had demonstrated moments ago. The two men, she noted, did not shake hands. "Yes, you're right, I was certainly expecting someone else."

"Perhaps a fellow American."

"An archeologist named Stephen Kaine."

"A good and accurate guess," Stone said. He turned, his eyes settling upon Jaymin. "And I was told you'd be arriving alone."

"The lady is in my employ, Doctor. That's really all you need to know."

"If my being here makes you uncomfortable, Doctor, I'd be glad to wait downstairs," Jaymin said, knowing she meant the lounge.

"Not at all," Stone replied, but Jaymin could see pangs of both discomfort and anxiety.

"Then to business," Turnbull said.

"Professor Kaine believes me to be his accomplice in a bit of cloak-and-dagger mischief he's evidently gotten himself involved in," Stone replied.

"Believes you to be? That's an interesting bit of phrasing."

"Interesting, but accurate."

"Where is he?"

"Gone." Stone used an open palm to indicate the nearest seat. "Sit down, Colonel Turnbull. I'm of a mind that we can be of some service to one another."

"How?"

"One of your friends has a serious problem. You came here to see how seriously the problem affects you. You came here to see what it would take to buy off Professor Kaine. On the one hand, you underestimated him. He's hardly the kind to be bought off, I'm afraid. On the other hand, you overestimated, at least for the moment, exactly how much damage he is capable of. Please don't make the same miscalculations with me."

"I'll do my best to remember that, Doctor," Turnbull said softly. "Please continue."

"Yesterday, in Dover, a tugboat operator named Tanner Thorpe was killed at close range by three low-caliber bullets."

Turnbull's shoulders tensed. Jaymin shook her head in disgust. "Perfect," she said. "Just perfect."

Stone's eyes widened. "So you didn't know," he said. "But you do know who this Mr. Thorpe is, I assume?"

Turnbull didn't answer the question. "What are we doing here, Stone?"

Jaymin saw that the directness of the question had unnerved Stone for a moment. He squirmed in his chair. Finally, he explained about the photo. He switched off the desk lamp. Upon the face of the overhead projector he placed the distorted image of Angela Kaine's Polaroid as produced by the computer. Stone explained in short about the image-enhancing capabilities of parellel processing. "What you see on the screen now is what Professor Kaine expects me to show you, Colonel."

"And I'm supposed to make a guess as to exactly who the hell it is that I'm looking at. Is that right?"

"You're looking at the killer, as portrayed by the computer six hours and forty minutes into the enhancing process. Two hours later, the computer came up with this face." Now Stone placed a copy of the finished print into the overhead. This face produced a momentary gasp from Turnbull, and then a controlled, exasperated sigh. Stone said, "You recognize him, of course."

"Blundering fool," Jaymin said.

"The plus side is that Kaine didn't recognize him."

"You're certain of that?" Turnbull asked.

"This is not the most recognizable face in London. And fortunately for you he generally keeps a low profile."

"A low-profile killer. That *is* good news," Jaymin said with patented sarcasm. "And now there's another face involved."

"Mine," Turnbull said. "Does Kaine know me?"

"By now I would say yes." Stone didn't explain.

"You said that we could be of service to one another," Turnbull said directly. "How?"

"I have already been of service, Colonel. And with the help of my computer, there is considerably more I can do."

"I'll bet there is," Jaymin said. She was thinking of Kaine, how very out of his league he had stepped. "And out of the goodness of your heart, I'll bet, too."

Turnbull silenced her with a raised hand. "Your cooperation is worth a great deal to us, Doctor. Rest assured."

"We've got company!" the guard at the control booth said a moment after Turnbull and Jaymin had gotten on the elevator. "Scotland Yard. Three cars. This have anything to do with you?" he said to Kaine.

"We've got the necessary papers, Sergeant," they all heard the Scotland Yard detective say to the guard at the entrance. "Don't make me go over your head. His name is Kaine. An American. We know he's here."

"Be my guest," the outside guard said, raising the gate.

"I guess it does, doesn't it?" the one at the control booth sneered. "Bloody Yard. Like they own the place. No notice, no nothing."

"I need a way out of here," Kaine said.

"You're looking at the only way out of here, mate. One gate, one entrance."

The other guard in the booth was on his feet. He was peering into the television monitors. The Scotland Yard policemen had climbed out of their cars and were dispersing. "I don't believe this. Bloody bastards," he said. "Wait a minute. Wait a minute. There's the fire escape exit over by the elevators. Takes you downstairs to a private garage. Follow the yellow arrows. You'll see a metal door, another emergency exit. We'll open it from up here."

"Hold the hell on," his partner argued.

"The stairs behind the metal door lead to a service shed in the parking lot where your car's parked. I don't know what you'll do then. But from there, the main gate's the only exit."

"Have you lost your mind?" his partner said.

"Go, go, go," the one guard shouted, physically directing Kaine toward the emergency exit.

Kaine ran. The door was solid and heavy. He threw his shoulder into it. The stairs were concrete, the air still and cool. Not a dozen cars populated the underground garage. Red, green, and yellow arrows ran across the surface in three directions. Kaine tracked the yellow ones diagonally across the lot. He saw the door and lunged for the handle. It didn't budge.

Sweat broke out on his forehead. He was panting. He tried again. Nothing. Then he heard a low buzz, straight from the handle. The buzz stopped, then sounded again. Kaine wrenched the door open. The stairs beyond rose to a bedroom-size maintenance shed filled with tools and a thin layer of dust.

Kaine opened a second door and came face to face with a uniformed policeman. The policeman was already swinging his billy club and it caught Kaine square in the midsection. He doubled over. His knees buckled. The club came down hard on his back. All Kaine saw through the pain were the policeman's spit-polished shoes. He lunged, wrapped his arms around the man's ankles, and drove his shoulder into his knees. The policeman toppled forward. Kaine drove a knee into his rib cage. The billy club dropped to the pavement and Kaine retrieved it.

"Get in the shed," he ordered.

"I can't. My legs."

"Crawl." Kaine raised the club, wondering if he could really strike the man. "Down the stairs and into the garage. Close the door behind you."

When Kaine heard the door lock behind the policeman, he stumbled into the parking lot. He dodged from car to car until he found the Honda.

He was fully prepared to crash the gate at the entrance, but for some reason the barricade had been raised. Why? Had his ally at the control booth inside prevailed upon his reluctant partner? Or was it a trap? As Kaine approached the gate, the guard turned his back to him, focusing his attention on the pages of his log book. Kaine didn't stop, nor did he hurry. When he was a safe distance away, he glanced into his rearview mirror and saw the barricade closing behind him.

20 The longer Kaine pondered the computer image of Tanner Thorpe's killer, the more convoluted his thinking became. He had seen the face, but where? Could the man have been associated with Karmin-Yar? A part of Kaine insisted it was so; an equally persuasive part argued that Kaine was pushing too hard, that the answer was more likely to come if he turned his attention elsewhere for a time.

Kaine's connections were now three in number. The telephone numbers from Joseph Jankowski's wallet had led to the new chief archeologist at the Karmin-Yar site on the Black Sea, Maurice Dreyfuss. Now he had put a name to the Arlington, Virginia, connection: William F. Turnbull, a U.S. Army colonel assigned to the National Security Council and a member of the Foreign Intelligence Advisory Board, positions of considerable influence, also of considerable access to information. The third connection was the unnamed man in Angela's photo, First Skipper Thorpe's murderer.

Amateur detective, Jaymin had called him.

And what of Jaymin? Had she merely knocked on Turnbull's door one day and said, I'm one hell of a pilot and need a job? Were her connections in the drug trade that strong? Or was her role something more? It occurred to Kaine that his biggest mistake might have been in underestimating her role.

Simply because he hadn't known where else to go, but knowing the Medway towns were no longer safe, Kaine had taken the highway east. When he saw an old pickup truck parked out front of a petrol station with a For Sale sign in the window, he pulled over. He parked the Honda toward the rear of the station, out of sight of the road. A woman in dungarees met him at the door.

"Good evening," Kaine said. "I'm interested in your pickup truck. Can I take it for a short ride? I'll be glad to leave you the keys to mine."

The woman walked around back. Her appraisal of the Honda consisted of a grunt and a shrug. "Fine," she said, exchanging keys with Kaine. "I'll be closing up in about forty-five minutes, so don't be late. She's all gassed up. Clutch is a bit sloppy. Give her a good ride. She can take it."

A diverging two-lane road placed Kaine and the pickup on a course for the Isle of Sheppey. He pulled off among the paper mills of the Swale River. He found a deserted gravel lot a quarter of a mile down the road. He climbed out of the truck and sat on the guardrail along the riverbank. His midsection ached. He couldn't straighten his shoulders. An acrid, chemical odor drifted up from the water. Smoke curled from the chimneys of two or three mills; the rest stood silent. Kaine lost himself in the flow of the river. Moments later, a train whistle filled his ears, at once provoking a vivid image of Tanner Thorpe lying in a pool of his own blood, and Kaine leapt to his feet.

He found a call box outside a grocery store a mile down the road. He dialed Jaymin's hotel in London. As expected, the operator at the front desk informed him that she had checked out. No, she had not left a forwarding address or phone number.

He placed a second call to the Dover flat that Tanner and Connor Thorpe called home. Kaine had not spoken with the first skipper's son since the shooting, and he was consumed with guilt.

A woman answered the phone, her voice muted and serene.

Kaine identified himself and asked for a quick word with Connor
Thorpe, a chance to offer his condolences.

Incredibly, Connor's first words were about Angela. "Where is
she? Is she all right?"

"I sent her away. Which is what I should have done in the first
place."

"You're blaming yourself. Don't. My dad lived a good life. He
liked what he did. He knew what it meant to love; he always told
me that. My mother. She died when I was twelve, but Dad never
took her picture off the wall. There was never another woman. He
said there was never a need for another woman after her. And me.
Bloody hell, we fought and battled like alley cats, but I respected
him and he loved me."

Kaine looked out into the deserted street and heard thunder.
Rain followed close on its heels, like a wave thrown across the city
by an angry sea.

"I respected your father, too," Kaine said. "More than respected
him, Connor. The things he did for my daughter, and me. And no
one should die like that."

"You don't understand. It's more than that," Connor said.
"When my mother died, something in my dad died right along with
her. This mischievous streak he had. It was like a little kid that
came out once in a while, if I'm making any sense at all."

"You are," Kaine assured him.

"All of a sudden he's raising this twelve-year-old hellion, and
the mischievous streak is lost, trampled by events he had no control
over. For a few hours last week I saw that streak again, Mr. Kaine.
When your daughter was on board."

Kaine shook his head. The rain played against the glass like
fingers pecking a grand piano. He saw a man running with a newspaper over his head. A car pulled up in front of the grocery, an
immaculately kept Volkswagen bug. An attractive young woman
jumped out and ran inside. The car and its driver put Kaine in
mind of Shelley Christian, the woman he had followed from the
Tower Hamlets in London to the American embassy, and he stood
bolt upright.

"I know who did it," he said.

"Did what?" Connor said. "Mr. Kaine? Did what?"

"I think I know who killed your father, Connor."

"My God." Kaine could hear a shuffling sound, then a clatter, and finally a door closing. Connor's voice changed, at once astringent and yet a notch lower in volume. "The police haven't said anything. Who? Tell me. If you know, you have to tell me."

Kaine related the story behind Angela's Polaroid. "I knew the face, or thought I did. But there was no where or when . . . until now."

"And?"

"Earlier this week I was in the American embassy tracing the whereabouts of the car I found on the vehicle deck of the *Spirit of Long Life*. Remember?"

"That Mercedes."

"I saw a photograph on the wall."

"Of?"

"Of a man posing with Margaret Thatcher and George Bush. Very official. It's him. Who he is, I don't know."

"You've gone to the police?"

"I'm not on the best of terms with the police right now. Maybe Superintendent Preble in Dover. But I need confirmation first. And a name. Unfortunately my standing with the embassy isn't very good either."

"But mine is."

"No," Kaine said.

"We're talking about the man who murdered my father. Don't tell me no."

"Out of respect for your father—"

"Out of respect for my father let me do something besides sitting around in the house he built doing nothing. My cousin has a car."

Kaine forced air into his lungs. "Do you know London?"

"I know that the American embassy is across from Hyde Park, and I can find Hyde Park."

"On the northeast corner of the park is a monument called the Marble Arch. I'll meet you there tomorrow morning, first thing. The Embassy opens at nine."

Given that the Marble Arch had once been the grand entry into
Buckingham Palace, its relegation to a traffic island outside Hyde
Park seemed insulting. History compounded the insult; this had
also been the location of the Tyburn Tree, from the middle ages to
the seventeenth century the site of ten thousand executions.

The arch's function now was purely ornamental; tourists min-
gled and cameras flashed. A waste, Kaine thought. The arch was
modeled after the Constantine in Rome. Time had tinged its marble
with a mottled patina, stone and mortar melded together like a
castle wall.

Kaine was running a hand over one of the columns when he
heard Connor Thorpe's footsteps. He was jogging, out of breath,
and startled pigeons opened a path for him.

"Late," he said. "Sorry."

Kaine studied him. Connor's appearance put Kaine in mind of
a figure out of a late work by Delacroix, fragility and determination
haphazardly drawn together in one picture. His hands were buried
in his pockets as he regained his wind; his hair tangled. His feet
were spread, his eyes narrowed and focused, his jutting jaw nervously taut. Kaine didn't know whether to put his arms around him
or harness him with a leash.

He said, "Your dad was there when he was needed, Connor,
and he didn't ask questions. He just acted. He knew what was
right. I'd like to find the man who cut his life short."

From his shirt pocket Kaine carefully unfolded the print produced by Dr. Daniel Stone's computer, the enhancement from Angela's Polaroid. "If the man we're looking for has his picture on the
embassy wall posing with your prime minister and my president,
then he has influence."

"I get your message," Connor said, demonstrating his impatience by reaching out for the print.

Kaine demonstrated his by holding onto it. "I'm pissed off, too,"
he said. "Who wouldn't be?" Then he shook out the print again
and added, "But I don't think you *do* get my message. If we're right,
then you can be certain that this very influential individual will
have someone inside the embassy very much on the alert. For what?
For someone acting edgy or careless or just plain nasty. Three

things you're on the verge of falling victim to right now. If you want to do this, we'll do it my way."

Connor turned and walked in a slow circle. He stopped, pinning Kaine with stern eyes. "I'm a student at the University of London. I'm studying international management. I'm doing a comparative thesis on the ferry systems of Great Britain and the United States. I'm using the Washington State ferries as my main point of reference in the States. Can the embassy provide me with information on the subject or a means of acquiring such information?"

Kaine tipped his head. "Good." He passed over the print of Tanner Thorpe's killer. "Memorize it."

Connor took the print, pacing now like a man in a body cast. A full minute later, he returned the print in its folded state.

"Got it."

"They'll ask for ID at the entrance. You'll pass through a screening device. We Americans expect you Brits to be sullen, correct, and courteous. Don't disappoint them. The embassy attaché occupies a cubicle at the rear of the lobby. The photograph is on the wall off to your right."

Connor Thorpe crossed the Park Lane thoroughfare.

The American embassy fronted the west flank of Grosvenor Square. The compound was elaborate and showy. Gardens were canopied by plane trees and walks mosaicked in flagstone and granite. A black wrought-iron fence, twelve feet high and intricately detailed, encapsulated the entire area on four sides.

The military guards at the front gate asked unimposing questions as to Connor's purpose. They surveyed his identification. When they were satisfied, Connor walked unescorted to the entrance. He stood for a moment beneath the columned portico. The screening device inside resembled those at Heathrow Airport; Connor had been there twice, both times collecting visiting relatives from Aberdeen. He passed through the device without incident. In awe he gazed up at the vaulted ceiling, at the scrollwork and the rich molding. Black and white tiles led him across the room to the cubicle Kaine had described.

The attaché was the same one Kaine had encountered, thin-boned and glassy-eyed, but he gave Connor a kind of attention he had not displayed toward the American. In a voice that sang and jousted at the same time, he said, "You're either a very lost boy or a tourist looking for just the right place to stay, but without spending everything you have. And you think I can help. Am I close?"

Though momentarily taken back, Connor Thorpe actually managed an amiable, even a spirited laugh.

"A student, quite honestly," he replied, "but still one in need."

"Not a place to stay for the night then." The attaché put a hand to his chin.

"Nothing so pressing as that," Connor admitted. He allowed a wave of his hand to help locate the photo. It hung in a gilded frame, but he would need more than a momentary glance. "Well, not at the moment at any rate."

"All things in their time," the attaché said. "So tell me."

Connor did. In response, the attaché stalled; the address of a Washington State ferry line would be easy enough to find, but that would also cut Connor Thorpe's visit very short. The attaché toyed with his computer.

"We'll give it a chance to work. Sometimes these things can be so stubborn." He dismissed the machine with a lilting wave. "Ferries. A fascinating subject," he said. Now the wave included a chair at his desk. "Would you like to sit?"

The chair was perfect. Connor leaned back on two legs. He chose a challenging smile, then allowed his eyes to wander. They came to rest on the photograph. Margaret Thatcher gazed back with puckered lips and keen eyes; George Bush flashed his avuncular smile; Tanner Thorpe's killer stood proudly between them, beaming. The brass plate on the frame was too small to be read from this distance.

"I feel like we're being watched," Connor said, tossing a more confidential glance toward the photo and smiling shyly.

The attaché didn't even look back. "Oh, them. I don't know about Bush or the Iron Lady, but Mathers has been after my sweet ass for a year now."

"Really? Doesn't look your type."

"You know my type," the attaché said, shifting in his seat.

"Who the hell is he?" Connor asked the question in an offhand manner.

"Only the bloody U.S. ambassador. And just between you and me, a worm. And at the moment the last person on earth I want to be talking about."

"Louis Mathers." Kaine said the name without emotion. Mathers had signed the papers supporting Kaine's banishment from Turkish soil six months ago. Kaine's appeals had been denied; his requests for an audience with the ambassador had gone unanswered.

"You know the name," Connor said. They had the Marble Arch to themselves now; a drizzle had driven the tourists into hiding.

"The name. And the reputation."

"A worm, the attaché called him. A fucking worm that's due a serious squashing."

"A dangerous worm that's due a serious squashing," Kaine corrected. "And only when the time is right."

"And exactly when might that . . ." Connor caught himself. For the moment, he buried the fury. "Okay. You tell me how."

Kaine handed him the computer printout of Louis Mathers's face. "Keep this. Keep it well," Kaine said gently. "Go back home. Go back home and be with your family. Wait for my call."

Connor clenched his fist, and only when the fingers relaxed again did he say, "We Scots are slow to anger, Mr. Kaine, but when aroused our anger burns like an unforgettable fire. Revenge is a consequence. Actions breed consequences. For me to forsake the consequences due that man, given what I know, would be to dishonor my father. That I won't do."

Kaine laid his hands on Connor Thorpe's shoulders. He said, "My father was Scottish, too. Pure bred, from Lochinver. My mother was Sicilian. I hated my father. He was a shark. He once said something that I thought was fairly perverse, at least at the time. Now it makes sense. He was comparing the Sicilian and Scottish temper. He said that the Sicilians were too quick with their vendettas. He said that they had no sense of relishing their triumph over an adversary. He said that an adversary should see the blade coming. He should see it coming so clearly that the reflection of the cutting edge blinds him. He should see it coming so clearly that there can be no mistake as to the wielder of the blade. My father called it Scottish rules.

"No one is asking you to put out the fire of your anger, Connor. Only to be certain that when the blade falls that Mr. Mathers knows exactly where the blow came from, and who struck it."

Connor Thorpe broke down. Tears churned from his eyes. Kaine drew him near, allowing Connor's head to rest upon his chest. When the young man's head came away a minute later, the eyes were fiery red but dry and coldly determined.

"I'll wait for your call," he said. Connor had taken a step away when he stopped. "It will come, won't it, Mr. Kaine?"

"Count on it."

PART II

21 For every person, Jaymin thought, there should be a place of safety, a place of warmth, a place of solace. A dimly lit room in the corner of one's home. A hidden lake in the mountains. The pages of an irreplaceable book. Someplace. For Jaymin, it was the cockpit of an airplane. Her airplane.

In the air, among the clouds, she felt totally at peace. Even on the ground, moored as she was now, along the tarmac of a ramshackle airport at the edge of Istanbul, with the doors locked around her, there existed, if not peace, at least a sense of place. Her place.

Jaymin had flown so many hours in this plane that every dial, every indicator, every switch was like an old reliable friend. The control wheel was like an extension of herself.

Over the last two years, as her heroin addiction had grown, and as her paranoia had festered, the airplane had also served a secondary purpose. Here she could step away from her cover and listen to the tapes she had recorded and process the notes she had become so obsessed with. She felt impervious, immune. She was surrounded by her friends. An empty syringe lay on the passenger seat next to her. A pint bottle of Scotch nestled between her legs.

Across the face of a cassette, she penciled the date and time of the telephone conference that had taken place less than an hour ago. She closed the cassette inside the player and put on the headphones. She ran the tape back again; by now she had marked the spot she was looking for on the tape counter. When the counter reached zero, she punched the play button.

". . . we're on schedule, gentleman. We're close. We're this goddamn close."

"Except we now have three very nice, very annoying problems."

"Kaine is my problem, and I'll take care of it. Ras Haydar and his brother were my doing, and none of this would have happened if I'd been a little smarter about them."

"That's a very humble admission." Jaymin stopped the tape suddenly; the sound of her own voice never failed to amaze her. Over time, she had grown to loathe it. On the other hand, Kaine had complimented her on it. *I like your voice,* he had said during those awkward, frightening hours before Angela's rescue. *I like your voice.* Sister Immaculata would have surely reminded her that something as simple as that shouldn't mean so much. But why shouldn't it? Jaymin thought. What's so wrong with something feeling good for a change?

She punched the rewind button, then play. "That's a very humble admission." There, it didn't sound so bad this time. "If you two didn't find it necessary to come out with your guns blazing every time someone irritated you, we wouldn't have these problems."

"Thorpe was a mistake. I should have never involved him."

"We have to find the girl."

"We'll find her."

"Not just find her, take care of her."

"The girl can't harm us. Don't be ridiculous."

"That's not your picture on that photograph, Jaymin. And what's more, you've gotten yourself emotionally involved. I don't know which of us is the more stupid."

"The photograph is being taken care of. But we need the copies. And Jaymin knows where to draw the line. Don't you, my dear?"

"The line has already been drawn," Jaymin heard herself say, and she pressed the stop button.

She punched rewind and then play.

"We have to find the girl."
"We'll find her."
"Not just find her, take care of her."
Stop. Rewind. Play.
"Not just find her, take care of her."

22 Kaine entered a pub on Oxford Street called the Black
Lantern. It catered to a curiously mixed crowd, children
even, but the music was distinctively modern. Festooned with
heavy timbers and cut-glass lighting, people sat at long communal
tables.

Laughter rose above the music, and political discussions bested
the laughter. Kaine stood at the end of a solid oak bar. He ordered
Irish whiskey. He had no intention of drinking until the heat of
the first swallow erupted in his stomach. He had neglected himself,
and the whiskey served as both a reminder and a tonic. When he
caught a reflection of himself in the mirror, however, he realized
that the neglect showed more in his dress than on his face. He had
thrown a loose-fitting jean jacket over a gray work shirt and blue
jeans. Yet his dark eyes were focused and clear. His long chin had
a predatory set to it. Danielle had commented on his hair; she liked
it long. Kaine finished his whiskey and carried a second round into
a call box at the back.

The operator in London connected him with one in Dodman
Point, the coastal town in Cornwall where he and Danielle had
taken a belated honeymoon fifteen years ago. Kaine exchanged his

credit-card number for the telephone number of the White Rain motel. When the switchboard answered, Kaine asked for Danielle Aslund's room.

Danielle answered after a single ring. "Stephen?"

"You made it."

"A miniadventure. The only private charter we could arrange out of Folkestone at that time of night was a sea plane. The pilot took nocturnal coastal photos for some government agency, and most of the time the plane flew itself. We got here in one piece, though, and for a mere two hundred pounds. What do you think of that?"

"Which government agency?"

Danielle heard the suspicion in Kaine's voice and translated it into concern. "He said something about the environment. Tracking the residuals of an oil spill that happened up north last year sometime. Why? Does it matter?"

Kaine sighed; he was becoming his own worst enemy. "I've been seeing too many ghosts lately, that's all. I'm just glad you're there. Angie okay?"

"Sleeping. The kid's a rock. It scares me to death."

"How about you?"

"You always had a way of making life interesting, I can't deny that." Danielle's laughter had a sarcastic ring to it that Kaine had always misunderstood. This time he laughed with her. "Where are you? At a party?"

"Still in London. In a pub."

"You never did like drinking alone. That was my bad habit, wasn't it?" She didn't allow for an answer, saying quickly, "What have you found out? Anything?"

"More than I hoped," Kaine admitted. Yet here, he realized, was an opportunity to unburden himself, and he welcomed it. He started with his visit to Julian Persoff's chemistry lab at the University in London and ended with Connor Thorpe's discovery at the American embassy. Yet he left out the scene in Jaymin's hotel room, and wondered why. Was it the confused state of the emotions he was feeling for both women? Or was it . . .?

Unknowingly, Danielle saved him from the questions with one of her own. "The U.S. ambassador to England and some colonel on the National Security Council? Are you serious?"

"Both very dangerous and, unless I'm mistaken, very driven."

"Stephen, you can't be serious. No, don't answer that. I know when you're serious. At least I used to think I always did. Which was a mistake, wasn't it? How are they involved with Karmin-Yar?"

"I don't know that yet."

"Have they been arrested?"

Kaine finished his whiskey. He finally mustered the energy to reply. "I haven't talked to the police yet."

"You have to, Stephen. Won't they find out the same thing you did from their copy of Angela's photograph?"

The answer seemed obvious, but Kaine was no longer convinced. "Eventually," he said.

"Is she going to have to identify this Mathers?"

"If it gets that far."

"Goddamn it, Stephen." A prolonged pause festered; it became a nagging silence. Finally, Danielle said, "You're not through, are you?"

Kaine answered with a question of his own. "Do you remember Jurgen Spire?"

"The Soviet. Of course. I liked him." Danielle had met Spire at the International Archeological Conference in New York six years ago; he had been full of compliments for both her and Kaine, and had extended an invitation for a future visit to Leningrad—one which, unfortunately, had never materialized. "Spire's somehow involved?"

"I have to find out."

"And we have to stay here until you do."

"How did you get from the airport to the motel? Taxi?"

Danielle sighed again. "No. Our pilot had a car. He dropped us. Not good?"

Kaine stared into his empty glass. "Stay off the beaches," he said in time. "If you have to go out, go to the country."

"Call," Danielle said.

"Tell Angela she's my special one." Then he added—though not as an afterthought—"You're rather special yourself."

Detective Superintendent Preble affected an attitude of nonchalance over his meeting with Kaine, but Kaine recognized his eagerness. Kaine ordered, but hardly touched, a third whiskey. He left a bowl of chowder half-eaten. Ordinarily a man of patience—he had parlayed a lifetime of waiting into an almost eerie awareness of details and an acute sense of when to act—he toyed with his spoon and drank coffee one cup after another until Preble arrived.

"You could have picked a less conspicuous place than the Black Lantern," the superintendent said, ordering a draft and a roast beef sandwich before taking a seat.

"Am I in need of being inconspicuous?"

"You mean above and beyond the arrest warrant the Chatham police have issued for you?" Preble grimaced. "Bring another," he said to the waitress who left his beer. He drank like a man whose pleasures had been narrowed and honed over the years, and drinking had survived the process. He scanned the pub much as he had the interior of the harbor tug upon their first meeting.

"Hennagan's dead," Kaine said.

Now Preble gave him his full attention. "Your information is good," he said soberly. "How is that?"

"I saw it happen."

Preble consumed the remainder of his beer, eyes locked on the man across the table, and used one hand and then the other to wipe the corners of his mouth. He said, "You better tell me what the bloody hell you know, mister. And you better tell me all of it."

"He was moonlighting," Kaine said. He related the incident on the dock the night the ferry went down, seeing the man and his two bodyguards leaving Tanner Thorpe's tug. Inexplicably, he didn't mention Louis Mathers by name.

Preble pushed his mug aside. He leaned heavily upon the table. "You identified Hennagan then and didn't bother to say anything to me?"

Kaine shook his head. "I only got a close look at the one, Jankowski. From the phone booth. Even that didn't register until later.
The other one was either Hennagan or you."

Preble's face flared. "What the fuck are you—"

Kaine subdued him with a raised hand, surprised at the strength
of Preble's reaction. "That was an unfortunate play on the obvious,
Detective Preble. It only means that you two were like bookends.
Same build, same slouch, same walk. Nothing personal. The three
of them got into a car, a rental. I tracked it down. Hennagan had
rented it two days before."

"Another fact you failed to share."

"I'm sharing it now." For an instant, Kaine wondered why. Still,
he said, "But it doesn't make sense. When he died, Hennagan was
delivering shoes to a homeless shelter."

"The shoes were filled with drugs. The pants were lined with
the stuff. Cocaine," Preble said quickly. His sandwich came, but
he pushed it away. "Hennagan had been on the pad for nearly a
year. He had gambling debts that would choke a horse. I made a
mess of it. I tried talking him out of it, giving him some time. He
wouldn't budge. Told me to bugger off."

"You knew? His superior? And you kept it quiet? You two must
have been good friends."

Preble took offense. "We were more than just friends, Professor.
We were family. Cousins. Satisfied?"

"What have the police done with Angela's Polaroid?" Kaine
realized that in asking the question he was also putting himself in
the position of mentioning the second photo, the one he had with-
held from Preble earlier.

Now Preble reached for his sandwich. He talked out of the side
of his mouth. "We've been jacking around with the negative sheets.
You soak it in this sodium sulfite solution. Wash away the developer
residue. The catch is doing it without disturbing the emulsion layer
below. Do that and you get essentially a clean negative which you
essentially reexpose. You go through the process of reversing the
image and then enlarging it. In some cases the results are worth
the time . . ."

The procedure was not new to Kaine. He shook his head. "Except you're only reproducing the original image. A man without a face."

"You've got a better idea, I suppose." Preble's nonchalance had returned.

Kaine placed the second of Daniel Stone's computer-enhanced prints next to Preble's plate. The pendulum of the detective's emotions swung again, to anger, but also to disbelief. At what, Kaine wasn't sure.

"You know him, obviously," Kaine said. "First Skipper Tanner Thorpe's killer."

The sandwich was now a forgotten extension of one hand; Preble drew the print near with the other. "You, mister, are truly remarkable. Do you realize—"

"Keep it," Kaine said, throwing an exasperated glance at the print. "You'll need it." Then he rose. "And I need a ride to the airport."

"Where's your daughter, Kaine?" Preble was still entranced by the sight of Ambassador Louis Mathers's face.

"We'll talk more in the car," Kaine said.

The London night had succumbed to a London fog. The car was like a coffin. Lights were weapons without power in this mass. Kaine remembered crossing the river, twice, he thought. Heathrow International Airport lay twenty miles to the west of central London. The ride took an hour and ten minutes.

Preble demanded to know why Kaine had held out on the second Polaroid, and in reply Kaine questioned the failure of Scotland Yard to implement the most modern forensic techniques in identifying the killer's face.

"Doesn't a tugboat operator warrant such treatment? Would you have done it if the dead bastard owned a sixty foot yacht and a membership in the Westminister Yacht Club?"

"It was a mistake," Preble admitted. "A screwup. We don't have that kind of equipment; I admit I'm not even familiar with the technique, but I should have been more thorough. Blame me, not the Yard."

Preble asked about Angela again, and Kaine questioned him
about the procedural problems of bringing a diplomat of ambas-
sadorial ranking to justice.

"Without your daughter's testimony, a photograph spun out by
a quick-witted computer isn't going to bring Louis Mathers or even
Mickey Mouse to trial." A damp gloss formed under Preble's thick
hands; his grip on the wheel didn't suit a man who spent a good
part of the day driving, Kaine thought. "You say you saw the man
climb aboard a helicopter. It was getting dark and you were a
hundred meters away. Your daughter was in distress. You were
dodging bullets. Can you identify the son of a bitch?"

Kaine looked aside. Preble had the profile of a rounded Buddha;
a rope of flesh formed under his chin.

"Whose side are you on?" Kaine asked.

Preble blinked. "Stupid question."

"Who was Hennagan working for when he was watching our
hotel Friday night? You or Mathers?"

"You gave me your word that Angela would be available. I can't
figure you Americans. For an Englishman, his word would have
been enough," Preble replied. But Kaine didn't honor the insin-
uation with a response, and finally Preble capitulated, saying, "It
was Hennagan's night off, all right."

They fell in behind a tour bus. The fog christened its shell with
an aura of mist and haze. They found the expressway and a caravan
of tentative motorists. Preble said, "This car may be headed in the
direction of the airport, Professor Kaine, but if you expect it to get
there, you better fill me in on the whys and wherefores."

"Remember the wallet I took off of Joseph Jankowski?" Kaine
said. "There was a reference to a colleague of mine. His name is
Jurgen Spire. Jurgen is an archeologist with a strong interest in
the city of Karmin-Yar. Also a wealth of knowledge on the subject.
He has a winter home on the Black Sea in the Crimea."

"The Crimea? In the Soviet Union? Three days ago I made it
very clear that you're not to leave the county much less the country.
Yesterday you punch out a cop in Chatham, and now you're suggesting I allow you on a plane for the Crimea?"

"That's exactly what I'm suggesting."

Preble relaxed. "And you hope to find?"

Kaine fell silent. Preble seemed content, even relieved to push the conversation in a different direction. He said, "Professor Stephen Kaine. An expert on the rise and fall of the Persian Empire. I've heard it from more than a few people recently. A title you accept?"

"An expert is someone who's stopped learning," Kaine replied. He stared out the window and saw only his reflection. "I'm a novice in that department."

"The greatest empire in history, the Persians. I've heard that, too. True?"

"From the Danube River and the Aral Sea in the north to the Arabian Sea in the south. From the Indus Valley in India as far west as Egypt. Twenty-three nations. It lasted a paltry three hundred years."

"They managed to dominate everyone but the Greeks, the way I hear it."

"The Athenians defeated Darius the First at Marathon in 490 B.C. They repelled the fleet of Xerxes ten years later at Salamis. It's a dilemma, however. Half the historians you talk to argue that the Mediterranean Sea was more responsible than the Greek army."

"Yeah? What do your historians have to say about Alexander the Great?"

"Alexander was one of the most inspirational leaders in history; no one argues that. He only had two failings: shortsightedness and booze. Unfortunately he drank himself to death and left behind him an empire with no foundation and nowhere to go but down. The Greeks have been fighting the legend ever since. But Karmin-Yar was defeated long before Alexander the Great. Mother nature saw to that."

The expressway took them to the edge of greater London and through the last vestiges of the fog. Heathrow Airport gobbled up the bulk of the traffic; the rest dispersed into the undulant hills of southern England and Kaine envied them their eventual destinations. He was tired. His body ached. He felt utterly alone.

A series of ill-marked thoroughfares funneled them toward the international terminal. Kaine would employ the services of Aeroflot, as he had many times, and Preble located the appropriate entrance.

He climbed out of the car but didn't turn off the engine. From his wallet, he produced a business card. "You're crazy, you realize. Utterly foolish." Preble offered the card anyway. "You'll sure as hell be in need of a friend before this is all over. For what it's worth, figure the number here will get you one."

Kaine expected him to ask about Angela again, but he didn't. Curious. When the detective superintendent's car was out of sight, Kaine ventured inside.

He had flown into the Soviet Union four different times, and never without complications. The Soviet Intourist office was located on the first floor of the main concourse. They required three photo IDs just to begin the process. Kaine offered his passport, driver's license, and the Archeological Society card he always carried. The latter was not well-received. Still, a computer check confirmed his prior trips into the Soviet Union: as a visiting graduate student at the University in Moscow in 1972; as a noted researcher in Leningrad in 1977; and twice on site at an exploratory dig near Tashkent in Soviet Central Asia. All but his student visit had been at the invitation of the Moscow Institute of Antiquities, and this expedited matters considerably. An Intourist number was issued and a visa application was accepted. The required hotel reservations and hourly itinerary were filed.

An Aeroflot flight number 459, with stops in Warsaw and Odessa, boarded at two ten Monday morning.

It was an excruciating flight. Kaine vacillated between bouts of fitful slumber and the restless onslaught of old, recurring dreams. Danielle had often theorized that his nocturnal habits suggested a man who wished to be in any bed except his own. Despite the health of their own sex life, she had been obsessed with the possibility of his infidelity. She once said that no man who spent half of every year in tent cities halfway around the globe could be faithful. She didn't blame him. Nor did she ever ask him straight out.

Since the divorce, there had been three women, relationships that had suffered most from a prevailing indifference on Kaine's part. The first had been a carbon copy of Danielle, less the spunk and the sex drive. The second had provided such long and salacious nights—Kaine remembered a never-ending stream of soaking wet sheets—that it had taken three months for them to realize that they had nothing in common to see them through the days. The third had been a colleague, a woman at Karmin-Yar. Carol was smart, funny, and possessive, and twenty-hour work days had convinced her that Kaine's first love was two thousand years old and half-buried in sand.

The problem wasn't the women, it was more like a disease Kaine had determined to be malignant. The indifference he felt subsided only when the women—like Jaymin, or even Danielle—were inaccessible.

In Jaymin's case, he wondered what he would do if the scene in the hotel could somehow be replayed, or if the events surrounding the crown of Sharana Ni had been different? But that, Kaine realized, was a fantasy he couldn't afford. Jaymin *had* taken possession of the crown and the coins; she was deeply involved, and people had died. He still cared. He still wanted to reach out to her. He saw a part of himself in this woman seemingly so set on self-destruction, and wondered if he could save either of them.

As for Danielle, he simply hadn't given her up completely, and this had undoubtedly contributed to his indifference toward other women. Angela had wisely observed that it was obvious her mother and father still liked one another. Well, it was true. He did still like Danielle, still desired her.

In Odessa he booked a seat on a twelve-passenger prop plane. In the day's aborning hour, a bank of heavy fog lay upon the waters of the Black Sea; the first rays of sun filtered through it like veins of blood. From the air, the Crimea was a diamond-shaped peninsula dangling from the Soviet mainland, a dark and rugged land. Simferopol, its inland capital, nestled at the foot of the Crimean Mountains.

Kaine passed with minimal encumberance through customs. He was questioned most fervently about his lack of luggage; a duffel bag contained a single change of clothes and shaving gear. He carried two magazines, *The Economist* and *Newsweek*. He had glanced at the cover story in the first and not so much as opened the second.

An Intourist guide directed him to the bus to Balaklava. The sixty-mile drive to the coast carved inexorably through dense cedar forest. In quarries, miners unearthed huge slabs of pink and white marble; trucks laden with the stone traveled inland under heavy escort. As the bus neared the coast, there were views of broad valley floors and herds of horses. Beneath the prevailing fog, the waters beyond the coast writhed like a sea of black eels, and closer, glistened like a sheen of crude oil.

Elistara, north of Balaklava, was a harbor town as yet undiscovered by tourists. Here, cedars had abdicated to magnolias and grape vineyards. Whitewashed buildings were stacked with an odd symmetry across the coastal rim. The dachas and villas of the Soviet elite nestled in the low hills surrounding the town.

The bus made one stop, at the entrance to a clapboard hotel called the Sula. Kaine and one other man disembarked. The guide helped them check in, and for the second time, Kaine's lack of luggage was viewed as disturbing. The guide passed a copy of his itinerary into the hands of the desk clerk. A second copy, Kaine realized, had already been forwarded to the local police.

23

Now things got tricky.

Kaine spoke a smattering of Russian, but he couldn't cope with the Crimean dialect, its cumbersome mixture of Ukrainian and Georgian. The police would, of course, know of Jurgen Spire's whereabouts, but by simply asking Kaine would elicit undesirable fanfare and inevitable suspicions. If a man is on your itinerary, then you shouldn't have to ask directions; good, solid, Soviet logic.

A phone directory covered the entire peninsula. In the end, Kaine was forced to seek the assistance of the concierge and discovered that Jurgen Spire was not listed. This was not significant, Kaine decided; a Soviet as prominent as Spire needn't advertise his winter home.

The sounds and smells issuing forth from the hotel's tiny but crowded restaurant evoked a memory. A handwritten sign outside the swinging doors of the entrance referred to fresh herring, and the memory blossomed. Like a man discussing his favorite avocation, Spire, Kaine recalled, had talked with as much zest about food as he had his chosen profession. The fresh herring was an Elistara tradition.

Jurgen Spire was an archeologist of research and theory; unlike

Kaine, he rarely transformed his theories with a pick and shovel. Spire favored bow ties. His hands were manicured. He wore jewelry. Kaine transformed this profile into a question for the hotel concierge.

"I'm looking for a restaurant with clean tablecloths, fresh herring, and no tourists."

The concierge frowned. When the translation became clear, his frown deepened. He volunteered two names. Both were seaside cafés located east of town.

Kaine left his duffel bag at the desk and ventured outside.

Elistara was a town of fishermen and loggers. Kaine wore blue jeans and the jacket he used on site, and still felt conspicuous.

A ten-minute walk along the town's main thoroughfare brought him eventually to the Café de Crimea. It was stoutly constructed of cedar logs, and smoke belched from a stone chimney. Inside, ten wooden tables surrounded a central fireplace. Tablecloths did indeed cover every table. All were occupied, and the occupants looked nothing like tourists. They drank beer from wooden mugs. Their bursts of laughter were uninhibited.

It was the music more than anything; the music was beer garden music, and Kaine could picture Jurgen Spire cringing at the tinny sound. He left without a word.

In contrast to the café, the Goblin's Hut was situated on a low promontory. A stretch of white beach opened up on its left, the piers of a small harbor on the right. It was constructed of cedar, and its rounded front and a bank of mullioned windows presented a spectacular vista.

Men in suits and women in hats were sprinkled among an otherwise casual crowd. The music was classical. Brahms, Kaine thought. He saw crystal wine goblets.

Kaine sat at a wooden bar with the high gloss of many polishings. The bartender wore a vest and a string tie. Kaine ordered vodka. The bartender pointed blandly to a row of sixteen different brands and flavors. Kaine pointed in return and received a peppered variety.

With the aid of the translation dictionary he had picked up before leaving England, Kaine had written his questions out on a piece of hotel stationery. When his vodka was served, Kaine turned the paper in the direction of the bartender. He laid the dictionary beside it and the bartender smirked.

Kaine's first question read, "Is Mr. Spire expected this afternoon?" This was an attempt to appear knowledgeable despite the language barrier.

The bartender answered via the dictionary, as well. "Tonight."

Second question. "Does he have a telephone at his dacha, please?"

Answer. The bartender used his chin to indicate a phone on the counter near the kitchen. He held up ten fingers and said, "Ten rubles."

In reply, Kaine laid twenty American dollars on the table. His written question was already prepared. "Can you help me find his number, please?"

Expressionless, the bartender held up the Crimea phone directory. Kaine shook his head, and the bartender nodded his as if he had known all along. He disappeared into the kitchen; Kaine heard bits and pieces of a muted conversation. When the bartender returned he held up the telephone receiver, inviting Kaine over with a wave of his hand. He offered the receiver, dialed the number, and turned his attention to a polishing cloth and crystal wine goblets.

Jurgen Spire answered the phone on the sixteenth ring. Though the archeologist's Russian was beyond Kaine's comprehension, it was clear that he was not happy about the interruption.

Remembering Spire's hearing aid, Kaine spoke in concise, clear English. "Mr. Spire. I'm sorry to interrupt you, sir. This is Stephen Kaine. The American archeologist, from the United States."

The pause that followed this introduction made Kaine suspect some difficulty with the phone. He tried again. "Jurgen Spire? Do you remember me, sir?"

"Yes, Stephen Kaine, I remember you. Not a person I'm likely to forget despite my advancing years." The voice droned. The weight of the words fell like stones from the receiver. "It's about Karmin-Yar, isn't it? Where are you calling from?"

"Here in Elistara. At a restaurant called the Goblin's Hut."

"Your memory serves you well, sir. As does your ingenuity."

"Our conversations were memorable."

"Indeed they were, weren't they? Also enlightening. Unfortunate that the circumstances aren't different now."

The bartender worked his polishing cloth absently over the same wineglass; he stared into the mirror at the back of the bar. Kaine turned his back to him. Into the phone he said, "What are the circumstances?"

Spire spoke with a sense of urgency, also an edge of futility. "You have no notion of what you have become involved in, Stephen."

"If it has anything to do with Karmin-Yar, Jurgen, which we both know it does, then I have been involved half my life."

"Yes, and of course I respect that. But there is more here than simple archeological discoveries." The anger Kaine heard in Spire's voice was self-directed. Then it flared out at Kaine, as well. "Why have you come here? Why?"

"The crown of Sharana Ni," Kaine said simply.

Now Kaine heard only urgency. "This is not a matter for the telephone."

"A visit to your dacha is on my itinerary."

Silence, a silence eaten by turmoil and ambivalence, gave way eventually to a profound sigh. When Spire said, "I would welcome you to my house, Stephen Kaine," the tone of his voice said, "I had hoped it was over."

"And I would be honored," Kaine replied.

Now abrupt and businesslike, Spire said, "May I assume you have ordered lunch or a drink?"

"A drink, yes."

"You must not appear to be in a hurry. You have already brought attention to yourself by using their phone. Finish your drink and return to town. There is a market and an apothecary shop, a . . . a druggist, you call it, at the first stop. There is a dirt road which leads directly north from there. Into the mountains. A signpost reads Rya Peak. Yes?"

"Yes."

"It is a nine-kilometer walk, perhaps five or six miles, but don't worry. I must change first, but then I will meet you. In Leningrad I drive a Zhiguli, but in Elistara I drive a panel truck. A dirty gray color. You'll see none other like it."

The bartender had forsaken the mirror. Now he focused his attention without reservation on Kaine; the polishing cloth dangled at his side. Kaine stared back. "I'll look for you," he said softly into the phone.

"Stay off the road as much as possible. Talk to no one," Spire ordered. "Do you hear?"

Kaine laid the phone carefully back in the cradle. He stopped at the bar. He lifted his vodka glass. He swirled the contents, taking occasional sips. He studied the view. Then he drank, consuming what remained of the liquor in a single swallow. He was halfway to the door when he turned suddenly and said to the bartender in English, "Thank you."

"You're wel—" The bartender caught himself, his accent coarse and unwieldy. Then, as if it didn't matter, he said, "You're welcome, Mr. Kaine."

The midday sun had taken the heart out of the Black Sea fog. Only wisps survived, like lonely ghosts. The water rippled with colors, swells of emerald and indigo. Troughs of silver and whitecaps as pure as snow.

There were people on the road back to town. A pair of women in long skirts and with scarves on their heads carried baskets of vegetables. A man on horseback tugged a stubborn donkey and two goats. A group of kids on bicycles drank Coca-Cola from glass bottles. Two heavily loaded logging trucks lumbered past. Kaine counted a half dozen cars.

Conversely, there were neither people nor vehicles on the dirt road to Rya Peak. At least in the beginning.

On the left side of the road an olive grove filled the valley, its leaves a steely blue. On the right side, cedar trees perfumed the air. It was not hot, but Kaine felt sweat rising on his skin. He forged a path through the trees, but stayed within sight of the road. Though his route was hardly strenuous, it was also not the swiftest of choices. Flowers in the underbrush brought to mind bluebells and lilies of the valley.

This is not a matter for the telephone, Spire had said. The very mention of the crown of Sharana Ni had shaken Spire. But there was no surprise in his voice. He had known.

Kaine had walked for thirty or forty minutes when the hum of an oncoming vehicle caught his attention. He fell in behind an outcropping of gray limestone, then worked his way to the edge of the forest. The hum became a wail. Would Jurgen Spire, a man who wore bow ties and relied on a hearing aid, drive with such abandon? Kaine doubted it. Then he saw them. Not one, but two cars hastening down the mountain; their tires bit into the dirt and a wall of dust pursued them. Kaine expected teenagers in junkyard heaps. But the cars were newer than that. The drivers, from Kaine's vantage, looked more like white-collar workers.

When they had passed, and only a pall of dust remained, Kaine took to the road. He convinced himself that sounds—sounds of cars, surely—were amplified in the hills, and that he would have sufficient time to retreat if necessary. It was a theory; the anxiety he felt, however, was far from theoretical.

Kaine fortified himself with bits of Crimean history. In 501 B.C. Darius the First sent an exploratory force of a hundred ships across the Black Sea; they found the Scythian tribes hard at war with one another and easily defeatable. Two thousand years and seven or eight conquering tribes later, the Ottoman Turks made the ruling Tatars of the Golden Horde a footnote of history. In the process, the Crimea became a cornerstone of the Ottoman empire. The Ottomans themselves survived only until 1783, when the tsar made the peninsula a part of the ever-expanding Russian umbrella . . .

It didn't help, Kaine removed his jacket and jogged. At the top of the next rise he slowed. He used the trees again to gain a secluded vantage point. A breathtaking view brought him momentarily to a halt. A sea of green swept out before him, holding at its heart a field of yellow flowers. The arrow piercing it was the road, now straight and narrow.

Kaine caught sight of Jurgen Spire's gray panel truck two miles off and lumbering toward him. Dust eclipsed it. He bounded out of the trees and started down the hill, trotting, then walking as the car neared. He held up a hand. The apprehension he was feeling over the encounter evaporated, replaced now by genuine anticipation. He found himself smiling and waved again.

Then the smile froze; his hand dropped.

One moment gliding along the valley floor and preparing for its ascent of the next rise, Jurgen Spire's gray panel truck was, in the next moment, consumed in a fountain of orange fire. The explosion was so sudden and so fierce that Kaine was momentarily thrust backward. His feet absorbed the tremors. The truck rose into the air, settled again, and then broke into a thousand projectiles hurling in a thousand directions. An impenetrable cloud of black smoke funneled skyward. Bits and pieces of metal and glass rained down and forced Kaine to cover his head.

What remained seconds later was a naked chassis and four flaming tires.

Stunned, Kaine staggered forward. Then ran. He halted ten feet from the car, the destruction nearly bringing him to his knees. The air shimmered with heat. An acrid scent like cordite filled his nose. The silence was so complete that there was about it an unreality, hints of a terrible joke. In a daze, he circled. He saw a patent-leather shoe; it smoked. He saw a steering wheel. A charred and dented bumper had been flung thirty yards from the car. He saw a distorted mass and recognized it as a hand.

Kaine didn't know which came first, the panic, or the message at the edge of his conscious mind that the cars he had seen before were returning. He moved like an angry cat.

From the road to the shoulder and up the loose soil of the embankment took only seconds. Kaine scurried into the trees. He hid behind the low branches of a cedar, hurling himself down on his stomach. To the south, the cars broke the horizon. They descended into the valley, one behind the other, slowing. Kaine snaked farther in among the trees.

Thirty yards from the naked remains of Jurgen Spire's truck, the cars stopped.

Two men emerged, one from the passenger side of each vehicle. They wore suits in need of tailoring and the wind tugged at the flaps of their jackets and the cuffs of their pants. They moved incautiously toward the truck. One bent down and stupidly swept up a charred piece of metal from the ground; he dropped it immediately, shaking his hand and wincing. His partner chuckled. He stopped at the chassis and casually rested a foot upon it. He lit a cigarette. He scanned the valley the way a man on a mountain hike eyes an unimpressive stretch of prairie. Had Kaine a gun in his possession he would have shot the man dead for that look alone.

Neither man made an effort to find the remains of a body. Body? Or bodies? Kaine whispered the words, suddenly struck by their significance. Had the explosion been premature? Had they known that Jurgen Spire was in the process of meeting him? Had it been their intent that both he and Spire die in that explosion?

The tires flared in a sudden gust. Overhead, a hawk carved a wide circle above the valley. The man crushed out his cigarette. Wordlessly, he and his partner returned to their vehicles. Their drivers turned around and drove like model citizens back toward town.

The moment the cars disappeared over the rise, Kaine was on his feet and hastening for Jurgen Spire's house. He jogged, then walked, then jogged again. The jogging helped stave off his alarm and delirium, both of which were very real. No matter that he was on a peninsula with the beauty of a Victoria Island or a Rocky Mountain National Park; no matter that it was the age of *glasnost;* he was an American in the Soviet Union and his business here was not so easily explained.

Through the trees he saw lakes. They were so still that upon their surfaces he could make out the minuscule wakes of geese and eiders. The dachas surrounding the lakes were more log cabins than villas. Ramparts of cut and stacked wood encapsulated them. Smoke rose from chimneys, and twice Kaine was confronted by barking dogs. Kaine the American looked for mailboxes with names painted on them, or gates with signs hung above them; had he been in Rocky Mountain National Park he knew he would have found them proudly exhibited. Here they were nonexistent.

In lieu of mailboxes, Kaine found something almost as telling:

roadside markers that calculated the distance from the main road in Elistara. They did so in kilometers. Spire had said about nine kilometers.

Kaine opened his pocket watch. He brushed his thumb across the glass, an old habit, a superstition. It was one thirty Greenwich time. The Crimea was three hours ahead. It would be dark in two hours.

Kaine jogged past the eight-kilometer marker, and five minutes later slowed to a walk. Now there were streams coursing down the hills. Their music brought Kaine a false sense of equanimity. The nine-kilometer marker shoved the feeling of calm inexorably aside.

From the road Kaine spied two dachas. A terraced lawn surrounded the first. Potted plants filled out the porch. A Ukrainian flag hung above the plants. Parked alongside the wood pile were two bicycles. Jurgen Spire was not Ukrainian; nor could Kaine picture him pedaling a bicycle through the Crimean Mountains.

The cabin on the right was smaller, yet neat and seemingly well tended. A grove of slender white birch protected it on the windward side. A stream rambled past on the other. A rutted drive was empty of cars. An open door exposed an empty garage. The cabin, Kaine was sure, belonged to Spire. A wisp of gray smoke snaked from the mouth of the chimney. The Soviet archeologist had, he decided, thoughtfully stoked the fire before venturing out; the irony of it all left Kaine feeling sick and defeated, and only a spate of anger kept him going.

He left the road on the far side of the stream. He held to the shadows of tall cedars. Thick brambles of willow clung in places to the bank. The serenity of the scene was disturbed only by Kaine's imagination; Jurgen Spire would step out on the front porch at any moment chewing on the stem of his pipe.

Kaine pressed on. The caroling of the stream covered his footsteps. Curtainless windows stared out from the walls of the cabin. A generator, now visible as Kaine circled, was situated in a shed off the back porch. An electric light illuminated the interior of the cabin with a faint yellow glow.

Thirty meters from the house, a pair of fallen trees formed a footbridge across the water. A rope had been strung waist-high for balance, and Kaine crossed into the wild grass that grew in the backyard.

An easel and chair stood like abandoned theater props among this growth. An unfinished canvas leaned against the easel; upon it, a background of magnolias had been sketched. A palette and brush had been consigned to the chair—where Spire had probably set them when Kaine had called.

Warily, Kaine circled the house again. He peered into four double-paned windows accessing four different rooms, all small, all sparely furnished. In the bedroom, a gray and blue quilt covered a four-poster bed. In the bathroom, a straight razor and shaving brush lay beside a porcelain bowl and water pitcher. A shower and stool suggested a well system more sophisticated than Kaine would have anticipated. A tiny kitchen, with hot plate and copper teakettle, opened onto a tiny living room. Kaine could see a marble-topped table adjacent to a spindled rocker; a rack of pipes and a humidor rested upon the table. Through the last window he observed what obviously represented Spire's library away from home.

He saw no sign of intruders.

Kaine found the front door had been chained, but the screen off the back porch was propped open and the door was unlocked. He went inside. Other details leapt out at him. In the kitchen, a pan of soup cooled on a one-burner stove. In the living room, an album cover for Tchaikovsky's *Swan Lake* rested against a turntable built twenty-five years ago. A Russian translation of *Grapes of Wrath* lay open on the floor next to the rocker. How strange to pass into the domain of a man whose existence had, only an hour before, been scattered among the ruins of a demolished panel truck. Such a loss. A man who had given to the theater of archeology dozens of telling discoveries. A man who had ushered a thousand eager kids into the field. Kaine shuddered; another good man dead. He told himself he was to blame, but there was no conviction in the words.

He bypassed the bathroom. If there were any evidence here to explain Jurgen Spire's death, and the prominence of his name in the wallet of a former New York City policeman named Joseph Jankowski, then it would surely be found in the library.

Like the rest of the cabin, the library was small, but seemed smaller due to the clutter and warmth of wood and books. Against the near wall stood a heavy oak desk. Oak filing cabinets decorated with fine scrollwork stood like sentries on either side. Floor-to-ceiling bookshelves lined two other walls, and the size of the collection suggested the many years Spire had wintered in this tiny cabin. An overstuffed chair, damask-covered, and matching ottoman made the room whole and complete.

With a certain reverence, Kaine positioned himself in front of the desk. Reams of paper were neatly arranged. Files were stacked in three wire bins. The tabs on all these files referred to the ruins of an iron-age city in Soviet Armenia called Tern Baia, Jurgen Spire's most recent project. Squares of yellow notepaper were tucked along the folds of a smooth leather desk pad; each square suggested to Kaine the stages of development of a newly organized expedition to the city. Geological charts and seismic readings all focused on the Caucasus Mountains west of the Caspian Sea: Tern Baia again. But the subject at hand was Karmin-Yar, not Tern Baia.

Kaine moved to the filing cabinets. Rubric cards attached to the face of each drawer suggested a system based simply on the alphabet. Or three alphabets: Russian, ancient Greek, and English. Kaine tugged at the top drawer of each cabinet; he expected them to be locked, and they were. Out of a sense of decorum, perhaps, before resorting to more drastic measures, Kaine yanked at the drawer labeled H–L. To his great surprise and the sudden skipping of his heart, it opened. A cursory examination of the lock revealed that it had been jimmied. Now his heart galloped.

The bulk of the drawer was dedicated to the letter *K*. Karmin-Yar, of course. Seven files bore the Karmin-Yar heading. All were now empty.

Kaine dropped into Jurgen Spire's chair. The exhaustion he had been able to ignore for the last twelve hours caved in on him. Among his American colleagues, there was a saying in the archeological field: "To search and be destroyed." And another equally appropriate: "Prepare to be disappointed, expect the unexpected, and when all else fails, pour a drink."

Kaine found brandy in the bottom drawer of the desk. Four bottles. Obviously, Kaine thought, Soviet archeologists followed a similar credo. Four bottles but only one glass; he and Spire had more in common than he had thought. Kaine drank sparingly despite the urge to do otherwise. A slice of his phone conversation with Spire came back to him. *There is more here than simple archeological discoveries.* Kaine knew that. Greed, avarice, drugs, deceit, delusion, death, dirt, and more dirt.

Kaine raised his glass mockingly. "To a perfect world."

He turned the cynicism in on himself and set the glass aside. He took the saying in reverse: Drink first, then expect the unexpected, then prepare to be disappointed.

He stood up again. He thumbed through the other three files in the H–L drawer: one labeled "Knossos," the capital of the Minoan Empire two thousand years before Christ; the second labeled "Ife," the first capital city of the Yorubas, located west of the Niger River in Nigeria; and third, speculative documentation on the elusive continent of Lemuria. The contents were all duplications, but this only suggested to Kaine that the Soviet archeologist had thought better of leaving original material in a remote dacha in the Crimean Mountains. Still, something very intuitive told Kaine that if there was anything to be found among these files, anything not already pilfered by the men in the cars he had seen, it would be original material.

He found a screwdriver in the kitchen. He popped the lock on the file drawer labeled A–F. This was scientific thinking taken to its most primitive level: When there is neither a clue to follow nor a sixth sense to rely on, start at the beginning.

As he plunged through the files, Kaine recognized projects Spire had either contributed to, consulted on, or initiated. Alexandropol was the location of funeral barrows of the Scythian warlords of the Ukraine. Anuradhapura was the ancient capital of Sri Lanka mysteriously abandoned in 550 A.D. Cappadocia was the beehive dwellings of ancient Turkey. The names were all familiar to Kaine; had circumstances been different, he would have treasured the opportunity to read on. The Dolmens of Drenthe were five-thousand-year-old underground chambers in Holland, unheard of until Spire's team unearthed them thirty years ago. The Externsteine were enigmatic rock pillars in the northern forests of Germany containing caves and carvings that even Spire had been hard-pressed to explain. "The Fire Theft"? A designation Kaine couldn't place. The name suggested an occurrence as opposed to a location or site.

Kaine drew the file from the drawer. The pages within were sheets of thick parchment, not the work of a copying machine. The sketches and notations were all drawn or written in Jurgen Spire's own hand. The file heading was dated exactly six months and three weeks ago, just days prior to Kaine's termination as project director and chief archeologist at the Karmin-Yar site.

Knowing at once that he had stumbled upon a document of immense significance, Kaine cleared a space for himself on the desk. He opened the file. The sketch at the beginning was enough to steal the air from his lungs. It was an exact replica of the blueprint Ras Haydar had taped to the back of a Janet Jackson poster and passed on to Angela a week ago.

Kaine threw himself back into the swivel chair in front of the desk. He calmed himself with a second brandy, and this time the elixir proved a stimulant. *Expect the unexpected.*

He laid open the file, felt the heat of discovery on the back of his neck and the simultaneous cool of a clear and open mind. The file contained five pages of handwritten notes, the blueprint, and a second sketch. Kaine studied them in reverse order. The second sketch depicted a floor plan of the king's court of Darius the First, a structure as yet uncovered by the site team working at Karmin-Yar, at least prior to Kaine's inauspicious departure. Below the floor plan was written, "See test." Kaine placed the sketch and the city blueprint side by side and then turned to Spire's notes. He read.

I should be thrilled.

I have set foot in the dank and dark caverns that lie beneath the Ancient Archives of Antiquities in even more ancient Istanbul. I am, or so I was told, the first non-national to be thus allowed since World War II. Ironically, my search for Karmin-Yar has ended here. Oh yes, it is true that the American archeologist, my nemesis and equal, Stephen Kaine, has truly located the site. A brilliant find. A deserved find which, without the blueprint of the city, will take a lifetime to unravel. Yet, the lost blueprint is mine. No. Was mine. As were the actual foundation records written in Darius's own hand, and in such condition. Dear God. Now I wish with all my heart that both had been forever lost.

But no, no. This is not the way to start. I must begin, so as to satisfy my indignation, or at least to channel my anger, with the fire theft. For that, ironically, is the crime to which I have contributed.

It is true that throughout history, the fire theft has taken many forms. The classic theft is an act of pure heroism; a sacrifice lent to the achievement of some greater good, and what greater good than the gift of light and warmth? There is, first and foremost, the Greek myth of Prometheus. Upon a horse of silver and gray it is said that Prometheus rode into heaven's domain and, from the very hand of Zeus, stole fire which from that day forth brought eternal light to earth. A powerful tale, to be sure.

The Polynesians have long lived with another version of the story. That of the human, Maui, who by some magic transformed himself into the god Maui. Whereupon, for a single day, he summoned unto himself the strength of all his people, reached daringly into the soul of the sun, and returned with a single flame that achieved much the same result that Prometheus' fistful of fire did.

The Belgians, obviously a people of great imagination, believed in the tale of the cockatoo. The story tells of this great bird storming into the endless night and fooling the moon into believing he was a courier from the sun. The bird, by hook or crook, no one knows for certain, returned sometime later with a bolt of lightning tied around his neck. Same result.

The story evolved. The Germanic tribes of Middle Earth

claimed the right to all fire via a battle of wits with Dradarius, king of all dragons. The ancestors of Lyonesse claimed a similar victory. As the story goes, once defeated, the dragons vowed eternal devotion to these brave folk and thus assured their place as the foremost keepers of the flame. After all, what better source of fire?

The story took on new meaning. Death. Man first took the life of his own kind in a battle over fire. The killing of his own species was from that moment on a curse never to be escaped.

Finally, the definition of fire itself took on new meaning. The diamond was the first symbolic fire. The tribes of southern Africa referred to it as "white fire"; its power was distinguished from that of the real thing by its indestructibility. Medieval folklore called the sapphire "Blue Fire made whole." A sapphire held high in battle and made to reflect the sun was a sign of invincibility; armies were said to have fled in its path, soldiers to be forever struck dumb by the sight.

In ancient China, it was the flesh, called the "fire unleashed." To possess the flesh of a woman was to touch the essence of fire. Yet to possess the flesh of another man's woman warranted the death penalty, though not the offending man's death, rather the offending woman's; a nice slice of hypocrisy.

Gold was late in becoming fire symbolically represented. And here my unfortunate part of the story unfolds. No, Darius the Great was not the first to proclaim gold a deity. That distinction belongs to the Minoans, seafaring rulers of the Mediterranean two thousand years before Christ. Then the Taurus Mountains of Asia Minor glistened with gold, and seeing this spectacle from their ships, the Minoans believed the mountains to be consumed by fire. It was they who first placed gold beside the eternal flame in their temples of fire, but as a tribute to the flame, not as an insult.

Darius, not a perverse man by nature, nonetheless perverted this practice. In one of his Foundation records he went so far as to call his precious gold "the Incarnate Fire." His vehicle for this perversion was the great city that he himself conceived and constructed, Karmin-Yar. Darius, history verifies, taxed his vast empire heavily; tributes were paid in gold and silver. He even managed to create the world's first inflation. How? Because once collected, the gold was never recirculated. The treasure house at Persepolis bulged; old story. Not so the treasure house at Karmin-Yar.

Beads of perspiration tinseled Kaine's forehead as he read the account. He reached for his brandy and paused even as the glass reached his lips. He listened, then strained, certain he had heard the passing of an automobile. He came quickly to his feet. He crossed to the room's one window, the file held zealously in his hand.

Outside, early evening had taken possession of the land. A breeze pushed tall grass in waves; it agitated the pencil-thin branches of the willows along the creek. The gray shadows of Kaine's late-afternoon arrival were now pockets of black. He hastened into the living room. From his vantage point at the window, the road was clearly visible. And quiet now, though remnants of dust sparkled in the sun's last light, telling him his hearing had not deceived him.

He reclaimed his chair in the library. He read, almost as if the words had been written in his own hand.

The conquered tribes of the Persian's northern empire were nomadic, hateful people. Darius wasted a fourth of his army keeping them in order. Yet, it was worth the trouble. Nomadic, the tribes were also the possessors of great wealth, for gold was an easily mined commodity in areas of the Black and Caspian seas. The tribes of the north paid their tributes while openly swearing retribution.

To haul hundreds of ingots of gold eleven hundred miles to his own backyard in Persepolis or Susa made no sense to Darius. Inviting the nomads to plunder his Karmin-Yar treasure house made less sense yet. Therefore, Darius followed the Minoan's lead. He chose the fire temple, the house of the eternal flame and inviolate even to the nomadic tribes of the north, in which to secrete his gold. It was an act of supreme cunning, though an unspeakable breach of all the religious tenets of his time. And yes, the gold was there when the earthquake of 412 B.C. changed the coastline of the Black Sea and effectively wiped Karmin-Yar from the face of the earth.

The enclosed drawing details the floor plan of the king's court of the palace of Darius, named Tachara after its counterpart in Persepolis. It is the key to the fire theft I have unwittingly helped perpetrate. The enclosed plan is much like the plan used in the great shrine in the temple of Angkor, and as deceptive. Yes, and further reminiscent of the secrets surrounding the Potola in Tibet.

A similarity between Karmin-Yar and Angkor, the Hindu temple city hidden in the Kampuchean jungle, and the Dalai Lama's palace in Tibet? Unlike the Karmin-Yar blueprint given to Angela on the day of the ferry disaster, the original here gave no indication of an underground link between the treasure house and the fire temple. Kaine tapped his memory. At Angkor, legend suggested an undiscovered passageway that supposedly allowed the spirit of the great King Suryavarnam II access to the outer world. At the Potola a similar legend flourished: the existence of a subterranean tunnel reputedly linking the palace with the utopian society of Shangri-La.

Kaine didn't speculate. He turned to the last page of Jurgen Spire's notes. It was written in a different hand, less readable. A purple stain discolored it. Wine, Kaine guessed. The account began abruptly.

They will steal the incarnate fire of Karmin-Yar, and I am helpless to stop them. What plans they have for the gold I honestly do not know. Is this a confession or a meager

attempt at purging myself of guilt? I imagine in some respects both. They threatened my life, which left me unaffected. They threatened my reputation, which, I confess,
affected me greatly. I know that it is my everlasting bane
to carry upon my shoulders the lack of courage I displayed
in resisting them. Them?

I know not the men responsible, only their henchmen. I
know only that Dreyfuss is involved; I should never have
shared the blueprint with him. Never. That dispirited fag-
got, now chief archeologist where once a man of Stephen
Kaine's character prevailed. Dreyfuss. Maurice Dreyfuss. I
should have ruined the son of a bitch the moment I discovered he was involved with that anthropology professor
in Paris. . . .

Outside, Kaine heard a rustling sound that was surely not the
wind. And then a sound that just as surely was footsteps.

He jumped to his feet. Acting purely on instinct, he replaced
the first four pages of Spire's account, and the original blueprint
of the city of Karmin-Yar, back into the file labeled "The Fire Theft."
He stored this again in the top drawer under F. The last page of
the account, containing Spire's assertions about the theft, and the
floor plan of the king's court, he slipped into the file labeled "Dolmens of Drenthe." Kaine closed the drawer.

He took the brandy glass in his hand, walked casually into the
living room, and then out the back door onto the deck.

The policeman was young. His uniform was dark brown and
ill-fitting. He wore a fur-lined cap with an insignia on the upturned
bill, and held a nine-millimeter pistol at arm's length. He sited down
the barrel at Kaine's head. He was excited, shocked, and scared;
he bounced from one foot to the other, breathing hard.

Kaine in return opened his arms and hands in a gesture of
innocence and curiosity. Inside, his heart throbbed, his mouth was
bone dry.

"Don't move," the boy shouted in a dialect Kaine understood
only by the universal fervor in his voice. Then he shouted louder,
"Captain Medvedev. Captain Medvedev. I have him."

The police detail was six in number. Like spooked rhinos they scrambled through the tall grass surrounding the house. Cut from the same mold as the first policeman, they wielded similar pistols and similar masks of inexperience.

Not so Captain Medvedev. He was a fleshy, obese man. He wore black leather gloves. He carried a bamboo stave. And he was in no hurry; with each step he slapped the stave against his thigh. His smile, one of irony and satisfaction, spread thick jowls in layers below his chin. He looked out from behind round steel-rimmed glasses. The bill of his cap was upturned, exposing a pronounced widow's peak. He smoked.

"You are Kaine," he said in English. The words seemed to ooze from his mouth. He gave no indication of calling off his youth brigade; their guns were trained on Kaine even now. "You are an American archeologist seeking a Soviet counterpart, citizen Jurgen Spire. Where is he, Mr. Kaine? Where is citizen Jurgen Spire?"

Kaine had already committed himself to lying. He said, "Jurgen is expecting me."

"That is an answer?"

"We spoke on the phone earlier this afternoon—"

"From the Goblin's Hut. That we are aware of. Where, I will ask again, is citizen Spire?"

"He gave me directions to his house. I arrived twenty minutes ago. Jurgen wasn't here." Kaine's arms were still spread at his side; surprisingly, the glass had taken on a terrific weight. "He told me to make myself at home."

Medvedev blew smoke through his nose; his lips were ruby red and slick with moisture. "Odd, don't you think? The host leaving like that. Rude, some would say."

Kaine didn't blink. "Jurgen mentioned some errands he needed to run."

"Run?"

"To do. To get done."

"Mmm." Medvedev adjusted his spectacles. "Allowing his guest to walk nine point two kilometers through unfamiliar country."

Sweat rolled from under Kaine's arms. "It was a beautiful day. I didn't mind."

"You noticed nothing unusual on the road?"

"I stayed off the road. Jurgen suggested it."

Medvedev was interested. "Why?"

Kaine shrugged. "Guns make me nervous."

"Do they? Good." Now Medvedev stared; the fatty folds of his cheeks made minute slits of his eyes. He drew on his cigarette. Finally, he made an exaggerated gesture with his hand, like a conductor bringing a great symphony to a close, and the six guns withdrew.

"You have my itinerary," Kaine said, his own arms dropping. "The visit with Soviet citizen Jurgen Spire is on it." Then he lied. "My itinerary is also on hand with the English government and the American embassy in London. I'm expected back in that city tomorrow morning."

A blush of deep scarlet washed over Medvedev's face. Two lumbering steps brought him chest to chest with Kaine. Sweat beaded upon the Soviet's brow; his breath reeked. He grabbed a handful of Kaine's hair and forced his head up. With surprising speed, Medvedev drew the nine-millimeter pistol from the holster at his side and thrust the barrel beneath Kaine's chin. He cocked the hammer. His upper lip trembled. "You may be delayed, Mr. Kaine," he whispered. "You may be delayed."

24 Kaine spent an uncomfortable night in a holding cell in Elistara. At noon on the following day, the American consul from Simferopol was finally called in. His name was Fred Collins. He sat together with Kaine in a dimly lit room across a wooden table from Captain Medvedev. The police had been busy. Already evidence from the explosion had confirmed the identity of the victim and his vehicle.

Fred Collins was not the ally Kaine had hoped for. In fact, he provided documentation of Kaine's relationship with Jurgen Spire, their mutual—or as Collins put it, diverse—interests in Karmin-Yar, and also the "facts" surrounding Kaine's dismissal as chief archeologist of the project.

"You and he go back a long way," Collins said. "But it sounds like you come from two different schools of thought entirely."

"Our methods varied," Kaine said. "Our goals were the same."

"Really now? Characterized how, exactly?"

Exasperated, Kaine said, "Historical facts correctly interpreted."

"You were rivals," Medvedev broke in coldly. "You were fired from the most important project of your career. A project which he knew more about than you did. A project which most of the archeological community believed he should have been in charge of. You killed him because of it."

Collins held up a hand. "Hold on now, Captain. You'll concede that, though jealousy is often a motive of considerable impact, it is also a tough one to support when it comes to evidence."

The bartender from the Goblin's Hut was called in and questioned. He repeated Kaine's conversation with Spire most accurately. Then added, "They whispered a lot. It sounded like hush-hush business. Very important."

"Which proves nothing," Kaine said, looking to Collins and seeing that the consul was in no hurry to lend his support again.

"Which proves urgency," Medvedev said when the witness was gone. "Which indicates need, which suggests desire."

A phone call was placed to Detective Superintendent Preble in Dover. It was put on speakers. Medvedev conducted the interview with a jocularity Kaine didn't think the Soviet possessed, peer to peer. Preble confirmed Kaine's involvement in the ferry accident. Ras Haydar's name was mentioned, as was Angela's. When Kaine heard Preble describing the contents of the metal tube Angela had been given, he cringed. Preble made it clear that Kaine's visit to the Crimea was directly related to the blueprint, and that Kaine had felt certain Spire was responsible for its existence.

"Whose side are you on?" Kaine shouted.

Medvedev intervened at once. "Another outburst of that nature and you will be bound and gagged."

"I don't think that's necessary," Collins said mildly. Then, glancing at Kaine, he asked, "Is it?"

The interview with Preble was concluded.

Soviet Captain Medvedev announced that they would await the final results of the forensic investigation currently in progress at the bomb site.

"And that will be when?" Fred Collins said meekly.

"Oh, by tomorrow morning, almost certainly." Medvedev smiled, warming to the American consul.

"As a gesture of goodwill, Captain, I would like to request that Mr. Kaine be allowed to remain in my custody until then, with my assurance that we will, well, stay within shouting distance of your office."

"So be it," Medvedev agreed. "This office at eight tomorrow morning. Sharp," he said tersely. "Until then."

"Blowfish, leech, mealworm, asshole!" Collins spat as they walked out the station door and into the street. As if to stem the tide of his fury, he jammed his clenched fists into his pockets. "That, by the way, represents the Soviet police at its very best. They're bred in some sewer in Siberia, I think."

Perplexed, Kaine tried protesting. "Then why didn't you—"

"Don't say a fucking thing, mister." Collins threw open the door of his car, a mistreated Triumph Spitfire. When Kaine was seated next to him, he said. "Don't question my methods, Kaine. Don't ever question my methods. You're the stupid one in this car. Act like it and keep quiet."

Collins slammed on his brakes in front of the Sula Hotel. He tossed Kaine an icy look. "We've got a room. Stay in it. I've got things to arrange and not a hell of a lot of time to do it. I'll pick you up here at six, on the nose. Be in the lobby; that's as close as I come to a house call. Understood? We'll start with dinner."

Collins was true to his word. He arrived on time and seemed less bellicose. They drove in silence to the Café de Crimea, the first restaurant where Kaine had sought out Jurgen Spire. The workday was over, and the noise level had risen accordingly. Flames swelled in the central fireplace. The consul believed in the politics of local tradition and ordered beer. Kaine settled for vodka straight up.

From their window seat, Kaine studied the harbor. A dockside crane dropped a last container into the hold of a Turkish freighter. The ship's running lights splashed yellow light upon the backs of three or four deckhands. Single funnels fore and aft belched smoke into a growing fog bank. Kaine looked wistfully away.

Their drinks arrived. "You won't be drinking," Collins said, resting an open palm over Kaine's shot glass. "The last thing you'll need in your system tonight is alcohol."

"If you say so."

"I say so." Collins downed the shot himself and winced. "You saw Spire die?"

"It wasn't pretty."

"At least it was quick," Collins replied. "As soon as Captain Medvedev's forensic people finish their work, they'll place you at the scene and that, my friend, will be that. President Bush won't be able to intervene on your behalf. My problem is, I'm receiving mixed messages from people in high places. Some would very much like to see you right where you are—"

"Who?"

Collins put on his best diplomatic mask, giving away nothing. "On the other hand, some think you deserve better."

"Who are you talking about, Consul?"

"So," Collins said briskly, "in a moment, I'll be ordering another drink. You'll excuse yourself for the rest room; do so in front of the waiter. The rest room is downstairs. Hanging on the inside of the door is a mackinaw. Put it on. Inside the pocket is a stocking cap. Put it on. There's a door next to the bathroom. It's for employees. Use it. Walk straight down the stairs to the pier and then to that freighter you've been looking at so longingly."

"Why?"

"Because it's going take you the hell away from the Crimea, and I hope you understand that you won't be welcomed back." Collins sipped his beer; his knee bounced under the table, betraying the anxiety he was trying so unsuccessfully to conceal. "The freighter has agreed to take you on as an additional hand. There will be a man waiting on deck. He'll be wearing a stocking hat exactly like yours. He'll get you on and he'll get you off. That is unless someone else has paid them more money than I have, to see that something goes awry; and I should tell you that it's been known to happen."

"Why?"

"Because loyalty isn't one of the top ten virtues in this business, that's why."

"I mean, why are you doing this?"

Collins ignored the question. "The freighter there is destined for Istanbul. Your old stomping grounds."

"I'm not exactly welcome in Istanbul."

"No, you're not." Collins smiled. "You're not exactly welcome anywhere on the whole godforsaken Turkish mainland. You'll have no papers, and the American consulate there won't even acknowledge your existence. But you won't be wanted for murder there either, and nobody gets extradited back into the Soviet Union. Not for any reason."

"And if I'm shot trying to escape?"

"Then I can go back to Simferopol and do what I do best," the American consul said guilelessly. "Play golf and drink vodka."

Kaine nodded. "I'll need money."

"In the other pocket of the mackinaw, assuming it hasn't been stolen. A thousand Turkish liras."

"Fifty dollars," Kaine said dubiously.

"It'll be enough." Collins held up his empty glass to the waiter. "Once you're on shore, your friend from the freighter will find you a taxi. If all goes according to plan, your driver will be sympathetic to your cause. Whatever the hell that cause might be. And don't tell me, I personally am not the sympathetic type."

"Who put you up to this?" Kaine asked.

"A friend of yours," was all Collins would say. He slipped back in his chair.

"A friend?"

Collins didn't answer. Instead, he reached into his coat pocket and produced Kaine's wallet, passport, pocket watch, and a pewter chess piece in the shape of a dragon.

"You may need these," Collins said. Kaine clutched his watch—the wallet, he noticed, was empty. "And they weren't easy to come by, just in case you're thinking Captain Medvedev suffered a moment of goodhearted weakness. He didn't."

"Thanks."

"Don't thank me." They saw the waiter approaching with a beer in his hand. "Now do as I said. And have some faith, Mr. Kaine. Have some faith."

The waiter set the beer in front of Collins, and Kaine mumbled something about the rest rooms. Collins translated, and the waiter tossed his head in the direction of the stairs.

At the head of the stairs, Kaine glanced back. Collins responded by holding up his beer, tipping his head, and grinning feebly.

The bathroom reeked of urine. The mackinaw was huge and Kaine pulled it on over his own coat. He hated stocking hats; this one was olive green and oil-stained, and there was no mirror in which to examine himself. A rubber band held the liras in a bundle. The stairs Collins had referred to were wooden, and they traversed the side of the escarpment in the same fashion as a fire escape descends the side of a tenement house in London or New York. The handrail was loose and wavered in the wind.

At the foot of the steps lay a narrow dirt path. The path led to the waterfront. When Kaine heard the echo of his feet on the concrete, he had to call on every ounce of his restraint not to break into a run. Instead, he thrust his hands in his pockets, hunched his shoulders, and walked. The Turkish freighter lay at anchor three hundred yards away. A swirl of mist caused its running lights to sway and quiver. The harbor crane lowered a last pallet into the hold. Its boom arm swung in the direction of another vessel. From the water, Kaine smelled diesel. A shift in the wind wafted an aroma of frying fish from shore.

A man driving a forklift pulled up alongside him. His voice rang with irritation; he gestured to the unlit cigarette in his mouth and threw up his hands. Kaine went through the motions of searching his pockets for matches, then shrugged, and held up his palms apologetically. Then he did something bold and, he would think later, stupid. He threw a finger out toward the pier and the freighter, and then used his thumb in what he hoped would be taken as the universal request for a ride.

The operator crumbled a half dozen indistinguishable words but didn't immediately drive off, so Kaine jumped aboard one of the vehicle's horizontal forks. They sped off.

The freighter was a four-hundred-ton vessel with many thousands of miles of wear on it. The hull hinted of a past coat of blue paint. The word *Karaman* had been superimposed in black across the side. A gangplank extended from the bow end of the main deck to the pier, and the forklift drew to a halt a dozen paces from it. Kaine jumped off. The operator accepted a silent wave as a sign of gratitude.

No sooner had the forklift pulled away than a man was calling down to Kaine from the head of the gangplank; his stocking cap was a dirty olive color. He used both hands to express the urgency of their situation. Kaine took a last glance back toward shore. A glow of muted orange emanated from inside the Café de Crimea. Smoke curled invitingly from the chimney. Suddenly, a wave of fear overwhelmed Kaine, fear born of a situation over which he had lost all control.

Yet not even this fear could compel him to walk back into the hands of Captain Medvedev and the Crimean police. Kaine turned and sprang up the gangplank. The sailor greeted him with a traditional bearhug. The grit and grime of manual labor covered him; it hovered like an aura around him.

"In five minutes you would have been stranded." His accent, excited and urgent, was one Kaine had grown familiar with over the last five years, one he now found comforting. The man's laugh, strained and fitful, surprised him. "Plan on a long night. You dressed warm. Smart. We've got the watch. We'll get to Istanbul about the time your Crimean friends start to panic."

An enclosed bridge deck was positioned at the stern end of the vessel. The sailor raised a hand in that direction, and must have received some positive signal in reply, for a moment later he and Kaine were hoisting the gangplank aboard. Jets of smoke erupted from the twin funnels at the rear of the ship. A verbal order was issued over the ship's loudspeaker; it unnerved Kaine that he didn't understand it. Not that Turkish was a second language, necessarily—he was better versed in Greek and Latin—but after five years he could make out most of what he heard. His companion led him toward the bow end of the ship. Two small derrick cranes were positioned astride the sealed holds, and they found a protected niche at the base of one of these.

"Your name for now is Silvanus. Lukas Silvanus," the sailor said. From the pocket of a heavy yellow slicker, he passed Kaine a well-worn seaman's purse. Inside were the papers and identification of one Lukas Silvanus. A stained and cracked photograph showed a dour, unshaven man in his thirties. A stocking hat worn low on his brow was the one feature likening him in any way to Kaine. "You've been drunk for twenty-four hours. You overstayed your leave. The first officer is very unhappy. Fortunately, making haste out of Soviet waters will come before any reprimand. If the fog is anything like it was last night, the reprimand will have to wait until we reach Istanbul. If not, he will have to be bought off. You have money?"

"A thousand liras," Kaine admitted. The sailor groaned, regret knotting his tired face. "The police confiscated everything else," was all Kaine could say.

A black cigarette materialized from the sailor's coat. He shielded a butane lighter with his hand. A true Turk, he offered the lit cigarette to his guest. Kaine shook his head.

"You'll smoke by the time this night is over," the sailor predicted; he had still not offered his own name, and Kaine didn't inquire.

The freighter made a wide circle and plunged into a shroud woven of fog, a bitter chill, and a moonless night. "What happened to the real Lukas Silvanus?" Kaine asked.

"Don't worry," the sailor assured him. "Lukas has been in worse situations."

25

Kaine froze, but he never did resort to the cigarettes.

The worst of it was the sensation of being trapped in a vacuum. If they were moving at all, Kaine couldn't detect it. The fog not only robbed one of the sense of sight, it also destroyed one's sense of equilibrium, of motion. The one evidence of their crossing was the remote and frightening contact with a second freighter. The ships were within fifty yards of one another when a halo of spotlights unexpectedly materialized. A horn sounded, a quick and unnerving shriek. Then a second horn emitted a sharper and more piercing scream because it came from the transmitter directly overhead; the sailor at Kaine's side merely hung his head and crossed himself. He resigned himself to a fitful sleep.

Kaine, in return, listened to the sound of the sailor's heavy breathing. He took out his pocket watch; it wasn't the time that interested him, it was the comfort of the gold, of the snow-white face, of the muted ticking. Angela had already put her claim on the watch; she would wait until he was gone, of course. "Gone" meaning dead. Kaine considered that a fair arrangement. He had taught her about the time zones and the conversion charts, and Angela had, in return, set her own wristwatch on Greenwich mean time. It was a simple connection they had forged as father and daughter, a bridge. But then all life was a series of bridges, wasn't it? Kaine thought. Some without foundation, some as tenuous as a spider's web, some as everlasting as gold. He missed her. He would have given anything, even his watch, for word of her safety.

Dawn was marked by a change in the color of the fog. The black mass took on a ceiling of purple. When the ceiling blushed pink, the sailor stirred. Kaine's watch reminded him that in Dodman Point it was only one forty-six; Angela and Danielle were surely fast asleep. In Istanbul, however, it was four forty-six and a new day was fast approaching. Kaine snapped the watch shut and the sleeping sailor jumped. Unhappy, he aroused himself with a cigarette.

"The fog is lifting," was all he said.

Within minutes, a drowsy, ironclad sea revealed itself, land masses closing in on three sides. The Black Sea fed eventually into a narrow strait called the Bosphorus. Europe stood on the western shore, a wooded, rolling expanse; the plateau of Asia Minor stood to the east. Kaine followed his companion to the bow. A cathartic breeze swept over him. It carried upon it the scent and spindrift of the sea, and Kaine inhaled greedily. Every muscle in his body ached, and he realized it was as much the tension of the crossing as it was the cramped quarters they had kept all night.

For a moment he forgot his status as an escapee from the Soviet Union. A palace from the days of the Ottoman empire overlooked an eighteenth-century fishing village aglow with the flames and smoke of a hundred morning fires. Oddly, neither palace nor village looked out of place. Suspension bridges and ferries linked East and West. It was dawn and already the strait seethed with barges and frigates and trawlers. Dolmus boats dashed among them like taxis in New York City.

Kaine had traveled to Istanbul many times. It remained a mystery to him. The influences were overwhelming. The Romans had left their arches, the Greeks their columns, the Byzantines their great domes. The Turks had filled the skyline with minarets and mosques, and now skyscrapers that could easily have been imported from midtown Manhattan. The morning sun tinged them all with its blood-red fire.

The harbor was home to one of the oldest fishing fleets on earth, trawlers and yawls and ketches stacked one upon the other and squeezing through narrow channels toward the open sea. The harbor was home to one of the filthiest fleets of freighters on earth, each jockeying for miles of docking space and spewing clouds of black into the diminishing fog. And puttering among them all, one of the most efficient tugboat fleets on earth managed to sandwich passenger vessels and tankers into spaces meant for steamers and cargo ships.

The freighter *Karaman* plunged into this melee. Around it rose a deafening cacophony. Of voices shouting and engines roaring, of whistles and horns piercing the air and bells clanging, of water moving and resisting, of cranes straining, of metal thrashing against metal, of wood splitting and cracking.

For every sound, a smell of equal potency seemed familiarly attached—wood rotting, diesel burning, garbage festering, sweat pouring off the bodies of stevedores and crewmen and longshoremen. Exhaust fumes spewing skyward, lamb and fish boiling, coffee brewing, the stench of sheep and goats and cattle languishing in pens on shore.

A tugboat singlehandedly escorted the freighter to a dock site on the Asian side of Istanbul. The police were waiting. Kaine saw them. He counted seven in uniform, and wondered how many others were disguised as civilians. The sailor at his side saw them at the same moment.

"Don't panic," he said. "They're harbor police, not security."

"There's a difference?"

The sailor used his stocking cap to mop a sheen of sweat off his brow. "Some."

"What?"

"Drugs mainly," the sailor said without conviction.

"Coming from the Crimea into Istanbul?" Kaine's tone took a sarcastic turn. "You're right. There's no reason to panic."

Pallets of cargo emerged in huge nets from the freighter's hold. A harbor crane hoisted them from the deck to the dock. Forklifts ferried the pallets to the boxcars of a waiting train. Two of the policemen boarded the freighter via the gangplank.

"We go now or we don't go at all," the sailor said. "Follow me."

He jumped aboard one of the pallets, his hands clinging to the net. At the exact moment when the net went taut and the pallet began to rise from the deck, Kaine joined him.

The net swung wildly, one instant high above the deck, then twisting above the water, finally dropping gracefully to the dock. The sailor joined the stevedores in the task of removing the net. He spoke with them in hushed whispers, then laughed, slapping his side. He came back, took Kaine by the arm, and spoke close to his ear.

"Not drugs after all," he said. "Not stowaways or fugitives or murder suspects. That ship we almost rammed last night? Remember? It was a Soviet steamer. The filthy beggars filed a complaint against our captain. Negligence."

Kaine felt sick with relief. The sailor had thrown his arm around him and they were ambling toward the train tracks, two sailors with a few hours of shore leave.

When the police were behind them, he returned his grip to Kaine's arm and their pace quickened. They entered an open market on the wharf, melding with merchants preparing for a day of brutal competition. Kaine was bombarded by the pungent smells of curry and garlic, of animal droppings and coal fires, of collusion and cunning.

That such a tumultuous din could persist at such an early hour struck him more than anything. Donkeys brayed, pigs snorted, sheep whined, men and women shouted and laughed. The sailor moved doggedly toward a line of idling taxis.

"Your driver's name is Lenci."

"You know him?"

"Only enough not to trust him."

Lenci's cab was a yellow station wagon. He had painted a large orange star on each front door. He and the sailor fell into a deep bear hug, but Kaine could see that they were both in a hurry. They exchanged muted whispers that Kaine could put no meaning to. Then Lenci raced around to his side of the cab. The sailor opened Kaine's door for him. He whispered, "Be careful."

"I will." Kaine embraced him. "Stay well."

"And you."

Lenci didn't ask for directions. He plunged into the throngs. The wharf gave way to an old business district and streets of cobblestone. The traffic was sobering. Beyond Kaine's window the city put on its day face.

"Your name is Lenci. Anything else I should know?" Kaine asked in time, his Turkish ragged and out of practice.

"For one, I speak English, at least better than you do whatever language it was that you were just butchering," Lenci replied. He was a large man. His head was thick and brutish, unshaved and sunburnt. He wore a skull cap over a stubble of black hair. There was an odor in the taxi and it came from its driver. "I am also a man who trusts his instincts. I drive a taxi. But since there are ten thousand taxi drivers in Istanbul, I do small favors on the side, as well. Good enough?"

Kaine turned out a sardonic grin. "More than enough."

"Excellent."

"Where are we going?"

"I was thinking about something to eat. For me as well as you, unless of course your unlikely passage across the Black Sea included a complimentary meal of some kind."

"I ate yesterday sometime, but I can't remember what," Kaine admitted. "Food sounds good. But I need to use a telephone first."

"Why?" Lenci asked. "You have relatives here in Istanbul? I wasn't told."

"What were you told?"

"To feed you, to clothe you, to see to your transportation. Simple and to the point."

"Told by whom?"

"An American. I was paid handsomely. Very handsomely, so I understand that your problems are of the big variety."

"An American? What American? From the embassy?"

Lenci didn't answer. He stopped the car on a side street in front of a small market and a butcher shop. There was a public phone on the wall between them. Lenci provided the coinage Kaine needed to dial the operator. The taxi driver was not pleased, and it had nothing to do with the money.

"If I may be permitted a bit of unsolicited advice," he said. Kaine stopped halfway out the door. "Whoever it is you're calling, do watch what you say."

There were two million people in Istanbul and the phone system was relatively sophisticated. Kaine's call to Dover took less than five minutes. It rang once, as if Preble had been standing by the phone waiting.

And though there was nothing remarkable about his greeting, neither, however, did it reflect the two hours' difference in time zones. "Superintendent Preble speaking."

"It's Kaine."

"Good Lord. Calling from where?"

Kaine didn't immediately respond to the question. Instead, he said, "For someone who said I might need a friend sometime, you weren't much of one with the Crimean police."

"What did you expect exactly? For me to lie to a law enforcement agency that already knew the answers to the questions they were asking? Exactly how much help would that have been to you?"

"How did they know?"

"You were arrested on a Monday night. It took the American consul in Simferopol how long to get to you? Almost fifteen hours, if my calculations are correct. What do you think he was doing all that time? Just so you won't feel left out in the dark, I'll tell you. He was finding out everything there was to know about you. And I'll tell you why. To see just how bloody far to stick his neck out." Preble regained his breath. "How bad is it?"

At this moment, Kaine's only ally was a taxi driver whose credentials he'd been warned against. Which suggested a lack of places to turn. Preble had not made excuses for his blunt behavior with the Crimean Captain Medvedev, only a candid explanation. Yet Fred Collins, the American consul Preble was berating, had in fact stuck his neck out a considerable way. Wasn't Preble aware of that?

Up to this moment, Kaine had given Preble credit for having effected his escape. Now he wasn't sure.

"I'm in Istanbul," Kaine said directly.

"Impossible."

"Then you didn't know." Now Kaine's confusion was coupled with suspicion. "I got out of the Crimea on a Turkish freighter."

"How?"

Kaine decided against mentioning the American consul. "A friend of a friend," he said.

Preble was mute for a brief, uncomfortable moment. "You're on the Turkish government's hit list. You said that yourself."

"I'm calling from a phone outside a butcher shop. There's a beggar on every corner and a mosque on every block. It's Istanbul."

"Your leverage is gone, you realize," Preble told him. "You've got nowhere to go. According to Captain Medvedev, the only meaningful information you may have acquired comes from a bloke everyone thinks you killed. Your ability to walk into the American embassy in Istanbul or London or anywhere else for that matter went up in smoke when Jurgen Spire died. It doesn't matter what kind of information you've discovered. As a matter of fact, as the prime suspect in Spire's death, you'd probably serve as a natural point of cooperation for two governments that are making history out of cooperating with one another for the first time in decades. I hate to make so much sense."

"I gave you direct evidence implicating Louis Mathers, the U.S. ambassador to your country, in the murder of one of your countrymen. What have you done about it?"

"First Skipper Tanner Thorpe was Scottish. Don't confuse the two."

Kaine was incredulous. "What?"

Preble chuckled. "We're putting together a case against Mathers based on your photo. When your daughter comes forward to confirm it, then we'll have something to act on. In the meantime, the ambassador is indisposed. On a brief vacation, his office says. As he was on the day Thorpe was killed. Do you get the picture, Kaine? I need to know where your daughter is."

"And Colonel Turnbull? On vacation, too?"

Preble's sigh had a fatalistic quality to it that Kaine didn't believe. "The man has connections on top of connections," Preble said. "He was out of the country an hour before you and I talked the other day."

"And you don't know where to?"

"Tell me your plan," Preble replied. "I'll see what I can do to help."

Kaine thought a moment, mostly about hanging up. Then the image of Jurgen Spire's dacha passed before him. The intimacy, the innocence, the solitude. His library, his books, his research. And finally, the "Fire Theft" journal. Which led him to say, "There's an anthropology professor at the University of Paris. I need his name, and I need it in an hour."

"What? Why, for God's sake? Have you lost your senses? There's probably fifteen anthropology professors at the University of Paris."

"This one gave a lecture tour in Leningrad sometime in the last ten years. I just need his name. It's important."

"Important how?"

"When I have the name, I'll tell you how. You'll hear from me again in one hour."

"I need to know where your daughter is, Kaine, and I need to know now."

"I'm going to get some breakfast," Kaine replied. "I'll call back later."

He hung up.

The operator returned to the line. Now he gave her the phone number of the White Rain motel in Dodman Point, in Cornwall. He asked for Danielle's room, then let it ring at least fifteen times before losing count.

26 Not only had Danielle avoided the beaches, as Kaine had suggested, but she had taken it upon herself to rent a small cabin five and a half miles west along the bank of the Fal River. She had, however, not given up the motel room in Dodman Point, nor had she informed the manager of any intent to do so. She had rented a car.

She felt safe. The cabins were out of season, and, as far as she could tell, only one other was rented. The occupants were an older couple; the man wore a felt hat and sat by the riverbank with a fishing line dangling in the water. Every morning, the woman walked in the opposite direction, into the woods. They were the types who nodded their heads pleasantly but kept to themselves.

The river had tributaries, more like streams, lined with willows and cottonwoods. Angela and Danielle confined themselves to these. Angela explored; there were tiny dams created by fallen branches and enterprising beavers. Well, at least one beaver. Angela had spotted him upon the bank one morning and made a study of his work habits all that day. Danielle borrowed a deck chair from the cabin and found a shady spot next to the stream. She worried most about the pilot who had ferried them from Folkestone to Dodman Point. Kaine had fed her anxiety with his questions about the man's government connections. Why in the hell had she spoon-fed this complete stranger knowledge of the White Rain motel? He had literally carried their bags into their room for them. If nothing else, the move from the motel to the cabin had given her some sense of well-being.

That morning, Danielle paid a visit to the old couple in the cabin down from them. The woman was preparing for her walk. The man was sewing a hole in his creel and packing marshmallows for bait.

"My dad called marshmallows the best bait you could find that didn't come straight out of the ground," Danielle told them.

"Especially if you have no intention, nor desire, to catch any fish," the woman answered. She laughed, but her mate only scowled.

"That's a pretty young lady you're keeping company with," he told Danielle.

"Thank you. That's Angela," Danielle replied. "She has this urge to drive into Tregony, farther up the river. She thinks we can have lunch in some cozy diner. I was wondering about the road."

"Terrible," the woman replied.

"Not with that little thing you're driving, I wouldn't," her husband added.

The woman snatched a set of keys from the kitchen counter. She tossed them halfway across the room to Danielle. "Take our truck. We're not going anywhere for at least a week."

"You will be back by then, won't you?" the fisherman said with raised eyebrows and a crooked grin.

"Promise," Danielle said.

She was pleased. Her expression was a childish one she had often used with great success on Kaine. As she walked back to their own cabin, his face filled her head. He was smiling that god-damn smile that she yearned for and therefore loathed. She felt a stirring inside, one she hadn't felt for some time, one she had patiently, painfully, almost surgically cut out of her life. She stopped dead in the middle of the parking lot and clenched her fist, willing away her longing for him, cursing the wetness she felt between her legs. The next time you need a man, he'll need you for the same reasons, she told herself. It was a litany. The next time you allow yourself to be that vulnerable, he'll want the same things you want. The next time . . . The next time . . . When she unclenched her fists, she was still wet and still wanted him, and realized it didn't hurt so bad after all.

The moment Angela climbed into the old couple's truck she sensed her mother's distraction. There was a distant look on her face that Angela couldn't translate. Her mom drove in silence, which was not like her at all. If Danielle felt Angela's eyes upon her, she didn't yield, keeping her own eyes on the road.

"I need something to read," she said. "Maybe they'll have a bookstore in this place."

"You haven't been dating that jerk from the bank for a while," Angela said. "How come?"

"Maybe we could find a cassette for that new tape player of yours," Danielle replied. "Anybody new you've been wanting to get?"

"Do people sometimes date just to date?"

"It's called insecurity, babe. When you're forty, you wonder if anybody wants you anymore. At least, anyone worth having."

"Was Dad worth having?"

Danielle stared at the road, biting her lower lip. "The price was too high."

"But—"

"End of discussion."

"Do you want him back?"

"End of discussion, I said."

"You do, don't you."

The café in Tregony perched on a steep cliff. The river below tumbled along a path of huge boulders, found refuge in clear deep pools, and then continued on at its harried pace. The weather was cool, but mother and daughter both felt adventurous; the man who was both waiter and maître d' led them out onto the deck. He seated them at the railing. A breathtaking view of the river and the farmland beyond reminded Danielle of a Corot painting.

They were halfway through the huge chef salads they had both ordered when Danielle saw the man who had flown them to this lonely, isolated part of England. He was seated inside by the window contemplating a menu.

Danielle dropped her fork, then covered the side of her face with her hand.

"What is it?" Angela said in alarm. "You look like—"

"Don't look back. We've been followed. By the man who flew us here from Dover."

"Our pilot? The photographer? But . . ." Angela had liked the man. He had pointed out landmarks to her. He had let her peer through the camera and even steer the plane for a few minutes. He had called her mom "miss." He wasn't like that man in the car, the one who had tried driving them off the road. He wasn't like that at all. Was he? "What are we going to do, Mom? What are we going to do now?"

"I don't know, babe. I don't know yet."

"Profitable?" Lenci asked when Kaine had returned to the cab. Kaine assumed he was referring to the phone calls he had just made.

"Educational," he replied.

"Not the same thing," Lenci scoffed. He shook his huge head and belched. "Never mind. Let's get food in our stomachs before you do any more thinking."

They ate boiled lamb, dates, and cold rice at a diner owned, ostensibly, by Lenci's uncle. The diner was perched on a hill at the outskirts of Asian Istanbul and looked down upon a thriving bazaar. An undistinguishable odor permeated the air, and Kaine realized that it came from the vaporous cloud rising above the bazaar. In the distance, pencil-thin minarets scored the horizon like spears.

After eating, Kaine sat outside at a wooden table with a mug of strong black coffee. He borrowed a paper and pencil from one of Lenci's cousins. The letter he composed was addressed to Maurice Dreyfuss, the new chief archeologist at Karmin-Yar. Kaine intended delivering the letter in person. He realized that Preble was right, that he was no longer in a position to present the information he had obtained at Jurgen Spire's dacha to the authorities. Still, Kaine realized, he was not without leverage. Spire had given him some, in particular where Maurice Dreyfuss was concerned. A last piece of information was needed, and Kaine was counting on Detective Superintendent Preble to provide it. He assumed the information would not come without a trade-off of some kind, and Kaine only had one thing to trade, Angela's whereabouts. That wouldn't work.

The diner was not equipped with a telephone; Kaine walked across the road to a cobbled street lined with booksellers and textile shops. He was forced to spend his first lira "renting" a phone from one of the former.

Preble was waiting. He said, "Your man's name is Georges Tournier. He's the assistant dean of anthropology at the University of Paris. He's forty-five years old. He's visited Leningrad twice. Once on a research project, a fossil find of some kind or another in 1978. And then again in 1984, a lecture tour with a combined group of anthropologists and archeologists. I assume that's the tour you're referring to."

"Who was your source?"

"I have many, Professor Kaine, and I had to spend a few favors getting this. If there's another anthropologist at the esteemed Paris University with the qualifications you mentioned then you'll have to do the research yourself."

"That won't be necessary," Kaine replied.

"Happy to hear it," Preble said magnanimously, "because we have a more immediate problem. We presented our copy of Angela's Polaroid to your friend at the Chatham Institute of Technology . . . what's his name?"

Kaine felt a knot tightening in his throat. "Stone."

"Quite right. Daniel Stone. At any rate, we presented Dr. Stone with Angela's second photo, the one you gave me at the dock the day of Thorpe's killing. I'm afraid the doctor came up with quite a different image than the one you showed me on the way to the airport. No resemblance to Ambassador Mathers at all."

For a moment, Kaine felt like someone had kicked him in the

stomach. He couldn't breathe. In time, he managed a meaningless reply. "End of story, I suppose."

"Not necessarily," Preble said quickly. "The good doctor said there was a second copy of the computer printout you gave me. I hope you know where the other one is because the institute requisitioned mine, and they don't seem too eager to relinquish it. Evidently, Dr. Stone overstepped his authority in putting that photo of yours into their system. The whole thing makes me nervous. Don't let that other copy out of your sight."

At this point, Kaine had no intention of mentioning Connor Thorpe, so he lied. "It's a little late for that," he said. "A certain Captain Medvedev confiscated it."

"Just dandy," Preble said. "In that case I might as well tell you about a last problem. The Turkish secret police are now aware of your presence on their soil. They seem very eager to have you in custody. The U.S. embassy in Istanbul is lending their full cooperation."

"Naturally."

"Don't make light, Professor. You're running on empty about now, and it's my impression that you don't seem particularly eager to accept a helping hand when it's offered."

"You?" Kaine wanted to laugh. Right, he thought. "What do you suggest?"

"I have a friend in the British embassy there. The secretary of legation. Stuart. Alden Stuart. It's totally against protocol, but he has agreed to see you back into my hands. From there, we'll make a case of it. It's your best chance, and all I can—"

Kaine hung up. It took him nearly a minute to extract himself from the chair at the back of the bookstore. His first thought was of Angela. Her name had never been mentioned. Why? Would the introduction of a contradictory computer image exonerating Louis Mathers be enough to discount her direct testimony? Or was that merely a ploy bent on forcing her testimony? Or worse, had she and Danielle been found without Kaine's assistance? The very thought of this left Kaine numb.

It was not difficult reasoning out the contradictory computer image. Obviously Daniel Stone was not the man Kaine had hoped he was. A creature for sale, after all. And you, a great judge of character, Kaine thought.

Lenci was waiting for him, propped against the fender of his taxi, a plate of oily mutton in his hand.

"You don't look happy," he said. "Come on! The sun is out, the breeze is cool, the smell is almost tolerable, and your stomach is full. Why this look of total disgust? I'll tell you why. Your puzzle has too many pieces, that's why."

Kaine smiled; it was either that or curse. "You're an insightful man."

"Let's just say my information is good. You've been offered a deal. Yes? A deal your head says to take. A deal something deep down in your gut says forget."

"Any advice?"

Lenci brushed breadcrumbs off his shirt. "A friend of yours, one who shall remain nameless, called you the singleminded man. Which makes you, for better or worse, the kind of man who can't seem to ignore those deep-down-in-the-gut kind of messages. Therefore, you've already decided."

Kaine contemplated that. In the end, he said simply, "I need a car."

"We know," Lenci replied. "You're going east, up the coast. The car is old, but it should get you where you're going. Be careful who you trust," he said, and added: "Trust your instincts first and foremost and you'll do fine."

27

The singleminded man. Only Jaymin had ever called him that. So there it was. Lenci was connected to the sailor on the *Karaman*. The sailor was bought off by the American consul, Collins. It was simple logic that Jaymin and Collins were connected, too. Jaymin was a heroin addict and far too unforgiving of herself. She had called herself a liar, a cheat, and a thief. Yet all along Kaine's gut had told him there was more to her than that. A Turkish taxi driver tells him to trust his instincts. For twenty years Kaine had been *taught* to trust the facts. Yet, for twenty years his most reliable source had been simple gut reaction.

The car was a Renault of a vintage Kaine could only estimate by the pitted wheel wells and the odd slope of the trunk. A smart man entered from the passenger side because the driver's-side door was held shut by fencing wire. An athletic man, one who had never completely accepted growing up, entered feet first through the driver's-side window, where there was no glass. Kaine managed the latter, using the luggage rack on the roof as a handgrip. Lenci's cousins cheered. A woman who had spoken not a single word in Kaine's presence placed a basket on the seat next to him.

"It's not much," Lenci explained. "Almonds and pine nuts, raisins and dried tomatoes. All she has really. But she must have a feeling for you because she tells me there is also a piece of baklava, and if it's the baklava I think it is, it's like nothing you've ever tasted. Also a small bottle of a liquor we call raki; but be careful, the stuff sits for two years and . . . and you'll know when you taste it."

Kaine knew the way. He had driven from Istanbul to Cide many times. A subtle elegance captured the Black Sea coast east of Istanbul. Today there was sunshine and the water was a slate gray. The deception was that the water, rising and falling like a sleeping animal's chest, often seemed higher than the land. In the sun, the coastal sand was a soft gold color and surprising flecks of purple radiated from it.

The farms scattered among the rolling hills on Kaine's right produced corn and nuts, fruits and tobacco. During the months of harvest, roadside stands littered the highway. The farmers used their children as vendors, which made it impossible for Kaine to bypass them. Today the stands were empty. If the rumors were correct, the only harvest taking place this time of year was in the mountains high on the Anatolia plateau. But the bounty there was neither corn nor fruit nor tobacco. The bounty of this harvest was opium poppies.

The site workers at Karmin-Yar used to laugh over a saying Kaine never took seriously. "Bring a strong back to the mountains for three weeks and celebrate by burning your tobacco crop to the ground when you return."

The road was tarred, but badly worn and deeply pitted. A bridge had given way over a narrow stream, but the spring thaw was still a month away and Kaine found a passable spot a half mile inland.

He stopped in every town that had a petrol station, because most didn't. In Karasu he found an American naval outpost. He stopped at the commissary and bought two gallons of bottled water; it took months to condition the body to the waters here, and dysentery wasn't something Kaine needed to chance right now.

Though Cide was only two hundred miles from Istanbul, it was well after noon by the time Kaine arrived. In contrast to Istanbul, Cide was a broken-down fishing hamlet. The spires of Muslim minarets were ignominiously supplanted by the mainmasts of yawls and ketches. The freighters and cargo ships Kaine had seen by the hundreds in the Bosphorus were here represented by a single funnel steamer and a hundred-ton oiler anchored a half mile from shore.

Kaine hated the town. It represented everything the city of Karmin-Yar didn't. Clapboard shanties had displaced architectural vision and palaces cut of stone. The people of Cide drank mercury-tinged water; in Karmin-Yar they had built a system of interlocking clay pipes to transport springwater from the Karmin-Yar River and its tributaries. The people of Karmin-Yar had traded gold for silk; in Cide a pizza parlor established simply as a means of catering to spoiled Americans was the most financially sound enterprise in town. More than anything, Kaine hated the town because it was here and Karmin-Yar was history.

The Black Sea Inn had been built along the coast at the eastern end of town. Fifteen freestanding units stood in a half-moon formation around a gravel parking lot. At the heart of the lot a plot of ground had been turned over, but no one had ever gotten around to planting the flowers destined for the plot. The single-story dwellings were constructed of adobe. Some years back they had received a coat of terra-cotta-colored paint. Each unit had a small porch and a screen door. The screens fronted solid wood doors equipped with deadbolts.

Unit numbers had been painted above the doorframes. Unit three belonged to Maurice Dreyfuss. The curtains had been drawn aside. Beyond, the unit was dim and dingy. Kaine parked across the road next to a granary. He climbed out and stretched. In the heat of midday, the town was virtually deserted.

At the edge of town a neon light flashed, in red vertical letters, PIZZA, and below in horizontal green letters, BEER. Kaine stared at the blinking lights, waiting for the evocation of some memory or some emotion. Instead, he was struck only by a vivid picture of Angela and Danielle and the stark realization of their dilemma; the ringing of their unanswered telephone haunted him. Kaine walked halfway to the beer hall and then turned back.

There were good things happening to him. Life and death in the present were putting a new face on life and death in the past, a more realistic face. He was forty-two years old. He stood before an ever-expanding past that was his very own. He was highly respected by his peers, but where were the lifelong friends he had given second priority to for so long? He had changed the course of archeological thinking in several major areas, but how many lives had he made a difference in today? He had unearthed four sites previously unknown to modern man, but when was the last time he had used the earth's bounty to cultivate a garden? He had given a hundred dreadfully serious lectures, but what about simple laughter? And then a chill raced down his spine and the shiver infected his whole body. My God, was he turning into his own father?

The sun took refuge behind a high ceiling of thunderheads, a gust of wind rushed in off the water, and the temperature plummeted. He retreated to the car. He uncovered the food basket given to him in Istanbul. The raki had been stored in a large canning jar. Kaine broke the seal. The liquor was syrupy and the color of weak coffee. He expected a sugary taste and found instead a flavor as biting as that of straight vodka. The first swallow exorcised the chill he had felt. He stopped after three sips because his eyes were watering.

He forced himself to eat.

He watched the motel for ten more minutes. Finally, he put his mackinaw on and climbed out again. From a rudimentary tool kit in the trunk he secured two different-size screwdrivers, a pair of pliers, and an oil-stained rag.

Jogging, he circled the complex. The bathroom and bedroom of every unit faced the dunes that fronted the sea. There were no backdoors, but a window in each room. The beach was deserted; it was too windy and too cold. Kaine stopped at the bedroom window of Maurice Dreyfuss's unit. In his youth, he had been a reader of Dashiell Hammett mysteries. In these, the thieves always seemed to Kaine to be ruthless and indiscriminate, and they were never caught in the act. A novice, Kaine employed the Hammett approach. The window screen was secured from the inside. He jammed the largest of the screwdrivers between the windowframe and the screen and bent it out. He used two hands to wrench the screen from the moulding. Acting on pure adrenaline, he wrapped the rag around his fist and punched a hole in the window. He cranked the window open from the inside. He was crouching on the floor of the bedroom with the curtains drawn when he remembered the flashlight he had seen in the glove compartment. It was too late.

He closed the bedroom door and switched on the dresser lamp. There was a porcelain figurine of the Madonna and child on the dresser. An oft-burnt candle stood in a clay holder next to it. A book of matches. An open pack of Kent cigarettes.

The top drawer of the dresser contained two changes of clothes and a Bible. The other drawers were lined with paper, which Kaine glanced beneath. He took the drawers out and looked beneath them, as well. He searched the bed and the bedframe. He pulled a free-standing oil heater away from the wall.

In the dining room there was evidence only of a man who spent little time on leisurely endeavors. A sweater had been thrown over the back of a chair. A two-week-old London *Times,* a faded *Newsweek,* and a half-used notebook lay upon the table. Kaine thumbed through the magazine. He shook out the empty pages of the notebook. A radio sat upon a small side table. Kaine switched it on. It was set to a news station broadcasting out of Istanbul and the reception was horrendous. He switched it off again.

In a kitchen the size of a closet Kaine found two empty pizza boxes, a bottle of expensive whiskey two-thirds empty, and four glasses containing traces of the liquor. One glass, Kaine noticed, seemed hardly to have been touched. A second showed traces of lipstick on the rim. Kaine tried the stove. The gas had been disconnected. He opened it anyway. Beneath the broiler pan he found a nine-millimeter pistol, an Italian Beretta. A full magazine lay beside it. Kaine didn't touch it. In the cupboard, he found a bottle of cleaning fluid, a sponge, and an open carton of French cigarettes, Gauloise Caporals. Eight packets out of ten remained. Beside the cigarettes lay a plastic wrapper containing one of two butane lighters.

In the bathroom, there were two towels provided by the inn and two others, newer and fluffier, that obviously belonged to the renter. In the shower Kaine found shampoo and conditioner bought, almost certainly, in a city considerably more diverse than Cide. Kaine hand-searched the towels and even opened the shampoo. On the counter next to a bar of scented soap lay a razor, blades, and a can of shaving cream. On the stool lay a second magazine, a recent issue of *Gentleman's Quarterly.*

Kaine hastened into the dining room again.

On the floor, immediately inside the front door, he laid a copy of the first page of the letter he had written to Maurice Dreyfuss only hours before. It described the evidence presented by Jurgen Spire of the wrongdoings taking place at Karmin-Yar.

Then he climbed back out the bedroom window and returned to his car. He indulged in two swallows of raki.

Twenty minutes later a car rumbled into the lot of the Black Sea Inn. It was a late-model Ford. It was too clean for this part of the world. It came to a halt in front of unit three. Maurice Dreyfuss climbed out. A small man, he wore a well-tailored suit, another anomaly. Before locking the car door, he tossed a pair of sunglasses and a straw hat onto the front seat. A cigarette dangled from his lips. Looking fatigued and old, he lugged a briefcase to the front door.

He unlocked the door, pushed it open, and switched on the interior light before going inside. He didn't get far. Kaine saw him stop, bend down, and reach for the letter.

Kaine waited five minutes, then crossed the street. He knocked aggressively at the door. He reached for the handle; in Dreyfuss's distracted state of mind he had forgotten to lock it behind him. Kaine walked in. Dreyfuss had fallen into one of the dining room chairs. He had not removed his coat, his briefcase lay nestled on his lap, and he had exchanged his cigarette for a pair of bifocals. The first page of Kaine's letter lay unfolded on the table before him.

"In the name of God," he said. "You! You! Stephen Kaine, the wonder boy."

"Maurice, you look terrible."

"What are you doing here? You've been permanently deported."

"The word *permanently* strikes me as a bit inaccurate, doesn't it you?" Kaine went to the kitchen and returned with the nine-millimeter Beretta, the whiskey bottle, and one glass. He filled the glass and placed it next to the letter. "Have a drink, Maurice. You and I have some things to discuss."

"What are you doing here, Kaine?"

"I don't think you've been acting like the archeologist you were trained to be, Maurice. I've come back to make sure my city hasn't fallen into the hands of people with ill intent. Like Ambassador Louis Mathers, for instance."

Dreyfuss's mouth fell open. "Mathers."

"You'll have to excuse the lack of detail in my letter. It doesn't mention that Scotland Yard is eager to talk to the ambassador about the murder of a Dover tugboat captain named Tanner Thorpe," Kaine said. "It also doesn't mention Colonel William Turnbull."

"You've been a busy man, Kaine. As usual." Dreyfuss removed a handkerchief from his breast pocket, wrapped it around two fingers, and worked the fingers into his eyes. He used the gesture and a deep drink of whiskey to calm himself. "So you've made your grand entrance. Now what?"

"Read the letter," Kaine said. "It explains a lot."

"I've done so. It's nothing but lies. I wouldn't use it to kindle a fire."

Now Kaine lied. "A copy of the letter has been sent to Henri Pare, the chancellor of the University of Paris. A second copy has been sent to the president of the Archeological Society of Europe, William McGuckin, and a third copy has been sent to Turkish Minister of Internal Affairs Mihil Rytting. Their instructions are to open the letter within forty-eight hours unless they hear from me before. I doubt they'll consider using the letter to kindle a fire, however, unless it happens to be one that destroys your career."

"This is preposterous. Why hasn't Spire come forward with this information concerning Karmin-Yar? He hasn't been heard from in months."

"Jurgen is dead. Murdered."

"That's a . . . How do you know this? Spire—"

"Scotland Yard and the Crimean police are cooperating on the matter. They have two names. Mathers and Turnbull. They're looking for a third, Maurice."

Dreyfuss focused on the table. One hand worked furiously knotting itself into a fist. "All right, wonder boy, what do you want?"

"You've located the fire temple."

"Yes."

"Via the king's court."

"Like I said, you've been busy."

"How much gold?"

Dreyfuss wiped his mouth. He reached into his pocket for cigarettes, Gauloise Caporals, not Kents. He lit one. When the smoke emptied from his lungs, he said, "By my estimate, one hundred thirty tons, mostly coins. Also ninety or a hundred tons of silver ingots."

Kaine didn't blink. He calculated. At two thousand pounds to the ton: two hundred sixty thousand pounds. At sixteen ounces to the pound: roughly four million ounces of gold. On today's market, at approximately four hundred dollars to the ounce, it would be worth well over a billion and a half dollars. This was only half the amount found by the Greeks in the Persepolis treasure house when Alexander the Great razed it in 330 B.C., but still not bad. Kaine didn't bother figuring the silver.

"How are they getting it out?" he asked.

"You're too late."

"Then it doesn't matter. How?"

Dreyfuss chuckled sourly. "You fool. On a Colombian freighter. All right. Does that satisfy you? For the last six months those people have been policing Karmin-Yar like it was their property. For all I know, it is."

"Nasty companions, Maurice. Very nasty. What's the deal Mathers has made?"

Dreyfuss shook his head adamantly. "No, don't even think about it. If it's money you want, half of my share is yours. It's enough to see us both through the rest of our lives in a style Darius himself would have envied."

Now Kaine nodded. He did it slowly, pensively. "You're right."

"The gold is nothing."

"Heroin."

"It's perfect, Kaine." Dreyfuss was suddenly excited, like a caged animal who detects a narrow gap in the bars; Kaine had seen this odious side of the archeologist before. "How does one go about disposing of such a visible commodity as gold and do so without detection? Think about it. It's perfect. Believe me."

Kaine partook in Dreyfuss's whiskey, a show of communion. "How?" he asked, his voice affecting genuine confusion.

With gathering impatience, Dreyfuss said, "You simply exchange the gold for a less visible commodity. One parlayed every single day on the streets of every major city in the world, and for five or ten times the price."

"It's beautiful," Kaine said.

"Then you see it." Dreyfuss drank. The liquor pushed him on. "The gold, in turn, is laundered by the most sophisticated laundering organization the world has ever known."

"The Colombian drug lords."

"Whatever the hell you call them," Dreyfuss answered, still impatient. "But you see the sense in it, don't you? The inevitability."

"Yes. I do." Kaine drank again. Now he reached into his jacket pocket and withdrew the pewter chess piece he had taken from Ras Haydar's personal effects at the church in Dover. He set the dragon down on the table and said, "Your chess game must have suffered without this."

"Where in the world . . . ?"

"Ras Haydar," Kaine answered. In response, Maurice Dreyfuss pressed his palms together; his hands came to rest upon his lips. After a moment, Kaine said, "I am curious about one thing, though. How did Ras Haydar come by a blueprint of the city?"

"It was foolish. We hired him to get rid of you, to set you up. I'm sorry to say it, but it's true."

"Don't be sorry."

"When Ras found out the reason he'd been hired, he developed a sudden case of conscience. And worse yet, it was a sacrilege to allow the crown of Sharana Ni to leave Asia Minor. I couldn't convince certain parties just how seriously such an act would be taken." Dreyfuss swallowed hard. A sip of whiskey gave him the energy to continue. "It was a mistake to tell Ras about the blueprint in the first place. When we found out he'd made a copy—"

"He deliberately sank a ferry in the middle of Admiralty Harbor in Dover. Twenty-four people died, Maurice. Over a blueprint and a crown?"

Dreyfuss sighed. "Ras Haydar had a brother. His name was Mikkel. Turnbull hired them both. The brother was more fanatical than Ras, but not as smart. In short, he made threats he shouldn't have. I'm sorry to say it cost him his life. Ras blamed Turnbull. Ras was a Turk. To avenge his brother he would have gone to any lengths."

"And Turnbull was on the ferry. Of course." Kaine hung his head. To be driven to such extremes, he thought. One would have to experience it to understand it. He had heard enough. He said, "How and where will it take place, Maurice?"

"I've told you too much already, don't you see?" The French archeologist's eyes darted around the room—they rested only momentarily upon the gun—and Kaine knew he had missed something in his search. "You can't stop the transfer of the gold. It's unimportant, believe me. And I promise you no harm will come to Karmin-Yar. No one has ever believed in the existence of a gold treasure at Karmin-Yar anyway. You've written that yourself. Jurgen Spire supported the theory. The archeological world believes it; an empty treasure house is expected, Kaine."

"True."

The relief Dreyfuss felt expressed itself in a deep sigh. He lit another cigarette; Kaine stared at the Gauloise packet.

"We have both given our share to the world's archeological past, Kaine, to its history even," the Frenchman said. "Is it so unfair that we receive something back in return?"

"With no damage done really."

"Exactly. With no damage done."

"Except the drugs."

"Those drugs are destined for the scum of the earth." Dreyfuss blew smoke aggressively into the air. He waved a hand through it, gathering momentum. "That's another world. Those people don't concern you or me. We've studied the greatest races the world has ever known. To bother with the likes of those—"

"You smoke Gauloises, I see," Kaine said, rising.

"Well, yes," Dreyfuss said. "Oh, how rude of me. Would you care for one?"

Kaine declined. He slipped the second page of his letter from the pocket of his coat. It was short and brief, outlining Jurgen Spire's accusations of Maurice Dreyfuss's homosexuality, and alleging Scotland Yard documentation of his affair with Georges Tournier, the assistant dean of anthropology in Paris.

"I lied," Kaine said. "There's more. This is page two of the letter I sent. I thought you'd like to see it."

Kaine traded the paper for the briefcase on Dreyfuss's lap and the archeologist didn't protest. While Dreyfuss read, Kaine sorted through the case. The transfer papers necessary for entrance into and out of the Karmin-Yar site were sealed in a plastic binder. Kaine wasn't concerned about the discrepancy in the photo. He had been through the Karmin-Yar gates enough to know the cursory approach given to ID inspection. The binder itself was the most important component. He slipped it into his coat.

Maurice Dreyfuss had finished reading the second page of Kaine's letter. He slumped back in the chair, removed his glasses, and pinched the bridge of his nose. He protested meekly, "You insinuate matters concerning my private life of which you have no proof. How dare you?"

"Georges Tournier has already confirmed the facts with Scotland Yard. He's protecting himself at your expense, Maurice," Kaine lied. "I personally don't have an opinion on the matter of who you choose to screw, but I imagine the evidence in that letter concerning Karmin-Yar is in itself enough to see you behind bars. And if you end up in a prison here in Turkey, you won't survive a month. On the other hand, I have no desire to see this letter made public. It's up to you. I need forty-eight hours."

Kaine took the Beretta and walked into the unit's tiny bedroom. He stopped at the dresser. For a moment, he stared at the Madonna and child. Then he scooped up the packet of Kent cigarettes. A gut reaction.

Seeing the packet in Kaine's hand, Dreyfuss gasped, and Kaine knew he was right; there was something here.

"Not your brand," he said. "I couldn't help but wonder."

"I won't let you ruin my life, Kaine."

"It wasn't worth much to begin with, Maurice." Kaine put the cigarettes in his pocket. He lifted Maurice Dreyfuss's car keys and briefcase from the table. As he was turning to leave, Dreyfuss sprang from his chair. With a desperate cry, he dove for the gun in Kaine's hand. His fingers were like claws; the nails cut into Kaine's skin. Kaine swung the briefcase, catching the side of the French archeologist's head, but Dreyfuss hung on, stronger than his meek appearance suggested. They toppled to the floor, rolling, legs flailing. The gun discharged. Maurice Dreyfuss's head hit the floor with a dull thud.

"Jesus!" Kaine untangled himself. He scrambled to his feet. Blood poured from a hole in Dreyfuss's neck; the round, wide eyes of surprise stared back at Kaine.

Kaine didn't hurry. He calmed himself with a swallow of whiskey. He locked the door behind him. He paused for a moment on the porch. He made a thorough survey of the street. Then he crossed the gravel parking lot as if he had done so a hundred times. He climbed into the car and looked at himself in the rearview mirror. He hadn't expected to feel remorse. But he did. After all, a life was a life, and no one should die like that.

He started the car. He drove east two miles to a roadside rest area. A copse of flowering fruit trees formed a canopy under which he parked. He threw the Beretta as deep into the woods as he could. He took the packet of Kents from his pocket; he had no idea what he was looking for, but his search was brief. Inside the packet were four cigarettes and a section of brown paper rolled into a tight cylinder. It was a short note.

The words were written in French. Kaine couldn't speak the language well, but he could read it. The note was printed in blue ink.

My Dearest Maurice:
For you to come the entire way to Larnica makes no sense. Your presence is unnecessary, the way is treacherous, and to leave Karmin-Yar unattended would only arouse suspicion. Our rendezvous remains Ano Kliston on the ninth. I

will arrive by plane on said date due to unexpected complications here. Remain true to your station.

L. M.

Kaine rushed to interpret. L. M., Louis Mathers. Unexpected complications here. Here being England. Complications being First Skipper Thorpe and Angela. On the other hand, the words Larnica and Ano Kliston, obviously locations, made no impression. And for the moment, they were of no consequence. For Karmin-Yar was only a heartbeat away, and it called to him like a lost child.

28 Angela was perplexed. She wanted to walk right up to the pilot and ask him how he happened to be in Tregony, eating at the same restaurant they were, on precisely the same day. Was he, in fact, following them? Hadn't it been his plan to return to Folkestone and Dover the day after he had flown them to Dodman Point? Isn't that what he had told them? Why was he here?

"Let's just ask him and get it over with," she said to her mother.

Danielle vetoed the idea. He was here because they were here. He was here because of Angela's involvement in the ferry accident. He was here because she had unwittingly witnessed a murder. Danielle didn't need to ask him.

They waited. The maître d' worried because they didn't appear particularly interested in their food. Was there a problem? Danielle insisted there was no problem, but she asked, "Is there an airport nearby?"

"No, ma'am. You'd have to drive to Truro, or Portloe off Dodman Point, which might be five minutes closer. They're both on the coast though, a fair drive away in any case."

The pilot ordered and ate and read the newspaper. He refused to make eye contact.

Angela stopped talking. She sensed her mother's growing ap-

prehension and the seeds of it settled in her stomach and blossomed. Danielle put twenty pounds on the table. She took Angela's
hand and they walked back into the café. They used the rest room.
When Danielle peeked back into the restaurant, the pilot was gone.

It occurred to Danielle to leave the old couple's truck and set
out on foot. They did neither. Instead, they walked into the village
as planned and found a pharmacy that also sold liquor, homemade
chocolates, and books.

Remarkably, the pilot was at the counter purchasing a bottle
of English gin. When he turned, Danielle was staring at him with
eyes as stern as a winter's night.

"Hello," he said. He bore the face of an accountant just returned
from a vacation in the sun. His smile conveyed genuine warmth.
"You've discovered Tregony. How marvelous. I thought only fly
fishermen knew about this river."

He reached out and shook Angela's hand. "My co-pilot. I don't
think flying will ever be quite as much fun."

"What are you doing here?" Danielle asked. "Why in the hell
are you following us?"

The pilot pushed his glasses up the bridge of his nose. "Excuse me?"

"You didn't see us at lunch?" It was a demand, not a question.

"At the Riverside Café? No. You were there?"

"We were sitting outside—" Angela began to say before her
mother cut her off.

"We were sitting thirty feet away from you."

"Then I not only owe you an apology, I must confess to some
regret at not joining you." He shrugged. His hand went toward his
glasses again. "Unfortunately, I wasn't wearing these. I can read
without them, but not much else."

"He's right, Mom. He wasn't, I remember." Angela beamed,
glancing at the pilot again. Her belief in him was a matter of necessity, she had been through so much. "I knew I should have said
something to you."

"I wish you had," he answered. He graced Danielle with a
solicitous tip of the head. "Is everything all right? You seem
frightened."

"You were on your way back to Folkestone," she replied. "It was my impression that you were on a rather tight schedule."

"Your impression was correct," he said evenly, now twisting the top of the bag around the neck of his bottle. "They canceled my contract. The government. They do that, but usually with a bit more notice. I'm escaping. Fly fishing and drinking. Two safe ports of call."

"Sorry."

"It happens. Sorry I startled you," he said, taking his bottle and sauntering out the door.

Danielle watched him from the pharmacy window. A block down the road, he climbed behind the wheel of a bruised and battered Land Rover. He drove north out of town.

Mother and daughter put on a cloak of relief, trying to convince themselves, trying to convince one another. They bought their books. Danielle chose a mystery by Agatha Christie; she hated mysteries. Angela decided upon a revised edition of *Swan Lake*. She was still hungry, she said, so they bought cheese and crackers and a large bottle of fruit juice.

They walked back to the truck, window shopping as they went. Danielle tried on a hat in a used clothing store. They put gas in the old couple's truck.

At the station, Danielle sat with her hands on the steering wheel, dreading the trip back to the cabins.

"You believed him," she said to her daughter, who sat beside her, sipping juice. It was an accusation, a fleeing from the ambivalence she herself felt, and Danielle recognized it the moment it left her mouth. "I'm sorry," she said quickly. "I didn't mean it to sound that way."

"I wanted to believe him," Angela said. Her voice still clung to a thread of optimism. "I really did. But it was that thing he said about the fly fishing."

Now Danielle turned in her seat. "What do you mean?"

"Back at the cabin, by the river, there's a sign," Angela replied. "You know, one of those signs with all the warnings written on it. At the top of the sign it said, 'Fly Fishing Absolutely Prohibited.' The old guy in the cabin next to ours said something about it, too.

He thought it was great. He said fishing with flies was like cheating at checkers."

Angela held the juice bottle in two hands on her lap. A strand of auburn hair hung loosely across her face. Her lips were damp but she licked them anyway. Then she met her mother's gaze and said, "Right outside of town, when we were driving in for lunch, I saw the exact same sign. 'Fly Fishing Absolutely Prohibited.' "

29

The ancient city of Karmin-Yar was 2,329 years old.

The archeological site surrounding the city was not open to the public. Tourists viewed it from a roadside observation point at the edge of the Pontic Mountains 2.2 miles away. Today, Kaine stood alone at the point. A cutting wind swept up the hillside off the sea, and he welcomed it despite the cold. His sunburnt face tingling, black hair flagging wildly, his chin thrust forward.

The distance was healthy; it gave him the perspective of an outsider, which was exactly what he had become.

To his left, a city of tents flanked a river surprisingly untamed for this part of the world. The river had many names. The Phrygians called it the "Carving Hand." The Lydians talked of "Water Without End." The cuneiform tablets of the early Cappadocians referred to the restless river as the Yakmach. The Persians before them had, however, christened it the Karmin-Yar. Five hundred years before Christ, the Karmin-Yar River dropped down from the Pontic Mountains and brought fertility to the gentle hills along the coast. The Persians, though not the world's foremost farmers, had recognized the potential of the land. Yet agricultural promise was not paramount in the mind of Darius the First when he decided to build his city here. His thoughts turned more toward control and expansion: to control the vast and nomadic northern reaches of his empire; to access the sea as a means of pushing his empire into the Balkans to the west and Asia to the east.

Stonecutters from Persepolis and Susa had built the city, named for the river, block by block from bright gray limestone. The palaces of Darius and Cyrus, his father, were housed within tall stone columns. The audience palace of Xerxes consisted of a square hall enclosed by thirty-six columns, three arched porticos, and towers rising at each corner. An amphitheater held two thousand patrons. The local bathhouses were cut of marble imported from quarries high on the Anatolia plateau beyond the mountains. Crenellated mudbrick fortifications encapsulating the inner city were as thick as fifteen meters in places, rising along the exposed southern flank to a height of twenty meters.

Artisans from as great a distance as Egypt were hired to decorate the city walls with glazed brick frieze. There were reliefs of dragons and archers, palm trees and seagulls. There were reliefs depicting each Persian king and every subservient tribe. A system of aqueducts for moving the water from the river, and cisterns for collecting and storing it, gave the Persian nobility the world's first indoor plumbing. The Persian working class built thatch-roofed cottages from timber secured from the forests of the Pontics. They rode horses and bartered with merchants from as far away as the Danube River.

Unfortunately, the Persians had no way of knowing that every two or three thousand years the forces beneath the ground here changed the nature of the landscape, sometimes drastically. In 421 B.C., exactly one century after Darius assumed the Persian throne, an earthquake of immense magnitude did just that. It reduced the mountains surrounding the city by half their size, and threw the Karmin-Yar river off course by nearly a mile. The city literally sank into the soft ground upon which it had been built. Mudslides engulfed it. A hundred miles of coastline suffered such extensive damage that coves were now cliffs and promontories were now sandbars.

The reduction of the mountains, the alteration of the river's course, the redesign of the coastline, and the burial by mud all contributed to the mystery of the city's disappearance.

The last hundred years had yielded fourteen serious expeditions bent on unearthing the lost city of Karmin-Yar. Thirteen failures stirred rumors questioning the city's very existence. Kaine's attempt was the fourteenth. The Turkish government consented to the expedition only because it was privately sponsored.

Kaine had employed neither archeology nor geology in his search; he chose oceanography. The discovery of pottery shards in a coral reef a half mile out to sea, and a theoretical estimate of the tides prior to and after the earthquake, led Kaine to a startling revelation: previous to the quake the Karmin-Yar River had emptied into the sea east of the city; its current location was now an unspecified distance west of the city. So the previous thirteen expeditions had all been searching in the wrong direction.

Furthermore, the same coral reef revealed fragments of an ancient shipwreck. The wreckage offered another clue. Since the Persians had been fond of launching their ships from protected river basins, the wreckage suggested to Kaine the previous location of the river. He was right.

Four months later a team of thirty diggers had begun preliminary work. A timbered cottage led to a mudbrick fortification. The ruins of a stone temple were unearthed shortly thereafter, and a full-fledged excavation commenced. Diggers were hired from Ankara and Istanbul. Students came from as far away as San Francisco. Anthropologists, biologists, lithicists, and ecologists were all recruited.

They had established a base camp near the river, a mile from the city. Tents were pitched. A trestled aqueduct system carried water to the site. Nearby acres were given over to farm and grazing land where vegetables were planted and cattle reared. An irrigation system gave the project a taste of self-sufficiency. Graders and haulers, water trucks and cranes, Land Rovers and Jeeps arrived from Istanbul.

Excavation of the site had been like searching blindly through a chest for a crystal goblet and finding it. Workers pushed shovels and spades, and the makings of a city were uncovered. The broken wall of the audience palace's north portico revealed an intricate relief of Cyrus the Great and fifteen throne bearers. Five months later, an untouched façade along the eastern doorway of the great treasure house was uncovered, showing a delegation of Ionians offering a circular shield, a lance, and a cart filled with treasure to the King of Kings, Darius himself.

Now a chain-link fence surrounded a half-buried city of stone. Scaffolding formed a cincture around the columns and towers of the palace of Darius. Ladders rose along the side parapets of the high temple. Experts working with dental picks and tiny brushes painstakingly revealed the scrollwork on a bathhouse cut of marble. A suspension bridge connected the fallen walls of the palace of Xerxes with the stone stairs traversing the *apadana*.

Kaine employed the platform binoculars at the edge of the observation point; he spied a second chain-link fence, this within the compound itself. The fence enclosed a new find, one he had only dreamed of unearthing. A round courtyard spanned fifty or sixty feet; at its heart, the remnants of a center throne stood upon a stone dais. A series of rounded arches hinted at the walls that once enclosed the courtyard. This was the king's court, the very one cited by Jurgen Spire in his "Fire Theft" journal, and depicted on the blueprint given to Angela. Despite a wave of outrage, Kaine stared in awe at the court. Darius himself had sat upon that throne, as had Xerxes and Artaxerxes after him. And Darius had built the tunnel that connected it with the fire temple, as yet still buried. And it was Darius who had violated the sacrosanct nature of the temple by secreting his gold hoard there. So the fence was no surprise.

Kaine forced his attention elsewhere. The wind had driven the clouds inland. Beneath a sky of brilliant blue, he surveyed his discovery. Five years' work and still the project was little more than a third done; and now it was turning on the whim of a theft and a drug deal. Yet the project had controlled Kaine's life for years, ruined his life in many ways. Maybe, he thought, it was for the best after all. Maybe he could make a last statement and walk away from it, a free man at last.

Kaine heard the shrill report of the camp bell. Out of habit, he retrieved his watch. It was exactly twelve-thirty, Greenwich time; three-thirty here at Karmin-Yar. Work began at five-thirty in the morning; it was often too cold to begin earlier. Conversely, the afternoon sun could be torturous even this early in spring.

The bell sounded again. Good.

In an hour, the flow of traffic back to the tent compound, for sleep and camp duties, would cross with the flow of technicians destined for station assignments within the site. They would be conducting geological examinations of rock, soil, and brick samples; botanic reviews of pollen, carbonized seeds, and living plant material; anthropological studies of animal bones. Every pottery shard would be saved, counted, washed, mended, and catologued as if the balance of history hinged on it.

Kaine played it all out in his mind. At four-ten, he turned away.

Kaine had never before achieved a sense of detachment from his work, and this inability had often led to unexpected and damaging consequences. Now he had achieved it, and it spurred him to action. He slid behind the wheel of Maurice Dreyfuss's polished Ford. The chief archeologist would be recognized as much by his vehicle as by any scrutiny of identification; for five years, Kaine had driven a battered Jeep with a zebra-striped roll bar, his personal trademark.

Maurice Dreyfuss was known for his straw hat, and it lay now on the passenger seat. Kaine tried it on. It was too small and he tugged at the brim. Sunglasses were hooked behind the visor; Kaine filled out his disguise with these, as well.

He drove east on the highway for a half mile. A RESTRICTED AREA—DO NOT ENTER sign marked a gravel road that plunged north toward the sea and the city.

At the perimeter of the Karmin-Yar site there was a high fence. Within it stood a freestanding, flat building. It was the area's only entrance, its only checkpoint. The area beyond the fence, however, was under constant surveillance by men on foot and horseback.

What additional precautions Maurice Dreyfuss and his associates had put in place since his dismissal, Kaine could only guess.

Yet since drawing attention to their operation was not in its best interest, Kaine expected that little had changed.

A one-armed barricade blocked the road. A man in khaki shorts with a clipboard in his hand stood beside it as Kaine approached. The man waved the clipboard in greeting and raised the barricade without a moment's hesitation. Kaine tipped his hat as he passed.

The road forked. Kaine took the right fork, past idle earthmovers and a fleet of small tractors. He threw aside the straw hat and sunglasses. In the distance, cast in the haze of early evening, stood the brash contrasts of old and new: a derrick crane, a pallet dangling in midair from its boom arm, rose above the limestone columns of a Persian palace.

Kaine parked behind the lithicist station. Martha Perrimore had been the second person hired by Kaine when the dig was officially approved four and a half years ago. She was an expert in stone: its age, its content, its history, its purpose.

A notoriously overweight fifty-year-old, Marty took extreme pleasure in a sharp, sardonic tongue. Unfortunately, she also suffered from distinctly masculine features, which, hand in hand with her chosen profession, contributed to a longstanding nickname: the Stonemaiden.

The lithology station consisted of clapboard walls, a wooden floor, and a canvas roof. Rocks covered three sorting benches of graduated sizes. Washtubs and screening tables filled out one corner of the station. A spectrometer, chromatograph, microscopes, and a computer huddled behind a plastic screen in the other.

Kaine climbed out of the car, considering what he would say and how. He stood momentarily at the open station door, peering in. Marty was hunched over a sorting table. She was humming the Beatles' "Norwegian Wood."

Kaine stepped inside. The floor creaked but the lithicist moved not a muscle.

"Don't tell me you're still drinking that same cheap whiskey?" he said. Kaine watched her back stiffen. A low groan caught in her throat.

When Marty Perrimore turned, it put Kaine in mind of a carousel revolving, matters of bulk and grace in equal proportions. Indeed, she cradled in one hand a stemmed goblet, three inches of a lustrous brown liquid in the bottom. The rock in her other hand had all the appearances of an unwashed crystal.

There was never a time, Kaine thought, when a sheen of sweat didn't glaze the Stonemaiden's forehead, and it glistened there now. From deep within her, she produced a laugh reminiscent of distant thunder, but the laughter was insufficient to disguise her shock.

She thrust the goblet toward the floor and a cardboard box half hidden beneath one of the screening tables. The words "Wild Turkey, Kentucky Straight Bourbon Whiskey, 101 proof," ran across the side of the box.

"Same shit," she said.

"I don't know why they lie like that and call it whiskey, when they mean poison."

The Stonemaiden guffawed. "Want one?"

"Absolutely," Kaine answered. "A double, if you can spare it."

Marty found a second goblet and poured. Her laughter filled Kaine with an odd sense of mirth, but he had always mistrusted it. Marty had served him as consultant and counselor, but also as devil's advocate and voice of dissension. She had been the only member of Kaine's team spared the purge that had cost him his position six months ago. Inwardly, he had found it curious. He had, however, openly and hardily expressed satisfaction that "at least one of us survived."

Her response had been a flippant "Who wants to be the last man on a sinking ship?" though everyone knew the project was too vital to let flounder.

Marty arranged two canvas-backed chairs alongside the screening table. She hoisted her glass, eyes pinched together as if in contemplation of the perfect toast.

"Back from the dead," she muttered, chortling. "The magic man who gave us all a lifetime's worth of work. Very gutsy, old salt. Couldn't stay away? Like a woman's voice in the dark, is she, your Karmin-Yar? That it? England too boorish for the cosmopolitan professor? Nobody to pour your guts out to in Glastonbury, that it? Or did you squander all that gold already, you silly boy?"

"Be nice, Marty," he said behind a guileless grin.

Marty had blamed him; that had been Kaine's reasoning when she withdrew so totally during the investigation of the gold found in his tent. As she saw the matter, it was he who had, in some way, deserted her. "Archeology isn't for greedy men," she had once said. "Are you a greedy man, Stephen? Lonely, despite that tramp you're humping every night? Vindictive?" Marty had complained about the pay scale every month. She would say, "I'd make more than this teaching one-hundred-level courses at Smith." Kaine would laugh.

There had been another woman in camp, a short blowsy brunette from Seattle, a student worker. One evening, Kaine had inadvertently walked in on them. They had both been naked from the waist up. The Stonemaiden was on top of her, a hand pumping the girl's crotch beneath her jeans. The girl had fled, embarrassed, and packed her bags for good a week later. Marty had been not only unforgiving but spiteful.

"Be nice," Kaine said again.

"Old salt, Marty's never been one to hold grudges. Not at all. A grudge is a vendetta left to rot in the sun. What good is it?"

"True," Kaine said.

"You outgrew the project, old salt." And then her eyes widened; her smile was quick, and sharp like a finely stropped blade. "Or maybe the project outgrew you. Either way, you're better off."

Kaine thought for a moment; he chose acquiescence over confrontation. "You may be right," he said, bowing his head. He drank sparingly of the whiskey, made a brief study of the goblet, and nodded his head with a measure of approval. "Better than I remember."

"Lots of things are better than you remember them, darling," she said.

"They've uncovered the king's court." Kaine graced her with his full attention.

"You've been up on the point."

Kaine nodded. "What's so special that it deserves its own barricade?"

The Stonemaiden didn't answer. She tossed him the rock she had been fondling since his arrival. She drank, forcing him to examine it. Kaine indulged her.

"Guess what Marty came across, old salt? An alluvial deposit along the basin where the original river used to run." Kaine studied the stone with more interest, actually wetting a finger and scrubbing the surface. "That's right, darling. Diamonds."

The pride Marty exuded was recognizably forced, as if she were trying to impress him with less than her best work.

"Congratulations," Kaine said, though in truth such a discovery would not have been totally unexpected. Diamond pipes were not unknown in the Pontic Mountains, and where there were diamond pipes and rivers there were often alluvial deposits along the coast.

Kaine set the stone on the screening table. He was getting nowhere. He needed an ally, even one involved in the theft. "Why is the king's court fenced off, Marty?"

"How did you get in here?" she demanded. "Have you lost your mind? You could be thrown in a Turkish prison for ten years."

"Why us, but not you?"

The folds around Marty's eyes threatened to block them out, so intense had her concentration become. Yet there was no conviction in her voice when she asked, "Us?"

"They fired us all. From the director to the head of anthropology. Fired and banished. All but the head of lithology." Kaine's voice was sympathetic, not accusatory. He rose, not quickly, but like a cat burglar entering a window. He retrieved the Wild Turkey bottle, replenished her glass, and then took himself out of her view. Finally, he asked, "Why? Why us, but not you?"

"You never once thought of me as a friend," she whispered. Kaine had to strain to hear her, so soft had her voice turned. "All those late-night chats. Hunched over that worthless backgammon game of yours. The confiding and the commiserating. All crap."

"You're wrong, Marty."

"Oh, our revered director. The discoverer himself. Oh, you manage people like a stonecutter wields a blade all right. Such skill, and always with a purpose." Now she besieged him with a burst of laughter. "You almost took the Stonemaiden in, you did. Very near."

Kaine reclaimed his chair. He pressed forward. He reached out for her free hand and she allowed him to take it. "This isn't your first time working with Maurice Dreyfuss, is it?"

"Maurice? No, no. He hired me when no one else would. I was ugly and I was queer, but it didn't matter to him." She tried to laugh. "Well, hell, why should it? He was ugly and queer, too. But he knew I was good. He hired me for an expedition to Teotihuacán, in Mexico." Teotihuacán was a lithicist's dream, a city of stone built a thousand years before the Aztecs. "But he used it against me. He had photographs, old salt. The disgusting bastard had photos of me and . . . and a friend. We weren't hurting a soul, not a soul. But he knew what those pictures would do to my career. My rocks are all I have, old salt. Without my rocks I'm just a drunk and a queer. The disgusting bastard stole things from the site, Stephen. From a place as holy as Teotihuacán. And as God is my judge, I not only turned my back, but I helped. I helped the bastard. Oh, I never took a cent, I just kept my mouth shut. Then he showed up here. He gave me back my friend. But it wasn't long before the demands started . . ."

"A lithicist is one of only four people with the authority to quarantine an area within an excavation site," Kaine said. It was so obvious that he could only shake his head.

"The director, the CA, the head of geology, and the head of lithology," Marty said. "We have no director, and we've gone through three geologists in the last six months."

"You, as lithicist, deemed the ground beneath the king's court as dangerously unstable, didn't you?" The ground *beneath* a site was an area where the chief archeologist had no authority. "Drey-fuss couldn't get a geologist to support your findings, so he kept firing them."

"That's the truth of it, I'm afraid."

"Don't be afraid, Marty. Maurice is dead."

"Dead?"

"An accident," Kaine said coldly. "And he may have done us a favor besides. The king's court is closed on your authority. Therefore, the order can also be reviewed on your authority."

The Stonemaiden nodded. "In this case, Maurice was playing it very much by the rules."

"In this case, Maurice was being *told* to play it very much by the rules," Kaine explained.

30

The dust of evening settled. Fog knitted its quilt of silvers and grays upon the waters of the Black Sea. Karmin-Yar took on the role of a forgotten castle emerging from the slopes of a sand dune. A palace wall, a broken arch, a stairway, all had their roots in the side of sedimentary hillsides. Scaffolding wove an intricate web around the doorway of an audience hall. The figures of a king, a lion, and an entourage of servants walked upon the surface of gray limestone. Grids were laid out in string. Yellow flags marked areas off limits to those of heavy foot. Red flags marked pathways safe for travel.

Kaine's vast team of four hundred men and women, with shovels and picks, with brushes and spades, backed by cranes and earthmovers and tractors, had worked straight into the sides of three distinct mountains, mountains which for two thousand years had acted as the city's ancient tomb. Less any formal blueprint, the method had proved the safest and most direct.

The discovery of the blueprint would normally have changed all that. Throw a transit up, pinpoint a structure, and set about uncovering it. A fifteen-year marathon becomes a seven-year sprint. But it was too soon for that; the blueprint had not been made public, and might never be.

Therefore, in the eyes of the archeological world, Maurice Dreyfuss had taken a daring new approach. His excavation team had leapt over the rounded peaks of the three mountains to a shallow plateau where the blueprint had informed them of the location of the king's court of Darius the First. Not that Kaine's pre-blueprint plan had been abandoned, that would have been too obvious; since his departure the north portico of the palace of Xerxes had been resurrected, its parapets nearly all intact. It was a magnificent site for the city's discoverer to behold.

The Stonemaiden saw the expression cross his face. "Yes, it's marvelous, isn't it, old salt? Wait till you lay your eyes on the eastern stairway of the *apadana*. We haven't been totally idle since we bade you farewell."

Marty had relieved Kaine of his mackinaw. In its place she had found him a heavy wool sweater and a tan smock that was the common garb of station workers. Most importantly, she had managed to secure the green lapel pin that identified the head of geology. Since geology and lithology worked hand in hand, their stations were built side by side. Since geology had been out of commission for the last five weeks, maintenance of its station had become the Stonemaiden's headache. She had found the lapel pin on the floor one day while on her hands and knees rummaging through the last geologist's liquor stash, which, as it turned out, consisted of a bottle of peppermint schnapps and a last inch of foul-smelling wine. She had poured both out in disgust.

They climbed a hillside overgrown with wild grass and yucca plants. A fallen sun brushed the sky with strokes of misty pink. Night bleached the sand of its iridescent purple flecks.

From atop the hill, Kaine glimpsed the ocean. A lone freighter was moored a half mile from the coast. Tiny breakers signaled the reef line a hundred yards farther inland. Though hardly more than a shadow in this light, Kaine could see a helicopter hovering above the ship's main deck. A pallet dangled from the chopper's undercarriage. Ghostly shadows tarried beneath it. A flag hung above the ship's bridge deck, but night had stolen away any identifiable colors. Kaine didn't need the colors. He had Maurice Dreyfuss's confession.

The freighter was Colombian, or at least it was flying the yellow, red, and blue flag that designated it as such.

Marty Perrimore watched it all at Kaine's side. Her confusion was genuine. "What is it, old salt? What's happening here? What have I done? Are we too late?"

Kaine didn't answer. The helicopter had delivered its parcel. Now it flew hurriedly back toward land.

In the plateau on the opposite side of the hill lay the site of the king's court. The fence enclosing it was masked by a sheet of black nylon which made viewing difficult; with the onset of night, it was nearly impossible. The enclosed area, Kaine estimated, covered three acres. This was three times the area of the court itself—under normal circumstances, an unnecessarily large area to fence off.

There was little left of the court's original building. It had been rounded and domed in its completed state two thousand years ago. What remained today was the intricately scrolled floor, the marble throne and dais, and a series of finely carved arches.

From their vantage atop the hill, Kaine also glimpsed the boom arm of a derrick crane, inactive at the moment. The helicopter was clearly visible now. It swept low over the area, cables dangling loosely below, and landed thirty seconds later, seemingly at the crane's feet, out of sight.

Kaine set out again, the Stonemaiden straining at his heels and gasping for wind. A well-worn path led eventually to the graded road that gave sole access to this canonized segment of the Karmin-Yar project.

A single gateway led to the excavation of the king's court itself. The gate was a galvanized frame set on wheels, large enough to admit the earthmovers and backhoes and tractors which sat idle now inside the compound.

The man who patrolled the entrance carried a clipboard; Kaine had expected an automatic rifle or at least a sidearm. Then he realized that almost any action within an archeological site could be justified and explained as scientific or historical as long as the right people proclaimed it so. The beauty of this was that the Stone-maiden, with her lithology lapel pin and unforgettable face, and

Kaine, presumably the latest in an ever-revolving parade of geologists, were among the right people.

The man at the gate was, however, not so easily impressed. He asked for Kaine's identification, and Kaine produced the papers he had taken from Maurice Dreyfuss.

"You're not wearing your glasses, Professor Dreyfuss," the man inquired. It was a skillful way of saying the picture looked nothing like Kaine. "Mind if I ask why?"

"Would you like him to pop out one of his contact lenses for you?" the Stonemaiden snapped. "Or could we get on with our work?"

"No, he's right to wonder," Kaine replied. "In fact, your conduct is worth mentioning to the head of security. Give me a second to look at your identification. I think a commendation is in order."

The head of security at Karmin-Yar was a member of the government's secret police; no one actively sought his approval, much less his attention. Kaine knew this. The man turned the clipboard over and over in his hands. His face twitched, as he pondered how to retract his previous statement.

The Stonemaiden saved him. She said, "He's a good boy, really. The commendation isn't necessary. The head of security already knows of his excellent efforts."

"Thank you," he replied, and opened the gate an extra foot for their benefit.

Kaine and the Stonemaiden entered the compound. They circled the gridded perimeter, following the unexcavated walks on the north side of the court. In archeological parlance, these were called "balks." Balks were necessary for reading the changes in soil patterns, in its color and density. Excavation of the balks also resulted in narrow ditches on either side, and when Kaine and Marty were out of sight of the gate, they took shelter in one of these. The king's court of Darius the First lay fifty yards to the south.

Now it became clear. A landing pad had been constructed adjacent to the excavated portion of the court. The helicopter had put down there. The boom arm of the crane hovered over the circular floor of the court. A ring of floodlights illuminated the heart of the circle, and a group of site workers gathered there. A slab of stone the size of a coffin had been uprooted from the floor and laid aside. Peering over the rim of the balk, Kaine could only imagine the opening that led to the tunnel below the court.

The man shouting directions at the crane operator was unmistakably Colonel William Turnbull; he moved a cigar like a baton with his left hand and orange embers danced. Now a pair of men emerged from the opening in the floor; from where he and Marty crouched, one of them looked so much like the late Detective Hennagan that Kaine felt the hair on the back of his neck stand on end.

At last, the rotors of the helicopter came to a halt. The pilot jumped down from the cockpit. Jaymin. Kaine recognized her as much by her confident, audacious stride as by her lithe frame. A flood of excitement washed over him. She confronted Colonel Turnbull with her hands on her hips and her feet spread, and Kaine was swept back to their abrupt parting at the hotel. *You know what I was hoping you'd say, Stephen? I was hoping you'd say, "At this moment, I'm interested in you, Jaymin. In making love to you. In making love to you until we both collapse from exhaustion."* But he hadn't, and now he wondered why.

The Stonemaiden's voice was a grateful reprieve. "Are you going to tell me about all this now, or should I just go back to my bottle of Wild Turkey and pretend I've been working too hard?"

"Jurgen Spire called it the fire theft," Kaine replied, "and it cost him his life."

"Dreyfuss. Spire. A lot of people dying around here, old salt." There was no jocularity in Marty Perrimore's voice. "Are you next, or am I?"

Kaine had little choice but to confide in her, a woman who had betrayed him, had professed her disdain for him, had confessed her jealousy toward him.

When he was finished, Marty swore openly at the man who had created the fire temple and the king's court and the city of Karmin-Yar in the beginning, Darius the First.

"A warmonger, a mercenary, and a pimp," she growled. "I've said so all along. And now history proves him a foolhardy miser and a sacrilegious hypocrite to boot." Marty spat on the ground. "Spire knew about this from the start and didn't say a word?" She grimaced. "Darius may have been a warmonger and a miser, but I'd take that over a coward any day."

Kaine listened without comment. The site workers they had seen were now crossing the court and lumbering toward the exit. The man at the gate, Kaine saw, was checking the identifications of a second group, obviously the next shift. This second group entered the compound only after the first had been individually checked out. Very efficient. Now Kaine followed the progress of the new arrivals. They walked doggedly toward the court and the crane and the tunnel. Abruptly, one of them veered away. His compatriots seemed neither to notice nor to care. A cigarette dangled from the man's mouth. He trudged toward the perimeter of the excavation and what Kaine now recognized as a row of outhouses.

Suddenly excited, he took the Stonemaiden by the arm. "Marty, do you remember Cyril Davenport?"

"The animal bone guy." Marty was perplexed, also exasperated. "A real loser. Thought he was God's special gift to the female species. From what I heard, it was an unwarranted accolade. Why?"

"He scuba-dived in his spare time. Remember?"

"Like I said, he thought—"

"He kept his diving gear in an old oil drum in anthropology."

"He didn't think anyone knew about it. The truth was no one wanted it."

"I do," Kaine said. He watched the worker disappear behind the outhouse door. "Get it. All of it. Air tanks, wet suit, everything. Meet me at the cargo bay on the east quay."

"You're serious."

"Can you get a key to the explosives depot?"

The Stonemaiden hung her head. She moved it from side to side. "I was just going to sit with my rocks and make love to my Wild Turkey. Why'd you have to show up?"

Kaine kissed her on the forehead. "The cargo bay at the east quay. Two hours."

Then he was running along the balk toward the outhouses. There were five units in all. The man had gone into the one on the far end; the door stood ajar. Kaine heard singing. He wrenched open the door and hit the man square in the jaw. So stunned was the worker that a protest never reached his lips. He crumpled against the back wall. Kaine hoisted him by the collar and dragged him out beyond the outhouses.

He stripped off the worker's shirt and gloves and the scarf he had tied around his forehead. Kaine put these on. But there was something missing. He went back into the outhouse and found the protective goggles dangling from the door handle. The scarf and the goggles concealed the upper half of his face. He and the site worker were both unshaven. Still, he thought, a weak disguise. Finally, Kaine stuffed the worker's mouth with one of his own socks and tied it off with the other. Then he used the man's belt to strap him to the tow bar of a pickup truck beyond the outhouses.

With an air of nonchalance, Kaine walked toward the circle of light illuminating the center of the king's court. He was scared. Marty's words were like pistons in his head: "A lot of people dying around here, old salt. Are you next or am I?"

Kaine saw that the crane operator had climbed down from his cab. He and Jaymin were smoking cigarettes; she was gesturing out toward the freighter and the running lights that gave life to the ship. Turnbull had retreated to a canvas tent at the edge of the court. He was hunched over a small table dimly lit by a gas lantern. Next to him stood the man who so resembled the policeman Kaine had seen electrocuted two days earlier. The site workers were dropping into the tunnel one by one. Kaine saw a flicker of artificial light rising from the opening.

The crew foreman was standing on the huge stone slab that had once hidden Darius's secret passage. His hands were on his hips, and his eyes followed Kaine with a look that convinced Kaine he was not for a moment fooled by his disguise.

Yet the foreman's voice, though heavy with exasperation, delivered a different message. "What's this? The night's just starting, mister." Distinctively American, Kaine thought. He made a show of checking the strap on his goggles, his head bowed. "You start the shift out in the goddamn outhouse? What does that tell me? You gonna run off for a shit every time we get a five-minute break?"

The foreman didn't wait for an answer. He jumped off the stone and climbed disgustedly into the tunnel. Kaine followed. The tunnel, not surprisingly, testified to the sheer extravagance of the Persian architect. Kaine estimated its width at six feet. The walls shone with black limestone. They were periodically adorned with frieze-work honoring the eternal flame. Iron sconces, once the bearers of great candles, were now empty.

Thick pine timbers reinforced the ceiling. A string of incandescent bulbs had been strung from timber to timber. The air felt cool, and it moved; every hundred yards, forced-air generators churned. The air was also damp, and it left the walls glistening with condensation.

The tunnel floor consisted of bits of loose gravel upon which thick railroad ties had been laid. Narrow-gauge railroad tracks ran its entire length; as with the lights and the generators, this was not the work of the Persian architect. Kaine jumped aboard a motorized flatcar six feet in length. He sat with his back to the foreman. The foreman released a hand lever on the engine mount and the car moved slowly down the tracks. Kaine marveled at the sophistication of the operation.

Ahead, he heard the low rumble of two other cars. The voices of the other workers filtered back, as well. Yet to call them site workers was an obvious mistake; they were hired thieves as surely as Maurice Dreyfuss, Louis Mathers, and Colonel Turnbull were the architects of the conspiracy of which they were a part. Now he heard laughter, and the foreman assailed them with a burst of profanity. "Shut the hell up. What do think this is? A goddamn party?"

As the flatcars took them deeper into the tunnel, Kaine visualized the city blueprint. The tunnel ran east, away from the existing excavation, beneath the town square and the ruins of the cathedral of the Achaemenids, and surfaced a half mile later at the base of the fire temple. Here the flatcars stacked up one behind the other.

Four stone steps rose to a new opening. The slab that had concealed the opening for so long had been wrestled aside. The six workers clambered up. The room beyond was circular, as Kaine knew all Persian fire temples to be. Its ceiling arched magnificently above walls of limestone. An altar and font stood at the room's heart. The crucible of the eternal flame, a lantern forged of gold and bejeweled with rubies and emeralds, graced the altar as it must have done twenty centuries ago.

Here too the walls glistened, but neither from condensation nor age. Rather, from gold. Persian gold. The harvest of a century's worth of taxation and tributes swallowed by the earth over two thousand years ago. Kaine could only stare in amazement.

Chests were filled with darics, the gold coins bearing the image of Darius himself. Silver ingots were stacked in neat rows against two walls. Dreyfuss had estimated one hundred thirty tons of gold. How much of it had been removed over how many nights, Kaine could only guess. But much had; Kaine was left with the feeling that, had he arrived a night later, the temple would have been empty.

The thieves were methodical and businesslike; they neither acknowledged nor questioned Kaine's presence. He was a body, a strong back, nothing more. They worked in teams of three, in three stages. First they hauled a chest of coins or a tray of ingots to the stairs. Next they lowered each parcel to the tunnel floor. Finally, they maneuvered each onto the back of a flatcar. Each car held three chests and six trays, an hour and ten minutes' worth of back-breaking work.

Caked with grit and sweat, the workers walked the flatcars back down the tunnel. At the king's court the chests and trays were strapped to wooden pallets. The crane hoisted the pallets and the boom arm carried them to the helipad. From there Jaymin and the helicopter were the final conduit to the freighter moored a half mile out to sea.

The entire scenario was played out while a city of tents slept a mile away, and stations of busy scientists obliviously plied their skills beyond an unexcavated hillside. For the second time, Kaine found himself admiring the shrewdness of the men behind it all.

Yet their efficiency also played into his hands. When his team emerged from the tunnel the second time, the first shift had returned. The second shift was granted a two-hour break; the foreman threw out a stern warning regarding punctuality and focused most of his attention on Kaine. The team dispersed. Kaine wandered back to the balks. He tore off the shirt, gloves, and headband of the worker he had replaced, and left the compound again under the guise of the head of geology.

31 Little, if anything, came or went from Karmin-Yar by sea. The reef patterns offshore were simply too treacherous. Still, a pier had been built at the east end of the site with the intention of seeing minor items delivered to and from the tent city a mile down the coast via skiff or shallow-water launch.

The pier was constructed of wooden pilings and cuts of untreated pine, now fast rotting. A concrete slab had been poured along the shore, however, and two small warehouses, built of cinder block and reinforced with steel bars, stood upon it. They, along with Darius's own stone fortifications, were the most substantial buildings within miles. They were also well away from the actual excavation site and out of view of the camp work stations.

The largest of the two buildings provided storage for canned food, an item highly coveted among the native population. The other, though smaller in size, was a windowless chamber whose singular purpose was the storage of the site's favorite target of theft: explosives. The array was both eclectic and impressive; that, in and of itself, was odd, because explosives were rarely used on an archeological dig. Yet geologists and archeologists were keenly attracted to them. The Turkish military had provided the Karmin-Yar project with a virtual arsenal.

By Kaine's watch he had spent two hours and twenty minutes hauling gold from the fire temple to the King's Court. As he stood now outside the fenced compound he was overwhelmed with the desire to run, for his faith in Marty Perrimore was not absolute. Yet running on the grounds of an archeological site was prohibited simply because what lay beneath one's feet was often unknown. Kaine ran anyway. He knew the grids well, and reached the east quay in ten minutes.

Marty's truck was parked between the two warehouses. She wallowed in the front seat, drunk and irate. Kaine startled her.

"You crazy man. You inconsiderate crazy man." She did her best to climb contemptuously out of the truck. "I've been sitting here for an hour and a half looking stupid."

"What's stupid about sitting by the sea on a night like this, toasting the fog and the good fortune of being alive?" Kaine replied.

"My good fortune ended about six hours ago with the rediscovery of your face."

"You're drunk." Then Kaine saw the bare-chested young man crouching in front of the smaller of the two warehouses. He was dark-skinned and emaciated, his ribs clearly outlined beneath the skin. He was dressed in a tattered pair of drawsting pants. He wore no shoes. An overstuffed duffel bag lay at his feet.

"His name is Treas," Marty said quickly. "Ethe Treas."

"Get rid of him."

"He knows the arsenal, Kaine. And he dives."

Treas rose, approaching Kaine with quiet, confident steps. "I have known for some time that matters were not right here at Karmin-Yar. Perhaps I can help make them so again."

"A man who conceals his knowledge in a maze of unspoken words is a man of little confidence," Kaine said, quoting Cappadocian folklore. He climbed into the bed of the pickup truck and rummaged quickly through the diving gear. He held up a full-body wet suit and found it very near his own size. A nylon tote contained flippers, weights, depth and pressure meters, an underwater watch, and a waterproof flashlight. There were two air tanks, one full, the other nearly so. Kaine checked the intake valve on the mouthpiece of the full tank. Satisfied, he jumped down again. He carried the tote, the wet suit, and the full tank down to the end of the quay.

He jogged back with his hand out. "The key."

The Stonemaiden was wearing a down vest. Swaying on unsteady legs, she fumbled for a ring of three keys from an inside pocket. "I couldn't just sit there, half frozen," she said, now meekly holding out his mackinaw to him. "I hadn't intended bringing my Wild Turkey with me."

Kaine wasn't sympathetic. "The bottle just jumped into your hand as you were walking out the door."

Then he sighed. He grasped her gently by the shoulders, kissed her forehead, and smiled. "You did good, Marty. Real good. Go back to your station. Get some sleep. If this all goes according to the plan I haven't made yet, we'll have a shot with breakfast."

"A plan you haven't made yet." Her massive head moved back and forth. Tears rolled down her face. "Improvise, you always told me. Improvise." She stumbled back toward the truck. As she opened the door, she looked back at him and said, "The first man ever to accuse me of having instincts. I did so love that, old salt."

"Go home," Kaine said to Treas when the truck was out of sight.

The three keys unlocked a padlock and two deadbolts. A reinforced steel door revealed a pitch-black room maintained at a constant fifty-eight degrees. For the first time, Kaine realized he was sweating; the cool air struck his skin and he shivered momentarily.

The same generator that ran the cooling system also provided electric light, and Kaine discovered a pull chain in the center of the room. A single hundred-watt bulb cast an insufficient light over the arsenal, an arsenal Darius the First would surely have put to better use than the discoverer of his lost city.

Darius was a descendant of nomadic herders. The herders eventually settled the land and took to farming. Some became landowners. His ancestors were the first people of the civilized world to break and ride horses; they learned the art of the short bow and dagger and how to wield a spear or javelin on horseback. They worked in bronze and clay, in silver and gold. They perfected warfare by chariot. Darius was born of Cyrus the Great, called the master of the bloodless coup, a title Kaine recognized as one of history's great euphemisms. Darius was a born warrior; he reigned over an army of two million men. His empire stretched from India to Egypt, from the Black Sea to the Arabian Sea.

Kaine stood in the half-light of this well-stocked arsenal comparing himself to the man known in his time as the King of Kings. Kaine believed in self-defense, not in conquest for its own sake; he would gladly give up his life for those he loved. Did that make him more or less a man than Darius? Darius had created a cuneiform system of writing made up of over three thousand signs, called Old Persian. Kaine had been one of the first to make the system accessible at the university level. Did that make him more or less a scholar than Darius? Darius the Second had taken up arms against his father. Angela hadn't spoken a word to Kaine their last day together; she had as much as blamed him for Tanner Thorpe's death. Did that make him more or less a father than Darius? Darius had driven his people toward bankruptcy in his quest for gold. Kaine was considering a plan that would see that gold lost once more, perhaps permanently. Did that make him more or less unscrupulous than Darius?

The explosives, ironically, were almost all Soviet-made; the Soviets had been benefactors to the Turkish government for years. The markings on the sides of wooden crates and heavy cardboard boxes had been scratched out with black markers, and the English translations penciled in. The translations were only slightly less confusing than the Russian.

NITROGLYCERIN DYNAMITE—SHOULD NOT BE USED UNDERGROUND DUE TO AFTER BLAST FUMES. VELOCITY: 17,400 FEET PER SECOND. 50 POUNDS PER CASE. Kaine counted four cases.

ASTROLITE—PRIMARY USE, DEMOLITION. APPROXIMATE RATE OF DETONATION, 26,200 F.P.S. DO NOT USE WITH TETRYL BOOSTERS. Two cases.

FLEX-X—PRIMARY USE, CUTTING CHARGES FOR IRREGULAR OR CURVED SURFACES. FLEXIBLE, WATERPROOF, EASILY CUT, AND INSENSITIVE TO SHOCK. One case.

There were others. Kinepak, Pentolite, TNT, smokeless powder. Kaine read the instructions and the warnings and realized an expert in the field would have hit upon a hundred different vehicles of destruction. For every one of them he found accessories necessary to facilitate the process. Detonators, boosters, blasting caps, safety fuses, casings, fillers, primers, cartridge sticks, igniters, crimpers.

Kaine was not an expert in explosives; his confusion manifested itself in a self-deprecating grin.

"It's right in front of you," a voice at his back said.

Kaine was past being startled; he came about in a slow circle. The young man called Treas stood in the open door, slender arms folded across his chest.

Kaine had heard neither the opening of the door nor his entrance. "Close the door," he said.

Treas did so. "You are confused," he said, "and these kinds of things are nothing to be confused about. As our mutual friend said, I can help."

He spoke an educated English, his accent similar to Ras Haydar's. By now Kaine had become wary of locals so adept at his language.

"It's right in front of me," Kaine said flatly. "Where, right in front of me?"

"Whatever your purpose, the tools are here," Treas answered. "Tell me your purpose, and I will provide the tools."

How would Darius have advised him? Kaine wondered. *Tell him your purpose, reap his knowledge, and then dispose of him.*

Kaine took the first step. "There is a freighter at anchor off the coast, flying a Colombian flag. I intend to sink it."

"Very well. It can be done." Treas moved quickly to the back wall of the warehouse. He found a small stepladder, spread its less-than-stable legs, and climbed to the third rung. He reached for the top shelf, pushed one box aside and then another. "When and where?" he asked.

Kaine answered by saying, "Questions that have nothing to do with my purpose."

Treas paused, facing him momentarily. For the first time, Kaine saw signs of life in his dark eyes. "Very well," he answered again.

Eventually Treas's search ended with a single wooden box. It was heavy and he required Kaine's help in moving it from the shelf to the floor. The Soviet nomenclature had been translated to read, C4 EXPLOSIVE PLASTICIZER—SELF-CONTAINED, MAGNETIZED

LIMPET MINES. INDIVIDUAL UNITS. PRIMARY USE, LONG-RANGE DEMOLITION. WATER RESISTANT. RADIO WAVE DETONATOR, TYPE E-27 ONLY. FREQUENCY 72.320.

Treas found a rusted screwdriver and split the top of the box. Inside, neatly packed in straw, were eight twelve-inch round steel casings, convex on one side, flat on the other. Attached to the flat side of each mine was a four-inch square magnet. Also on this flat side they discovered a square panel held in place by four screws. Treas used the screwdriver to expose the interior and found the frequency controls: five tiny dials and an activation switch.

The type E-27 detonators were wrapped in plastic bubble paper. They resembled common remote-control units. Flat and rectangular, a single unit fit in the palm of Kaine's hand. Each came equipped with a collapsible antenna. A warning was printed across the face: NOT RESISTANT TO WATER. The frequency controls matched those found inside the panels on the explosives. The remote was equipped with two activation devices, mere switches really. The first activated the frequency mode. The second activated the explosive.

"This is very good." Treas tapped the switches eagerly. "This means that a single unit can be employed to control more than one mine."

Kaine had already deduced as much. He unpacked a second mine and, as Treas had on the first, used the screwdriver to remove the panel from the back. Then he set both mines to the same frequency. This done, he replaced the panels again.

"Two will not be enough," Treas said. A trace of agitation crept into his voice, and Kaine puzzled over it.

"It's all I can carry," he said.

Treas thrust a hand at his own chest. "And two is four."

Kaine stowed the remote control in his coat pocket. "No."

"Where will you place the mines?" Treas asked. "Do you seek only to damage the ship or is your purpose truly to sink it?"

"Where?" Kaine asked.

"Where can only be answered underwater," Treas replied. "If your purpose is truly to sink the ship and you find a suitable location for the mines, how will you activate them given that radio waves

refuse to travel through water? These are simple questions which
I pose to you. I assume they are redundant. But perhaps not."

Treas didn't wait for a response. He uncovered two more mines
and a second remote unit. He placed them at Kaine's feet. Then
he crossed the room and threw aside a large tarp. Beneath it he
found a large spool wrapped with many yards of flexible antenna
wire. From this, he cut four pieces fifteen feet in length. He
searched again, throwing aside clamps and straps and settling in
time on a thick roll of tape.

He carried his cache back to the center of the room.

"Now you will learn," he said. "The explosive is primed by an
electric blasting cap. The antenna wire picks up the radio signal
from the remote unit. The wire sends a minor electric current to
the blasting cap, which ignites the plastic explosive. Simple."

"*If* the antenna wire is above the waterline."

"You learn quickly." The compliment was delivered without
enthusiasm; Treas was busy connecting the sections of antenna
wire to the contact points on the explosives. "The tape is waterproof
and like glue when stuck to metal. That is not our problem. Our
problem is setting the antenna wire above the waterline without
exposing ourselves to the men on the freighter we intend to sink."

When his task was finished, Treas looked up. He spread his
arms and opened his palms as if to say, "Now the decision is yours."

Once Kaine made his decision, he moved swiftly. He set the
frequencies on the second pair of mines to match those of the first.
Then he tied in the frequencies to the second remote-control unit.
The second pair of mines and the adhesive tape he placed in Treas's
care. Kaine stored the second remote unit, along with the first, in
the inside pocket of his coat. Together they repacked the box and
placed it on the shelf well out of sight. Finally, Kaine switched off
the light, closed the door, and restored the three locks.

They carried the mines to the end of the quay. Treas hurried
back for his duffel bag.

Night deepened, and the temperature plunged. Kaine's watch
read eight fifty-seven, nearly midnight Karmin-Yar time. The
freighter lay at anchor a half mile west, and by Kaine's estimate,

nearly the same distance out to sea. Its running lights were now shadowy filaments in the thickening fog.

They stripped down to their shorts. Kaine stowed his clothes in the arms of his mackinaw and hung the bundle over the side of the quay, out of sight of anything less than a thorough search. The wet suit proved a good fit. He stored the remote-control units in a waterproof hip pack and clipped the pack to his weight belt.

Treas emptied his own gear from the duffel bag. His wet suit was a dirty olive green, small and worn. He dressed quickly. The knife he hooked to his weight belt had both straight and serrated edges. He said, "It will do us no good for you to have both remote controls. The other could serve as a backup in case something happened to the first."

"Like what?" Kaine slipped the underwater watch around his wrist and squeezed into the flippers. He studied Treas all the while.

"Things happen," was all Treas said.

"You're right," Kaine agreed. "Things do happen. Once the mines are set, you and I will separate. Do you know the place they call the West Block?"

Treas nodded. The West Block was the name given to the remains of a Persian bathhouse situated at the mouth of the original Karmin-Yar river. What remained, essentially, was the most beautiful slab of marble Kaine had ever seen, and fragments of two collapsed walls. A cove had developed over the centuries and now the site workers used it as a launch for skiffs and sailboats.

"Go directly there," Kaine said. "When you're out of the water, hide the second remote in the cistern beneath the block. Then go home. Go home and stay there."

"It's a good plan," Treas said excitedly. "It's a very good plan. And you?"

Kaine didn't answer. He adjusted his oxygen tank. He checked the regulator on his mouthpiece. When his mask was in place, he jumped off the quay with two of the four limpet mines in the nylon tote over his shoulder and a flashlight in his hand. Treas was in the water beside him moments later.

They swam straight out from the quay, Kaine with an eye on

Treas's shoulder, a body length between them. The water was silty and dark, and as cold as the chilling waters of the Strait of Dover. The cold brought back memories of the ferry, of a child grasping a headless doll, of a mother cradling her shivering baby, of the sound of a drowning man's last breath: images Kaine had to escape. He drove himself harder out to sea. Tiny fish, like flecks in the eye, darted in and out of the beams created by their flashlights. A dense barrier of coral reef emitted muted colors even in the dead of night, a red like dried blood, a yellow like sun-bleached paper, a blue like deep bruises.

They crossed the reef and then followed it west. Treas was a strong swimmer; he moved out of range of Kaine's beam. For nearly a minute Kaine saw no sign of him. He felt a burst of panic and switched off his light. He dove. The explosives propelled his descent. Near the bottom, he swam in a westerly direction for fifty yards, feeling his way in the pitch black, breathing intermittently. Eventually, he saw the muted beam of Treas's flashlight, ten or twelve feet below the surface. It was clear that the young man had stopped, for the beam moved sporadically, panning the water around him. Kaine came upon him slowly. At the last instant, he switched on his own light and played it upon Treas's face. There was no readable reaction; Treas stared back blankly, no alarm, no confusion. To the contrary. The confusion and alarm, Kaine realized, were his own.

He pointed toward the surface. There, they located the freighter. The fog, Kaine realized, was his ally now. If he could only be as confident of the man beside him.

Surfacing a second time, they heard the tumultuous warble of Jaymin's helicopter. It passed directly overhead. The fog churned under the downdraft of its rotors. Shafts of white poured from the spotlights mounted on its rounded nose. The beams cut through the fog, scored the sea, and eventually found the deck of the freighter.

Treas dove, and Kaine followed. He led them away from the reef line into deeper water.

From below, the filthy hull of the freighter loomed huge and out of place in the soft grays of sea and night. Thick anchor chains hung taut from stern and bow. In his mind, Kaine pictured the twin funnels of the freighter rising from the stern end, directly aft of the bridge deck. Which meant the holds of the vessel ran from the bridge deck, midship, to the bow.

Treas swam intently alongside the vessel. He drew up near midship, approximately ten feet from the waterline. He gestured toward Kaine's tote, and together they removed the first mine. Like a greedy suction cup, the magnet at the back latched onto the ship's side; the sound of metal on metal echoed dully and the two men stared ominously at one another.

Though the echo faded as quickly as it had come, there was no solace in the ensuing silence.

Kaine fed the antenna wire up the side of the hull to the surface. He dug the waterproof adhesive tape from his tote and tore off a series of six-inch strips, then spaced these along the upper third of the wire. Finally, he broke the surface, the end of the wire in one hand, reached up the hull, and sealed the uppermost strip to the steel. He followed the remaining strips back into the water, sealing each against the hull as he descended.

They waited. There was no way of knowing if he had been seen. Kaine calculated the odds; it was night, the fog was heavy, the men on board the freighter were occupied, and he had seen no sign of Jaymin's helicopter. Treas tugged at the wire and it held. They moved on.

They attached a second mine thirty yards closer to the bow. It occurred to Kaine that he could be placing the mines in the ship's least vulnerable spots and never know it.

Nonetheless, they followed the same procedure on the ship's starboard side, without incident. For a brief moment before they parted, the two accomplices illuminated one another's faces with their flashlights. Treas was smiling.

And then he was gone, powerful kicks propelling him in the direction of the West Block. Kaine followed his departure until all he saw was black water.

Then, as a matter of precaution, Kaine dove straight for the ocean floor. He found a patch of sea grass beside which he took shelter. He extinguished his light.

Resting, even for a moment, was a mistake in one sense. Fatigue and the blunt realization of his actions over the last hour seemed to come at him from all directions. He sucked hard on the mouthpiece and the flow of oxygen left him lightheaded.

There was something else, as well. To accomplish his task, he had no choice but to return to shore. And even at that, were he successful at bringing down the freighter, the task would truly then be only half done.

For you to come the entire way to Larnica makes no sense, the message Louis Mathers had conveyed to Maurice Dreyfuss said. *Your presence is unnecessary, the way is treacherous, and to leave Karmin-Yar unattended would only arouse suspicion. Our rendezvous remains Ano Kliston on the 19th.* The meaning behind the references to Ano Kliston and Larnica had, until this moment, eluded Kaine. It was only here, alone and sheltered by a patch of fitful seagrass, that he was able to put it together with a second message, the one given to Angela by the stowaway Ras Haydar. "Tell your father that the deed will happen the third week in March. Tell him that's all I know."

Even then Kaine had recognized the time frame suggested by the message, the week of the opium harvest; it was only now that he recalled that Larnica was a mountain village at the heart of the most prodigious poppy-growing region in Asia Minor.

The first message also brought to mind that Mathers, whatever his long-range plan, had for now been held up in England, that he was not, as Preble had said, on vacation. Oddly, Kaine perceived Mathers, though physically unimpressive, as a more formidable foe than a Jankowski or a Hennagan, more so even than a Colonel Turnbull. This perception was no doubt rooted in Mathers's barbaric execution of Tanner Thorpe, but it was just as strongly influenced by the fact that Mathers remained in England, where Danielle and Angela were in hiding.

When his breathing stablized, Kaine set out again, traversing the bottom in an eastward direction away from the freighter and eventually turning toward the coast. He surfaced before the reef line and found he had gone a short distance beyond the east quay. Though his vision was obscured, he could see two men standing upon the rotting dock. They were scanning the sea and the fog and smoking cigarettes.

Kaine did not believe in coincidence; they knew he was here. But did they know where? There was, he decided, nothing about their actions to suggest he had been spotted. After a moment, the men flicked their half-smoked cigarettes into the water off the quay. They turned away, brisk steps taking them inland, and were soon out of sight.

Without hesitating, Kaine deposited his oxygen tank and air hose at the coral reef, drew a deep breath, and swam directly for the quay. He surfaced only when he could stand, and then only for a breath of air and a last gauging of his target.

The end of the quay stood in four feet of water. Kaine came up beneath it, straddled the pillar upon which his clothes hung, and exposed himself only long enough to remove them. With the clothes held aloft, he swam east away from the quay. He encountered a sandbar fifty yards farther on and came out of the water there. He used a sand dune for cover, shedding the wet suit and flippers. When he was dressed, Kaine removed the remote-control unit from the waterproof pouch in which he had been carrying it. He fondled it momentarily, glancing briefly out to sea and the ghostly outline of the freighter. Finally, he stowed the unit in his coat pocket.

It was too soon to trigger the mines, Kaine knew that. The water in which the freighter was anchored was far too shallow and much too close to shore. To sink the freighter now would only wound the operation. Kaine's intent was far more ambitious.

32 Night imposed a strange magic on Karmin-Yar. The pale yellow of a waning moon, the wisps of fog creeping inland; it was like viewing a Michelangelo sculpture in its first stages of creation, a rough cut of the upper torso punching its way out of a block of marble. In this archeological wonder, columns supported only air, arches rose without rooftops, porticos entered upon rooms with a single wall, stairways without destinations. All were masked by the fog and by the forbidding shadows cast by its pale counterpart in the sky above.

Kaine climbed the hills east of the site. He paused in the shadow of a bent and gnarled juniper, then circled a bramble of thorny shrubs. He stopped at the foot of a low mesa and crawled on his stomach to the edge. From here, he was blessed with a full view of the original site. He was also able to glimpse the newly resurrected king's court, and upon the water a misty rendering of the Colombian freighter.

Then he saw flames. They erupted at the heart of the scientific work stations. The fire spread into a neat square, as if some unseen power had mandated dimensional limits on the flame. The lithicist's station. Kaine knew it at once.

"Marty!"

He leapt to his feet. He had taken only two steps when the startling sound of his own name brought him to a halt. The call rose up from the vicinity of the fire, obviously projected by a bullhorn.

"Professor Kaine." The familiarity of the voice was like a sucker punch catching Kaine low in the stomach. Bile rose in his throat. Preble. Detective Superintendent Preble. The worst of it was the lack of faith Kaine had shown in his own powers of insight. His anger evoked an ancient Persian saying: *The fool who knows, but does not believe, is a fool for all time.* So it seems, Kaine thought.

"Professor Kaine," the voice boomed again. "We will ask you to come forward of your own accord. Miss Perrimore has already been put in jeopardy, as you can surely see. For her sake, if not for yours, please make your way down the hillside. There'll be no trouble, I assure you."

At the same time, Kaine heard the clamor of Jaymin's helicopter. He saw one of its spotlights come to life; a circle of light blossomed at the edge of the smoldering work station. Within the circle Marty Perrimore, the Stonemaiden, knelt, head thrust down, arms clasped behind her. Hovering over her, a hand grasping the back of her shirt, stood Detective Superintendent Preble.

"Bastard." The word came from the depth of Kaine's throat, a terrible whisper. Then he shouted it. "Bastard."

He vaulted down the hillside. In the gravel lot behind the work stations, among idle road graders and earthmovers, he paused momentarily. Reaching into his coat pocket, he removed the remote-control unit and laid it between the grooves of the tractor tread of a huge bulldozer. Then he jogged through the lot and the still blackness onto the road approaching the stations.

The clapboard walls of Marty Perrimore's station sent flames licking at the night. The machinery within the walls smoldered. The canvas ceiling and doorflaps had been swept from existence; the stench of gasoline permeated the air. The rotors of the helicopter sent dust and ash skyward in wild pirouettes.

Kaine halted in the penumbra at the edge of the light. Finally, the helicopter moved on, taking the light with it, and set down on the road thirty yards away. Even before the blades had stopped, he saw Jaymin and Colonel William Turnbull climbing down from the cockpit.

Now there was only the light of the fire. A timber cracked and popped. Another sizzled. A wall collapsed, taking a sorting table with it to the ground. Stones spilled like tumbling dice across the floor.

"So this is the elusive Professor Kaine," Turnbull said when the rotor was quiet. He carried an automatic rifle on his hip. "Well, at least we know where your weakness lies, Professor."

"He means with other human beings," Jaymin added.

"Let her up," Kaine said, tipping his head toward Marty Perrimore.

"You're not in a position to be making demands, Mr. Kaine," Turnbull said.

Kaine stared. His voice tumbled a notch and was that much colder for the change in pitch. "The woman's spent enough time on her knees."

Turnbull swung the rifle as if it were a dismissing wave of the hand. "Let's indulge the professor, Detective Preble. We don't want to scar his sensitivities."

Preble released the Stonemaiden's shirt. She labored to her feet. "They got nothing from me, old salt," she said to Kaine, dusting herself off and spitting at Preble's feet. "They knew you were here, but they didn't get it from me. Even dead drunk, I'm a tough old bitch. You know that."

"I know," Kaine said.

"Search him," Turnbull ordered Jaymin.

"Search him yourself," Jaymin replied. She struck a pose Kaine recognized, feet spread, hands lost in the pockets of her leather jacket. "Or have King Kong do it, if it's that important."

"Do it," Turnbull told the detective.

"With pleasure," Preble said. He circled, kicked Kaine's feet apart, and slammed a fist into his kidney. Kaine's knees buckled. "I don't care much for being called a bastard," the detective superintendent said quietly.

"Tough one to swallow, I'll bet," Kaine responded, his teeth clenched. A second blow drove him to the ground. "Then I've known snakes with more loyalty, so maybe 'bastard' is a little generous."

"Really?" Preble sent the toe of his shoe plunging into Kaine's rib cage, forcing him into a ball. Kaine tried rolling, but Preble caught him with his thick hands, drove him back to the ground with his knee, and used his hands again to search him head to foot. "And how does it feel to be a card played by every player at the table, smart boy?"

Preble hoisted Kaine to his feet. "Clean," the detective superintendent said.

Kaine staggered, but behind his faltering steps he showed Preble a crooked smile. Then he turned. Oddly, he found that Colonel Turnbull had paid no attention to the encounter between himself and Preble. Instead, Turnbull's eyes were fixed upon the side of Jaymin's face, and the intensity of his gaze made Kaine afraid for her. Had she provoked him so easily?

"I think Professor Kaine is in for a surprise, Detective Preble," Turnbull said. He used Preble's name, but his focus had not changed. "He has been far too involved in our affairs, and it's time his involvement was terminated. I think it's only fitting that his termination take place right here though, among the walls of the city upon which he has placed so much importance, and wasted so much of his life. Don't you agree, my dear?" he said to Jaymin.

Instead of answering, Jaymin strode forward, sweeping past Preble as if he were an inanimate object, and placing herself directly in front of Kaine. Gently, she unbuttoned his shirt and ran her hand over the bruised area of his side. With the fingertips of her other hand she touched his face, tracing the outline of his mouth, and drawing him slowly toward her. Her lips brushed against his, following the path her fingertips had just taken. And then she pressed against his cheek.

"Damn you. What are you doing here?" Her voice trembled, painful and low. "Oh, Stephen, we were so close to something special."

Kaine's arms encircled her. "I know that. I do. And I'm sorry."

"Me, too. For everything. Truly I am. Always believe that."

And then, as quickly as she had begun, Jaymin pushed away from him.

She walked halfway back to Turnbull, stopped, and glared over her shoulder. "Yes, I do agree, Colonel. An archeologist should definitely perish with his toys. And what more fitting toy than a city two thousand years old?"

Turnbull stared at her, his mouth slightly agape, confused, enraged, and aroused in the same volatile moment. "And?" he said.

"Not 'and.' But," Jaymin replied. "But not without a touch of irony."

Unlike Turnbull's, Kaine's rage was fueled solely by confusion. What was she doing, for God's sake? And why? He said, "Irony. That's your strong suit, isn't it?"

"My strong suit is the paradoxical, not the ironic," Jaymin answered. "Which brings us to the fire temple, the focal point of anyone who has spent half his life devoted to the Persian Empire. After all, the temple *was* the first structure built in any of their cities, right? The most revered, the most important, the most fiercely defended of all buildings."

"Information my thirteen-year-old daughter can recite in her sleep," Kaine said.

"The irony of the matter is that the esteemed discoverer of Karmin-Yar, the proud professor of things dead and gone, wasn't even the one to uncover that which he most sought. The paradox behind the matter," she went on, "is that the same fire temple would seem to be the perfect place for the proud professor to end his search."

"Permanently," Turnbull intoned.

"Naturally," Jaymin said. "But unless I'm mistaken, the proud professor won't approve of the method I have in mind. You see, Colonel, our archeologist here is a man of high standards. The problem with a man of high standards is an uncontrollable urge to pass judgment upon those you don't think quite measure up."

Kaine had fallen silent, numb. He met her steely gaze full on and held it, wanting to shout, "Why are you doing this? Is life that meaningless to you? Is death?" And then, as if in answer, Jaymin's expression wavered minutely; Kaine was convinced of it. A hesitation, the slightest tilt of her head, and despite himself he wanted to believe that she was reaching out to him.

He heard Colonel Turnbull say, "I see. Mr. Kaine knows about your nasty habit, doesn't he?"

Jaymin straightened. "He knows. Which leads me to the method I have in mind."

"Hold the bloody hell on. What are you talking about?" Preble snapped. "What is this?"

"I'm talking about at the end of a needle," Jaymin replied. "Don't you see? It's the only way."

"It's crazy, is what it is. Colonel, you're not listening to this, are you? We put a bullet in the guy's head and get on with our business."

"Use your imagination, Detective Preble," Turnbull said. "By the time the body's found, you'll be on a beach somewhere on permanent vacation. And if it's done right, they'll be calling the professor's death a suicide or an accident."

"It'll be done right," Jaymin assured him.

"I'm sure it will be," Turnbull said to her in a low voice. Then he turned toward the helicopter. "We've wasted enough time. Bring him," he said, gesturing in Kaine's direction.

Preble resorted to his gun, withdrawing it from his shoulder holster and using a wave of the barrel to set Kaine in motion. "And the woman?" the detective called out.

Turnbull paused. His gaze fell momentarily upon the Stonemaiden. She sat cross-legged among her rocks, fondling those that had been thrown to the ground. In her own world, she wept soundlessly, her huge head bobbing.

"Maurice was right," Turnbull said. "She's harmless. Not even a tool worth using anymore."

As Kaine backpedaled toward the helicopter, he didn't know whether to speak out in Marty's defense or not. It made no sense to leave her alive knowing what she did. On the other hand, removing her from the Karmin-Yar project, destroying her reputation, and thus ruining her life, would be more than adequate punishment. Maybe Turnbull saw that; a victim of her own small world, she was incapable of action.

It was a short ride. The helicopter rose less than a hundred feet above the ground. This was still high enough for Kaine to view the electric lights of the tent city and its oblivious tenants a mile away. The moon had worked its way down the western sky. Yet dawn was still three hours away. Kaine looked across the cockpit at Jaymin, but she refused to acknowledge him. His eyes drifted down to the controls at her fingertips. An instant later, he felt the barrel of Turnbull's rifle digging into his side.

"Please don't. You'd be dead before it made any difference," the colonel said. "What's more, I have news of your daughter that you just might want to hear."

Kaine glanced over his shoulder, pinning Turnbull with his eyes. It occurred to Kaine that the thought of killing a man with his bare hands had never possessed him before that moment. Had he come so far? The madness of it sent a chill along his spine, and he was forced to look away.

Seconds later, the helicopter set down on the pad next to the king's court. Jaymin seized a small duffel bag from under the seat and climbed out even as the rotors completed their last revolutions. Preble reached into the cockpit and unlatched Kaine's door. Kaine stepped down. There was no sign of the tunnel workers. The crane stood idle. He looked out to sea. The freighter was still at anchor, the water as placid as cast iron.

A wave of terror came over Kaine when his eyes beheld again the mammoth piece of limestone that for so long had concealed the mouth of the tunnel. It lay next to the opening, exactly as it had when Kaine ventured into the tunnel hours ago. A quarter of a mile away, the fire temple lay buried beneath tons of dirt and sand. A man trapped in that tunnel might die of thirst before the air ran out, but he would surely die a slow death. A lethal dose of heroin wasn't necessary.

"Perhaps Professor Kaine would be more comfortable with his hands tied behind his back, Detective Preble," Turnbull said, retrieving a length of nylon cord from the helicopter and passing it into Preble's hands. "I'm counting on you to make sure this thing goes right, Detective. No slipups. Understood?"

"I still don't like it," Preble replied.

By now Preble was merely a machine with limited purpose in Kaine's eyes. He gave his attention fully to Colonel Turnbull. It was a waiting game—dangling news of Angela before him would keep Kaine in line better than any shackle—and Turnbull played the game well. The barrel of Preble's gun prodded Kaine in the direction of the tunnel. They were halfway down the steps when Turnbull held up his hand.

"Oh, Professor Kaine. About your daughter," he called out. "You vacationed some years back in a small harbor town on the coast of southern England, did you not? In Cornwall. Dodman Point. As I understand it, you stayed in a motel called the White Rain. It seems your daughter and ex-wife checked into the same motel only a few days ago. I hope they've enjoyed themselves."

Turnbull dropped his hand. His words followed Kaine into the tunnel like a rabid dog.

33 Preble caught Kaine by the back of the jacket and propelled him past the flatcars stacked up at the mouth of the tunnel. Kaine stumbled. A kidney punch drove him to the tunnel floor, and he cried out. With a quickness that belied his bulk, Preble was on him, a knee coming down hard on Kaine's back. Jaymin stood over them, drawing the polished Smith & Wesson from her shoulder harness, and peering down the site at Kaine.

"If he moves, kill him," Preble said.

"I know how the game is played," Jaymin replied.

His arms drawn roughly behind him, Kaine felt the sting of the nylon cord biting into his wrists. The instant Preble let up, Kaine rolled to his knees. His head came up and the detective superintendent hit him with a blow that echoed throughout the chamber.

"I look forward to seeing you dead, Professor Kaine," Preble said. He raised his hand again; it closed into a meaty fist.

"That's enough," Jaymin shouted an instant before the blow fell. "We're doing it my way."

Preble hesitated, his arm cocked; he stared at her with contempt. "We're doing it my way," she said again.

"I heard you the first time." Preble arose. As a last gesture, he drove a toe into Kaine's side. "Count your blessings, Professor. You got off easy."

"Keep your distance, Preble. And I mean it," Jaymin said. "I don't need a fucking bodyguard, and if I did, I wouldn't go to Scotland Yard for applicants. Got it? Keep your distance."

Preble stepped back toward the mouth of the tunnel. He smiled grimly. "Have it your way, if you like. I'll be here. Do remember though, that in a tunnel like this, with no back door, distance is a relative thing."

"Yeah. Yeah it is. You're a true scholar." Jaymin helped Kaine to his feet.

"Don't keep me waiting long, Jaymin. Turnbull said . . ."

"I heard him," Jaymin interrupted. "He said, 'Make sure.' And when you put your fingers on Kaine's wrist and realize he no longer has a pulse, then you'll be sure. In the meantime, stay out of my way."

"One other thing, Jaymin." Preble propped a leg up on one of the tunnel cars. "I'll kill you before this whole thing is over. Consider it a promise."

"And I'll kill you if you come anywhere near that temple before I say," Jaymin replied mildly. "Count on it."

Jaymin backpedaled a moment and then turned her back to him. She latched onto Kaine's elbow. They walked in silence for nearly a minute. Jaymin listened for the echo of Preble's footsteps, but heard only their own.

Eventually, she whispered, "You have to trust me."

For a moment Kaine said nothing. "Trust you? What about my daughter?"

She cut him off. "I haven't forgotten about Angela."

"Neither have Turnbull or Mathers."

"Shit, Stephen, who do you think got you out of the Crimea?" A sharp breath lent exasperation to a question already heavy with it, but she didn't wait for an answer. "Obviously it wasn't your favorite Scotland Yard detective back there, was it?"

"I know who got me out of the Crimea, Jaymin. I do."

Jaymin was frightened. Not by Preble, nor by the passivity of

Kaine's reply. She was frightened by the strength of her own feelings, feelings for a man she hardly knew, or knew too well because he was such a mirror image of some hidden part of herself. Divulging those feelings frightened her even more. "I liked it when you held me," she said.

"I know," he said quietly.

A voice crept into Jaymin's head. As always, it belonged to Sister Immaculata at the orphanage. Sister Im would say, "You complicate things so, child. A woman's duty is to serve, and to do so without question. Passion and pleasure of any kind have no place in a woman's life; do not mock yourself or life by thinking otherwise."

"Make love to me, Stephen," Jaymin whispered. "Let me make love to you, even if it's just for a short time."

She glanced aside and watched his expression, puzzling, contemplating, rebelling. As always, she interpreted it. Was he dealing with a child or with the most confused woman he had ever met? But for once she held her tongue, and held her breath in anticipation, and felt not for a moment that she was mocking herself or life.

A mask of sadness and longing fell across Kaine's face. "And then you'll stick one of your needles in my arm. Is that it?" he asked.

He answered her inquisitive gaze with one so penetrating that Jaymin could hardly speak. It was all she could do merely to say, "Yes. Yes. Make love to me and then trust me to stick one of my needles in your arm. I'm sorry, Stephen, but there are so many . . . so many things . . ." She could no longer contend with his eyes. She found the railroad tracks in front of her a soothing retreat. And then the words flowed from her again, calmly now, content. "Make love to me. Say you will."

"I will, Jaymin. You know I will," Kaine whispered. Then he also gave himself up to the ribbons of steel at their feet, and they walked the rest of the tunnel in silence.

At the temple entrance, Jaymin glanced back. There was no sign of Preble. She urged Kaine inside. Kaine stumbled up the stairs and into the empty fire temple. All that remained was the altar, the font, and the crucible of the flame no longer eternal. He sprawled on the floor at the foot of the altar, his strength depleted.

Kaine forced himself into a sitting position. The side of his face throbbed. He glanced quickly about him. Gold and silver by the ton had been removed to the last ingot, the last coin. The walls of the temple shone now only with the luster of black limestone. In this, its natural state, the temple exuded the peace and calm of an empty church, as if it had been relieved of some terrible burden. The stone of the altar felt warm to the touch.

Jaymin entered the temple quietly. He was unaware of her presence almost until the instant she was upon him. She knelt beside him. With fingertips as warm as the stone she caressed his face, gently circling the bruise upon his cheek. Her breath was hot and sweet; with each movement of her hands the sound became more desperate, more avid. She kissed his lips, fully, gently biting. Her tongue filled his mouth and he felt the heat building within him. Now her hands traveled to his chest, her lips to his neck, as she moved fluidly to free him from the bonds of the cord.

He felt her hands on his, soothing, even as they struggled with the knot, her urgency compounding the struggle. A moment later he was free, his hands stinging with the rush of new blood.

When Jaymin returned to him, Kaine grasped her roughly by the shoulders, holding her at arm's length. She didn't resist. Instead, she held his gaze until the moment of anger subsided. Then he drew her to him, kissing her wildly, drinking in the scent of her.

They shed their clothes, never losing contact. He arose, lifting her in his arms. He carried her to the altar, lay her upon it, and entered her.

Her head rested upon his chest. Tears pooled in her eyes and dampened her cheeks. Kaine held her. He stroked her hair. His hand traveled down the length of her back and her hips moved against him. He took her hair in his hand and tipped her head back.

He brushed aside the tears, but nothing could stem their flow. Her lips parted. She straddled him and he filled her again. Through the tears she came and came.

To his amazement, Kaine allowed Jaymin to bind his hands again, this time using a leg of the altar. "It has to be this way," she whispered. "Forgive me."

A prisoner once more, Kaine watched her lay the implements from her duffel bag on the temple floor next to him.

A plastic bag contained two hypodermic needles. A candle stood erect in a tiny ceramic stand and Jaymin struck a match to it. The flame wavered in a breeze Kaine had been unaware of until that moment. She lay a bent spoon next to the needles; a film of black carbon stained its surface. She opened a white envelope and they both stared at the powder that lay within it. She drank from a water bottle, filled Kaine's mouth as well, and then set it alongside an eyedropper. A collection of three bandannas materialized at her fingertips. Kaine had seen the blue one before, in the hotel room in London; the other two, one white and red, the other a solid black, fell in a heap next to a swatch of cotton.

There were other things he hadn't seen before. Packets of sugar. A plastic packet containing four small, sealed ampules. A miniature gram scale with tiny steel weights.

Jaymin worked at a feverish pitch.

"We have to hurry," was all she said.

Kaine said nothing. It was as if the use of words had become a dangerous device, in an arena where nothing could express what had just occurred between them. Perhaps it was because they both realized that it could not possibly happen again, not like that. Perhaps because they both realized that it wasn't meant to happen again.

Jaymin tied a bandanna around his bicep, and then did the same to herself.

Kaine's eyes widened. But again he said nothing, and he could see, in the minute softening of Jaymin's face, that she was oddly gratified by his silence. His instincts told him to trust her; his instincts told him the trust was mutual.

She opened the water bottle, dipped into it with the eyedropper, and filled the spoon. She used the tip of a nail file to transport the white powder from the envelope to the water. She stirred momentarily, then cooked the mixture above the flame for a matter of seconds. A sulfuric stench filled the temple, and the odor seemed to have a calming effect on Jaymin. With her free hand she rolled cotton into a tiny pellet, dropped it into the spoon, and watched it absorb the mixture. Finally, she buried the tip of one needle in the cotton and drew the serum into the cylinder. Kaine remembered the golden brown color.

He watched her tighten the bandanna on her own arm. Watched her make a fist, heard the quickening of her breath, and saw beads of sweat rising from her forehead. There were tiny scabs along her forearm; they rode the ridge of a purple vein. Jaymin guided the needle into her arm. A show of blood in the syringe signaled the successful tapping of the vein. She eased the plunger forward. Her emerald eyes rolled and her head tipped backward. Now the sweat was a sheen covering her entire face. When her eyes opened again, they were pinned and glassy. She groaned.

A minute passed.

When her breathing was under control again, she opened a packet of sugar. Then she tore into the packet of sealed ampules. She cleaned the spoon with water and wiped it dry with the third bandanna. She retrieved the eyedropper and filled the bottom of the spoon with a measured amount of water.

"What you'll feel is this," she said, her voice thin and ragged. "One moment you'll feel lightheaded, the next sick to your stomach. Breathe through it. There'll be an itchy sensation. Expect it. It's not very pleasant, but it won't last. Then you'll feel as if your body has been sent to heaven and given a lifelong massage. Then you'll be floating. You'll wonder why you've never done this before and thank God you haven't."

Jaymin used the scale to measure out a sprinkling of sugar. She added this to the water. She cracked a single ampule and a stream of clear liquid filled the spoon. A sweet scent redolent of cinnamon billowed forth.

Finally, Kaine spoke. "What is it?"

"Trust me," Jaymin said.

When Kaine saw her guiding the fingernail file toward the China White, his stomach tightened. His shirt clung to the rivers of perspiration flowing from under his arms and down his back. Yet what she brought forth from the envelope was less than half the heroin she had just fed into her own vein. She used the scale again, then scraped the powder into the spoon.

When the mixture was thoroughly diluted, she circled the spoon above the flame. For the first time since their lovemaking, she gave him her full attention. Her smile was excited, yet strangely warm, and it helped stem his fear.

"Close your eyes, my love."

With his eyes shut tight, Kaine's thoughts traveled through time to Angela and Danielle. As a family, they had been at their best when they still had the place in the mountains outside Denver. They should never have left. Now, to consider the jeopardy they might well be facing at this moment was almost unbearable. In contrast, Jaymin had unlocked a part of him that very likely only she could have touched. She had helped him see Angela in a new light, as a young woman. Oddly, Jaymin had somehow also freed him to miss Danielle, something he had not admitted to in five years. His mind was a jumble of contradictions—Jaymin, Danielle, Angela—and yet he felt stronger for it.

Cotton absorbed the serum. The needle drew it into the cylinder of the hypodermic. Jaymin tightened his bandanna.

"Make a fist," she said in his ear. She kissed his mouth, gently, languidly. Then she whispered again. "Breathe deeply, slowly. Just relax."

Kaine felt the prick of the needle on his forearm. Momentarily light-headed, he was then swept up by an overwhelming sensation, as if his body were being flooded from the inside out.

He heard Jaymin say, "Don't forget me, Stephen."

And he remembered no more.

PART III

34 Danielle drove the old couple's pickup truck into Meva-gissey, north of Dodman Point. She felt bad abandoning it at the curb in front of a boarded-up movie house, but the pilot had seen the vehicle. It wasn't safe. She felt better when they were on the bus to Plymouth, better yet when they reached the coast.

Plymouth smelled of the sea. It smelled of the fish hauled daily onto its rotting docks and the processing plants that made the fish market-ready.

It was a deceptively large town, old and overgrown. Spawned by the industry that made it a vital community, its citizens were a diverse lot. Plymouth's first fishermen had migrated from Aberdeen, in the north of Scotland. Its first shipbuilders had emigrated from Alaska. Financiers had relocated from London, and dock workers had been imported from as far away as Lisbon.

The bus dropped Danielle and Angela at the Plymouth bus station, within sight of the harbor. Evening was fast settling upon the coast, and Danielle gave thanks for that even as she cursed the English and their antiquated transportation system. She was in that kind of mood. She cursed archeology and everything associated with it. She cursed airplanes and everyone who flew them. She cursed ferries and gold and heroin. Lastly, she cursed her ex-husband even as she longed for his presence. Five years ago he had given her freedom when what she had wanted all along was to bring him to his senses, not to his knees, a point of contention they had never come to terms on. But for now Danielle drove the past from her mind; it was too consuming, and she had other things to think about.

They sat in a pub on Saint Charles Street and ate corned beef sandwiches. Danielle hated corned beef. Ordering it had been a punitive measure, she decided, like buying that ridiculous mystery novel. She was holding Angela's hand, something she hadn't been allowed to do since her daughter turned thirteen.

"There were five buses out of Mevagissey today," Angela reminded her. "I saw the map. One followed the coast down toward Falmouth. One went inland to a place called Truro. They both left Mevagissey about noon and were scheduled to arrive about now."

"I can still read, young lady."

"All three of the others followed routes along the coast and eventually ended up right here in Plymouth. There were inland buses all the way along the line but they all basically ended up nowhere. That pilot knows we're not going back to that stupid motel in Dodman Point. Or back to those cabins."

Angela had acquired her gift for the obvious from her father, and Danielle resented them both for it. "I know that," she said calmly. "You're right."

"Can't we get out of the country?"

"Not according to your dad, who seemed to have a certain amount of faith in that detective. Preble, wasn't that what he called him?"

"I didn't like him," Angela said quickly.

"I hope you mean the detective." They both laughed, and Danielle was pleased to see it. There had been little conversation between them since the scene with the pilot, and no levity; the pressure was intolerable. She gave Angela's hand a quick squeeze. "You're right. We can't stay here."

Plymouth, depressing and colorless, was not a tourist town. Yet the group at the long table next to them was certainly American.

They were boisterous and their voices carried; Danielle heard accents straight out of the Midwest.

One of them, a man in a gabardine coat and felt hat, had been staring at her. The stare turned into a smile; the smile seeded an idea. If logic and a recognition of the obvious were strong suits of Angela, Danielle's was the ability to see a crack in the door of opportunity and to slip through it. In five years, on that very strength, she had risen from the ranks of a regional sales staff at IBM, to the rank of regional manager, and finally to her Paris position.

She returned the man's smile, tossed her head back, and said, "Are you American?"

As she had hoped, the man rose, crossed to their table, and politely removed his hat. He was balding and, by Danielle's estimate, in his mid-fifties.

"I must apologize," he said. "I honestly couldn't hear you over the melee my companions have created, and they're not even drinking yet. You should see them after the cocktail hour."

Danielle rested her chin on her hand, accenting her long neck. "You're American."

"As apple pie."

"On holiday."

"We're pretty obvious, I suppose. I'm John Hopkins."

"Hopkins. Sounds like a name straight out of an old English novel." Danielle smiled lightly. "I'm Danielle Kaine. This is my daughter, Angela."

John Hopkins shook their hands. He cocked his head slightly. "Kaine, you say. Now that sounds pretty English to me."

"Scottish," Angela said.

"Join us." Danielle said. She patted the seat cushion of an empty chair. "What brings you to Plymouth?"

John Hopkins sat down. "That's our cruise ship out in the harbor there. We were headed for the Isle of Wight when all hell broke loose. Some mechanical failure or another, they tell us. So here we sit. Could be worse. And you two ladies?"

"Yes, we're American, as well. Also on holiday. Though nothing so well planned as yours, I'm afraid. A cruise? How romantic,"

Danielle replied. Now her smile filled out her entire face. "Do you realize, Mr. Hopkins, that my poor daughter has never been on a cruise ship? You don't suppose there would be some way she might have a peek, just for the fun of it?"

John Hopkins beamed. "I think you should both have a peek, Ms. Kaine. Just for the fun of it."

"Call me Danielle, please."

"Danielle. As my guests. And while your daughter explores, perhaps I could interest her mother in having a drink with me."

"That would be lovely."

The waiter approached their table. "Anything more I can bring you two ladies? Dessert? Tea?"

"Just the bill," Danielle answered.

"You can put the ladies' tab with ours, young man," Mr. Hopkins said nobly. "They're honorary members of the cruise ship *White Mariner,* now. It's the least we can do."

The waiter shrugged. Danielle graced Mr. Hopkins with a polite tip of the head. "You're very kind."

Ten minutes later, a city bus drew up in front of the pub and the touring Americans were called aboard. Mr. Hopkins took hold of Danielle's arm. Angela held her hand.

"What are you up to?" she whispered in her mother's ear.

"We're getting out of Plymouth," Danielle answered.

They walked aboard the cruise ship *White Mariner* in a group of forty or fifty people. They were immediately taken for passengers. A steward went so far as to apologize to Danielle for any inconvenience their delay had caused them.

Danielle sipped a martini with Mr. Hopkins in one of three dimly lit lounges. The lounge menu offered American entrées, and Angela ordered a cheeseburger and french fries.

When the ship's departure was announced, John Hopkins prepared to see them off, but Danielle said, "Let's be daring and have a quick second round."

Mr. Hopkins was delighted. Twenty minutes later, the ship disembarked with an additional two passengers.

"Oh my, what'll we do with you now?" The gin had made Mr. Hopkins a little giddy by this time.

"Stowaways," Danielle replied mischievously. "You won't tell, will you?"

Angela's imagination flooded with images of the *Spirit of Long Life*. She ate until she was sick. Then she explored. The entertainment center on deck 2 offered video games and pay-per-view movies. Angela boldly charged a movie rental to Mr. Hopkins's room. When the movie ended, she played video games until midnight, when her mother turned up. Alone.

"Didn't he proposition you?" Angela asked.

"Of course." Danielle winced. "Poor man. Three martinis was about his limit. I had a steward walk him to his room."

Her mother looked exhausted; she didn't like games, Angela knew, and stringing Mr. Hopkins along had probably been a more difficult game than any Angela had played in the last two hours.

"We'll sleep here," Danielle said. "Pick a couch."

"The ship was a good idea, Mom."

"We'll see, babe. I hope so."

Angela didn't sleep; she would never sleep on a boat again as long as she lived. She had been sincere when she told her mother that the ship was a good idea, but she was also furious with her for ever allowing her daughter to board another ship of any kind. Yet, by now, they were many miles from Plymouth. Earlier, it had been announced over the ship's intercom that a brief layover would be made at the famous port at Sandown-Shanklin on the Isle of Wight.

At six thirty in the morning, unable to stand the claustrophobic atmosphere of the entertainment center another minute, Angela struggled out of her couch. She was stiff and bleary-eyed. Her mother lay on the couch next to her. She slept soundly even now, and Angela dared not wake her.

She took the stairs to the main deck. Behind a wall of stubborn thunderheads, the sun fought its way into the eastern sky. Two women swam laps in the ship's pool despite a biting wind.

Angela walked to the bow. A light spray rose from the water and caressed her face. The spray revived her. A fishing trawler, cut low in the water and rusted from stem to stern, lunged out to sea ahead of them. The coast lay off the port side. Hills contoured in deep shades of green stretched over the island for as far as Angela could see. Sheep grazed in one valley; horses frolicked in another. A farmhouse, severely whitewashed, threw back a snowy reflection. A barn was painted black; it rose like a medieval fort above a fenced corral.

The first thing she noticed about the town of Sandown-Shanklin was the steeple of a Gothic church.

The second thing she noticed was a dual-prop airplane with a blue tailfin dropping from the sky in preparation for a landing, and Angela knew at once they were in trouble.

She backpedaled, turned, and bounded across the deck, nearly running head on into Mr. Hopkins. He called out to her, but Angela didn't answer. She charged down the stairs, raced through the corridor to the entertainment center, and shook her mom awake.

"He's here," she said.

Kaine awoke.

In the beginning, he was aware only of an immense pressure on his eyes; it seemed to come from inside his head as well as from without. His eyelids refused to open. He lay on his back, the stone beneath him brutally hard, and cold. His hands were drawn awkwardly behind him, bound and numb. The pain in his arms and shoulders was excruciating.

A sulfuric smell registered in his nostrils. The smell tripped his memory, and the muscles in his chest constricted.

Jaymin!

His fingers played over the knotted rope restricting his hands, and he realized it had been loosely tied. When his hands were free, Kaine rolled onto his side, drew his knees up to his chest, and groaned. The pain he had moments ago only recognized in his eyes spread indiscriminately over his entire body. He made fists of his hands and pressed them against his eyes. The pressure subsided. His eyes opened. He was alone. The tools of a heroin addict were scattered on the floor before him. A syringe lay next to a spent candle. A carbon-black spoon cradled the tip of an eyedropper. A fingernail file was pressed between the folds of a bandanna. He searched for the envelope and the ampule and the packet of sugar, but they were nowhere to be found.

The thought of the ampule triggered another memory: the sweet cinnamon scent the clear liquid inside had given off. The picture was complete.

Jaymin. She had done this. The ampule, the sugar, the heroin. Something in that odd combination had produced a reaction sufficient to convince Preble of Kaine's death.

When he was able, Kaine struggled into a sitting position. A haze of yellow light lay upon the temple; a film of dust coated the bulbs incongruously strung from the ceiling. The air was stale and clung to his skin. Jaymin had also left the duffel bag and the water bottle. It was a task merely to grip the bottle; to squeeze water into his mouth was nearly impossible. He used two hands. The water was lukewarm, but he had never tasted anything so sweet. He got better at it. He filled his mouth. He played the stream over his face and eyes and hair, and used his hand to massage it into his pores. Then he drank again.

When the bottle was empty, he found the strength to stand. An onslaught of dizziness passed. He drank in the air like a man resurrected. His first piercing thought was that Turnbull had discovered the whereabouts of Angela and Danielle. Did this discovery also signify that they were now his captives, or more likely, Mathers's captives?

The panic that followed was exorcised by an impotent anger, and seeded again by a feeling of utter helplessness. Then came the most immobilizing thought of all: Were they alive? The aftereffect of the heroin had dulled his mind; if it stole his will to act, he was in trouble.

He focused on the fire temple, the dank walls, the cold stone of the altar, the flawlessly smooth surface of the font. To a man of archeology, what stuck Kaine next was very much a revelation. The temple no longer represented life, nor death. It represented a slice of ancient history, and history was not worth dying for.

Kaine reached into his pocket for his watch and instead withdrew a rectangular piece of paper which he was certain had not been there before. The size of a business card, its worn texture suggested a long stay in someone's wallet. Nearly illegible type read, *Car Repair, Body Work — Tosya — Every Day*. In one corner the letters *ATE* suggested a trademark or business logo. Kaine flipped it over. Someone had handwritten "Tony" on the back. In his convoluted state of mind, the card was meaningless, and Kaine quickly stored it again in his pocket.

His watch, on the other hand, if only by virtue of its familiarity, restored a sense of order. He rubbed the gold case with his thumb and then flipped open the top. It was five forty-five Greenwich time, an hour later in southeastern England, and eight forty-five here in Karmin-Yar. He had lost half a day.

Kaine walked unsteadily across the temple to the tunnel entrance; he would never look upon it again, he realized, and didn't look back now. He climbed down the steps. Had his legs permitted it, he would have run.

Despite the removal of the gold, nothing had been done to rid the tunnel of the apparatus that now served as evidence of the deed. The cool-air generators still churned. There was almost a breeze, and Kaine found it revitalizing. The string of incandescent bulbs dusted the stone walls with tawny highlights. Removal of the steel tracks and the flatcars would be a major undertaking, as their installation must have been, and Kaine realized the task would have fallen to Maurice Dreyfuss, were he alive. Kaine wondered momentarily if Dreyfuss's fellow conspirators were aware of his death yet. If so, would it affect their plans in any way? No, Kaine decided, Maurice had served his purpose. If anything, there was now one less piece of the pie to consider.

Kaine rounded a slight bend and in the distance saw a shaft of sunlight burrowing through Darius's secret entryway. His fears of being forever trapped in this most unlikely ossuary vanished. He tried jogging and his legs responded. But he was weak and starving.

He climbed up the steps to the king's court; it was deserted. The sun had driven away the fog. To his dismay, the Colombian freighter was gone.

35 Beyond the King's Court, the site swarmed with people. They could be seen on scaffolding cleaning walls with paintbrushes, scrubbing the friezework of artisans born before Christ, hauling dirt in buckets, wielding shovels and picks and pushing wheelbarrows. Cappadocians, Europeans, Americans, Japanese, Soviets. A prevailing energy, one Kaine had always marveled at, pushed them on. Most of them earned room and board and not a penny more. It wasn't money. It was discovery. It was camaraderie. It was the revelation of history beneath every stroke of the brush and every shovelful of dirt. Turning his back to it, Kaine knew he would never look upon history the same way again.

He stayed near the perimeter. It was essential that he avoid contact with the many workers familiar with his face, for he was branded. It had never been proved that Kaine had stolen the gold found in his tent six months ago, but the indictment had been enough. Kaine remembered the disappointment he had felt in seeing how easily his word was dismissed. As he drove away from the site that last day, a chorus of jeers had followed him out the gate. Someone had thrown a rock at the windshield of his car. A note had been lodged under the wiper blade. It read, "You put the world of archeology to shame. Good riddance."

A crowd gathered before the charred remains of Marty Perrimore's lithology station. Four blackened posts and knee-high walls stood like defeated sentinels. A dozen broken whiskey bottles formed a mound at the station's heart. "Marty and her Wild Turkey," Kaine heard someone say. The sorting table had been righted, and the stones restored to their trays, but there was no sign of the Stonemaiden.

Kaine fled the scene for the motor pool. The bulldozer upon whose tractor tread he had hidden his remote-control unit had been moved. The tracks of its departure were firmly engraved in the dirt. Kaine followed the right tread back into the lot. He used a stick as a probe. When the stick snagged upon something rectangular and flat, Kaine crouched down. He dug the remote unit out with his fingers. It was encrusted with dirt and badly smashed. For a despondent moment, he could do no more than stare at the ground. Then he slapped the unit against his thigh and tossed it aside.

Kaine returned to Maurice Dreyfuss's car. Where he was going, the immaculate blue Ford would mark him as a lost tourist or an indiscreet thief. He found an oil-stained rag in the trunk. Methodically, he ran the rag over the door handles, the steering wheel, the gear shift, the console; any surface upon which he may have left his prints. The precautions of a criminal, he thought, or of an innocent victim, yet he felt like neither of these.

Finally, Kaine pressed the dead man's straw hat down on his head and wrapped the wire-rim sunglasses around his eyes. He left the keys in the ignition and walked to the terminal. The terminal was a huge tent equipped with long, narrow benches and a deep-rock water cooler. From here, four yellow schoolbuses ferried workers back and forth between the site and the tent city a mile to the west.

A bus with its engine running was parked next to the tent. There were no more than a half dozen passengers aboard. The driver was closing the door when Kaine jogged up. He rapped on the door, and the driver responded.

"Thanks," Kaine said, climbing aboard.

"Gonna be a hot one." Kaine recognized the man. His name was Alexi; he had lost an arm in a freak accident the first year of the dig. His choice had been either to drive a bus or to return to the barren fields of Anatolia and the life of a herdsman. Kaine could offer him no more than that. He remembered Alexi breaking into tears of gratitude and throwing his one arm around Kaine's shoulder.

"How's the *good* arm?" Kaine said, nodding at the stump that was all that remained of his left arm. For years it had been a running joke between the two men.

As the bus ambled down the hill in the direction of the tent city, Alexi stroked his chin. His eyes bulged with excitement. Kaine crouched down in the aisle next to the driver's seat. He removed his sunglasses momentarily.

"How are you, Alexi?" he asked in a low voice.

Alexi's glance, though furtive and quick, could not conceal his recognition. "I have heard nothing of the chief archeologist's return," he said matter-of-factly. Alexi, Kaine remembered, had always been a cool one. "Should you be here?"

"No, I shouldn't be here," Kaine admitted. "Nothing's changed."

"Then why? Have you lost the remainder of the little sense you may have once been blessed with?"

"I need to get to Larnica."

"Larnica! In the name of God, why? My good and faithful friend, Larnica is called Hell's Backyard, and with good reason. The poppy fields have returned, and so have the wars. The Colombians have moved in. Government troops won't go anywhere near Larnica, why would you?"

"That's because the government's found it more profitable *not* to send their troops to Larnica, Alexi."

The bus lumbered to a halt in front of a prefabricated building at the outskirts of the tent city. The passengers climbed down. At this time in the morning it would be a full bus for the trip back, and there was a long line. Alexi closed the door and pulled up next to the gas truck before anyone could board. He told the attendant to check the tank.

"I did that two hours ago. Where ya been? Istanbul?"

"Do it again," Alexi demanded. "And check the oil while you're at it."

Alexi turned in his seat. Kaine had taken off the hat. "You look like death's second cousin," Alexi said. "I'm sorry, but it's so."

"A rough night," Kaine replied.

A moment of silence made Alexi noticeably uneasy. "You're in need of my help, yes?"

Kaine knew that in Alexi's mind a debt was owed. He tried making it easier on the one-armed man. "I ask a favor."

"You have been a friend. A favor to a friend is a gift to the bestower." He tapped anxiously at the steering wheel. "Ask."

"A means of transportation to Larnica, a map, food and water for two or three days."

Unconsciously, Alexi released a breath of considerable relief. "A car will only take you as far as Iskilip. There are a few roads into the mountains around the Larnica district, most are impassable. There is a train, but it is controlled by the trade. They are very well armed and ruthless. There is no law in the opium fields but theirs. Horseback is the only other alternative. I have a friend in Iskilip who can probably lend some assistance with that. I will give you his name. I can come by a map, but it will only be close at best. Food and water is not plentiful, but I will share all I have."

"And I am grateful," Kaine replied, knowing he would have to acquire transportation of considerably greater speed than a horse.

"When will you leave?"

"An hour. I have one stop to make, at the West Block,"

"You need food and a shower before you set out," Alexi, now relaxed and paternal, said. "There is food in my tent. Please wear your hat and sunglasses. You are not a popular figure at Karmin-Yar, it saddens me to say. The communal showers will not be busy at this time of day. It may be your last for a while. Enjoy it." Alexi started the bus again. "I have another round to drive and then preparations. Be patient. I will be as quick as possible."

The Karmin-Yar tent city was enclosed on two sides by full-size trailer vans. The trailers had been hauled to the site years ago by truck and permanently moored. A refrigerator car sold meats and dairy products. A moving van had been converted into a grocery store. Another tastefully recreated the ambience of a clothing store. Yet another had been transformed into a general store selling everything from tape players and the latest in rock-and-roll music to light bulbs and candles.

From its inception, however, Kaine had seen to it that the views to the west and north of the city remained undisturbed. To the west flowed the rambunctious Karmin-Yar River, along a course forced upon it two thousand years ago. At night, in particular, the music of its tumbling water filtered up to the city, and Kaine had fallen asleep to its melody many times. Along its banks cottonwoods and elms had taken root and now flourished.

To the north, down a sloping hill, lay the vast and mysterious Black Sea. Its perpetual blanket of fog had lifted momentarily. Steel-blue swells rose and fell for miles in the distance. A twenty-foot ketch, under full sail, skimmed across its surface, a singular grace note.

Kaine stood on the verge of the hill and imagined the course the Colombian freighter must have taken. To go east would have been fruitless, for there were no waterways in that direction worthy of such a vessel. North led to the Soviet Union, and Kaine could not fathom the transportation of a hundred tons of gold across Soviet territory. The single alternative was the Bosphorus, the strait connecting the Black Sea with the Aegean Sea, leading out through the Greek islands, and eventually to the Mediterranean.

The gold, Kaine decided, would still be under Colonel Turnbull's sphere of influence, and if this were true then an exchange for the heroin remained a thing of the future. Larnica, not a pleasant prospect, represented Kaine's one and only recourse. The message from Louis Mathers to Maurice Dreyfuss that Kaine had found in the packet of Kent cigarettes had made direct reference to Larnica; it was his only clue.

Finally, Kaine allowed his eyes to wander down to the coast and the cove off which the West Block was built. He had spent the last ten minutes thinking of a ship he would almost certainly never see again, mined with explosives he would no longer be able to detonate. There was an ironic twist to it all. Kaine had never trusted Treas, the diver who helped set the charges. When he had directed him to hide the second remote unit beneath the West Block, it had simply been a means of ridding himself of the man. That Treas might actually have done so hadn't been important until Kaine's discovery of his own damaged unit. Now that it hardly mattered, Kaine found himself hoping he had been wrong about Treas.

He followed a winding path through patches of thick grass and tufts of wild oak down the hill to the shore. The ocean was not rough here; it curled and lapped among slabs of limestone. The cove off which the West Block was located lay a quarter of a mile east.

Kaine traversed the shore on the high ground above the boulders. A cool breeze tugged at his matted hair. A promontory flared out into the water and the path followed it. On the point, at the headland of the cove, the sea took a rambunctious turn, slamming against the rocks and sending fountains of spray into the air. Kaine edged near, stripping off his shirt and taking the full force of the spray on his face and chest. His motor functions were close to normal again; the sluggishness and the mental fog he had been fighting for the last two hours were lifting.

He saw the body lying face down in the water, trapped between two boulders, arms raised limply at its side. Kaine recognized the wet suit immediately, old and worn, a dull, olive green. Treas. The incoming tide slammed the body against the rocks. Kaine sank to his knees.

He would have ten to fifteen seconds in which to avoid the force of the tide, grab hold of the body, and drag it out of harm's way. Stowing his watch and wallet on dry ground, he dropped from one boulder to the next. He endured the incoming tide's onslaught once, and realized he would have only one opportunity. He climbed to within ten yards of Treas. The tide returned, throwing him against the mussel-infested rocks, then making every effort to drag him back out to sea with it. When the tide had retreated, a calm pool formed around the body, lifting it gently to the surface. Kaine lunged into the pool, found it momentarily waist-high, grabbed the collar of the wet suit, and pulled. He beat the returning tide by seconds.

Atop a granite ledge, smoothed by a million years of erosion, he turned the body over. Treas's face was hardly recognizable; he had taken a severe beating before being dumped into the sea. The handiwork of Detective Superintendent Preble, Kaine knew at once.

He stared at the bludgeoned face and thought of Poe. Revenge, Poe once said, should not be mistaken for retaliation. Revenge is a stripping away of dead skin, revenge is a renewal of faith, revenge is a return to the river of the living. Revenge is the goal of every man at least once in his life. Yes, Kaine thought coldly, revenge; a noble undertaking, one he had spoken of with Connor Thorpe, yet one he himself had never considered before. Yes.

He was too weak yet to carry Treas's body. He dragged it into a narrow alcove above the rocks, and out of reach of the breakers. He would send the bus driver, Alexi, back for it later. Kaine retrieved his watch and wallet.

The backside of the promontory gradually gave way to the sandy beach of the cove. The marble floor that represented the West Block was marked by the remains of two adjoining walls, a graduated right angle that came to a peak at what was once a corner of the original bathhouse.

The Persian upper class had plumbing. Water was diverted from the river into the underground cisterns, also made of stone, and subsequently directed into the bathhouse. The Persians had developed a method of heating ceramic bricks that eventually led to the first sauna.

Three feet of marble had been laid for the bathhouse floor. Cracks ran the length of the slab in six or seven directions. That a corner section of two walls had escaped the earthquake remained, in Kaine's mind, a miracle. The underground aqueducts that fed the cistern had been dug out by hand two years ago and the cistern had been dredged. Both were lined with slabs of limestone and sealed with a mud-based cement.

Kaine found Treas's diving gear hidden behind a hedge of wild grass at the mouth of the aqueduct. Despite himself, he was cheered by the discovery. Anyone entering the aqueduct would surely have seen the gear. Was it possible that Treas had died without revealing to Preble the cistern and the purpose it had served him? Could Kaine have misjudged the young man so completely?

He secured the flashlight from Treas's gear. The aqueduct was a narrow chute that required Kaine to propel himself on his stomach. It burrowed directly into the side of the hill, eventually exiting into a huge pit faced with cuts of perfectly masoned limestone. The cistern radiated an everlasting cool.

The flashlight was weak; its beam revealed a straight drop but no bottom, and, as Kaine explored with the light, no means of climbing out. The workers charged with the resurrection of the cistern had used rope ladders and buckets, a filthy, undesirable task that had been little appreciated. It had been Kaine's plan to rebuild the pumping system, which had long since rotted, but it had never come to pass.

Kaine put himself in Treas's place. He had been instructed to hide the remote unit *in* the cistern. Treas was Cappadocian; he would have taken the instructions literally. Kaine searched the walls on either side of him. The stone was smooth as glass. Above him, a tiny ledge protruded, not deep enough, however, to hold the remote. He passed the beam over the wall below him and followed it as far down as the light would allow. He spied what appeared to be a silky thread. Kaine stared at it, then traced it back up the wall. It ceased to exist a foot below him. Kaine ran his fingers down the wall and realized the thread was secured to the stone by something flat and glossy. It was a piece of the waterproof tape they had used in securing the antennas to the side of the freighter. The silky thread wasn't thread at all, but nylon fishing line. Kaine wrapped it around his finger. Like a night fisherman, he reeled the line in on faith. He held his breath. The flashlight flickered. In its last light, the object of Kaine's search materialized. He reeled slowly, reached out with his free hand, and clutched the remote-control unit firmly. He wanted to kiss it.

The flashlight died. Kaine backed out of the aqueduct in the dark. Outside, he inspected the unit and found it in working order. Range, three miles. A freighter, he thought dispiritedly, at full steam since dawn, would be in sight of the Bosphorus by now, two hundred miles away.

36

The tent of Alexi, the one-armed bus driver, had been pitched the first year of the site's existence. It was, therefore, close to the river; only a single row of earlier dwellers obstructed his view. The city had grown up behind him. The tent was small and ragged, but inside amenities abounded—electric light, a small refrigerator, a seven-inch fan, a hot plate, and stores of canned food. Most people ate in the communal dining hall. Not Alexi. Though he would never admit to it, Kaine knew that the stigma of his one arm haunted him still.

Ravenous, Kaine cut two slabs of yellow cheese from a packet in the refrigerator. He tore a loaf of bread in half. Then he opened two cans of beef stew. He poured them into a saucepan and turned the hot plate on low. He searched Alexi's medicine chest. He found a razor and shaving cream, an Ace bandage in an unopened box, and a towel that had surely been used more than once. He took the bread and cheese and walked toward the communal showers.

Before dressing, Kaine used the Ace bandage to secure the remote-control unit to the small of his back, wrapping the bandage twice around his waist and tying it off in front.

He returned in a considerably improved condition, to find Alexi tending to his bubbling stew. Kaine's first impulse was to impart

346

the news of Treas and the need to remove the body. Alexi took it well. "I'll take care of it," he said. "But this should settle my debt, I would think, my good friend."

In the refrigerator there were three beers and a bottle of river water. Kaine drank the water while he ate; Alexi made short order of the beer. He spread a piece of notebook paper on the edge of his cot: Kaine's "map."

"You take the coast highway to Inebolu," he said. "You don't need a map for that. There's only one road that looks like a road south out of Inebolu. Take it. Fifty or sixty miles. You're climbing fast now, so remember the car you're driving is kept together by strands of wire and lots of evening prayers. Ever been to Kastamonu?"

Kaine shook his head.

"You'll know it because it has two buildings that don't look like shacks, maybe even a paved road. Take the left fork out of Kastamonu, around Mount Ilgaz. Tosya is your next stop."

"Tosya!" At that moment, Kaine remembered the business card he had found in his pocket earlier, of the car repair shop located in Tosya.

"You know Tosya?"

Given Kaine's state of mind in the fire temple, it hadn't registered. Now it did. Tosya was an industrial town. Steel and coal. "Half the steel in Karmin-Yar comes from Tosya," Kaine said, a gross exaggeration.

Nonetheless, Alexi apparently accepted the reply. He said, "Well, here's where the map gets interesting." To this point the map had featured three intersecting lines and a two-dimensional rendering of Mount Ilgaz. Now it mimicked a hand-drawn spider's web; roads branched in every direction. "If the car's gotten you as far as Tosya, then you're done climbing for a while and it'll likely get you all the way to Iskilip." He jabbed a pinky finger at a city farther south along the River Kizil. "If you get as far as Iskilip, sell the car, drive it off a cliff, do whatever. You won't be needing it."

Near the bottom of the map, Alexi had scribbled two names. "They're cousins of mine," he said. "They run a granary on the west edge of town. Mention my name. They'll provide horses. It's the only way I know once you cross the river. It's slower than the train, but the train is pure foolishness. I wouldn't go near it. I've scrounged enough food for a week and plenty of water." Alexi raised his shoulders apologetically. "It's the best I can do."

"You haven't asked me why," Kaine said.

"Why what? Why you, here at Karmin-Yar? Why a body down by the cove? Why the map, why the food, why Larnica?" Alexi shuddered. "Thank you, but I'm not a curious man, my good friend."

Kaine finished his stew in silence. As they were walking out, Alexi threw him his mackinaw. "I wouldn't face the mountains without this. Who knows, it might even be enough. This time of year, I doubt it."

The car was a decade-old Peugeot, an indefinable blue or black, dirt-encrusted, and pockmarked with rust. The backseat was stocked with canned food and bottled water. Alexi held the door open for Kaine.

"I figured something out," Alexi said. He made a sweeping gesture with his good arm, taking in the river, the tent city, and extending it to encompass the unseen Karmin-Yar a mile to the east. "Six months ago, we traded a tyrant with brains and a sense of humor for an asshole with wet diapers. We all cheered. Nobody's cheering now, just so you know."

"If that's some kind of compliment, I accept it." Kaine slipped behind the wheel and started the engine. "Try to forget I was here, Alexi. We might both live longer. Take care of that arm."

In Inebolu, after a relatively uneventful ride, Kaine discovered a healthy telephone system. The owner of the town's oldest building, the feed store, provided him with the use of his back office. The connections from Inebolu to Sinope and eventually to Istanbul were completed in minutes. An open line to England took twenty more, but Kaine waited. The feed-store owner's buxom daughter served him three cups of a drink made with lime juice and sugar water.

Pure chance found Connor Thorpe at his father's cottage going through fifty-eight years of final effects.

Connor's spirits swung wildly. He wept like a good Scot, and laughed like one, too. His excitement rested primarily upon a diary he had found in an old chest in the crawl space.

"I never knew my father wrote anything but log reports," he said. "The diary talks about my mother. He sketched a picture of her. He says, 'The sun radiated from her fingertips. She deserved better than me. I hope she didn't quit on life because of the life we led. But she was no quitter.' "

"Good stuff," Kaine said, meaning it.

"It was like, in life, he wanted me to forget her. In death, he brought her back to life for me. Actually brought us together."

"A powerful gift," Kaine said, almost to himself. "From death comes life."

"He says in the diary that the day I docked my first hundred-ton ship—I remember it like it was yesterday; I was nearly seventeen—that I'd become a man that day. My coming of age, he called it. He bought me Glenfiddich that night, and from then on that's all we ever drank together. Except for his ouzo, of course. He also says that the day he dies—died—I'd feel loneliness for the first time. He was right on both accounts, Mr. Kaine. I knew I'd taken my first step into manhood that day. And now I've got a house full of pining aunts and half-drunk uncles and I wish they'd all go the bloody hell home."

"Tell them."

"Tell them what?"

"Say, 'I need to feel lonely for a while. Please go home.' "

"You don't know my family."

"I know the Scottish. They're like a light bulb. Sometimes they burn too brightly. They really don't mind being turned off. And they'll be there when you need them."

"I'll try it."

"Angela's in trouble, Connor," Kaine said, now impatient. "Ambassador Mathers knows where she and her mother are. Or were. Which is nearly as bad."

"That bloody bastard has to be dealt with, Mr. Kaine," Connor said. "You said you'd call and you have. Now what? Tell me."

"Become his friend," Kaine said at once.

"What? I'd rather die first."

"Scottish rules," Kaine said. "Remember? Know your enemy. Earn his trust. Then, when the time comes, you'll have the pleasure of feeding him his own poison as well as bringing about his downfall."

"Become his friend?" Connor's voice reeked with hypocrisy. A prolonged silence was punctuated by the agonizing resistance Kaine detected in the young man's breathing. Yet Kaine waited; to rescue Connor now would be to absolve his doubts. Eventually the first skipper's son committed himself, as Kaine knew he would. "How?" he asked.

"Walk into his office and spit on his desk," Kaine answered. "Then cry on his desk. Tell him you're sick of Americans bleeding your people. Tell him about your father, that he was killed by an American and nothing is being done about it. Tell him you know the man's name and that he's still alive."

"You."

"Me," Kaine said. "He won't be able to refuse. Connor, when a man needs to look into such dark places for satisfaction, he looks to it even when it's an illusion."

"That sounds like something the first skipper would have said."

"Do it today. Become his friend, and you'll have him. Along the way maybe we'll be able to save Angela and her mother."

37 The cruise ship *White Mariner* docked in Sandown-Shanklin at seven forty-five. A tour of the harbor and the town was scheduled to begin at nine. Mr. John Hopkins had ceased to be an ally. Feeling spurned, and probably hung over, he had reported Danielle's presence on board, as well as her daughter's. He seemed to take pleasure in informing her of this "act of good citizenship," as he called it.

Rather than wait for the dubious honor of being escorted off the ship, Danielle and Angela joined the first wave of disembarking passengers. Once down the gangplank, the two skirted the awaiting tour bus for the tumult of the harbor. And Sandown-Shanklin was a busy harbor. Pier after pier of fishing boats stretched in a semicircle to the west of the passenger quay. The delicate pattern of mainmasts and guide wires outlined a cobalt-blue horizon; a glorious sight neither Danielle nor her daughter could appreciate.

To the east, sailboats of every shape and size bobbed at anchor. A fertile breeze threw a caldron of scents into the air. Pleasure sailors attended their crafts, readying sails and sheets, stowing gear, and drinking beer.

To the unaccustomed eye, it was a maze of confusion. At the opposite side of it all, Danielle saw a harbor house that at once became the object of their wanderings. What she soon realized was that a narrow stretch of water separated them from the harbor house, and that a ferry ride was their only option short of swimming or commandeering another boat.

They walked along freshly whitewashed docks and found an open gate at pier 32; a weathered sign read PASSENGER FERRY. They passed through the gate. Sailboats filled docking bays on either side of them. Excitement swelled with the rising sun, a brutal contradiction to a mother's anxiety.

A chain stretched across the end of the pier. A second sign hung below it and swayed in the wind. A rusted border attested to the sign's permanence, and the words were weathered to the point of illegibility. Still, Angela deciphered them: "Ferry closed to passenger travel."

A speedboat raced to a stop at the foot of the pier, sending a wake into the pillars below; the rank odor of diesel spewed from its engine. The airplane pilot sat at the controls. He bore little resemblance to the demure fisherman they had seen in Tregony. His jaw was locked tight and his eyes blazed. Hurriedly, he clambered to his feet. Danielle froze. She grasped Angela by the shoulders.

"Get aboard," he shouted. "You're in great danger. Now climb aboard." When they didn't move, he pinned Angela with his eyes. "Jaymin sent me, Angela. She sent me to look after you. I've been watching you since Dodman Point. You took a bus to Plymouth. You went aboard that cruise ship; that's where you made your mistake. Now I can't protect you any longer. Climb aboard. Both of you. Do it now."

"Jaymin? No. You're lying. She—"

"Look behind you, Danielle," he ordered. Danielle turned. Three men in suits were lumbering down the pier toward them. She heard voices. One of the three held up a hand, imploring them. The pilot said, "Ambassador Mathers has had those men looking for you for days. I can't protect you any longer. Get aboard, or we're all dead."

Two of the three men broke into a jog. The faster of the two was shouting, motioning Danielle and Angela toward him with his arm. "Run. This way. Don't listen to him. Run. Run."

"Don't believe him," the pilot pleaded. "Trust me. You've got about five seconds. Jaymin sent me. We work together. She cares about you. You know that."

"Jaymin stole the crown," Angela screamed.

"She also helped save your life. Now make up your minds."

The two men were upon them now, handguns displayed, and it was too late. The pilot jammed the throttle forward and sped away. One of the men tracked him with his gun but then thought better of firing.

The two men hovered over them. One grasped Danielle's elbow. She winced and pulled free. The third man, obviously the senior member of the group, sauntered forward. He spoke behind a satisfied smile. "I admire your creativity over the last two days, Mrs. Kaine. Very elusive," he said.

"How did you find us?"

"Fortunately there is a waiter at a certain pub in Plymouth with a good memory. He said the old man from the cruise ship paid your bill. That you left with him."

The man spent a moment freeing a cigar from its wrapper, bit the end off, and spat it into the pristine harbor waters. He gestured magnanimously toward the pilot and the fleeing speedboat. "A very cunning man, your pilot friend. Also very dangerous. Your decision was a wise one. You and your daughter are American citizens. Therefore, the U.S. ambassador to England is the man in the best possible position to assist you in your time of trouble. Come with us."

38 The car survived the trek inland from Inebolu.

The gracefully sculptured knolls put Kaine in mind of the low hills skirting the Rocky Mountains back home. Under the coaxing hand of the Anatolian farmers, the fertile, green valleys produced an abundance of corn and fruit and tobacco. Though peasants, these were the blessed of Asia Minor's lower class. Some drove tractors. Some owned horses with strength enough to pull full wagons.

Yet the fields and the gentle slopes were a short-lived phenomenon, for the Pontic Mountains soon consumed him.

These were rugged peaks, slaves to blistering summers and brutal winters. Among the broken rocks lived hardy pines and oaks that rarely matured past the shrub stage. Huts clustered in the valleys, some founded on stone, others with thatch roofs. All attention was paid to the survival of the goats and cattle in the corrals adjoining the huts. Most were attended by bent women and small children. By now, Kaine understood. The men had emigrated to Larnica, or Alaca, or a hundred other places like them, for the monthlong ritual of the opium harvest. The women, he imagined, could only hope to see their men again as they had seen them before their departure. Their worst fear was that they would return with the glassy eyes of opium smoke and the empty pockets that were a byproduct of the habit.

A filthy town, Tosya survived in a different way. Competitive plumes of black smoke rose above the steel-producing factories that had caused Tosya to thrive, to putrefy, and to reek. Kaine drove past mountains butchered in search of coking coal. He followed trucks spilling over with the stuff. He hurried past the mills awaiting the trucks' arrival. The city was shadowed in a pall of ghastly gray. A soot of ash and smoke clung to every exposed surface, invaded every lung, and brought tears to Kaine's eyes.

Parking beside an abandoned trailer at the outskirts of town, Kaine faced a decision. He had purposely avoided the business card buried in his pocket next to his watch. And the questions: Where had it come from? What did it mean? What was he meant to do with it? Was it a trap or a false lead? For half a day, Alexi had done his thinking for him—the map, the food, the car. Alexi had advised driving as far as Iskilip, disposing of the car, and proceeding on horseback. There was something gloriously foolhardy about this, but deep down inside Kaine knew better. He retrieved the card from his pocket.

His immediate assumption was that Jaymin had placed the card there. Still, he searched for alternative explanations. While he and Treas had been busy mining the Colombian freighter, the Stonemaiden had returned to the east quay, taken his clothes from their hiding place, and slipped the card into his pants. Why? Kaine had said nothing to the lithologist about his plans to proceed into the high country above Tosya. Or perhaps Preble himself had put the card there after Kaine's apparent overdose. Why? To implicate someone named Tony in Kaine's death? To lead Kaine astray should the overdose, by some chance, be unsuccessful?

Kaine read the card again. *Car Repair — Body Work — Tosya — Every Day*. He stared at the monogram in the one corner, the letters *ATE*. And then the script on the back. "Tony." It was gracefully written, the letters tall and narrow. Kaine allowed his imagination to play upon the three possible players in this puzzle: Jaymin, Marty Perrimore, and Preble. There was no question. The graceful handwriting, he decided, fit Jaymin.

Before asking directions, Kaine decided upon a cursory tour of Tosya's main streets. By chance, the letters *ATE* were hand-painted on a sandwich board standing in front of a petrol station at the opposite end of town. Business was brisk; three cars lined up at the station's lone pump. Kaine parked off to the side and climbed out.

The weather had taken a turn for the worse. It was damp, a drizzle making mud of the soot. The station was a low, flat-roofed structure; its blistered walls longed for a coat of paint. A wisp of coal smoke curled from a stovepipe protruding from one corner of the roof. Behind the station, a chain-link fence formed a barricade around a small, dual-prop airplane.

Though logically the plane may have given meaning to the business card, Kaine would not allow himself the luxury of such a notion.

For a moment, he watched a man in blue jeans and a wool sweater attend the gas pump. He was a talker; he knew all his customers by name. He would take their money without counting it and shove it into his pocket. As Kaine approached, he raised the nozzle in greeting, then replaced it alongside the pump. He wiped his hands on his jeans, then cupped them in front of his mouth and blew, warming them. Cordiality gave way to an expression of straightforward suspicion.

Kaine held out the card for the man's inspection. He took it, turning it front to back, and shrugged. "Not many of these around," he said, his nonchalance well practiced.

Kaine considered responses. Lying wasn't an option—he was already committed to that—but he decided that lying without a valid cover would be foolish. "I'm an archeologist," he explained. "I have a project on line along the coast near Cide. I have some research to do in Larnica. I was told you had a plane to charter."

"Archeological research in Larnica." By his tone, the attendant could just as easily have said, "You are a liar, but at least a creative one." He blew on his hands again, his eyes settling momentarily upon Kaine's Peugeot. Then he said, "Come inside. We'll have a talk with my partner. You have money?"

"Not much," Kaine admitted.

"That could pose a problem."

"What does the ATE stand for?"

The attendant held open the door. "Anthony Theo Eddings." He laughed, sardonically. "It used to stand for Air Transport Enterprises. I was bought out."

A man lounged at the desk. He wore a salmon-colored coat, white tie, and white shirt. He tugged absently at a sparse mustache, more like a dirty shadow. Kaine had heard enough talk of the Colombians' presence in the mountains, and he assumed this man was one of them.

"This gentleman wants a ride up to the river," Tony said. He slid the card across the desk.

The Colombian surveyed it, shrugged, and tossed it absently aside. "Fishing, I suppose." He had the garbled, painfully slow accent of a migrant worker. Now he drummed impatiently at the desktop, and Tony interpreted this.

"If you'll do me the honor of leaning on the edge of the desk," he said to Kaine. "Pretend you're auditioning for a low-budget movie. I'm the cop, you're the bad guy. I frisk, you sweat. Know that scene?"

"One of my favorites," Kaine said. With a remote-control unit strapped to his lower back, Kaine didn't need to pretend; the moisture collecting beneath his shirt was very real.

Tony searched him. Brisk and professional. Arms, legs, hips, crotch, chest, back. His hand ran momentarily over the remote control, stopped for an instant, and moved quickly on.

"Boring," Tony said. He laid Kaine's pocket watch, passport, and wallet on the desk. The Archeological Society of America card inside the wallet seemed to impress the Colombian more than anything. Kaine decided now would be the correct time to pitch the Karmin-Yar project. "We're looking for the source of the river," he said.

The Colombian picked at his mustache again. He reached for Kaine's watch, lifting it by the chain and allowing it to dangle in the air. Like a great pendulum it swung, momentarily mesmerizing them all. Then he pinned Kaine with his jaundiced eyes. "Larnica is the kind of place where liars die hard deaths."

"I thought everyone in Larnica was a liar," Kaine said at once.

The Colombian threw his head back and laughed; Tony evidently felt safe in joining him. "I think you should give our archeologist a lift," his partner said, returning Kaine's watch.

"He's broke," Tony told him.

"I have the car," Kaine replied, gesturing toward the Peugeot. "It runs. Not great, but enough."

"Tony can make anything run great," the Colombian assured him.

It took imagination to envision what the poppy fields had looked like in full bloom. Valleys and mountainsides flooded by a river of fiery orange, a river seemingly gone far afield of its banks. The spillage of orange filled every basin for miles and sent its tentacles deep into every glen, valley, and meadow.

Jaymin's first sight of the fields had been from the air, two weeks before; today she walked among those fields and found every flower barren of its petals. Where weeks ago a triumphant creation of nature had flowered, now stood a four-foot-high tubular stem. The petals had formed a cushion at her feet, exposing, in turn, a green seed pod the size of a fist.

Colonel Turnbull strolled at her side.

"You do amaze me," he said. "You, of all people, marvel at the petals. Why? Here, the petals are merely a source of anticipation, not wonder. It is these ugly pods which are the source of marvel, my dear, the source of ecstasy."

The fields swarmed with workers. Men of all ages tarried beside women with babies strapped to their backs and teenagers who had finally been granted the privilege of participation in the harvest. The men wore sackclothlike pants and sandals. The women toiled beneath heavy robes. The boys were shirtless and wild-eyed. Each carried specially curved knifes, perfect for the task assigned them.

Turnbull was right. Once the petals died back and fell to earth, a phenomenon as yet unexplained by science transpired. Within the womblike pods the synthesis of a milky white sap occurred. The sap was opium.

Jaymin likened the scene in the fields to a war zone; for every worker there patrolled a soldier; for every soldier there were automatic rifles strapped over shoulders and holsters heavy with Soviet pistols and American revolvers.

Turnbull smoked, taking great pleasure in his cigar. Like a land baron, he walked among his charges. He strolled, grasping a shoulder, throwing out an animated smile, stroking the brow of a querulous newborn. He was in an expansive mood. Jaymin's nerves tingled and she knew better than to interrupt him.

"It's a life cycle, Jaymin. Everything you see here." He swept the area with his cigar. "Man seeks miracle cures just like he seeks easy money. He always has. The sap of the poppy blessed him with opium. It wasn't enough. Opium bred morphine which bred heroin. Each in turn labeled by medicine men and scientists as the next miracle drug. Each able to kill pain and sorrow in the time it took to smoke the stuff or pop the pill or jab the needle in your arm."

"Less a few unexpected side-effects, the medicine men and scientists weren't far wrong," Jaymin replied.

"Man's own self-inflicted side-effects, my dear."

"That's one way of looking at it."

The sun beat down on them. Turnbull toweled his forehead with a handkerchief. "Hell, Jaymin, raw opium goes back to the Neolithic Age. Opium superseded Christ as the great cure-all. Hippocrates used it in Greece, and Galen, poor devil, was addicted. In the eighteenth and nineteenth centuries you couldn't buy a cold remedy without an opium base. And the damn things worked."

"They worked all right," Jaymin replied. "In fact, people went out of their way to catch colds."

Exasperated, she paused a moment and peered over an old woman's shoulder. The woman moved from pod to pod, cutting upon the surface of each bulb a series of shallow, parallel incisions.

Turnbull blew a fountain of smoke toward the sky. When Jaymin was beside him again, he threw an arm around her shoulders. "All of nature's a gift, Jaymin. It's what we do with it that counts. The opium poppy was no exception. It just took man about three or four thousand years to pervert what nature had graciously granted him."

"Three or four thousand years. That's a pretty good record for man."

"Why someone ever decided to mix lime fertilizer with opium is beyond me, but there it was. Morphine. A more miraculous drug than opium ever thought of being. By the end of the century every pharmaceutical company from Ohio to Oslo was experimenting with it. Then what happens? Some chemist with nothing better to do boils the morphine down with a bit of industrial acid, and the course of history changes."

"History? That's a strange way of looking at the discovery of heroin, Colonel."

Jaymin had stopped again. The white sap was seeping out from between the incisions and congealing on the bulbs' surfaces. Even now she could see its whitish color transforming into the brownish black hue that signaled its readiness for harvest. She glanced back. A quarter of a mile behind them, a second wave of workers had congregated. Their tools were different, however; each carried a flat, dull-bladed knife especially designed for scraping the thickening mass from the bulb. Each worker carried a canvas bag over his shoulder. By the end of the day, the bags would be full.

"Here's some irony for you," Turnbull said, discarding his cigar and walking toward the camp a mile ahead. "My dearly departed mother used to take this store-bought product called Bayer aspirin. Remember it?"

"The orphanage used to pass it out like candy," Jaymin told him.

"So guess who coined the term *heroin*? The very same folks who brought you the aspirin." Jaymin laughed, which only encouraged Turnbull. "It was a marketing ploy. *Diacetylmorphine* just didn't sound right. Go into a drug store and try that one on the pharmacist. They needed a brand name the whole world could relate to. They settled on *heroin*."

"Test marketed in the south Bronx with unparalleled results," Jaymin said.

A musky odor weighed heavily on the air. It was the ripening of opium; it was the refining of morphine; it was the low blanket of stormclouds. The odor hovered like a transparent veil. The edge of anxiety Jaymin had been harboring sharpened. She had

learned that small talk with the colonel inevitably led to some unpleasantness, and, sensing that the unpleasantness lay close at
hand, Jaymin paused. She scraped a sampling of the opium from
the surface of a pod and touched it to her tongue. She grimaced at
the taste.

"Not quite your flavor yet, I don't imagine." Turnbull laughed.
"Tell me. How did Professor Kaine like his first taste of China
White?"

"His body shook like a leaf and he foamed at the mouth like a
horse dying of exhaustion. It was very pretty."

"Detective Preble agreed wholeheartedly. In fact, I think the
matter changed his perception of you." Turnbull set his narrowed
eyes upon her. "He thinks you're dangerous."

"And he makes threats like the neighborhood bully." Jaymin
delivered the reply with as much indifference as she could muster.
She sampled the opium again, this time rubbing it on her gums.
"Where did you find him, anyway?"

The question was more seriously received than Jaymin had
expected, and Turnbull answered by stepping back in time. He
said, "The governments of the world put an end to legitimate heroin
production fifty or sixty years ago. The League of Nations and the
Geneva Convention and all that bullshit. Stupid and ridiculous.
What more perfect vehicle for the criminal mind? Illegitimate lab-
oratories from Marseilles to Shanghai sprouted up like weeds. The
mafiosi sold the final product like cotton candy at a carnival. And
then World War II broke out and damn near put an end to it all.
The war shut down the supply. Patriotism shelved the demand."

Turnbull lit a fresh cigar. They walked on. At the head of the
camp there were six wooden huts built on stilts. Four armed men
stood on the steps of the fourth hut watching their progress. Preble
sat in a chair on the porch and popped candies into his mouth.
Behind the huts, trees had been cleared to accommodate a prefabricated warehouse constructed entirely of corrugated sheet metal.
The refinery. Smoke rose from two stacks. A security fence enclosed
it. A railway siding abutted it on one side and an engine and two
boxcars had been stationed alongside.

Turnbull stopped. He turned a distracted gaze back to the fields.

Jaymin surmised that there was still more to his story; the colonel never liked leaving a story unfinished. But her instincts told her there was something more here than an unfinished monologue. After a moment, he took her arm, tipped his head as if the refinery might be of interest, and led her in that direction.

"The war left the world order in a shambles. The east and the west were scrambling to fill the void of lost influences, or newly created opportunities. I was with the CIA back then. We embraced an anti-Communist ideology that didn't give a damn about principles or fair play or even common sense."

"Very profoundly put," Jaymin intoned.

"In the forties and fifties we backed the Sicilian Mafia simply as a means of thwarting the Italian Communist Party. We recruited the Corsican underground. Which meant supporting every illegal activity they chose to foster. In the late fifties we backed the Nationalist Chinese in Burma and the Meo mercenaries in Laos. The same bandits made heroin addicts out of half our troops in Vietnam and all we did was provide the financing and the expertise and the smiling face of a big brother. In Pakistan, George Bush put on his buddy-buddy act with General Zia, lent him a couple of billion dollars, and then stood by and watched the incorrigible general make his country into the biggest producer of heroin in the world. Who we threw our support behind didn't matter as long as they claimed an anti-Communist stance; the heroin was an afterthought."

"And two million addicts was a small price to pay for us all to sleep safe and sound in our beds at night," Jaymin said. Yet it wasn't a question or even a statement of fact, it was a place to hide. The colonel had never offered an iota of information about his history or his conversion to the *other* side. Why the fuck would he now? Because something's wrong, that's why, she chastised herself. Her unease was immense.

"Preble was working for British military intelligence at the time. We knew each other even then. We were the good guys, Jaymin. He went with Scotland Yard and I made a career of the army. But you can only see the shit thrown back in your face so many times, I suppose."

Perhaps for the first time in their two-year relationship, Jaymin studied William Turnbull with interest. "It's a deep hole to fall into, isn't it? I understand."

"I don't think you do, dear beautiful Jaymin." A note of true regret framed Turnbull's words. They climbed the steps to the refinery. "After all, you've managed to avoid the hole for the most part. I envy you that, I suppose. You see, we sent someone back to the fire temple this morning. Professor Kaine, as you well know, was not only not dead, he was also gone. Walked out under his own power was the way our people figured it."

Turnbull cut off Jaymin's reply with a restrained raising of the hand. He pushed aside a stiff curtain and the fumes of the refinery rushed up to greet them. If the setup was crude, it was also enormously effective. The simple fact was, the traffickers of this region preferred their morphine refineries as close to the fields as possible. Since compact morphine blocks were infinitely more practical to smuggle than bundles of pungent, jellylike opium, the process at Larnica had not been tampered with.

The floor was compacted dirt. Electric fans vented the air through holes in the walls. Sacks of raw opium had been stockpiled along the back wall. At the heart of the room, four wood fires roared. Oil drums filled with water were simmering above the flames. A man dressed from head to foot in white, his thick glasses framing a narrow balding head, moved from one drum to the next. Jaymin could see that he was judging the temperature of the water with a mercury thermometer, but making final decisions with an experienced index finger.

The chemist was French. He had two assistants for each drum. They were locals, dressed in loose-fitting cotton pants and wearing gloves. When the chemist deemed the water temperature appropriate, his assistants dumped two bags of opium into each drum. They stirred the contents with a wooden stick. The chemist added precise amounts of ordinary lime fertilizer. The morphine then was left suspended in the chalky white water near the surface; the organic waste sank to the bottom. They then filtered the water through a layer of common flannel cloth, draining it slowly into a second oil drum. Again the solution was heated and stirred. The chemist added concentrated ammonia, and its fumes left Jaymin light-headed.

She watched simply because she could not move. She had failed to calculate the odds of Turnbull sending someone back to the fire temple, and now she was a victim of her own lack of foresight. No, Jaymin thought, a victim of emotion, of love even. What a powerful force. No wonder she had avoided it for so long. She was scared, but she wasn't sorry.

The morphine solidified and dropped to the bottom of the drum. The chemist's assistants filtered the solution a second time, leaving kernels of white morphine on the cloth. With great care, they carried the cloth to a protected corner of the room. Spread like fine jewels over the surface of a large, covered table, the morphine would take less than four hours to dry. There were a half dozen such tables.

The dried morphine was then packaged in preformed bricks made of plastic, and wrapped in aluminum foil. The bricks were then stowed in ordinary gunny sacks and hand carried to the boxcars waiting at the loading dock.

Turnbull sampled the refined morphine with the tip of his finger. He snorted it expertly into his left nostril. After a moment, he repeated the procedure in his other nostril, then dabbed a tiny morsel on his tongue.

The chemist wasn't waiting for an opinion. "Number four," he said blandly.

"Congratulations," Turnbull said. Number four was the ultimate compliment; it referred to the quality of the heroin which would result from this particular batch of morphine, ninety to ninety-nine percent pure.

Turnbull escorted Jaymin back outside.

"Was it worth it?" he said to her eventually. "Worth two years of your life, Jaymin?"

"I don't—"

"Oh, it's too late for excuses," Turnbull interrupted. "We searched your plane. Also your hotel room in London. You were careless. We found several very damaging tapes. Also notes. Two years, an agent with the U.S. Drug Enforcement Agency. You gave them two years of your life, living with us, scheming with us, plotting against us. You were on the verge of becoming a wealthy woman, beyond your wildest dreams. Why?"

Jaymin neither hesitated nor excused herself. "It's my job," she said.

They moved passively toward the hut. Jaymin saw the anticipation on the Colombians' faces; Preble rocked forward. The heat enhanced his eagerness.

"You're used to the abuses of the world," Turnbull said as they reached the bottom of the steps. "I know that about you. The heroin loosens your tongue. I'm afraid our Colombian friends have their own definition of abuse. You won't survive it, but then I don't think survival is high on your list, anyway."

One of the Colombians jumped off the porch. He reached out for her, roughly relieving Turnbull of her company. A filthy, callused hand took hold of her shirt and in one clean swipe ripped it away, exposing her bare chest. He held her back by her arms. Preble stood at the top of the steps, thick hands in his pockets, grinning eagerly down at her.

"I made you a promise. Do you remember? In the tunnel?" he said, now carefully unbuttoning his coat. "I've never made a promise I couldn't keep."

39 "Let me interpret your silence for you," Tony said to Kaine after an hour of hopscotching among mountain peaks that reminded Kaine of central Utah. "See, your work is relatively straightforward. You look for something. You either find it or you don't. It either has value or it doesn't. You teach, you travel, you don't spend much time looking over your shoulder. Except for now. New game. New rules. Now you're spending *most* of your time looking over your shoulder. Concealing unknown objects under your shirt." Tony raised an eyebrow. "Things like that. Not very pleasant, is it?"

"It has its moments," Kaine said. A downdraft sucked the Cessna 170 into a pocket of turbulence. The plane shook.

"At first, I couldn't figure it out. I'm thinking, Jaymin really likes this guy. As a rule of thumb, she sticks her neck out for nobody, and all of a sudden she's calling in markers left and right trying to save your ass." Tony flew like most people ride a bicycle, like a kid on a spring day. "I don't know what the fuck she promised that jerk-off in the Crimea, Kaine. Collins?" Tony hissed. "I'll tell you about your esteemed Consul Collins. He's the type of lowlife who'd buy a front-row seat to his own brother's flogging. All of a sudden he's pulling strings to get you on a Turkish freighter. Now I've seen it all."

"What are you telling me?"

"You're kidding." Tony took his hands off the controls. He struck at Kaine with a vicious scowl. "You piece of shit. See if you can follow my reasoning. I'll go real slow so as to let your academically warped brain follow along. Consul Collins, the weasel, the garbage collector, the leech. Lenci, the taxi driver with the extended family and a thousand connections. Treas, now dead because you don't know the difference between a period and menopause. Those are the kinds of associates that help someone in Jaymin's business stay on the job for two years."

Had Tony hoped to bring Kaine humbly to his knees, he was mistaken. Unwittingly, he had opened an old wound.

"You seem to be in the mood to lecture, Tony," Kaine replied. "You seem to be in the mood to test your repertoire of insults. Well, I'll try providing you with some inspiration. I have a thirteen-year-old daughter whose life has been twice threatened in the last several days, and whose whereabouts at the moment is unknown to me. If you think the Treases or the Lencis of the world come before my daughter, then you've been pumping gas in Asia Minor for too long. If you want to lecture, talk straight. If you don't want to talk straight, then go back to your paymaster in Tosya and I'll walk to Larnica. I don't need you."

Tony's grip tightened on the control wheel, even as the muscles in his neck and jaw constricted. Suddenly, he cut the wheel sharply to the right, simultaneously jamming his foot down hard on the rudder pedal. The plane banked sharply. A moment later, he cut back on the throttle, setting the plane in a downward spiral. Kaine was drawn instantly up in his seat, momentarily weightless. On the verge of panic, teeth clenched, he jammed his feet against the floorboard. His hands instinctively reached out for something to brace against, and he eventually found them wrapped tight around his shoulder harness. The wooded mountains raced up to meet them. Kaine made a vain attempt at closing his eyes. Had he thought to protest or scream, he had neither the wind nor the muscle control to do so.

Spiraling wildly toward the valley floor, Tony suddenly drew back hard on the control wheel. He jammed the throttle forward. At the last instant, they pulled out, the nose of the plane following the mountainside in a vertical climb back toward the sky. An instantaneous surge of G-force drove Kaine back in his seat. Tony banked sharply again and eventually leveled off.

Kaine's shirt was soaked through. He fought wildly for breath. Tony, if anything, seemed to be freed of the tension that had overwhelmed him earlier. When he spoke again, his words were calculated and distant.

"For your information, Professor Kaine," he said, "my paymaster sits behind a desk in one of the Drug Enforcement Agency's cramped offices in Washington, D.C. So does Jaymin's. In the parlance of the DEA, we're called trash collectors. For two years we've been running down the trash you've come to know as Mathers and Turnbull and Preble. Two years. It's a big deal, maybe the biggest deal I've ever come across, and you've done just about everything in your power to put the deal on ice. In return, Jaymin has done just about everything in her power to see you don't die in the process. Don't ask me why."

"I know what she's done," Kaine answered, his face drawn tight, his voice a near whisper. "More than you can know. And you can't even begin to know what I feel for her in return. And I wouldn't explain it even if I could."

"Yeah, all right. I hear what you're saying."

"I don't know how to balance it out, though. She spends two years chasing down a heroin deal and becomes an addict in the process."

"And it pisses you off."

"I can't help it. Probably because I can't help her and I know it."

"It happens," Tony said quietly. "It's a shit business and Jaymin's been at it for six or seven years. That's a long stint. Too long. Don't get me wrong. That's not an explanation. It's not an excuse. It's a goddamn deep trap and Jaymin fell in it."

Kaine nodded. What could he say to that?

Tony must have interpreted his silence as passing judgment,

because he shook his head, disgusted. "Anyway, there's about two billion dollars' worth of heroin about to hit the streets of London and Amsterdam and New York, and one woman trying to prevent it. Try coming away from something like that without a few bumps and bruises. In my book it beats the hell out of digging up two-thousand-year-old tourist traps. And if you think your pet project at Karmin-Yar will end up being anything but, then you're living under some sort of delusion."

"I should have known," Kaine said. "An expert on all things past and present. Playing at some cloak-and-dagger charade in a town straight out of the nineteenth century. I should have known."

"For your information, I've spent eighteen months earning the faith of that grease monkey back in Tosya."

Kaine's ribs ached. "Let's forget it," he said. "I'm more concerned about Jaymin."

"I'm a conduit for information, that's all. Jaymin knows everything I know, but I can't help her any more than that. She's on her own, and she knows it. It's been her show to make or break from the beginning."

"You just called it a big deal," Kaine protested. "Maybe the biggest you'd ever come across. Now you say that Jaymin's on her own. Her show to make or break. You realize how little sense that makes?"

"I realize, okay. I realize. But the United States and this medieval piece of no-man's-land are allies of record," Tony explained. "Which means we give them ten or fifteen billion dollars a year and they in turn let us park a couple of B-1 bombers on their soil. Officially, they don't allow poppy planting for purposes of opium production; that's part of our friend-to-friend agreement. For us to accuse them of such planting would be a breach of faith. Officially, Jaymin and I don't exist. If she can nail Turnbull and Mathers outside this medieval piece of no-man's-land, then we become official. Okay? Making any more sense yet?"

Kaine didn't reply. Instead, he became a sightseer. Beyond the window, the mountains were rugged and faced with sheer cliffs. Tony flew along the floors of barren, narrow valleys sparsely populated with sheep and robed herdsmen with staffs in their hands. Kaine felt as if he had been written into a scene from the Old Testament.

Finally, he asked, "And me?"

"There's a road two miles from Turnbull's camp. A pickup point for minor shipments. It's the best I can do." Tony withdrew a geographical map from under his seat. He opened it, allowing Kaine to spread it out over his lap. "The red slash is the strip. Two hundred yards up the side of a hill. Very exhilarating. That winding blue line, the one leading over the mountain to the camp, is a horse trail. For the last fourteen or fifteen months it's been controlled by the traffickers. And believe me, they take a certain pride in the shoot-first-and-ask-questions-later way of doing things. Your best bet is simple avoidance; no, your only chance. What you intend to do if and when you reach the camp, I won't even try to imagine."

Kaine pored over the map. At the top of the strip, an eighth of an inch above the red slash, was a circle within a square, obviously another landmark. "And that?" he asked.

"Essentially, a hole. Six or eight feet wide, maybe three feet deep," Tony said. "Big enough to hide fifty or sixty gallons of fuel anyway. My private reserve. See, the grease monkey back in Tosya keeps track of my fuel consumption and my mileage. It's his private leash. But it's hard to do my job on a leash. The tach clock is easy enough to fix. The fuel's a bit trickier. Thus, my private reserve."

Kaine refolded the map. "The shipment is due to go out when?"

Tony stared at him; his expression was one of enduring suspicion, one reshaped many times by simple resignation. Finally, he sighed. "If they stay on schedule, and Turnbull and Preble will see that they do, it'll be on the move by tomorrow morning."

"By airplane."

"Not by plane." Tony sighed again, by now the bored instructor. "When I said they use this strip for minor shipments, I meant sample packages for prospective buyers. The Turkish government has its pride, after all. Though they get their cut on every ounce of morphine that leaves the country, they also make it clear that a certain protocol will be followed. The airlines and the harbors are public domain. Stay away. Horseback, stagecoach, camels, even magic carpets. Fine. Just keep it away from the airlines and out of the water. Heard of the Taurus Railway?"

"A transcontinental narrow-gauge built by the British back in World War II," Kaine replied. "It fell apart twenty years later, didn't it, when the Turks decided the farmers could find another way to get their crops to market?"

"As the story goes, the government claimed a lack of availability of spare parts for such an antiquated system. Blamed the British, of course. The Colombians brought the Taurus line back to life. They found an abundance of necessary parts in a rather unpopular country on the tip of Southern Africa. It took eight months to reconstruct the line and fifteen million dollars, a sum recouped twice over with the railway's first shipment."

"What happens when the train arrives at the coast?" Kaine asked. "You just said transportation via water or air was prohibited by the government. Protocol, as you put it."

Tony's laughter filled the cockpit, ironic and twisted. And something else, Kaine thought. Defeated.

"That's the beauty of it. The wonderful, crazy beauty of it," Tony cracked. "Originally, the line ended at the harbor town of Saria."

"On the west coast of the country," Kaine said. "I know it. A thriving little port until the war ended, wasn't it?"

Tony nodded. "Everyone uses Izmir now, up north. Or Cesme. Economics. Saria's a fishing village now. But the Greek island Ano Kliston is a mere two miles away, over a span of calm, clear turquoise water."

"Ano Kliston!"

"You've heard of it."

"On a note written by a certain U.S. ambassador and delivered to the late Maurice Dreyfuss in a package of Kent cigarettes."

"Theatrical."

"Very."

"Well, the Colombians bridged that mere two-mile span of turquoise water with the finest little trestle bridge you ever saw." Tony's laughter had recaptured the mirth of honest irony now. He said, "They didn't do it alone, of course. At the request of the then

U.S. ambassador in Istanbul, the U.S. Army Corps of Engineers was brought in to assist in the project. It was a very successful collaboration. Now the Taurus Railway slips right across the Turkish border into Ano Kliston."

"I assume Ano Kliston has an airport."

"A rather active airport."

"And the name of the U.S. ambassador in Istanbul at the time the bridge was built?"

"Louis J. Mathers." Tony said the name very slowly. He wasn't laughing anymore. "One of our president's first official acts after he was elected was to reassign the ambassador to a similar, but far more prestigious, position in London."

The plane rocked with turbulence. There were no valley floors over which to fly now; they bounced from mountain peak to mountain peak.

"Then they'll make the exchange for the gold and the morphine there, in Ano Kliston," Kaine said.

"After that, the morphine is destined for the labs in Marseilles, where, unfortunately, the DEA hasn't been welcome since Nixon called their police force 'a gang of bungling idiots' twenty years ago."

Tony pointed up ahead. "There," he said. "Buckle up."

Kaine saw a mountainside dense with pine trees. The first splash of night visited the sky. "Where?"

Tony didn't offer an answer. He banked and cut back on the throttle. He trimmed the nose. He dropped down near tree level and Kaine saw a strip of dirt hidden between tall forests, as if an ambitious farmer had given up clearing the land when the magnitude of his undertaking had finally dawned on him.

"You can't land a plane there," Kaine protested. "Nobody can."

"It's the only thing I'm good at," Tony assured him. He reduced power further, trimmed the nose again, and skimmed the tops of threatening pines. He dropped the flaps and cut power altogether. The plane fell like a feather, fluttering from wing to wing. But impact was less delicate, a sharp shock and then a series of apparent leaps. The upward grade of the strip brought them to an abrupt halt. Tony killed the engine.

He was smiling. Not proud, just momentarily content.

From behind his seat, he quickly hoisted two wedge-shaped wooden blocks. He handed these to Kaine. Then he shouted, "Now we turn her."

They jumped to the ground. "Grab a wing strut," Tony said, as he raced back to the rear of the plane. He pushed down hard on the tail, raising the nose wheel in front off the ground, and swung the plane a hundred and eighty degrees, essentially facing it downhill again. Kaine kicked the wooden blocks under the wing wheels.

A moment later, he flung a full canteen over one shoulder and the satchel of food he had gotten from Alexi, the bus driver, over the other. Tony's offering was a compass that had long given false information, and a bedroll.

"Sorry about the stunt I pulled up there earlier," he said contritely. "Couldn't help myself."

Kaine raised an eyebrow. "On the other hand, the history lesson was worth it. We'll call it even."

"Over that mountain," Tony said, pointing to the peak directly south. A log cabin nestled into the side of the hill at the head of the landing strip. Kaine looked for signs of life and saw none. Behind the cabin, a narrow trail led into the woods. When he looked back, Tony was already at the controls of the plane. He gestured to the wheel blocks, and Kaine retrieved them. A moment later, the engine ignited and the propellers were invisible blurs. Kaine threw in the blocks; he thought of shaking hands, but by now the plane was already in motion. Seconds later, it was airborne.

40 Alone, Jaymin lay bloodied and broken and yearning for death. Naked, battered, and beyond degradation, she sprawled on the hardwood floor, her hands tied to a center pole in one of the clapboard huts. Throughout her ordeal, she had never had the luxury of losing consciousness. She remembered crying out; she tried filling her head with images of Stephen Kaine. She had bitten back her fear by revisiting the chambers of Sister Immaculata at the orphanage. Sister Immaculata had used a broom handle on her; nothing those five had done to her, she thought, tears streaming down her face, could have been worse.

She didn't remember everything, which was good. She remembered the stench of them. She remembered the burning of the needle as it was jabbed inexpertly into her arm. She remembered trying to float and being dragged ignominiously down to the ground and her arms being pinned behind her. And she remembered fighting and clawing and spitting until some premonitory message crept into her head telling her that to fight back in this case was to die. It was a difficult debate, because a second, equally convincing message argued that death would be her final release anyway, so why not go for it. Yet, somehow, for the moment at least, the message of survival had won out.

The door swung open and she recoiled, quivering. It was Turnbull. He smoked a cigar and ignored her. He carried a tray of food, a duffel bag, and a blanket. He came up behind her and she flinched.

"It's not me you have to worry about, you silly fool. I've come to say good-bye." He slit the rope, freeing her hands. He laid the blanket next to her and left again. Jaymin tried standing, but couldn't. She covered herself and began to shiver uncontrollably. Turnbull returned with a mug of something hot. He pressed it to her lips, and she spit it back at him.

"Tea," he said calmly. He repeated the gesture and Jaymin relented. Turnbull wiped the spittle from his face with a black handkerchief. "You're brave and stupid and beautiful, and I can't protect you, even if I wanted to. You're alive because the Colombians paid Preble to keep you alive. You'd be surprised at your worth."

"I need a fix."

"You need a savior." He threw the duffel bag across the room nonetheless; she unpacked it furiously. "Even now I can't help but marvel at you. Two goddamn years. The most remarkable charade, and then to have it end like this."

"Every move you and Mathers made for the last two years is documented. Washington doesn't need me to get you. The minute you're out of Asia Minor, you'll be extradited and a full-blown grand jury investigation will be called."

"No," Turnbull said simply. He could watch the process, but the smell of the heroin cooking turned his stomach. "We found your safe house in London, Jaymin. No, not the Belgravia. That was a pittance. The flat on Malvern Street in Lambeth."

Even in her fury to fill the syringe with the golden serum, Jaymin was struck momentarily numb. It took every ounce of self-control for her to draw the plunger back. Still, the hammering in her chest signaled the crashing down of the house of cards she had built so precariously over the last twenty-three months, since the day her services had been unsuspectingly recruited by former New York City policeman Joseph Jankowski, liaison for certain interests who at the time remained nameless.

But the Malvern Street flat was merely a drop for tapes and notes, all, according to her bosses at the DEA, unofficial until the final deal was struck. Jaymin had been to the flat a total of three times in eighteen months. Visits so brief that they could be measured in minutes. Her one confidant had been Ira Crabtree, the DEA chief. A fail-safe, he had called it.

A fail-safe for whom? Jaymin shook her head bitterly. Then she said his name. "Crabtree."

"Yes. Poor, pitiful Ira is not the man he once was," Turnbull replied. "Crabtree and Mathers attended Princeton together, did you know? Their wives still play bridge when the opportunity arises. And of course Louis never loses touch with a potential ally. I believe he and Mr. Crabtree had drinks yesterday. At any rate, your notes, though hardly legible, have been thoroughly shredded. Your tapes have been erased."

Jaymin set the syringe aside; the drug proved a double-edged sword, easing her pain, compounding her despair. "I was hoping for a little more drama at the end."

"I personally abhor photo finishes," Turnbull said.

"And I concede," she answered. Her muscles twitched, and she prayed it wouldn't show in her voice. "But conceding doesn't mean giving up."

"I know you better than that," Turnbull agreed.

"And you know that my word alone would be meaningless at this point. Without my notes and tapes, I've been rendered harmless." Odd how the words sapped her of strength. "We've been through a lot together, you and I."

"I've learned the meaning of rejection because of you."

"Also respect," Jaymin ventured. "And I deserve better than being chewed up and spit out by four Colombian animals."

"I admit it, not a prospect I care to envision." Turnbull stood up. He tied her hands again. He said, "Unfortunately, I also abhor loose ends, and you, dear Jaymin, have become exactly that."

41

At dawn, the bulbs of the poppy fields looked like huge beads of water suspended in air. Dew-covered, they radiated an iridescence verging on lavender. Miles upon miles of them, an ocean bordered by fragrant pines.

At the forest's edge, Kaine stood upwind of the fields, a deer poised at the penumbra between safety and danger. An idle tractor, the rust of many blistering summers and bitter winters scarring its yellow body, stood in the fields twenty yards away.

Kaine had stumbled upon the camp two hours before dawn. He had used the fallen logs and dry gulches of the forest for cover. There was a sophistication about the camp that he hadn't expected. Six clapboard huts had been fitted out with screened porches. Three long, narrow barracks were fed electricity from a huge generator and rationed water via two water towers. The morphine refinery had the prefabricated presence of a warehouse in the Tower Hamlets of London. Plumes of rancid smoke poured from stacks rising above its roof. A helipad had been constructed beyond the loading dock. Kaine had recognized the helicopter parked within its concentric circles, and knew then that Jaymin *was* here. Just let her be safe, he said to himself.

It wasn't to be. Circling the compound minutes later, Kaine

had heard a cry, like that of a wounded animal, and had known instantly that the agony belonged to Jaymin. My God. She had spared him his life and in the process been discovered herself. It had taken all his self-control to remain rational, all his will just to keep moving.

An assembly line moved brick-filled gunny sacks from the sheet-metal building into the second of two boxcars, and Kaine knew that he was surveying the results of converted and packaged opium. An hour before dawn, the train's coal-driven engine had been fired up. The engineer wore the uniform of a soldier.

Dangerously exposed at the time—Kaine had crept within thirty yards of the workers' barracks—he watched as the engineer pored over a map. When he saw Preble and Turnbull approaching, he threw himself behind the trunk of a tree. He slid to the ground, breathing heavily. His fingers dug into the ground. Poe's words returned to him: revenge, not retaliation. He thought, your time will come, Preble; first things first. He whispered Jaymin's name again and again.

Finally, he glanced back. Preble had evolved; he looked to Kaine like an animal finally in tune with his habitat. No longer subservient to Turnbull, the former Scotland Yard detective did most of the talking. He stomped toward the loading platform, shouting orders, and even the Colombians responded.

Kaine had waited long enough to see the doors of the boxcars shut tight. Men with automatic weapons were stationed atop the cars. When Kaine saw Preble and Turnbull board the train, he retreated to the fields. The tractor and the prevailing wind, traveling through the valley like a chute, seeded an idea.

The bulbs of the poppies this far afield of the camp had already been scored and the congealed opium harvested, and there were no workers within a mile of the tractor. The gold of Karmin-Yar, Kaine realized, had accounted for most of the harvest.

In a low crouch, he left the safety of the forest and scrambled through the field to the tractor. He tapped at the vehicle's cylindrical fuel tanks and found one half full, the other depleted.

More promising were three twenty-liter cans of diesel strapped along the chassis between the rear wheels; two were full. Kaine lugged the first of these to the south side of the valley. He worked his way back toward the tractor, splashing a yard-wide swatch of diesel over the dried poppies. When both cans were empty, he siphoned off what remained in the tractor's one fuel tank. Surprisingly, it refilled both cans and most of the third.

Kaine glanced back toward the camp and saw the train pulling away from the loading dock. It labored at first, wheels spinning. Plumes of smoke mushroomed from its stack. As it picked up speed, Kaine returned to his task.

Now he worked away from the tractor, north toward the railroad tracks, dousing the poppy stalks until all three cans were again empty. He discovered a crowbar and a rusted screwdriver in a toolbox beneath the tractor seat. He experimented; he found that by driving the claw end of the crowbar over the length of the screwdriver, he could produce a flurry of sparks. The dried stalks were like kindling. They ignited at once.

Within thirty seconds, a river of fire raced across the valley floor. The wind drove it east toward the camp. The flames devoured the poppy stalks; even the dried petals on the ground burned.

No longer concerned with concealment, Kaine ran between the railroad tracks toward the camp. The alarm, he saw, was instantaneous. The fire brought the entire camp to life. Panic followed. Men sought out the water towers, but their implements were buckets and rubber hoses, no match for the wall of flames stalking them. Some tried saving the unharvested poppies; others focused on the refinery.

Like those pouring from the barracks, Kaine became a man seeking survival; grimy and tinged with smoke, he was no longer an Anglo among men of brown skin. Beside him, the fire reared up, a tidal wave of heat and flames. It roared, attacking the ears as well as the lungs and the eyes. Kaine pushed through the throngs to the six clapboard huts; Jaymin's cries echoed in his head. He threw open one door after another. He found an office with desks and maps and a dart board; a bedroom with four real beds and a water bowl and pitcher made of clay; a room with a dozen card tables, a wood-burning stove, and a wall filled with liquor bottles; a room with six cots in a row and a woman huddled beneath a blanket, her hands tied to the center pole, an empty syringe on the floor at her side.

"Jaymin!"

"Oh, my God," she said, lifting her head. "It's you. No, you can't see me like this. Please, Stephen, don't. Don't. I've made such a mess of it."

Kaine fumbled with the rope. "*I* made the mess of it, Jaymin." Kaine kissed her hair, holding her. Finally, he threw off the blanket and studied her naked body. Her flesh was a piebald of black and purple splotches. The hair raised up on the back of Kaine's neck. "Jesus. Animals."

Jaymin collapsed against his chest. "I don't want you to see me like this, Stephen."

He carried her across the room. "Can you sit?"

She nodded. "How did you get here?"

"Lenci. Treas. Tony. You."

Blood covered her panties and blouse. She whimpered when he forced her legs into her jeans. Welts rose from her shoulders and back, and blood oozed from them. A knife had been held to her throat, and the wound had festered. A patch of hair had been scraped from her head. He poured water from his canteen, cleaning the wounds and bringing tears to her eyes. He apologized and she wept tears in a commingling of regret, shame, gratitude. Kaine ripped off his shirt and laid it gently over her shoulders.

She shook. Not from being cold, Kaine knew, for the fire had now encroached upon the buildings. Was it the need for heroin? Or the memories? He eased her jacket over her arms and buttoned it up. Her feet were swollen. Kaine gently rolled wool socks over them. "They beat my feet with a stick. I don't know why."

Kaine had no answer. He cradled her like a baby, smoothing her hair. As he lifted her, she gritted her teeth.

"Good," Kaine said. "Fight back."

"They found my tapes. They burned my notes. Talk about a screwup."

"Maybe not," Kaine said.

He kicked open the door. The smoke was thick and rancid. The fire had engulfed the first of the six huts, and flames towered anew. Men fled for the forest. Kaine heard gunshots and men shouting heedless orders. He circled the huts and came up behind the refinery. Workers carried sacks of raw opium on their backs. A chemist abandoned his domain with a microscope under one arm and a handkerchief over his mouth.

Smoke mushroomed above the helipad, but the helicopter was still tied down.

Now Jaymin understood his intention, and she shook her head. "I can't fly like this," she said flatly.

"I'm flying."

"No. Not up here, Stephen. We'd be down in two minutes." Her voice rang with remorse. "I need you to go back."

He knew what she meant: the duffel bag in the hut, the syringe. "No. It's too late. You don't need it."

"Yes," she said simply. "I do."

Arguing now made no sense. He opened the door on the pilot's side and set her on the seat. Though she grimaced, her hands were immediately busy with the controls.

By the time Kaine reached the huts again, the first three had been literally swept away by the fire. Flames climbed the walls of the fourth. As Kaine raced toward it, the porch roof caved in upon the door. The thatch roof virtually exploded. A second blast followed, then a fountain of flames, and the entire structure collapsed.

It was unapproachable; the heat alone drove Kaine away.

He returned to the helipad empty-handed. The rotors of the helicopter revolved furiously. Kaine opened her door. He shook his head. Jaymin's eyes widened with disbelief. A glaze of sweat rose on her skin even as he watched her. Suddenly she reached under the seat. Her search revealed an unopened bottle of Scotch. Her hands shook as she cracked the seal. She raised the bottle to her lips and drank. Her face knotted and she gasped. Twice more she drank. With each drink, a measure of control returned to her breathing.

"Cut the moorings," she said finally, with a commanding element in her voice.

Kaine raced from tie-down to tie-down, disconnecting each, and tossing them to the ground. He climbed aboard. No sooner had his door closed than the helicopter rose from the pad.

When they cleared the smoke, Jaymin looked back at the carnage. "Are you responsible for all that?"

"I was improvising."

"You improvise well. All for me?"

"Too much?"

"I didn't say that."

"Where are we going?"

The Scotch rested on the seat between Jaymin's legs. She took a deep swallow and passed the bottle. She watched Kaine fill his mouth; the liquor had a medicinal effect, and the muscles in his shoulders and neck relaxed. Then she told him. "We don't have enough fuel to go anywhere."

Kaine glanced at the gas gauge. The needle teetered on empty. "Can we make it to Iskilip?"

"We won't even make it to the river."

Jaymin flew so near the tops of the trees that Kaine watched them sway beneath the downdraft of the rotors. He helped himself to a second swallow of whiskey. A numbness that had nothing to do with the alcohol crept over him, mind and body. But the numbness was no blessing; it opened avenues of thought that had been blocked in the past hours by adrenaline and momentum and the sheer instinct to survive.

He drew a parallel between his own survival and that of Angela and Danielle; it was a mind game with a logical premise. Louis Mathers would recognize the need for a confrontation with Kaine. Mathers would perceive Kaine as a loose end with dangerous possibilities. Angela and Danielle represented the perfect lure. In Kaine's state of mind, dangerously fatalistic at the moment, he would strike without thinking, an animal driven into a corner, baited by a savage hatred.

But the logic took an unexpected turn; it punched a hole in the numbness. "Tony's landing strip," he said all at once. "He has fifty or sixty gallons of fuel hidden there. He called it his private reserve."

4 2 The pub in Dover was called the Curious Cousins. Its popularity had decreased over the years because the cousins had both retired, and the establishment had been sold to a Welsh family with a history of miscreant behavior. The home-cooked food and personal service had been foolishly replaced by cheap liquor and backroom parlor games. After monthly raids by members of Scotland Yard, the Welsh family moved on. The pub was taken over by a Frenchman named Proust. He served fish and chicken lavished with yellow pepper oil, and only the best liquor. Still, the English resistance to change remained a stumbling block. Even in cosmopolitan Dover, it was not an easy transition.

It was ten in the morning. The breakfast crowd had gone. The occupants of a single booth remained. They still had not ordered, and the gentleman in the silk suit had made it clear to Monsieur Proust that he would be wise to wait for his signal. Two Scotland Yard men were stationed outside the door; they had displayed their credentials and suggested a measure of cooperation would be in the owner's best interest.

In a corner booth, Louis Mathers pushed a warrant for Stephen Kaine's arrest across the table. "I'm sorry to have to be the one to share this news with you," Mathers said, directing his words to Danielle, while Angela sat numbly at her side.

Danielle took the time to read the arrest order carefully. It had the look and the jargon of an official document; the signature and official seal at the bottom belonged to the Magistrate Ian McGrath. The arrest order cited Kaine as the primary suspect in the murder of First Skipper Tanner Thorpe.

"And you, the U.S. ambassador to England, are here in this deserted pub sitting across from the accused's ex-wife for what reason?" Danielle asked calmly. "You must have more pressing matters elsewhere."

Behind this façade of equanimity, she was confused and frightened. Much of her fear was a direct result of the overwhelming reaction Angela had suffered upon seeing the ambassador. Much of her confusion was a direct result of the dumbfounded reaction Angela had suffered upon seeing Connor Thorpe at the ambassador's side.

"I come on behalf of the accused," Mathers replied matter-of-factly. His eyebrows arched. He smiled, and Danielle wondered if he was aware of the smile's mocking quality. She doubted it. "I am the American representative here in England. Americans are my first priority. Stephen Kaine is being considered by the English authorities as a fugitive from the law. If I am allowed to intervene on his behalf, then considerations are possible."

Angela glared at Connor Thorpe and could no longer restrain herself.

"You sit next to the man who murdered your father and nod your head at his lies." Since being seated, she had not taken her eyes off the first skipper's son. Tears of rage, Danielle noted, had evolved into a muted scowl. Then Angela pleaded. "I was there, Connor. He shot your father in the chest while he sat helplessly on a bench in your tugboat."

Connor's eyes were unreadable; Danielle saw a myriad of emotions reflected in them. Mechanically, Connor now presented Angela with a computerized enlargement of a Polaroid negative, much like the one Kaine had received from Dr. Daniel Stone at the Chatham Institute of Technology. There was a difference. Where the results of the original enhancement had revealed the face of Louis Mathers, the face looking back from this enlargement belonged to her father.

"And this?" Connor said softly. "Explain this. It came from your camera. The police have said so themselves."

Angela's head moved from side to side, an indiscernible, yearning gesture. It occurred to Danielle that she and her daughter were experiencing a shared impulse, the impulse to reach out and touch the young man's face.

"This . . . this picture. It has nothing to do with your father," Angela said. "I can only imagine how much it hurts to lose your dad—I liked him so much, Connor, I really did—but this is a lie."

"After all my father did for you. You would have drowned had it not been for him."

"Oh, Connor . . ."

"What considerations?" Danielle said quietly; it took an extraordinary force of will to intrude upon this exchange and refocus on Louis Mathers.

In return, the ambassador assumed a brusque, businesslike air. "It's very simple," he said. "According to the deal I have struck with Scotland Yard, your lovely daughter here will not be held as an accessory to the crime."

"Angela!" Like a curtain falling, the blood drained from Danielle's face. "Have you lost your mind? An accessory?"

"It's not as difficult to fathom as you might think."

From his inside breast pocket, Mathers produced a second document. He opened it, smoothed it across his chest, and presented it for Danielle's inspection. It replicated the first order nearly to the letter, was equally as official in appearance, and bore the same signature. There was one outstanding addendum. It called for the arrest of Angela Kaine as an accessory to the same first-degree murder charge. A chill ran down Danielle's spine; she shook visibly.

At the same time, she was struck by a series of relentless, debilitating emotions: confusion, disbelief, helplessness. Her wandering gaze settled momentarily upon Connor Thorpe. Something in his dull, empty stare triggered a fourth emotion, a wave of maternal protectiveness.

She swept up the second arrest order. Staring coldly into Louis Mathers's eyes, she tore the document in half, then into fourths. The scraps slipped through her open fingers and settled featherlike upon the tabletop.

Danielle was no fool. She knew there was more, and said, "Now what?"

"Take the young lady outside," Mathers ordered Connor Thorpe.

"Mom?" Angela protested.

Danielle squeezed Angela's hand, then kissed her cheek. Her voice steady and reassuring, she whispered, "It's okay, baby. I'll be out in a minute."

Mathers watched them go. Then he scooped up the first arrest order. As Danielle had done with the other, he shredded it. He laid the strips in a neat pile and rested his hands ceremoniously upon them. Then he said, "It would not do much good for young Connor to see me do that. In his eyes, the arrest order is written in stone. He's very angry and very confused. But the fact of the matter is, I can see to it that no charges are brought against either your daughter or your ex-husband."

Danielle bit back her anger. "You've got that much pull, do you?"

"You would be surprised at the pull I have when the matter involves my fellow Americans."

"And the deal?"

"Your daughter signs a statement that says in effect that she doesn't know who was on that tugboat the day First Skipper Thorpe was killed. That she was in another part of the boat, that she was scared, that she was hiding. The deal is that she remains in Dover until your ex-husband returns, which, if he is able, he will do. We both know that. Part two of the deal is that Mr. Kaine also agrees to our conditions. That his signature also appears on the statement. I'm sure you can understand the need for that."

"I understand that you're a son of a bitch, Ambassador Mathers. That's what I understand," Danielle replied.

Mathers leaned across the table, his voice a cutting whisper, his breath peppermint-scented. "Oh, I can be a great deal worse than a son of a bitch, Mrs. Kaine. For example, I have witnesses ready to swear to the fact that they saw your ex-husband and daughter fleeing the scene of the crime moments after the murder. Statements have already been prepared and signed. I have witnesses ready to swear to my presence miles from the scene at the same moment. You see, I can make their lives, and yours, hell for a very long time, and will gladly do so."

Danielle considered the predicament. She considered the players. What were her options? If Angela persisted in her assertion that Mathers was the man on the tugboat that day, and if charges were indeed brought against him, Danielle could only imagine the ordeal of a trial. She had no idea what had become of the actual photos Angela had taken that day. Were they still in Scotland Yard's possession? Had Mathers bought the Yard off, as well? Did Stephen still possess a copy? If it came down to Angela's word against that of the United States ambassador to England, then what?

Answers without questions, Danielle thought. Yet she was left with a nagging unknown, and that was Connor Thorpe's presence here. There was something inconsistent, if not tawdry, about it. How had Connor been so completely turned? Was Mathers that persuasive? Or had he in some way threatened Connor, as well?

In the end, Angela's safety was all that mattered. The child had tempted fate too many times already. She had been through enough.

Danielle hung her shoulders, hating herself, and said, "I accept your deal."

43

"I'll explain it one more time," Jaymin said. She was exasperated. She was also caught in the grip of a mental and physical landslide that Kaine could see gaining momentum minute by minute. "We need a plane, one with some speed and a reasonable-size fuel tank. This Tinker Toy piece-of-nothing helicopter won't do; it's built for maneuverability, not speed, and not distance. We've already lost three hours. It's four hundred and fifty miles from here to the Aegean Sea by air. By train, maybe twice as much. This helicopter would need two refueling stops to cover that much ground. And that's the catch, or at least one of them. See, the only refueling stations I know of between here and Ano Kliston were built along the Taurus line by the traffickers. They're manned by their men and their guns, and truthfully I don't expect them to welcome us with open arms. But then, maybe you're a better talker than I am."

Tony's private fuel supply was buried in a shallow grave at the head of the landing strip where Kaine had been dropped sixteen hours ago. A certain amount of time and effort had been given to the pit's creation. It was a four-by-six-foot rectangle, slightly more than two feet deep, and perfectly level. Unfortunately, a dirt-covered canvas tarp, stretched from one side to the other, so well disguised the hole that it had taken them twenty minutes to locate it.

The fuel was stored in twenty-liter cans. The helicopter's tiny fuel tank held only forty-eight liters. Kaine emptied two and a half cans into the tank.

Jaymin drank Scotch in defense against the agonies of withdrawal, but the whiskey's half-life had long since passed. Kaine knew nothing about heroin withdrawal; Jaymin didn't want to be touched. She refused the damp cloth he offered when sweat rained down from her brow; she refused his jacket when her entire body shook.

"Where to, then?" he asked impassively. He quickly restored the pit's disguise, nailing down the tarp and spreading a layer of dirt and pine needles over it. "A detour to Tosya will cost another two hours, if Tony's there at all."

"Not Tosya," Jaymin snapped. "Not Tony's plane."

"Where?"

"Across the river. Iskilip." She climbed into the cockpit with an aggressiveness fed mostly by despair.

"What's in Iskilip?" Kaine strapped himself into the passenger seat. "An airplane or a fix?"

He regretted the question even as he spoke it. He felt helpless and angry, his compassion tarnished by cynicism. It was foolish. Jaymin turned her sweat-soaked face in his direction; the rotor spun furiously above them, but she held tight to the throttle. "If we're lucky, both," she said. "If we're not, it doesn't matter much anyway, unless you suddenly sprout wings."

She jammed the stick forward. The helicopter rose only a matter of feet above the ground. It shot down the descending pitch of the runway until she banked sharply and eventually leveled off in a narrow valley between ramparts of brown and black granite.

"Try not to kill us in the meantime," Kaine said, grasping a leather thong dangling from the crossbar overhead.

Jaymin eased back on the throttle; her grip slackened on the stick and her lungs emptied of air. Ironically, Kaine observed, flying seemed to provide her with a momentary shield against the withdrawal. He only hoped it would last. The helicopter steadied. Canyons of stone and pine carried them in a northerly direction. A wildly erratic stream coursed along the basin below them. Kaine searched for life forms and found none.

"I lied," Jaymin said without looking in his direction.

Kaine studied her profile. "It becomes a defense mechanism, doesn't it? Lying," he said. "Like hedging a bet or playing two ends against the middle."

"In this case, more like a self-perpetuating fairy tale."

Now she looked at him. Her face was taut and pale; her eyes glistened with moisture, pools of green. Her short hair was slick with sweat. She nodded toward the cigarettes on the console. "You'd better light it for me," she said.

Kaine did. "A self-perpetuating fairy tale," he said. "You're not talking about the plane then, or Iskilip. Lied about what, Jaymin?"

"The China White." She set the helicopter in a languishing bank. The canyons fell away in broken steps and the Anatolia plateau opened up before them, a breathtaking vista of weatherbeaten prairie. "I said before that it wasn't a problem. I lied. Not to you. To myself. I'm as snakebitten as an alley junkie in Harlem. We fall into the same death traps and use the same mind games to convince ourselves it's not happening."

"Tony said it's the business," Kaine replied. "He said it calls for some rather dramatic playacting."

"That's supposed to make me feel better, I know. But it doesn't. Mastering the part is one thing. Letting the part master you is another."

On the horizon, the Kizil River cut a meandering ribbon across the brow of the plateau. The sun beat down on it, and the water threw off iridescent sparks, like fish scales. A trail of smoke, from a bonfire on the far bank, gave notice of a town built amid a smattering of tall trees. Sheep grazed on land too stingy for cattle.

An airstrip of hard-packed dirt scarred an unscarrable track of land south of town. Two small planes were tied down next to a square, flat-roofed building and an empty hangar. A derrick-shaped radio tower sprouted between the two, but Jaymin made no attempt at ground contact. As they were landing, a man appeared at the hangar door. His hands were grease-stained and he made a vain attempt at cleaning them on an equally grease-stained rag.

Jaymin disembarked. She marched straight for the planes. She circled the first, a single-engine Skyhawk. She started at the end of the wing, reaching up and throwing her full weight against it. She toyed with the flaps. She ran a finger over the leading edge of the propeller in search of nicks. She gave a cursory glance to the engine, and tugged at the generator belt. She spot-checked the fuselage. She found a dip stick beneath a panel on the top side of the engine cowling, and tested the color and consistency of the oil. Then she stepped to the rear of the plane, studied the control cables on the tail, and shook her head. She turned on her heels and didn't look back.

The second plane was so classic in design that Kaine was himself drawn to it. A biplane with an open cockpit, it reminded him of every crop duster he had ever imagined. The word BECKELHOUSE was stenciled along the side. Jaymin inspected it as thoroughly as she had the first plane: the wings, the fuselage, the engine, the oil. Then she drained the fuel strainer. She tugged at the guide wires. She bounced on the tail wheel. In the end, she seemed most intrigued by the makeshift metal racks that had been installed between the wings on either side of the fuselage, and the fuel drums attached to the racks. She tapped on the drums and they echoed percussively, obviously empty.

The mechanic sauntered forward, a stout man with a heavy beard and teeth blackened by a steady diet of Turkish cigarettes. He wore a billed cap, front to back. Jaymin spoke to him in one of a half dozen Turkish dialects. The man laughed.

He answered in English. "Bad. Very bad."

Jaymin's physical and mental frame of mind were beyond jocularities. She gestured at the biplane. "Buy or rent?"

The mechanic shook his head. "The owner lives in Ankara. The plane is not mine to sell. Anyway, very bad shape." He made a magnanimous gesture to the Skyhawk. "Better. Much better."

Jaymin stripped off her leather jacket. To the amazement of both men, she ripped away a matching patch stitched to the inside of the garment. From behind the patch, a stack of American hundred-dollar bills fell into her hand. Jaymin held out three of the bills, more money than the man made in a year. She tugged at the lower wing of the Beckelhouse.

"Rent for three days," she said simply. "A full tank of gas. Fuel drums, too."

The mechanic was momentarily speechless. He stared at Jaymin, not at the money. But when he moved, it was his hand reaching out for the bills.

"Have it ready in fifteen minutes," Jaymin said before relinquishing the money.

"Three days and the plane is back. Same condition. Guaranteed."

Jaymin nodded. A liar, a thief, and a cheat, Kaine thought. Roles made necessary by her trade maybe, but when it came down to it, he wondered if he had ever known anyone as genuine. One thing was certain, he didn't feel cheated.

Then she was jogging toward the helicopter. "I'll be back," she shouted over her shoulder at Kaine.

The mechanic had the plane fueled and ready when Jaymin returned twenty-five minutes later.

Kaine was waiting in the cockpit. "You're late," he said without commenting on her dramatically altered state.

"Some things take time. I'm sorry." Kaine didn't reply, and he could see how powerful that omission was; Jaymin seemed to shrink in her seat. "I'm sorry," she said again.

They lifted off moments later.

Jaymin had seen something in the Beckelhouse that the mechanic had not admitted to, or had tried to conceal. Though it lacked stability, it was equipped with an engine capable of a cruising speed of a hundred and thirty miles per hour. A simplistic control panel featured an air-speed indicator, a magnetic compass, an altimeter, a tachometer, an oil gauge, and a radio. Nothing more.

Jaymin flew without a map or flight plan.

The trip required a single refueling stop. Jaymin put the plane down on a stretch of salt flats, the remains of a lake left dry by some natural catastrophe wrought by the earth a million years ago. The eerie whiteness, striated by a constant east to west wind, stretched for miles. The transfer of fuel took Kaine ten minutes. Simple garden hoses had been attached to the bases of the storage drums. The hoses had been cut to stretch without slack to the fuel tank at the side of the fuselage. There was no pump; Kaine removed a cap at the top of each drum and gravity drove the fuel through the hoses. Jaymin waited placidly in the cockpit, her eyes half-closed.

From the air, they looked for landmarks. They saw the outskirts of Ankara and knew that the coastal village of Saria, and the trestle bridge that linked it to the Greek island of Ano Kliston, lay west by southwest of them. An hour later, the snowcapped peak of Kemer Dagi, a rounded cone off their left wing, told Jaymin that an adjustment in course, due west, was necessary. The shoe-shaped Lake Atros, high in the mountains ringing the west edge of the Anatolia plateau, told her that the Taurus Railway, though as yet still hidden by forests of pine, was plunging toward the coast very near at hand.

Moments later, they sighted Colonel Turnbull's train, in a valley alive with yellow flowers and farmhouses painted white. The engine churned black smoke into the air, and the two boxcars followed with their cargo securely in place.

"Can we notify the border patrol or the police?" Kaine asked, nodding toward the radio.

Jaymin threw out a cynical laugh. "You don't quite get it, do you, my love?" She patted Kaine's knee. "They've already been notified, Stephen. Every border-patrol officer, every customs official, and every policeman within twenty miles of the town of Saria are, at this moment, occupying themselves with some mundane task that just so happens to put them an hour or two away from the Taurus line; and they've been well paid to do so. That halfpint train down there won't even slow down until it's on that trestle bridge over the Aegean Sea and within shouting distance of Ano Kliston. By then it'll be too late."

"Then we have to stop them before they reach the bridge," Kaine said.

Weary and bruised, Jaymin sighed. Her shoulders sagged and she turned. The strain of her ordeal had bled her face of all color,

leaving dark circles under bloodshot eyes. Even at that, Kaine saw
a beauty that went so deep no ordeal could mask it. His hand
traveled to her face, his fingers tracing the outline of her swollen
cheeks. He wanted to say the shipment didn't matter. But he could
see that it did matter. That maybe the shipment was symbolic of
the ordeal, and that stopping the former might somehow ease the
pain of the latter.

She took the plane into a forty-five-degree bank, leaving the
train off her right wing, and flew on toward Saria. As if the Aegean
Sea were of a calmer, more idyllic temperament than the Black Sea
to the north, the coast here boasted of broadleaf trees and fields of
orchids. From the air, the Greek islands rose from the Aegean's
blue water like rough-cut emeralds.

Saria was an anomaly, a city of commerce turned fishing village.
It perched on a bluff overlooking the sea. Breakwaters in the shape
of horseshoes surrounded a harbor busy with low-slung trawlers,
two-man ketches, and yawls that put Kaine in mind of Chinese
sampans. The trestle bridge that forged a connection with the Greek
island of Ano Kliston rose off the back of the bluff and settled upon
tall spiny legs that seemed to walk on top of the water. Hovering
forty feet above the sea for a distance of two and a half miles, it
was a visual delight, an engineering feat. Built solely of wooden
supports and blackened railroad ties, it was archaic beyond its five-
year history.

As they circled, Kaine's eyes were drawn to the trainyard on
the perimeter of town. It had become a graveyard for abandoned
boxcars and engines gone to rust. The switching stations were from
a half century past, with hand-operated levers at crossroads of in-
terconnecting tracks. Kaine had become familiar with such devices
in the trainyards beyond the University of Chicago, where he had
done his master's work. He had written a thesis on the evolution of
land transportation and the yards were the site of copious research.

"If we could get to those," he said, more to himself than to
Jaymin.

"The switching stations," she said, reaching into his thoughts.

"There," he said excitedly. He waved his hand toward the trainyard and a strip of land once dedicated to the loading and unloading

of freight, essentially a road two or three hundred yards in length. "Is it long enough?"

"With the right pilot, a plane like this one could land twice on a strip that long," she said. "You happen to be with the right pilot."

She cut back on the throttle and banked. The Beckelhouse lost a hundred feet in ten seconds and Jaymin leveled off. The road, pitted and worn, had been in disrepair for a long time. Kaine was no longer so confident. "It looks like the Turkish air force has been using it as a bombing run," he commented. "Is there any other place?"

But Jaymin was already into her landing pattern. She squared up with the road, eased the wheel back, and reduced power. She trimmed the nose. She worked the rudder pedals, adjusting to an inland breeze, and the plane drifted to earth like a feather under God's guiding hand. Finally she cut power altogether and the wheels touched down. They came to a complete stop almost immediately.

The ensuing moment was one Kaine would never forget. She touched his shoulder, then reached out for his hand. Their eyes met. Kaine read contentment in hers. How could he convey what he *felt* in such a brief glance? Then it occurred to him that maybe she already knew, and that was enough. That for now, it had to be enough.

"Be careful," she said. She kissed his cheek.

"You, too." He opened the cockpit door and jumped out.

"Good-bye, Stephen," she said, as the door swung shut.

As the plane rolled down the road, Kaine felt a sudden tightening in his chest and throat. Good-bye? No. *No.*

"Jaymin?" He called out her name. "Jaymin!" He started after the plane. It was too late. The breeze off the sea became a wind and it tugged at the flaps of his jacket, kicked a dust cloud into the air, and sent his dark hair flying. The Beckelhouse lifted off, wings wobbling. Jaymin banked to her left, downwind, and the plane surged skyward.

Kaine turned as the plane turned. Inland she flew, over a village half asleep, over farms restless for spring, over a meadow and a herd of cattle with heads buried in tall grass. He watched, transfixed, until the mountains consumed her and the biplane she commanded. Even then, he waited for her reappearance. When she didn't return, Kaine shook himself back to life. The switching station.

Even among the many tracks leading into the trainyard, the Taurus line was easy to find. It was the only one not deteriorating under a layer of rust and corrosion. He located the nearest switching station a hundred yards farther on, housed in a tiny shed not much larger than a phone booth. Gazing inland, Kaine saw a fountain of smoke, but no train.

He ran, reaching the shed in time to study the intersection of track. There was nothing complex about it. The switch, once activated, would direct the train onto a set of tracks leading into the yard and eventually to a loading dock that hadn't been utilized in two decades. What Kaine would do then, he didn't know.

He stepped into the shed. The switch was a device of few moving parts and little chance of malfunctioning—essentially a hand lever that moved a section of track back and forth. Kaine was reaching for the lever when the door of the shed opened behind him. Detective Superintendent Preble stepped into the light. He waved an automatic pistol in Kaine's face. He gazed down at the lever and shook his head.

"I'd only put a half dozen bullets in your head and then switch the track back," Preble said. "You at least deserve to die in the light of day."

He stepped away from the door. He used the gun to issue his invitation for Kaine to follow. Kaine did so; Preble was right about the switch, and the morphine wasn't worth dying for.

The train roared into view, out of a cradle formed by the walls of two mountains. The tracks spilled out before it, down the rolling meadow, through a pasture of cattle and horses, eventually skirting Saria and then entering the yard.

"You're like a cat," Preble said, his voice melding respect with hatred. "Too many lives and too much of a bloody nuisance. We heard you'd picked up a plane in Iskilip. Turnbull had a hunch you'd turn up here. Had me fly ahead. And sure enough. Like a bloody cat."

"And you, Preble, you're like a snake. Vile and spineless. One life. One life too many. You change colors at the drop of a hat. I've prayed for this moment. You and me. Why don't you put down that gun?"

Preble didn't move.

Kaine considered a head-on attack. Given the pounding he had put Kaine through at Karmin-Yar, it was clear that Preble relished the use of his fists. Kaine's odds in hand-to-hand combat with the detective were poor, but better than a bullet. What's more, Preble was right; Kaine had proved his resilience, and his confidence had grown. Though Preble's posturing with the gun, his distance, and his caution signified a change in attitude since Karmin-Yar, perhaps the Scotland Yard detective could be baited.

Kaine continued. "Honor? If you were squeezed dry, your honor wouldn't fill a thimble. Courage? Does forcing a fifty-year-old half-drunk stone collector to her knees count? What about loyalty? Yeah, I suppose if it has the color and scent of money you can be real loyal."

Preble studied him. The gun dropped to his side. He didn't move, but his expression changed. To dismay, not anger. Deliberation, not recklessness. Contemplation, not malevolence.

"I'll tell you a thing or two about honor, and courage, and loyalty, Professor Kaine." He spoke with an eye on the approaching train, but with Kaine's shadow lying across his field of vision. "In 1968, the British patched together a group of combat-ready soldiers and gave us over to the American Special Forces in Vietnam for whatever purposes they could manufacture, mostly of a destructive nature. I came home up to my elbows in heinous deeds, most of those perpetrated at the expense of a bunch of rice farmers, and they pinned the Victoria Cross on my chest. After Vietnam, I did a tour in Belfast disarming IRA pipe bombs. That came with a medal for valor. I spent twenty years with Scotland Yard, up the ranks and all that, and came away without the money to send my daughter to a decent university. My wife found Yard work too nerve-wracking and left me for a bookkeeper on Fleet Street. I've seen more heroin shipped into the port of New York by your own American CIA than that train, plus a half dozen more just like it, could ever hold. That gold you're so concerned with? Tell me, who was in line to profit from it if and when you and your massive team of do-gooders came upon it? Don't ask me to explain my motives to you, Kaine. And make sure your own nest is faultless before you get around to casting aspersions on the likes of me, why don't you?"

"Very high-minded rationale for criminal behavior," Kaine replied.

Preble shrugged. "Yeah, well, you're not about to goad me into doing something stupid at this point, Kaine. True, killing you with my fists would give me the greatest of pleasure, but we're too close to the end now. There's a cargo plane that's been freed and cleared by Greek customs waiting on a runway right across that bridge there. It's a big plane, with just enough room inside for two boxcars. And you know what, Kaine? Your archeological site won't come out of it any the worse for it. Minus some gold nobody's been missing for two thousand years, but not much else."

"And the people who died in that ferry accident two weeks ago? How does that fit into your neat package? A minor oversight?"

Now the train was more than a silent apparition. The clash of steel wheels upon steel tracks traveled out in front of it, a herald of time slipping quickly away from Kaine. He scanned the sky for Jaymin and the Beckelhouse, but saw only gulls circling high off the bluff, and, out over the water, formations of pelicans like bombers in search of a target.

"Take a half dozen steps back, Professor Kaine," Preble ordered. "Just to calm my nerves."

The train was slowing. Of course, Kaine thought—to pick up Preble. But also, he discovered, to deliver a message. The train rolled to a halt well beyond the switching station. Preble climbed aboard the rear platform of the second boxcar. He hooked an arm around the top rung of a steel ladder and glanced back.

Colonel William Turnbull leaned out the side window of the engineer's compartment. He looked weary, gaunt and chalky. He called Kaine by name. "Your chase leads you back to the beginning after all," he said. "Your daughter and ex-wife are in Dover. They are in the company of the U.S. ambassador to England, awaiting your return. I advise you not to do anything stupid, Kaine. Our accommodations to you and your family are fair. And for your daughter's well-being, I suggest you put yourself in an accommodating frame of mind, as well."

Kaine neither gestured nor spoke; apparently, he was to be spared the bullet. Preble had slung the automatic weapon over his shoulder; Turnbull had withdrawn into the engineer's compartment again. The train inched forward. Kaine walked in tandem with it, then gradually lost ground as the three-car caravan picked up speed.

The train lumbered through the deserted yard. Like a ride at an amusement park, it rose off the back of the bluff, onto the trestle bridge, and emerged high over the waters of the Aegean Sea.

Out of the corner of his eye, Kaine caught sight of Jaymin and the Beckelhouse. She was flying low and fast over the coast, seemingly on an intersect course with the train. Instinctively, he began to run. His eyes darted from the train to the Beckelhouse and back again. Preble, Kaine saw, had spotted the approaching plane, as well. He was climbing up the ladder. He crawled onto the roof of the boxcar and slipped the automatic pistol off his shoulder. He assumed the stance of an infantryman, crouching on one knee.

"No!" Futilely Kaine shouted the word. He stumbled over a railroad tie, caught himself, and continued to run, arms pumping. He reached the edge of the bluff.

He saw Preble sighting in on the swiftly approaching plane, now dangerously close. And then he was firing. The orange flash spewing from the end of the gun brought Kaine up short. He stopped, helpless. He saw Jaymin's face outlined in the cockpit. He called out her name. "Jaymin! Pull up, goddammit. Pull up."

She didn't. The cockpit window shattered. Smoke leaked from the engine. Without slowing, the plane slammed into the bridge fifty feet ahead of the onrushing train. The force of the collision and the ensuing explosion ripped a gaping hole in the bridge and sent an entire section of track into the sea. The squeal of the train's brakes rose above it all, but the engineer's efforts were fruitless. The train's momentum was too great. It tumbled over the end of the bridge, plummeted engine-first into the sea, and vanished from sight.

Heedlessly, Kaine followed the tracks of the bridge out over the water. The plane had obliterated a thirty-foot section; it was as if it had never existed. Splintered timbers ended in midair. The track had been ripped apart at a weld joint.

Kaine stared into the sea. He looked for a body among the floating debris of the Beckelhouse. None appeared. The sea, however, had evidently wrenched open one of the boxcar doors, for rising to the surface Kaine saw empty gunny sacks.

Though it was certainly only a matter of minutes, Kaine felt as if he had been standing at the end of the bridge for hours. He tried piecing it together. It had been Jaymin's intent to pull up at the last second. He wanted to believe that. She had been hit by Preble's gunfire and lost control of the plane. Yet a train on tracks was not like a car on a road; you didn't divert a train by intimidation or close calls. No, Kaine thought, Jaymin had been ready to sacrifice her life. Not for the sake of some job or a busted drug deal. This was something more, a last act bent on righting the life that had sucked her so far down. An act of purification even. And as desperate as that seemed in Kaine's eyes, he would grant her that.

For a time, he gazed out over the glistening waters of the Aegean Sea, at islands dotting its surface for miles, and allowed the questions to wash over him. He counted the islands and then lost count. His vision blurred momentarily. A stiff breeze funneled down the coast, and the bridge swayed. Kaine gazed down into the water below a last time, hoping in vain for some sign of Jaymin's body.

As he was turning away, Kaine saw what looked like a tiny island moving along the horizon. He paused. He raised a hand to shade his eyes. It was the Colombian freighter, two miles to the south, and steaming directly for him. A smile of disbelief spread across Kaine's face. Yet even then he saw that the freighter was slowing—as if the vessel's pilot had become aware, suddenly, that something had gone wrong.

Instinctively, Kaine scrambled for the remote-control unit that, for the last two days, had been strapped to his lower back. He extended the antenna. Standing on the precipice of a broken bridge forty feet above the open sea, Kaine held the unit out before him. He waited. The freighter cut a sweeping arc through the water. When the ship's starboard side was completely exposed, Kaine pressed the detonator button. Seconds passed. Nothing. He estimated the distance; it couldn't be out of range, not after all this. Dumbly, desperately, he held the button down, held it down until his thumb ached from the pressure. Finally, the sea roiled up around the vessel. Four distinct fountains of water broke the surface. A low rumble, like distant thunder, reached Kaine's ears.

Within moments, the freighter lay dead in the water. It was fast listing to the starboard side. Then it rolled painfully over, paused, and finally, as if the sea had opened its jaws, the vessel, and the gold of Karmin-Yar, slipped gracefully into a watery grave.

44

Kaine took the Hovercraft from Calais across the strait to Dover. Angela and Danielle stood on the dock awaiting him. Flanking them stood Louis Mathers and Connor Thorpe. Kaine counted two bodyguards.

He was the last to depart the craft. He walked up the ramp to a now deserted dock. Strangely deserted, he thought. But then he assumed this was Mathers's doing. Angela ran to greet him. She threw her arms around his neck.

"You're safe," she said.

Kaine held her a moment, head against his chest. Danielle walked slowly toward them. A defeated, fatigued expression tugged at the corners of her mouth and formed dark wells beneath her eyes. She leaned on his shoulder, Angela between them.

"Missed you," she said. "I kept thinking about Colorado."

"We should have never left," he said.

This caused Danielle to raise her head. She surveyed him with an unhurried curiosity. Then was content to rest her head again.

"We haven't done too well on this side of the English Channel," she said. "How about you?"

"Good and bad," Kaine answered. He followed the approach of Louis Mathers, and tried to summon the rage and the animal instincts he had experienced earlier. Oddly, the little man's presence excited no such response. Rather, Kaine was struck most strongly by the urge to draw Danielle and Angela closer.

"You're very resilient, Mr. Kaine," the ambassador said. He couldn't resist a thin smile. "Very resilient."

"Your colleagues weren't so fortunate," Kaine told him.

"So I've heard," he said dispassionately. "Fate, I suppose."

Connor Thorpe had stationed himself a few feet behind the ambassador, and the first skipper's son tipped his head steadfastly in Kaine's direction. Kaine read volumes into the gesture. In the days since his father's death, Connor had become a man. He had discovered new meaning in patience and justice and revenge. And he had succeeded in his appointed task without compromising his discovery.

Kaine acknowledged the gesture with the briefest of nods, then turned back to Mathers. He said, "Fate probably has more to do with it than you think, Mr. Ambassador."

"Well, perhaps not in this case." Confidently, Mathers withdrew an envelope from his breast pocket. "I'll let your beautiful ex-wife explain the situation. I think she has a rather firm grasp on the matter as it now stands."

"Scotland Yard is holding a warrant for your arrest," Danielle told Kaine. "The evidence they've accumulated suggests that you were responsible for Tanner Thorpe's death, and that Angela was an accessory to the fact."

The dock behind them was suddenly alive with people. But these were not, Kaine noticed, potential passengers for the ferry. These were fishermen, and stevedores, and longshoremen. Tugboat captains and harbor pilots. They made their way down the ramp even as Danielle continued.

"But the ambassador has agreed that we can avoid all that if Angela goes on record as having no knowledge of the events of that night. She's to say that she saw no one, that she was scared and hiding. You will sign a similar statement. A straight trade for the warrants."

"Very civilized," Kaine agreed.

"All that remains," Mathers concluded, "is a certain computer-enhanced image illegally obtained by you from the Chatham Institute of Technology."

"It's not mine to give," Kaine said.

"Oh?"

"As it turns out, it's mine to give," said Connor Thorpe, now stepping forward. "Rather, to give or not to give."

The coterie of harbor workers had formed a partition at the young man's back, and the sight of them caused Louis Mathers to falter. His bodyguards had disappeared. Connor took the original computerized enhancement from his pocket, unfolded it, and offered it for the ambassador's inspection.

"These men behind me come from as far away as Aberdeen, in Scotland. All friends of my father, and he had many. You murdered him. You shot him down like a dog." Connor spoke in a low, steady voice, his intense, dark eyes locked upon Mathers. "But our ways are different from yours. Our rules. You'll pay reparation for my father's death, Mr. Ambassador, but you'll pay for it out there."

Connor threw a hand out toward the English Channel and the North Sea beyond. "Out there on the sea that my father loved and respected."

Mathers snorted scornfully, but the ribbons of sweat on his brow betrayed him. "Have you lost your mind?"

The partition closed in. Connor said, "You'll be given a boat. A twelve-foot sloop that was my first boat. My father would take me ten miles out, out of sight of land, with only a canteen of water. And he'd leave me. We all went through it. All of us. It was the way you found out very early that the sea could be both friend and enemy. But you're a brave man. You'll go farther out. A hundred miles plus ten. And no water. The European coast is farther, by forty miles, but the North Sea is less violent in that direction. You'll have to decide. And in return, we will accept the decision of the sea. Life or death. Which was more than you offered my father."

"And you'll spend the rest of your lives behind bars when I get back." Mathers's voice rose with each word.

"*If* you get back," Connor said quietly.

His protests muted and unheeded, Mathers was now swept

away by the throngs of fishermen and sea captains and harbor workers.

"You knew all along," Angela said to Connor Thorpe.

"Yes, Angela, I did. And I'm sorry it had to be done that way. Not telling you."

Angela shook her head. "You don't have to apologize. I'm the one who's sorry. How hard it must have been for you, sitting across from the man who killed your father. Will he survive?"

Connor bent down and kissed her forehead. "We'll let the sea decide and be content with that."

Then he was gone, jogging up the ramp in pursuit of the others.

In time it was just the three of them—Kaine, Danielle, and Angela. The dock was as empty as it had been ten minutes ago. "Why don't you take us home now?" Danielle said, touching Kaine's face. "We've all been through enough."

"Home." The word had a flavor to it that Kaine hadn't experienced in a long time. He grasped Danielle's hand. He wrapped an arm around Angela's shoulder and together they walked up the ramp. "Yes."